THE BIBLE ACCORDING TO MARK TWAIN

IRREVERENT WRITINGS ON EDEN, HEAVEN, AND THE FLOOD BY AMERICA'S MASTER SATIRIST

Edited by Howard G. Baetzhold and Joseph B. McCullough

A Touchstone Book
Published by Simon & Schuster

TOUCHSTONE
Rockefeller Center
1230 Avenue of the Americas
New York, NY 10020

First Touchstone Edition 1996
Published by arrangement with University of Georgia Press

TOUCHSTONE and colophon are registered trademarks
of Simon & Schuster Inc.

Manufactured in the United States of America

20 19 18

Library of Congress Cataloging-in-Publication Data

Twain, Mark, 1835–1910.
The Bible according to Mark Twain : irreverent writings on Eden, heaven, and the flood by America's master satirist / edited by Howard G. Baetzhold and Joseph B. McCullough.—1st Touchstone ed.
p. cm.
"Touchstone book."
Includes bibliographical references (p.).
1. Twain, Mark, 1835–1910—Quotations. 2. Religion—Quotations, maxims, etc. 3. Quotations, American. I. Baetzhold, Howard G., 1923– II. McCullough, Joseph B. III. Title.
PS1303.B34 1996
818'.409—dc20 96-32351 CIP

ISBN-13: 978-0-684-82439-0
ISBN-10: 0-684-82439-6

For Nancy and Judy

Faith is the substance of things hoped for,

the evidence of things not seen.

—Hebrews 11:1

CONTENTS

Preface ix
Abbreviations xiii
Introduction xv
A Note on the Texts xxiii

Eden and the Flood

Extracts from Adam's Diary 3
Eve's Diary 17
Autobiography of Eve and Diaries Antedating the Flood 35
Documents Related to "Diaries Antedating the Flood" 85
Two Additional Pre-Deluge Diarists 91
Passages from Methuselah's Diary 97
Passages from Shem's Diary 107
Adam's Expulsion 111
Adam's Soliloquy 117

Heaven

Captain Stormfield's Visit to Heaven 129
Captain Simon Wheeler's Dream Visit to Heaven 189
A Singular Episode: The Reception of Rev. Sam Jones in Heaven 195
Mental Telegraphy? 203
Etiquette for the Afterlife: Advice to Paine 207

Letters from the Earth

Letters from the Earth 213

Appendices

Appendix 1. Original Continuation of "Autobiography of Eve" 263
Appendix 2. Planning Notes for "Autobiography of Eve" 275
Appendix 3. "Extracts from Adam's Diary" from the Original *Niagara Book* Version 278
Appendix 4. Planning Notes for Methuselah's Diary 287
Appendix 5. Passages from "Stormfield" Preserved in the Manuscript but Deleted from Typescript or Proof 299
a. Original Mrs. Rushmore and Daughter Episode 299
b. Stormfield's Trouble with Wings 302
Appendix 6. Discussion of the Fall from "Schoolhouse Hill" 306
Appendix 7. God of the Bible vs. God of the Present Day (1870s) 313
Appendix 8. Selected Passages on God and the Bible from Autobiographical Dictations of June 1906 318
Notes 333
Works Cited 381

PREFACE

This collection brings together for the first time works that reveal Mark Twain's almost lifelong attempts to deal—both humorously and seriously—with traditional religious concepts, primarily the problems raised for him by the Book of Genesis and by the Old Testament in general.

Our introductions to each piece do not attempt complicated critical analyses, but rather concentrate on when and how Mark Twain came to write and publish—or fail to publish or to finish—each of them. We are pleased that in many instances we have been able to correct or expand earlier accounts. In our discussions we have generally followed the practice of using Samuel Clemens when referring to the private person and Mark Twain when speaking of the writer and his works, though at times the distinction becomes blurred.

All of the works have been newly edited from the manuscripts, where available. The few exceptions are indicated in a note on the texts (following the introduction), which also briefly describes the editorial procedures.

In the notes at the end of the volume we have provided what we hope will be valuable supplementary information. We have identified persons, places, and quotations, defined terms not readily available in a desk dictionary, and in general have sought to explain and clarify certain references or passages in the text. In order not to interrupt the reader's attention with intrusive footnote numbers, we have keyed the notes to page and line number of this volume. Because of the complexity of the genesis and composition of "Captain Stormfield's Visit to Heaven" we have supplied notes to that story's headnote, the only instance in which a headnote has its set of notes.

Abbreviations used in citations may be found in the list following this preface. For full documentation of source references, see "Works Cited" at the end of this volume.

We wish especially to thank Robert H. Hirst and the staff at the Mark Twain Project, University of California, Berkeley, for their support and invaluable assistance throughout this project, and Donald Malcolm, whose co-authorship of two major articles together with his insights into Mark Twain's initial intention in the "Autobiography of Eve" and his assistance in the early stages of the manuscript have vastly improved this edition. In annotating and collating the texts we have been greatly aided by Pamela Cantrell and Kari Pitkänen, graduate research assistants for Joseph McCullough. For his encouragement and suggestions we are grateful to Louis J. Budd, James B. Duke Professor Emeritus, Duke University. Our many debts to other scholars are indicated in the notes.

We wish also to thank the Research Council and the Foundation of the University of Nevada, Las Vegas, for generous assistance to McCullough for travel to research collections; the Butler University Academic Grants Committee, whose assistance during the summers of 1986 and 1987 allowed Howard Baetzhold to accomplish research that became basic to this project; and John Kondelik and the staff of the Butler University Libraries for their assistance to Baetzhold both during the present project and over many years.

We are most grateful to the following persons and libraries for information and for other assistance: Nancy Johnson, Archivist/Librarian of the American Academy and Institute of Arts and Letters, New York; Dr. Lola Zladits and the staff of the Henry W. and Albert A. Berg Collection, New York Public Library, Astor, Lenox, and Tilden Foundations; and Louis A. Rachow, Librarian, Walter Hampden Memorial Library, New York.

Our deep gratitude, too, to the trustees of the Mark Twain Foundation and to the University of California Press for permission to publish heretofore unpublished materials and the other items to which they retain copyright; to the American Academy and Institute of Arts and Letters, New York, for permission to reedit the manuscript of "Captain Stormfield's Visit to Heaven" in their archives; to the Clifton Waller Barrett Library, Special Collections, University of Virginia, for permission to include the revisions made by Mark Twain in a copy of the Harper 1904 book version of "Extracts from Adam's Diary" in that collection; to Kevin Ray, Curator of Manuscripts, Olin Library System, Washington University, St. Louis, for that library's permission to publish the manuscript in its collection that we have titled "Etiquette for the Afterlife: Advice to Paine"; to HarperCollins Publishers for permission to reedit items originally published in *Europe and Elsewhere*, edited by Albert Bigelow Paine, 1923; *Letters from the Earth*, edited by Bernard DeVoto, 1962; and *Report From Paradise*, edited by Dixon Wecter, 1952.

We wish also to thank Madelaine Cooke and Kim Cretors of the University of Georgia Press and copyeditor Sally Antrobus for their expert assistance and pertinent suggestions in connection with this volume.

Finally, but most important, to our wives, to whom we dedicate this volume, our special gratitude, not only for help with the onerous task of proofreading and for other support throughout this project, but for their faith that this "thing hoped for" would finally achieve real substance and this "thing not seen" (for a long, long while) would actually become evident.

ABBREVIATIONS

AMT	*The Autobiography of Mark Twain.* 1959.
Berg	Henry W. and Albert A. Berg Collection. New York Public Library. Astor, Lenox and Tilden Foundations.
E&E	*Europe and Elsewhere.* 1923.
ET&S1	*Early Tales & Sketches. Volume 1, 1851–1864.* 1979.
ET&S2	*Early Tales & Sketches. Volume 2, 1864–1865.* 1981.
FM	*Mark Twain's Fables of Man.* 1972.
HH&T	*Mark Twain's Hannibal, Huck & Tom.* 1969.
Indians	*Huck Finn and Tom Sawyer Among the Indians and Other Unfinished Sketches.* 1989.
JRO	James R. Osgood.
LE	*Letters from the Earth.* 1962.
Letters1	*Mark Twain's Letters. Volume 1: 1853–1866.* 1988.
Letters2	*Mark Twain's Letters. Volume 2: 1867–68.* 1990.
Letters3	*Mark Twain's Letters. Volume 3: 1869.* 1992.
LLMT	*The Love Letters of Mark Twain.* 1949.
MSM	*Mark Twain's Mysterious Stranger Manuscripts.* 1969.
MTA	*Mark Twain's Autobiography.* 1923.
MTB	Paine, Albert Bigelow. *Mark Twain: A Biography.* 1912.
MTBus	*Mark Twain, Business Man.* 1946.
MTE	*Mark Twain in Eruption.* 1940.

MTH	Frear, Walter F. *Mark Twain and Hawaii.* [Contains all of Mark Twain's letters to the Sacramento *Union.*] 1947.
MTHHR	*Mark Twain's Correspondence with Henry Huttleston Rogers 1893–1909.* 1969.
MTHL	*Mark Twain–Howells Letters.* 2 vols. 1960.
MTL	*Mark Twain's Letters.* 2 vols. 1923.
MTLP	*Mark Twain's Letters to His Publishers.* 1967.
MTM	Mark Twain Memorial, Hartford, Connecticut.
MTMary	*Mark Twain's Letters to Mary.* 1961.
MTMF	*Mark Twain to Mrs. Fairbanks.* 1949.
MTN	*Mark Twain's Notebook.* 1935.
MTP	Mark Twain Papers, Bancroft Library, University of California, Berkeley.
MTQH	*Mark Twain's Quarrel with Heaven.* 1970.
MTS	*Mark Twain Speaking.* 1976.
MTTB	*Mark Twain's Travels with Mr. Brown.* 1940.
N&J1	*Mark Twain's Notebooks & Journals. Volume 1 (1855–1873).* 1975.
N&J2	*Mark Twain's Notebooks & Journals. Volume 2 (1877–1883).* 1975.
N&J3	*Mark Twain's Notebooks & Journals. Volume 3 (1883–1891).* 1979.
OLC	Olivia Langdon Clemens.
PH	Photocopy.
RP	*Report From Paradise.* 1952.
S&B	*Mark Twain's Satires & Burlesques.* 1967.
SLC	Samuel Langhorne Clemens.
SN&O	*Sketches, New & Old.* 1875.
TS	Typescript.
WIM	*What is Man? and Other Philosophical Writings.* 1973.
WWD	*Mark Twain's Which Was the Dream? and Other Symbolic Writings of the Later Years.* 1967.

INTRODUCTION

On 8 January 1870 Samuel Clemens wrote his fiancée, Olivia Langdon, to share a current enthusiasm:

> I have been reading some new arguments to prove that the world is very old, & that the six days of creation were six immensely long periods. For instance, according to Genesis, the *stars* were made when the world was, yet this writer mentions the significant fact that there are stars within reach of our telescopes whose light requires 50,000 years to traverse the wastes of space & come to our earth. And so, if we made a tour through space ourselves, might we not, in some remote era of the future, meet & greet the first lagging rays of stars that started on their weary visit to us a million years ago? . . .
>
> How insignificant we are, with our pigmy little world!—an atom glinting with uncounted myriads of other atom worlds in a broad shaft of light streaming from God's countenance—& yet prating complacently of our speck as the Great World. . . . Did Christ live 33 years in each of the millions & millions of worlds that hold their majestic courses above our heads? Or was *our* small globe the favored one of all? Does one apple in a vast orchard think as much of itself as we do? . . . Do the pismires argue upon vexed questions of pismire theology—& do they climb a molehill & look abroad over the grand universe of an acre of ground & say "Great is God, who created all things for Us?"
>
> I do not see how astronomers can help feeling exquisitely insignificant, for every new page in the Book of the Heavens they open reveals to them more & more that the world we are so proud of is to the universe

> of careening globes as is one mosquito to the winged & hoofed flocks & herds that darken the air & populate the plains & forests of all the earth. If you killed the mosquito would it be missed? Verily, What is Man, that he should be considered of God? (*LLMT*, 133–34).

The concerns expressed in this letter were to command Mark Twain's attention for the rest of his life. Over the years he wrestled with their implications in many works, both humorous and serious. Some of the pieces he published; others he failed to complete or held back because he felt them too radical for publication.

This volume brings together for the first time the most important fiction resulting from two of Mark Twain's literary endeavors: his many attempts to rewrite and supplement the biblical account of creation and its aftermath from the point of view of the characters involved, and his several efforts to revise the traditional portrait of Heaven and the afterlife. It also includes, in separate appendices, related fictional and nonfictional pieces that furnish additional important background material.

Composed over a period of almost four decades (1873–1909), the writings range from farce to fantasy to biting satire. While they do not constitute a comprehensive study of Mark Twain's views on religion and morality, collectively they reveal his varied efforts to synthesize his views of human nature and man's relationship to God and the universe. His own intellectual development from the fundamentalist Presbyterianism of the Hannibal Sunday school to a Deism molded by Thomas Paine's *The Age of Reason* and later modified by the evolutionary determinism of Darwin and his followers places Mark Twain in the mainstream of the nineteenth-century conflict between science and religion. Hence, these writings also form an important literary reflection of that conflict, which in some respects continues today.

The first section of this volume, "Eden and the Flood," presents Mark Twain's several portraits of the world before the Deluge and the difficulties faced by our earliest ancestors. These works are placed in roughly chronological order in terms of the events described. Here we mention them in the order of their composition so that the reader may place them in the context of Mark Twain's career.

Samuel Clemens knew his Bible well. Besides the exposure in the Presbyterian Sunday school, he had read through the entire work—or so he said—by the time he was fifteen (*MTB*, 1281). Biblical echoes abound in his works, and there are grounds for asserting that the Bible influenced him more profoundly than any other single book. There is no question that the problems posed by the fallacies he found in Scripture continued to trouble him throughout his lifetime.

His first fictional adventure into antediluvian times was a "Noah's Ark book," as he occasionally referred to it. Unfortunately the manuscript, which occupied him from time to time between 1866 and the early 1870s, has not survived. But the fragments from the diaries of Methuselah (written in 1873 and 1877) and those from Shem's (one from the 1870s and one from 1908 or 1909) are perhaps related to the "Noah's Ark book." "Methuselah's Diary" and its planning notes also reveal an ambitious proposal to develop the biblical narrative into a satiric examination of later eras, an ambition that would resurface in several instances in the 1900s.

"Adam's Expulsion," Mark Twain's first attempt to feature the Father of the Race as chief character of a sketch, also dates from 1877. Originally conceived as a letter to a friend apologizing for not having kept a promise, it plays fast and loose with familiar phrases from many parts of the Bible as it describes Adam's delay in fulfilling the fervent requests of his descendants that he preserve in writing his memories of life in the Garden of Eden. Later intended for *The Stolen White Elephant* collection (1882) but omitted at that time, it is here first published.

The first of the biblical narratives to see print during the author's lifetime was "Extracts from Adam's Diary," written in November or December of 1892. Failing at first to find a publisher, Clemens agreed (for a price) to contribute the piece for *The Niagara Book*, a volume of articles a friend was editing at the time of the Columbian Exposition of 1893 in Chicago to promote Niagara Falls as an attractive side trip. For that volume he revised his manuscript, adding a number of details and passages so as to set the tale in Niagara Falls Park and its environs. In doing so, he also weakened the ending by suggesting that the Fall of Man resulted from Adam's telling an old joke. Later, however, he published the story in the British edition of *Tom Sawyer, Detective . . . and Other Tales* (1897) without the Niagara Falls references and with a much more effective conclusion.

Because he clearly intended that the Niagara Falls details be omitted from future printings, though Harper and Brothers later ignored his desires, the piece is presented here as Mark Twain himself edited it in 1905 for a projected book that was to include the diaries of both Adam and Eve. (For the *Niagara Book* version on which the subsequent Harper publications were based, see appendix 3.)

In 1898 Twain posited a different version of Eden and the Fall in "Schoolhouse Hill," one of the three so-called "Mysterious Stranger" manuscripts. There, while emphasizing the vast disparity between human time and celestial time, Quarante-quatre, an unfallen son of the great Arch-Enemy, presents a somewhat novel explanation of his father's part in bringing about the Fall of Man (see appendix 6).

A few years later, probably in 1901 or 1902, Mark Twain decided that Eve should tell *her* side of the story. In his first attempt at the "Autobiography of Eve," his most ambitious return to Edenic times, he piled up some ninety-eight pages of manuscript in which Eve recalled her earlier experiences while looking back from a thousand years after creation. Beginning with a humorous but tender account of the first days, her wonderings about her own identity, her delight in nature, her search for and early life with Adam, Twain then had Eve discuss various developments that chronicled the growth and decay of the first great civilization and forecast the approaching Flood. In the later passages Mark Twain presents a number of parallels to his own times and introduces a cyclical theory of history that envisions the antediluvian problems and ensuing flood as destined to be repeated again and again.

Subsequently, however, he decided that his initial approach was unsatisfactory and recast the tale, deleting several passages, switching some of the segments to other narrators, and adding a number of new passages, including one from Satan's diary describing the Fall and another from Eve's account of events that followed. By doing so, he may have been trying to present the ideas in a more objective, almost documentary fashion, perhaps in an effort to add greater historical perspective. Planning notes for the continuation of the story seem also to reflect themes treated more fully in "The Secret History of Eddypus," an unfinished burlesque history of civilization written in 1901 and 1902. That piece, too, though in a wholly different context, deals with the fall of a Great Civilization.

Unfortunately, Twain never brought the "Autobiography of Eve" project to a successful conclusion. Nevertheless these materials are important as one of Twain's rare uses of a woman narrator, as a further reflection of his social, political, and moral concerns during the final decade of his life, and as the source of important elements later embodied in "Letters from the Earth."

Published in part by Bernard DeVoto in his collection entitled *Letters from the Earth* (1962), "The Autobiography of Eve and Diaries Antedating the Flood" is now published in full for the first time. Moreover, since the original form of the "Autobiography of Eve" manuscript, with deletions restored, provides additional insights into Mark Twain's revisionist view of our biblical beginnings, it is included here as appendix 1.

In late February 1905 Mark Twain again turned to Adam as narrator and in "Adam's Soliloquy" placed him in New York City to comment on the dinosaur exhibits in a natural history museum and to impress a young mother with the fact that the two of them were related. Adam's discussion here also satirizes the biblical account of the Flood, partly by impugning the judgment of Noah and his selection of species to be saved.

The following summer of 1905 Mark Twain took up Eve's story once more. This time he finished it to his own satisfaction in a shorter form that more closely parallels "Adam's Diary," and published it the next December in *Harper's Monthly.* Much less complex than the "Autobiography," the "Diary" treats Eve's story more whimsically and tenderly, so that besides touching on the development of fear and grief and love, the piece ultimately becomes a tribute to woman, to love, and, implicitly, to Olivia Clemens, who had died just the year before.

The second section, "Heaven," presents Mark Twain's vision of the hereafter, primarily through the reminiscences of visitors to the celestial realms via dreams.

Just as the tales of man's biblical beginnings were created at various times from the 1870s to the 1900s, "Captain Stormfield's Visit to Heaven" remained on Mark Twain's drawing board from about 1869 until 1907. Sparked initially in 1868 by Captain Ned Wakeman's colorful account of his own dream visit to the celestial realms and by Clemens's own disgust with the popular conceptions of Paradise, so out of place in the immense grandeur of the universe, the piece went through several versions during the 1870s and very early 1880s. At one point in late 1877 or early 1878 he adapted a version of the journey and celestial reception for his abortive novel, *Simon Wheeler, Detective.* That passage is included here as an analogue to the longer piece.

During the next two decades suggestions for the Stormfield story continued to appear among Mark Twain's literary notes, and sometime during the early 1900s, probably by early 1906, he added a new beginning and several additional segments that further emphasized the unimaginable distances in heaven and the vast differences between celestial and human time.

For many years, especially since his publisher once turned it down, Twain considered his rollicking satire too radical for publication. But since he wished to preserve it, he decided in June 1906 to include it in the autobiography he was currently dictating, a work which was not to be published until long after his death, and had a large portion of it typed and placed among that summer's August dictations. Obviously thoughts of the hereafter and of religion in general were much on his mind, for the June decision came just a few days before he launched into his most virulent diatribe—also for the autobiography—against man, the Bible, and the Deity (see appendix 8).

The following year, however, he changed his mind about publication, and an "Extract from Captain Stormfield's Visit to Heaven"—the portion of the tale written between 1878 and 1882, with a few late revisions—finally appeared in *Harper's Monthly* for December 1907 and January 1908.

The present text of "Captain Stormfield's Visit to Heaven" includes all of the later segments of the Stormfield tale, as well as the "Extract." Also added in appendix 5 are two substantial passages, one of which Mark Twain deleted from the typescript and the other from the proof sheets for the *Harper's* "Extract."

One other work featuring a dream visit to the hereafter, "A Singular Episode: The Reception of Rev. Sam Jones in Heaven," never saw print during Clemens's lifetime. Though he read it to friends on a number of occasions, Livy presumably thought its portrait of the boisterous evangelist and its irreverent treatment of the Archbishop of Canterbury too strong for public consumption. And "Mental Telegraphy?" links both the "Reception" and "Stormfield" to another story of the hereafter, "Aerial Football: The New Game," by George Bernard Shaw. Finally, as a sort of coda to the "Heaven" section, we here publish for the first time "Etiquette for the Afterlife: Advice to Paine," which Mark Twain wrote just a few weeks before his death on 21 April 1910, his last substantial piece of writing. We have added the initial phrase to the title to indicate the nature of that advice.

The third section—"Letters from the Earth"—presents a piece that in several ways provides a synthesis of the biblical writings, the Stormfield saga, and Mark Twain's religious thought in general. In 1909, just the year before he would discover for himself whether his depiction of the afterlife was accurate, Mark Twain returned once more to a biblical context. Into these "Letters," he poured his own latest reflections on religion, morality, and matters biblical. Drawing numerous elements from the earlier writings, he presented a new picture of Heaven and the Creator, an implicitly scathing account of the Creation itself, and a series of letters from the temporarily banished Satan to his archangel friends Michael and Gabriel, describing the human race and its irrational beliefs.

Among the most important borrowings from "Stormfield" was the vast discrepancy between celestial and earthly concepts of distance and time, already present in the 1870s segments, though developed more fully in "From Captain Stormfield's Reminiscences," one of the latest additions to the story. (Mark Twain had also dealt with these themes in the "Mysterious Stranger" manuscripts, written between 1898 and 1908). From "Captain Stormfield's Reminiscences," he also borrowed the notion that human nature resulted from random mixtures of some twenty-eight good and evil "Moral Qualities" (twenty-seven in "Letters from the Earth"), with each individual receiving varying amounts of each quality as chance and the whim of the "mixer" determined. And from the "Autobiography of Eve," he adapted Satan's discussion of the Fall as a consequence of a natural desire for knowledge and the total ignorance of Adam and Eve as to the meanings of the words good, evil, and death.

Though he had not dealt with the creation in the earlier biblical works, except incidentally, he was now able to construct a creation myth based upon these concepts of celestial time and of the mixing of the various "Moral Qualities" (see headnote to "Letters from the Earth").

Because of the differences between celestial and earthly time, the Creator, though interested in his new experiment, cannot be concerned with, or even understand, the limited perceptions resulting from the absurdly brief life span of human beings. Hence the confusion resulting from the remoteness of heaven leads to the sorts of problems on earth which Satan describes in his darkly humorous explanations of the anomalies and the ridiculousness of many earthly analyses of the nature of God and His relations with human beings.

Though this work, too, remained unfinished, it is important as Mark Twain's final "literary" word on the questions posed in the 1870 letter to Livy, a final attempt to get at the root of man's moral and existential dilemmas. And it does so by means of a more or less vernacular style in which the fundamental seriousness is skillfully leavened by Twainian humor and satire.

Finally, appendices 7 and 8 present two statements, one from the early 1870s and the other from 1906, which, in their comparison of the God of the Bible with Mark Twain's concept of the real God, complement "Letters from the Earth" and reveal their author's views of the Deity near the beginning and at the end of his literary career.

There are, to be sure, numerous inconsistencies among the works in this volume, but most of them reveal in one way or another Mark Twain's efforts to explain what he saw as the idiosyncracies of man and God. And he obviously felt a good deal of frustration, like that which he had epitomized some years earlier in chapter 9 of *Tom Sawyer Abroad* (1894). There, after Huck and Tom argue over whether the Sahara Desert was made or just happened, Tom declares that "the trouble about arguments is, they ain't nothing but *theories*, and theories don't prove nothing, they only give you a place to rest on, a spell, when you are tuckered out butting around and around trying to find out something there ain't no way *to* find out." But Mark Twain did keep trying.

A NOTE ON THE TEXTS

Most of the works in this volume are newly edited from the original manuscripts, or in the case of the Autobiographical Dictations, the original typescript. For those items published during Mark Twain's lifetime the manuscripts have been collated against typescripts (if extant) and the first published versions. Where no manuscript exists, the first published version is the copy-text. As a special case, "Extracts from Adam's Diary" is based on the 1905 Harper book publication, as revised by Mark Twain himself. The text of the original 1893 *Niagara Book* publication of "Adam's Diary" is included as appendix 3. As for the pieces published since Mark Twain's death, the exceptions to manuscript-as-copy-text are "Captain Simon Wheeler's Dream Visit to Heaven," "Letters from the Earth," and the discussion of the Fall from "Schoolhouse Hill" (appendix 6). In all cases specific copy-texts are identified at the beginning of the notes to each piece.

The presence of words, phrases, etc. in angle brackets (⟨ ⟩) in any quotation indicates material deleted by Mark Twain.

Emendations of the copy-text have been conservative. Mark Twain's spelling has been changed only in the case of obvious errors. Variant spellings, if once acceptable, have been retained (e.g., "woful" for "woeful," "ancle" for "ankle"). In general Mark Twain's original punctuation (including ellipses and asterisks) has been followed, except where the variant in a later text (typescript or first printing) seems fairly clearly to have been made by the author. Substantive variants in later texts have also been adopted in similar cases. In both instances, the choices have been based on extensive experience with Mark Twain's style and other practices. Mechanical corrections, such as addition of closing quotation marks, parentheses, or brackets, have also been made, except in appendices 2 and 4, where the punctuation of planning notes for "Autobiography of Eve" and for "Methuselah's Diary" is recorded exactly as written.

All of the changes have been recorded in a list of emendations, which because of space limitations and relatively limited reader interest, has not been included in this volume. It is, however, available from the editors to interested scholars.

Certain emendations have not been recorded. In the texts themselves Mark Twain's customary ampersands have been expanded to "and." In a number of instances a short dash occurs at the end of a line, clearly different from the punctuational dash. These marks are apparently a holdover from a convention of filling out a short line with a dash to avoid confusing the end of the line with the end of a paragraph. They have been silently dropped. Titles and chapter headings have been styled for this volume.

Eden and the Flood

EXTRACTS FROM ADAM'S DIARY

Mark Twain wrote "Adam's Diary" at the Villa Viviani, near Florence, Italy, where the family had moved in late September 1892, after a summer at Bad Nauheim, Germany. The atmosphere there proved inspiring, for by mid December, besides an eight- or nine-thousand-word article (later published as "A Cure for the Blues" in *The £1,000,000 Bank-Note, Etc.*, 1893), he had finished "Those Extraordinary Twins" and was about to rewrite the first two-thirds of that manuscript so as to make Pudd'nhead Wilson the major character. It was sometime in December, also, that Twain returned to his long-time interest in our biblical beginnings, and early in January 1893 he noted that both *Pudd'nhead Wilson* and "Adam's Diary" had gone to the typist (notebook 32, ts p. 53, MTP).

What brought Mark Twain to turn to Adam again in 1892 is not clear. It is obvious that during these years he was writing furiously and searching for literary material that could bolster the sagging fortunes of his publishing company and the Paige typesetter in which he had invested so heavily, and he doubtless thought that a version of Adam's experiences might be a fruitful subject. He had long been fascinated with the story of our First Parents. As early as 1852, he had introduced our mutual ancestor into his own works, when W. Epaminondas Adrastus Blab traced his lineage to a Blab "who lived in Adam's time and had a little falling out with that gentleman." And the next year, in the person of a cocky and loquacious "Son of Adam," young Sam Clemens supported his assertion that redheads were superior beings by arguing that because Adam was made of "red earth" as his name signifies, the first man, too, must have had red hair ("Oh, She Has a Red Head!" Hannibal *Journal*, 16 September 1852, 13 May 1853; Brashear, 118, 126; *ET&S*, 104–5). The first instance of more than passing consideration, however, came in *The Innocents Abroad*, chapter 53, where the narrator revels in "tumultuous emotions" at finding himself beside Adam's tomb, and bewails the fact that neither of them had had the opportunity to know the other. And in 1877 "Adam's Expulsion," though not published until this volume, marked his first attempt to present Adam as an actual character and to delve into his motivations and reactions.

Two years later in Elmira, New York, the home of his wife's family, he jokingly proposed that the town erect a monument to the Father of the Human Race who, certainly, was worthy of being honored. When, surprisingly, a number of businessmen saw some commercial advantage in such an undertaking, Mark Twain kept the joke going by preparing a flowery petition to Congress to grant Elmira exlusive rights to erect such a memorial. Some ninety-four of Elmira's leading citizens actually signed the petition—Sam Clemens did not—and General Joseph Hawley, a congressman friend, even agreed to present it to the House of Representatives. Unfortunately, the general soon had sober second thoughts about the possible repercussions and returned the document to its author.

Despite that failure Mark Twain continued to be intrigued for many years by the humorous and satiric implications of his idea. In May 1883 he expanded upon it in some detail in a speech entitled "On Adam," given before the Royal Literary and Scientific Society in Ottawa (*MTS*, 178–80). Six months later, when he was solicited for a letter to be raffled off for a fund to help finance completion of the pedestal for the Statue of Liberty, he sent a check, arguing at the same time—tongue-in-cheek—that a monument to Adam would be a far worthier project than the current one. Again, in the early 1900s, angered by the Presbyterian church's rejection of two young candidates for the ministry because they believed Adam to be a myth, he drafted a brief "Proposal for the Renewal of the Adam Monument Petition," satirically demonstrating Adam's intellectual superiority to such giants as Socrates, Aristotle, Shakespeare, Darwin, Herbert Spencer, and others (*FM*, 449–52). Finally in 1905, he featured his protagonist's dream of establishing a monument to Adam as a subplot of "The Refuge of the Derelicts."

When the copy of "Adam's Diary" was finished, Mark Twain sent it to Webster and Company manager Fred Hall on 13 March 1893, along with another recently completed story, "Is He Living or Is He Dead?," suggesting that Hall try to place them with the *Cosmopolitan* or *Century* magazine. The diary he declared "a gem, if I *do* say it myself that shouldn't" (*MTLP*, 342).

Unfortunately, though the *Cosmopolitan* accepted "Is He Living or Is He Dead?" it turned down "Adam's Diary." And if Hall then sent the story to the *Century*, it fared no better. But it soon found a home in *The Niagara Book*, a volume that Irving S. Underhill, the son of an old friend from Buffalo, was preparing in the hope of promoting Niagara Falls as a tourist attraction, especially as a side trip for the many travelers attending the International Columbian Exposition in Chicago that spring and summer of 1893. When Underhill asked him to contribute to the volume, Mark Twain was reluctant at first, but finally decided that he could revise "Adam's Diary"—for a thousand dollars—so as to establish Niagara Falls Park and its environs as the setting for the Garden of Eden, and on 14 April he sent Underhill a typescript of the original manuscript with several sheets of revisions to be inserted at appropriate places.

The *Niagara Book* project was not ultimately a success, however. Twain received only five hundred dollars of the agreed-upon amount, and ultimately forgave Underhill the remainder. For their part, the producers of the volume ultimately lost some six thousand dollars (Underhill, 14, 18–19).

Moreover, Mark Twain apparently never really liked the Niagara Falls portions of the story. In August 1895, near the beginning of his world lecture tour, he revised a copy of the *Niagara Book* piece, marking out the Niagara Falls passages and localized allusions and making a few additional changes (original owned by John M. Clements, Phoenix, Arizona; PH in MTP). This he sent to Harper's, noting that it was to provide copy for publication of the story in future collected editions of his works. Sometime the following year, also, he sent a version without the Falls references to Chatto and Windus for an English edition of *Tom Sawyer, Detective, As Told by Huck Finn, and Other Stories* (1897). But though Chatto honored his revisions, when the story was republished in *Harper's Monthly* for April 1901, the text used was the *Niagara Book* version, only slightly revised.

One possible reason for using the original text in 1901 was that in December 1900, Irving Underhill wrote that Doubleday, Page and Co. was reprinting *The Niagara Book*, and asked whether Mark Twain intended to use it in one of his books in the near future, or whether he wished to make any revisions for the Doubleday edition. He further pledged that he would pay the five hundred dollars still owing from the first publication, even though Clemens earlier had said he need not do so (Underhill to SLC, 12/29/00, MTP). Clemens replied on 1 January that there were no plans at present to include the piece in a collection, and even if it were to be published soon, it would not harm

Underhill's book since it would form only a small part of one volume in a set of twenty-two. Moreover, he had given his publisher instructions to use only the version published in the English edition (Berg; PH, MTP).

On 2 February 1901 in answer to a query by Clemens concerning possible publication of the piece in *Harper's Monthly*, Underhill replied that Doubleday had no interest in printing the story in a magazine and that Clemens could use the article as he saw fit, without credit to the *Niagara Book*. And his further comment may have been partly responsible for the April publication of the piece in its original form: "Now I want to recommend something. The book will be out in April. Get Harper's to print it for April, if possible, and if they pay little or big for it, you keep the money. . . . It is your due for every reason." After further commending his friend's great patience and long-suffering in the matter of the debt, Underhill suggested only one thing if there were any plans to revise the piece: "Make it as Niagara Fallsy as possible" (MTP).

Mark Twain made but few revisions in the piece for the magazine publication, only one of which was at all "Fallsy" (changing "Garden" to "Park"). And he obviously sent Underhill a copy, because in the relatively few cases where the 1901 *Niagara Book* differs from the 1893 edition, it follows the *Harper's Monthly* text.

Hence it may well be that Underhill's generosity and praise caused him to leave the story in its *Niagara Book* form, not only in the magazine, but also for the 1904 book publication, and the collected works (*My Debut as a Literary Person, with Other Essays and Stories* (vol. 23, The Autograph Edition, Hartford: American Publishing Co., 1903) and *The $30,000 Bequest and Other Stories* (New York: Harper, 1906). Moreover, when the time came for the story to be included in the collected works, Clemens thought Underhill should be paid for that permission, especially since he had not charged for the magazine publication (SLC to Underhill 12/3/01, Berg; PH, MTP).

But when he wrote "Eve's Diary" in July 1905, he reread "Adam's Diary" with an eye to publishing both as companion pieces in a separate volume, was almost disgusted with it, and decided to revise it once more. On 16 July he wrote to his daughter Clara: "This morning I gutted old Adam's Diary & removed every blemish from it" (PH, MTP). This time he marked up a copy of the 1904 Harper book, removing the Niagara Falls allusions and adding a few additional revisions. The same day he reported his activities to Frederick Duneka, then his chief contact at Harper's, and asked him to send an additional copy of the 1904 book "so that I can make 2 revised copies (*MTL* 2:775). On 20 July he sent the revisions to Duneka, with instructions that this was the version to be used along with "Eve's Diary" for the proposed volume. In acknowledging receipt, the publisher assured him that the corrections would be made at once and in mid September wrote that the stories would be published together as soon as matters would allow proper preparation of the volume (7/20/05, Berg, PH, MTP; 7/27/05, MTP; 9/18/05, MTP; the marked 1904 books are in the Barrett Collection at the University of Virginia, with corrections in Mark Twain's hand, and in the collection of John M. Clements of Phoenix, Arizona, with the same corrections in another hand).

Actually, "matters" did not allow that publication until 1931, when Harper's finally published them together as *The Private Lives of Adam and Eve.* But by that time, the Clemens-Duneka correspondence had obviously been forgotten, for Harper's once more reprinted the *Niagara Book* version of "Adam's Diary." Hence this is the first publication of the piece as Mark Twain finally wanted it to be. For comparison we have reprinted the *Niagara Book* version as appendix 3.

EXTRACTS FROM ADAM'S DIARY

Translated from the original MS.

Note.—I translated a portion of this diary some years ago, and a friend of mine printed a few copies in an incomplete form, but the public never got them. Since then I have deciphered some more of Adam's hieroglyphics, and think he has now become sufficiently important as a public character to justify this publication.—M. T.

Monday

This new creature with the long hair is a good deal in the way. It is always hanging around and following me about. I don't like this; I am not used to company, I wish it would stay with the other animals. . . . Cloudy today, wind in the east; think we shall have rain. . . . *We?* Where did I get that word? . . . I remember now—the new creature uses it.

Tuesday

I get no chance to name anything myself. The new creature names everything that comes along, before I can get in a protest. And always the same pretext is offered—it *looks* like the thing. There is the dodo, for instance. Says the moment one looks at it one sees at a glance that it "looks like a dodo." It will have to keep that name, no doubt. It wearies me to fret about it, and it does no good, anyway. Dodo! It looks no more like a dodo than I do.

Wednesday

Built me a shelter against the rain, but could not have it to myself in peace. The new creature intruded. When I tried to put it out it shed water out of its face and wiped it away with the back of its paws, and made a noise such as some of the other animals make when they are in distress. I wish it would not talk; it is always talking. That sounds like a cheap fling at the poor creature, a slur; but I do not mean it so. I have never heard the human voice before, and any new and strange sound intruding itself here upon the solemn hush of these dreaming solitudes offends my ear and seems a false note. And this new sound is so close to me; it is right at my shoulder, right at my ear, first on one side and then on the other, and I am used only to sounds that are more or less distant from me.

Saturday

The new creature eats too much fruit. We are going to run short, most likely. "We" again—that is *its* word; mine too, now, from hearing it so much. Good deal of fog this morning. I do not go out in the fog myself. The new creature does. It goes out in all weathers. And talks. It used to be so pleasant and quiet here.

Sunday

Pulled through. This day is getting to be more and more trying. It was selected and set apart last November as a day of rest. I already had six of them per week, before.

Monday

The new creature says its name is Eve. That is all right, I have no objections. Says it is to call it by when I want it to come. I said it was superfluous, then. The word evidently raised me in its respect; and indeed it is a large, good word, and will bear repetition. It says it is not an It, it is a She. This is probably doubtful; yet it is all one to me; what she is were nothing to me if she would but go by herself and not talk.

Friday

She has taken to beseeching me to stop going over the Falls. What harm does it do? Says it makes her shudder. I wonder why. I have always done it—always liked the plunge, and the excitement, and the coolness. I supposed it was what the Falls were for. They have no other use that I can see, and they must have been made for something. She says they were only made for scenery—like the rhinoceros and the mastodon.

I am too much hampered here. What I need is a change of scene.

Saturday

I escaped last Tuesday night, and travelled two days, and built me another shelter, in a secluded place, and obliterated my tracks as well as I could, but she hunted me out by means of a beast which she has tamed and calls a wolf, and came making that pitiful noise again, and shedding that water which she calls tears. I was obliged to return with her, but will presently emigrate again, when the occasion offers. She engages herself in many foolish things: among others, trying to study out why the animals called lions and tigers live on grass and flowers, when, as she says, the sort of teeth they wear would indicate that they were intended to eat each other. This is foolish, because to do that would be to kill each other, and that would introduce what, as I understand it, is called "death"; and death, as I have been told, has not yet entered the Garden.

Sunday

Pulled through.

Monday

I believe I see what the week is for; it is to give time to rest up from the weariness of Sunday. It seems a good idea. . . . She has been climbing that tree again. She said nobody was looking. Seems to consider that a sufficient justification for chancing any dangerous thing. Told her that. The word justification moved her admiration—and envy too, I thought. It is a good word.

Thursday

She told me she was made out of a rib taken from my body. This is at least doubtful, if not more than that. I have not missed any rib. . . . She is in much trouble about the buzzard; says grass does not agree with it; is afraid she can't raise it; thinks it was intended to live on decayed flesh. The buzzard must get along the best it can with what is provided. We cannot overturn the whole scheme to accommodate the buzzard.

Saturday

She fell in the pond yesterday, when she was looking at herself in it, which she is always doing. She nearly strangled, and said it was most uncomfortable. This made her sorry for the creatures which live in there, which she calls fish, for she continues to fasten names on to things that don't need them and don't come when they are called by them, which is a matter of no consequence to her, as she is such an unreflecting and irrelevant half-blown bud anyway; so she got a lot of them out and brought them in last night and put them in my bed to keep warm, but I have noticed them now and then all day, and I don't see that they are any happier there than they were before, only quieter. When night comes I shall throw them out-doors. I will not sleep with them again, for I find them clammy and unpleasant to be among when a person hasn't anything on.

Sunday

Pulled through.

Tuesday

She has taken up with a snake now. Nothing comes amiss to her, in the animal line. She trusts them all, they all trust her; and because she wouldn't betray them, she thinks they won't betray her.

Friday

She says the snake advises her to try the fruit of that tree, and says the result will be a great and fine and noble education. I told her there would be another result, too—it would introduce death into the world. That was a mistake—it had been better to keep the remark to myself; it only gave her an idea—she could save the sick buzzard, and furnish meat to the despondent lions and tigers. I advised her to keep away from the tree. She said she wouldn't. I foresee trouble. Will emigrate.

Wednesday

Escaped that night, and rode a horse all night as fast as he could go, hoping to get clear out of the Garden and hide in some other country before the disaster should fall; but it was not to be. About an hour after sunup, as I was riding through a flowery plain where thousands of animals were grazing, slumbering, or playing with each other, according to their wont, all of a sudden they broke into a tempest of frightful noises, and in one moment the plain was in a frantic commotion and every beast was destroying its neighbor. I knew what it meant—Eve had eaten that fruit, and death was come into the world. . . . The tigers ate my horse, paying no attention when I ordered them to desist, and they would even have eaten me if I had stayed—which I didn't. . . . I found this place, outside the Garden but she has found me out. In fact, I was not sorry she came, for there are but meagre pickings here, and she brought some of those apples. I was obliged to eat them, I was so hungry. It was against my principles, but I find that principles have no real force except when one is well fed. . . . She came curtained in boughs and bunches of leaves, and when I asked her what she meant by such nonsense and snatched them away and threw them down, she tittered and blushed. I had never seen a person titter and blush before, and to me it seemed unbecoming and foolish. She said I would soon know how it was myself. This was correct. Hungry as I was, I laid down the apple half eaten and arrayed myself in the discarded boughs and branches, and then spoke to her with some severity and ordered her to go and get some more and not make such a spectacle of herself. She did it, and after this we crept down to where the wild-beast battle had been, and collected some skins, and I made her patch together a couple of suits proper for public occasions. They are uncomfortable, it is true, but they are in the mode, and that is the main point about clothes. . . . I find she is a good deal of a companion. I see I should be lonesome and depressed without her, now that I have lost my property. Another thing, she says it is ordered that we work for our living hereafter. She will be useful. I will superintend.

Next Year

We have named it Cain. She caught it while I was up country trapping; caught it in the timber a couple of miles from our dug-out—or it might have been four, she isn't certain which. It resembles us in some ways, and may be a relation. That is what she thinks, but this is an error, in my judgment. The difference in size warrants the conclusion that it is a different and new kind of animal—a fish perhaps, though when I put it in the water to see, it sank, and she plunged in and snatched it out before there was an opportunity for the experiment to determine the matter. I still think it is a fish, but she is indifferent about what it is, and will not let me have it to try. I do not understand this. The coming of the creature seems to have changed her whole nature and made her unreasonable about experiments. She thinks more of it than she does of any of the other animals, but is not able to explain why. Her mind is disordered—everything shows it. Sometimes she carries the fish in her arms half the night when it complains and wants to get to the water. At such times the shining water-drops trickle down her face, and she pats the fish on the back and makes soft sounds with her mouth to soothe it, and betrays sorrow and solicitude in a hundred ways. I have never seen her do like this with any other fish, and it troubles me greatly. She used to carry the young tigers around so, and play with them, before we lost our property; but it was only play; she never took on about them like this when their dinner disagreed with them.

Sunday

She doesn't work Sundays, but lies around all tired out, and likes to have the fish play over her; and she makes foolish noises to amuse it, and pretends to chew its paws, and that makes it laugh. I have not seen a fish before that could laugh. That makes me doubt. . . . I have come to like Sunday myself. Superintending all the week tires a body so. There ought to be more Sundays.

Wednesday

It isn't a fish. I cannot quite make out what it is. It makes curious, vicious noises when not satisfied, and says "goo-goo" when it is. It is not one of us, for it doesn't walk; it is not a bird, for it doesn't fly; it is not a frog, for it doesn't hop; it is not a snake, for it doesn't crawl; I feel sure it is not a fish, though I cannot get a chance to find out whether it can swim or not. It merely lies around, and mostly on its back, with its feet up. I have not seen any other animal do that before. I said I believed it was an enigma, but she only admired the word without understanding it. In my judgment it is either an enigma or some kind of a bug. If it dies, I will take it apart and see what its arrangements are. I never had a thing perplex me so.

Three Months Later

The perplexity augments instead of diminishing. I sleep but little. It has ceased from lying around, and goes about on its four legs now. Yet it differs from the other four-legged animals in that its front legs are unusually short, consequently this causes the main part of its person to stick up uncomfortably high in the air, and this is not attractive. It is built much as we are, but its method of travelling shows that it is not of our breed. The short front legs and long hind ones indicate that it is of the kangaroo family, but it is a marked variation of the species, since the true kangaroo hops, whereas this one never does. Still, it is a curious and interesting variety, and has not been catalogued before. As I discovered it, I have felt justified in securing the credit of discovery by attaching my name to it, and hence have called it *Kangaroorum Adamiensis*. . . . It must have been a young one when it came, for it has grown exceedingly since. It must be five times as big, now, as it was then, and when discontented is able to make from twenty-two to thirty-eight times the noise it made at first. Coercion does not modify this, but has the contrary effect. For this reason I discontinued the system. She reconciles it by persuasion, and by giving it things which she had previously told it she wouldn't give it. As already observed, I was not at home when it first came, and she told me she found it in the woods. It seems odd that it should be the only one, yet it must be so, for I have worn myself out these many weeks trying to find another one to add to my collection, and for this one to play with; for surely then it would be quieter and we could tame it more easily. But I find none, nor any vestige of any; and strangest of all, no tracks. It has to live on the ground, it cannot help itself; therefore, how does it get about without leaving a track? I have set a dozen traps, but they do no good. I catch all small animals except that one; animals that merely go into the trap out of curiosity, I think, to see what the milk is there for. They never drink it.

Three Months Later

The kangaroo still continues to grow, which is very strange and perplexing. I never knew one to be so long in getting its growth. It has fur on its head now; not like kangaroo fur, but exactly like our hair, except that it is much finer and softer, and instead of being black is red. I am like to lose my mind over the capricious and harassing developments of this unclassifiable zoological freak. If I could catch another one—but that is hopeless; it is a new variety, and the only sample; this is plain. But I caught a true kangaroo and brought it in, thinking that this one, being lonesome, would rather have that for company than have no kin at all, or any animal it could feel a nearness to or get sympathy from in its forlorn condition here among strangers who do not know its ways or habits, or what to do to make it feel that it is among friends; but it was a mistake—it went into such fits at the sight of the kangaroo that I was convinced it had never seen one before. I pity the poor noisy little animal, but there is nothing I can do to make it happy. If I could tame it—but that is out of the question; the more I try, the worse I seem to make it. It grieves me to the heart to see it in its little storms of sorrow and passion. I wanted to let it go, but she wouldn't hear of it. That seemed cruel and not like her; and yet she may be right. It might be lonelier than ever; for since I cannot find another one, how could *it?*

Five Months Later

It is not a kangaroo. No, for it supports itself by holding to her finger, and thus goes a few steps on its hind legs, and then falls down. It is probably some kind of a bear; and yet it has no tail—as yet—and no fur, except on its head. It still keeps on growing—that is a curious circumstance, for bears get their growth earlier than this. Bears are dangerous—since our catastrophe—and I shall not be satisfied to have this one prowling about the place much longer without a muzzle on. I have offered to get her a kangaroo if she would let this one go, but it did no good—she is determined to run us into all sorts of foolish risks, I think. She was not like this before she lost her mind.

A Fortnight Later

I examined its mouth. There is no danger yet; it has only one tooth. It has no tail yet. It makes more noise now than it ever did before—and mainly at night. I have moved out. But I shall go over, mornings, to breakfast, and to see if it has more teeth. If it gets a mouthful of teeth, it will be time for it to go, tail or no tail, for a bear does not need a tail in order to be dangerous.

Four Months Later

I have been off hunting and fishing a month. Meantime the bear has learned to paddle around all by itself on its hind legs and says "poppa" and "momma." It is certainly a new species. This resemblance to words may be purely accidental, of course, and may have no purpose or meaning; but even in that case it is still extraordinary and is a thing which no other bear can do. This imitation of speech, taken together with general absence of fur and entire absence of tail, sufficiently indicates that this is a new kind of bear. The further study of it will be exceedingly interesting. Meantime I will go off on a far expedition and make an exhaustive search. There must certainly be another one somewhere, and this one will be less dangerous when it has company of its own species. I will go straightway, but I will muzzle this one first.

Three Months Later

It has been a weary, weary hunt, yet I have had no success. In the mean time, without stirring from the home estate, she has caught another one! I never saw such luck. I might have hunted these woods a hundred years, I never should have run across that thing.

Next day

I have been comparing the new one with the old one, and it is perfectly plain that they are the same breed. I was going to stuff one of them for my collection, but she is prejudiced against it for some reason or other; so I have relinquished the idea, though I think it is a mistake. It would be an irreparable loss to science if they should get away. The old one is tamer than it was, and can laugh and talk like the parrot, having learned this, no doubt, from being with the parrot so much, and having the imitative faculty in a highly developed degree. I shall be astonished if it turns out to be a new kind of parrot; and yet I ought not to be astonished, for it has already been everything else it could think of, since those first days when it was a fish. The new one is as ugly now as the old one was at first; has the same sulfur-and-raw-meat complexion and the same singular head without any fur on it. She calls it Abel.

Ten Years Later

They are boys; we found it out long ago. It was their coming in that small, immature shape that puzzled us; we were not used to it. There are some girls now. Abel is a good boy, but if Cain had stayed a bear it would have improved him. After all these years, I see that I was mistaken about Eve in the beginning; it is better to live outside the Garden with her than inside it without her. At first I thought she talked too much; but now I should be sorry to have that voice fall silent and pass out of my life. Blessed be the sorrow that brought us near together and taught me to know the goodness of her heart and the sweetness of her spirit!

THE END

EVE'S DIARY

Mark Twain wrote "Eve's Diary" in Dublin, New Hampshire, in July 1905, following a visit from Harper editor Frederick Duneka, who suggested he write the story for the magazine's Christmas issue. From the beginning he thought of the story as a companion piece to "Adam's Diary," with Eve using Adam's record as her "unwitting and unconscious" text (SLC to Duneka, 7/16/05, *MTL*, 2:775). That desire led to the revision of "Adam's Diary," as described earlier.

Though Duneka was immensely pleased with Eve's story, he somewhat diplomatically rejected Mark Twain's suggestion that *both* pieces be published in the Christmas *Harper's*, saying that they would be issued together in a single volume as soon as "matters" allowed doing the book properly, and that "Eve's Diary" itself would go into the Christmas magazine. "Let me say again," he added, "how beautiful I think that is,—beautiful and tender and as true as anything about Eve may be" † (Duneka to SLC, 9/18/05, MTP).

Mark Twain then decided to supplement "Eve's Diary" with a new "chapter" from "Adam's Diary." But he was too late, for Duneka wrote again on 26 September to say that the Christmas issue was already made up and that "it would entail a very great deal of expense and delay to make changes at this time" (MTP).

Shortly after the story's appearance in the December *Harper's*, Mark Twain granted permission for William Dean Howells and Henry Alden, another Harper editor, to include "Eve's Diary" in a collection titled *Their Husband's Wives*, to be published in March 1906. The following June, Harper and Brothers published a separate book version of Eve's story, this time adding numerous delicate nude drawings by Lester Ralph, and the "new" material that Twain had earlier wished to include in the magazine version, a brief italicized interpolation entitled "Extract from Adam's Diary."

Mark Twain, who has often been accused of excessive prudery, thoroughly approved of Ralph's illustrations. To Duneka he wrote on 26 March:

> We all think Mr. Ralph's pictures delightful—full of grace, charm, variety of invention, humor, pathos, poetry—they are prodigal in merits. It's a bonny Eve, a sweet and innocent and winning lassie, and she is as natural and at home in the tale as if she had just climbed out of it. *Now* do you think draperies are indis[pens]ible to picture women? . . . Isn't she stunning where she has been chasing Adam, and is looking after him in his flight? Do you note how charged with childlike wonder and interest? Clothes would vulgarize her—even a duchess's (quoted in Stoneley, 106).

Looking at the pictures, it is difficult to see why anyone would object. But the "indecent"drawings did evoke a brief storm of protest later that year from the trustees of the Charleton Library in Worcester, Massachusetts, who refused to allow the book on their shelves. A "Special to the New York *Times*, Worcester, Mass. Nov. 23" sarcastically described the Charleton Library decision, noting that trustee Frank O. Wakefield, in reviewing some 100 volumes recently purchased for the library, had, with the approval of two other trustees, barred the book:

> The other ninety and nine books are all right, but this one book Mr. Wakefield says, is objectionable. That is because there are pictures in the book of a kind to which Mr. Wakefield objects.
>
> Before "Eve's Diary" could go on the circulating shelves, the Librarian, Mrs. H. L. Carpenter, looked it through. She saw the pictures and made known to Mr. Wakefield that she "had her doubts."
>
> On every left-handed page is a picture, fifty of which represent Eve in Summer costume. Her dresses are all cut Garden of Eden style. In one of them Eve is seen skipping through the bushes unrestrained and not at all afraid. The bushes do not seriously cut off the view of Eve.
>
> After looking long and earnestly at one picture depicting Eve pensively reclining on a rock, Mr. Wakefield decided to act.

Though the *Times* article noted that "Mr. Clemens" had told their reporter that this matter was "not of the slightest interest to him," he did comment in a letter to the Washington, D.C., *Herald* on 8 December as to the Charleton librarians' "interest" in the pictures:

It appears that the pictures in *Eve's Diary* were first discovered by a lady librarian. When she made the dreadful find, being very careful, she jumped at no hasty conclusions—not she—she examined the horrid things in detail. It took her some time to examine them all, but she did her hateful duty! I don't blame her for this careful examination; the time she spent was, I am sure, enjoyable, for I found considerable fascination in them myself.

Then she took the book to another librarian, a male this time, and he, also, took a long time to examine the unclothed ladies. He must have found something of the same sort of fascination in them that I found.

As many readers have noted, "Eve's Diary" constitutes the author's moving eulogy to his wife, Livy, who had died a year earlier. Shortly after her death, the grieving Clemens wrote to her brother, Charles Langdon: "I am a man without a country. Wherever Livy was, that was my country" (6/19/04, MTM, quoted in Hill, 85). At the end of "Eve's Diary" Adam's eloquent tribute reads, "Wherever she was, *there* was Eden."

Unlike "Adam's Diary," this piece—which Twain once described to Duneka as "Eve's love-Story, but we will not name it that" (*MTL*, 2:775)—is tender throughout, though still focusing on the lighter, more humorous elements of Adam and Eve's courtship and "marriage." Both of these published diaries lack the darker implications in some of the other biblical pieces (largely unfinished) that Mark Twain wrote but did not publish during his lifetime. One of the most important among these latter was the "Autobiography of Eve and Diaries Antedating the Flood," which follows "Eve's Diary" here.

EVE'S DIARY

Translated From The Original

SATURDAY.—I am almost a whole day old now. I arrived yesterday. That is as it seems to me. And it must be so, for if there was a day-before-yesterday I was not there when it happened, or I should remember it. It could be, of course, that it did happen, and that I was not noticing. Very well; I will be very watchful, now, and if any day-before-yesterdays happen I will make a note of it. It will be best to start right and not let the record get confused, for some instinct tells me that these details are going to be important to the historian some day. For I feel like an experiment, I feel exactly like an experiment, it would be impossible for a person to feel more like an experiment than I do, and so I am coming to feel convinced that that is what I *am*—an experiment; just an experiment, and nothing more.

Then if I am an experiment, am I the whole of it? No, I think not; I think the rest of it is part of it. I am the main part of it, but I think the rest of it has its share in the matter. Is my position assured, or do I have to watch it and take care of it? The latter, perhaps. Some instinct tells me that eternal vigilance is the price of supremacy. [That is a good phrase, I think, for one so young.]

Everything looks better to-day than it did yesterday. In the rush of finishing up yesterday, the mountains were left in a ragged condition, and some of the plains were so cluttered with rubbish and remnants that the aspects were quite distressing. Noble and beautiful works of art should not be subjected to haste; and this majestic new world is indeed a most noble and beautiful work. And certainly marvellously near to being perfect, notwithstanding the shortness of the time. There are too many stars in some places and not enough in others, but that can be remedied presently, no doubt. The moon got loose last night, and slid down and fell out of the scheme—a very great loss; it breaks my heart to think of it. There isn't another thing among the ornaments and decorations that is comparable to it for beauty and finish. It should have been fastened better. If we can only get it back again—

But of course there is no telling where it went to. And besides, whoever gets it will hide it; I know it because I would do it myself. I believe I can be honest in all other matters, but I already begin to realize that the core and centre of my nature is love of the beautiful, a passion for the beautiful, and that it would not be safe to trust me with a moon that belonged to another person and that person didn't know I had it. I could give up a moon that I found in the daytime, because I should be afraid some one was looking; but if I found it in the dark, I am sure I should find some kind of an excuse for not saying anything about it. For I do love moons, they are so pretty and so romantic. I wish we had five or six; I would never go to bed; I should never get tired lying on the moss-bank and looking up at them.

Stars are good, too. I wish I could get some to put in my hair. But I suppose I never can. You would be surprised to find how far off they are, for they do not look it. When they first showed, last night, I tried to knock some down with a pole, but it didn't reach, which astonished me; then I tried clods till I was all tired out, but I never got one. It was because I am left-handed and cannot throw good. Even when I aimed at the one I wasn't after I couldn't hit the other one, though I did make some close shots, for I saw the black blot of the clod sail right into the midst of the golden clusters forty or fifty times, just barely missing them, and if I could have held out a little longer maybe I could have got one.

So I cried a little, which was natural, I suppose, for one of my age, and after I was rested I got a basket and started for a place on the extreme rim of the circle, where the stars were close to the ground and I could get them with my hands, which would be better, anyway, because I could gather them tenderly then, and not break them. But it was farther than I thought, and at last I had to give it up; I was so tired I couldn't drag my feet another step; and besides, they were sore and hurt me very much.

I couldn't get back home; it was too far and turning cold; but I found some tigers and nestled in among them and was most adorably comfortable, and their breath was sweet and pleasant, because they live on strawberries. I had never seen a tiger before, but I knew them in a minute by the stripes. If I could have one of those skins, it would make a lovely gown.

To-day I am getting better ideas about distances. I was so eager to get hold of every pretty thing that I giddily grabbed for it, sometimes when it was too far off, and sometimes when it was but six inches away but seemed a foot—alas, with thorns between! I learned a lesson; also I made an axiom, all out of my own head—my very first one: *The scratched Experiment shuns the thorn.* I think it is a very good one for one so young.

I followed the other Experiment around, yesterday afternoon, at a distance, to see what it might be for, if I could. But I was not able to make out. I think it is a man. I had never seen a man, but it looked like one, and I feel sure that that is what it is. I realize that I feel more curiosity about it than about any of the other reptiles. If it is a reptile, and I suppose it is; for it has frowsy hair and blue eyes, and looks like a reptile. It has no hips; it tapers like a carrot; when it stands, it spreads itself apart like a derrick; so I think it is a reptile, though it may be architecture.

I was afraid of it at first, and started to run every time it turned around, for I thought it was going to chase me; but by-and-by I found it was only trying to get away, so after that I was not timid any more, but tracked it along, several hours, about twenty yards behind, which made it nervous and unhappy. At last it was a good deal worried, and climbed a tree. I waited a good while, then gave it up and went home.

To-day the same thing over. I've got it up the tree again.

Sunday.—It is up there yet. Resting, apparently. But that is a subterfuge: Sunday isn't the day of rest; Saturday is appointed for that. It looks to me like a creature that is more interested in resting than anything else. It would tire me to rest so much. It tires me just to sit around and watch the tree. I do wonder what it is for; I never see it do anything.

They returned the moon last night, and I was *so* happy! I think it is very honest of them. It slid down and fell off again, but I was not distressed; there is no need to worry when one has that kind of neighbors; they will fetch it back. I wish I could do something to show my appreciation. I would like to send them some stars, for we have more than we can use. I mean I, not we, for I can see that the reptile cares nothing for such things.

It has low tastes, and is not kind. When I went there yesterday evening in the gloaming it had crept down and was trying to catch the little speckled fishes that play in the pool, and I had to clod it to make it go up the tree again and let them alone. I wonder if *that* is what it is for? Hasn't it any heart? Hasn't it any compassion for those little creatures? Can it be that it was designed and manufactured for such ungentle work? It has the look of it. One of the clods took it back of the ear, and it used language. It gave me a thrill, for it was the first time I had ever heard speech, except my own. I did not understand the words, but they seemed expressive.

When I found it could talk I felt a new interest in it, for I love to talk; I talk all day, and in my sleep, too, and I am very interesting, but if I had another to talk to I could be twice as interesting, and would never stop, if desired.

If this reptile is a man, it isn't an *it*, is it? That wouldn't be grammatical, would it? I think it would be *he*. I think so. In that case one would parse it thus: nominative, *he;* dative, *him;* possessive, *his'n.* Well, I will consider it a man and call it he until it turns out to be something else. This will be handier than having so many uncertainties.

Next week Sunday.—All the week I tagged around after him and tried to get acquainted. I had to do the talking, because he was so shy, but I didn't mind it. He seemed pleased to have me around, and I used the sociable "we" a good deal, because it seemed to flatter him to be included.

Wednesday.—We are getting along very well indeed, now, and getting better and better acquainted. He does not try to avoid me any more, which is a good sign, and shows that he likes to have me with him. That pleases me, and I study to be useful to him in every way I can, so as to increase his regard. During the last day or two I have taken all the work of naming things off his hands, and this has been a great relief to him, for he has no gift in that line, and is evidently very grateful. He can't think of a rational name to save him, but I do not let him see that I am aware of his defect. Whenever a new creature comes along I name it before he has time to expose himself by an awkward silence. In this way I have saved him many embarrassments. I have no defect like his. The minute I set eyes on an animal I know what it is. I don't have to reflect a moment; the right name comes out instantly, just as if it were an inspiration, as no doubt it is, for I am sure it wasn't in me half a minute before. I seem to know just by the shape of the creature and the way it acts what animal it is.

When the dodo came along he thought it was a wildcat—I saw it in his eye. But I saved him. And I was careful not to do it in a way that could hurt his pride. I just spoke up in a quite natural way of pleased surprise, and not as if I was dreaming of conveying information, and said, "Well, I do declare if there isn't the dodo!" I explained—without seeming to be explaining—how I knew it for a dodo, and although I thought maybe he was a little piqued that I knew the creature when he didn't, it was quite evident that he admired me. That was very agreeable, and I thought of it more than once with gratification before I slept. How little a thing can make us happy when we feel that we have earned it.

Thursday.—My first sorrow. Yesterday he avoided me and seemed to wish I would not talk to him. I could not believe it, and thought there was some mistake, for I loved to be with him, and loved to hear him talk, and so how could it be that he could feel unkind towards me when I had not done anything? But at last it seemed true, so I went away and sat lonely in the place where I first saw him the morning that we were made and I did not know what he was and was indifferent about him; but now it was a mournful place, and every little thing spoke of him, and my heart was very sore. I did not know why very clearly, for it was a new feeling; I had not experienced it before, and it was all a mystery, and I could not make it out.

But when night came I could not bear the lonesomeness, and went to the new shelter which he has built, to ask him what I had done that was wrong and how I could mend it and get back his kindness again; but he put me out in the rain, and it was my first sorrow.

Sunday.—It is pleasant again, now, and I am happy; but those were heavy days; I do not think of them when I can help it.

I tried to get him some of those apples, but I cannot learn to throw straight. I failed, but I think the good intention pleased him. They are forbidden, and he says I shall come to harm; but so I come to harm through pleasing him, why shall I care for that harm?

Monday.—This morning I told him my name, hoping it would interest him. But he did not care for it. It is strange. If he should tell me his name, I would care. I think it would be pleasanter in my ears than any other sound.

He talks very little. Perhaps it is because he is not bright, and is sensitive about it and wishes to conceal it. It is such a pity that he should feel so, for brightness is nothing; it is in the heart that the values lie. I wish I could make him understand that a loving good heart is riches, and riches enough, and that without it intellect is poverty.

Although he talks so little he has quite a considerable vocabulary. This morning he used a surprisingly good word. He evidently recognized, himself, that it was a good one, for he worked it in twice afterward, casually. It was not good casual art, still it showed that he possesses a certain quality of perception. Without a doubt that seed can be made to grow, if cultivated.

Where did he get that word? I do not think I have ever used it.

No, he took no interest in my name. I tried to hide my disappointment, but I suppose I did not succeed. I went away and sat on the moss-bank with my feet in the water. It is where I go when I hunger for companionship, some one to look at, some one to talk to. It is not enough—that lovely white body painted there in the pool—but it is something, and something is better than utter loneliness. It talks when I talk; it is sad when I am sad; it comforts me with its sympathy; it says, "Do not be downhearted, you poor friendless girl; I will be your friend." It *is* a good friend to me, and my only one; it is my sister.

That first time that she forsook me! ah, I shall never forget that—never, never. My heart was lead in my body! I said, "She was all I had, and now she is gone!" In my despair I said, "Break, my heart; I cannot bear my life any more!" and hid my face in my hands, and there was no solace for me. And when I took them away, after a little, there she was again, white and shining and beautiful, and I sprang into her arms!

That was perfect happiness; I had known happiness before, but it was not like this, which was ecstasy. I never doubted her afterwards. Sometimes she stayed away—maybe an hour, maybe almost the whole day, but I waited and did not doubt; I said, "She is busy, or she is gone a journey, but she will come." And it was so: she always did. At night she would not come if it was dark, for she was a timid little thing; but if there was a moon she would come. I am not afraid of the dark, but she is younger than I am; she was born after I was. Many and many are the visits I have paid her; she is my comfort and my refuge when my life is hard—and it is mainly that.

Tuesday.—All the morning I was at work improving the estate; I purposely kept away from him in the hope that he would get lonely and come. But he did not.

At noon I stopped for the day and took my recreation by flitting all about with the bees and the butterflies and revelling in the flowers, those beautiful creatures that catch the smile of God out of the sky and preserve it! I gathered them, and made them into wreaths and garlands and clothed myself in them whilst I ate my luncheon—apples, of course; then I sat in the shade and wished and waited. But he did not come.

But no matter. Nothing would have come of it, for he does not care for flowers. He calls them rubbish, and cannot tell one from another, and thinks it is superior to feel like that. He does not care for me, he does not care for flowers, he does not care for the painted sky at eventide—is there anything he does care for, except building shacks to coop himself up in from the good clean rain, and thumping the melons, and sampling the grapes, and fingering the fruit on the trees, to see how those properties are coming along?

I laid a dry stick on the ground and tried to bore a hole in it with another one, in order to carry out a scheme that I had, and soon I got an awful fright. A thin, transparent bluish film rose out of the hole, and I dropped everything and ran! I thought it was a spirit, and I *was* so frightened! But I looked back, and it was not coming; so I leaned against a rock and rested and panted, and let my limbs go on trembling until they got steady again; then I crept warily back, alert, watching, and ready to fly if there was occasion; and when I was come near, I parted the branches of a rose-bush and peeped through—wishing the man was about, I was looking so cunning and pretty—but the sprite was gone. I went there, and there was a pinch of delicate pink dust in the hole. I put my finger in, to feel it, and said *ouch!* and took it out again. It was a cruel pain. I put my finger in my mouth; and by standing first on one foot and then the other, and grunting, I presently eased my misery; then I was full of interest, and began to examine.

I was curious to know what the pink dust was. Suddenly the name of it occurred to me, though I had never heard of it before. It was *fire!* I was as certain of it as a person could be of anything in the world. So without hesitation I named it that—fire.

I had created something that didn't exist before; I had added a new thing to the world's uncountable properties; I realized this, and was proud of my achievement, and was going to run and find him and tell him about it, thinking to raise myself in his esteem—but I reflected, and did not do it. No—he would not care for it. He would ask what it was good for, and what could I answer? for if it was not *good* for something, but only beautiful, merely beautiful—

So I sighed, and did not go. For it wasn't good for anything; it could not build a shack, it could not improve melons, it could not hurry a fruit crop; it was useless, it was a foolishness and a vanity; he would despise it and say cutting words. But to me it was not despicable; I said, "Oh, you fire, I love you, you dainty pink creature, for you are *beautiful*—and that is enough!" and was going to gather it to my breast. But refrained. Then I made another maxim out of my own head, though it was so nearly like the first one that I was afraid it was only a plagiarism: "*The burnt Experiment shuns the fire.*"

I wrought again; and when I had made a good deal of fire-dust I emptied it into a handful of dry brown grass, intending to carry it home and keep it always and play with it; but the wind struck it and it sprayed up and spat out at me fiercely, and I dropped it and ran. When I looked back the blue spirit was towering up and stretching and rolling away like a cloud, and instantly I thought of the name of it—*smoke!*—though, upon my word, I had never heard of smoke before.

Soon, brilliant yellow-and-red flares shot up through the smoke, and I named them in an instant—*flames!*—and I was right, too, though these were the very first flames that had ever been in the world. They climbed the trees, they flashed splendidly in and out of the vast and increasing volume of tumbling smoke, and I had to clap my hands and laugh and dance in my rapture, it was so new and strange and so wonderful and so beautiful!

He came running, and stopped and gazed, and said not a word for many minutes. Then he asked what it was. Ah, it was too bad that he should ask such a direct question. I had to answer it, of course, and I did. I said it was fire. If it annoyed him that I should know and he must ask, that was not my fault; I had no desire to annoy him. After a pause he asked,

"How did it come?"

Another direct question, and it also had to have a direct answer.

"I made it."

The fire was travelling farther and farther off. He went to the edge of the burned place and stood looking down, and said,

"What are these?"

"Fire-coals."

He picked up one to examine it, but changed his mind and put it down again. Then he went away. *Nothing* interests him.

But I was interested. There were ashes, gray and soft and delicate and pretty—I knew what they were at once. And the embers; I knew the embers, too. I found my apples, and raked them out, and was glad; for I am very young and my appetite is active. But I was disappointed; they were all burst open and spoiled. Spoiled apparently; but it was not so; they were better than raw ones. Fire is beautiful; some day it will be useful, I think.

Friday.—I saw him again, for a moment, last Monday at nightfall, but only for a moment. I was hoping he would praise me for trying to improve the estate, for I had meant well and had worked hard. But he was not pleased, and turned away and left me. He was also displeased on another account: I tried once more to persuade him to stop going over the Falls. That was because the fire had revealed to me a new passion—quite new, and distinctly different from love, grief, and those others which I had already discovered—*fear.* And it is horrible!—I wish I had never discovered it; it gives me dark moments, it spoils my happiness, it makes me shiver and tremble and shudder. But I could not persuade him, for he has not discovered fear yet, and so he could not understand me.

Extract from Adam's Diary

Perhaps I ought to remember that she is very young, a mere girl, and make allowances. She is all interest, eagerness, vivacity, the world is to her a charm, a wonder, a mystery, a joy; she can't speak for delight when she finds a new flower, she must pet it and caress it and smell it and talk to it, and pour out endearing names upon it. And she is color-mad: brown rocks, yellow sand, gray moss, green foliage, blue sky; the pearl of the dawn, the purple shadows on the mountains, the golden islands floating in crimson seas at sunset, the pallid moon sailing through the shredded cloud-rack, the star-jewels glittering in the wastes of space—none of them is of any practical value, so far as I can see, but because they have color and majesty, that is enough for her, and she loses her mind over them. If she could quiet down and keep still a couple of minutes at a time, it would be a reposeful spectacle. In that case I think I could enjoy looking at her; indeed I am sure I could, for I am coming to realize that she is a quite remarkably comely creature—lithe, slender, trim, rounded, shapely, nimble, graceful; and once when she was standing marble-white and sun-drenched on a boulder, with her young head tilted back and her hand shading her eyes, watching the flight of a bird in the sky, I recognized that she was beautiful.

Monday noon.—If there is anything on the planet that she is not interested in it is not in my list. There are animals that I am indifferent to, but it is not so with her. She has no discrimination, she takes to all of them, she thinks they are all treasures, every new one is welcome.

When the mighty brontosaurus came striding into camp, she regarded it as an acquisition, I considered it a calamity; that is a good sample of the lack of harmony that prevails in our views of things. She wanted to domesticate it, I wanted to make it a present of the homestead and move out. She believed it could be tamed by kind treatment and would be a good pet; I said a pet twenty-one feet high and eighty-four feet long would be no proper thing to have about the place, because, even with the best intentions and without meaning any harm, it could sit down on the house and mash it, for any one could see by the look of its eye that it was absent-minded.

Still, her heart was set upon having that monster, and she couldn't give it up. She thought we could start a dairy with it, and wanted me to help her milk it; but I wouldn't; it was too risky. The sex wasn't right, and we hadn't any ladder anyway. Then she wanted to ride it, and look at the scenery. Thirty or forty feet of its tail was lying on the ground, like a fallen tree, and she thought she could climb it, but she was mistaken; when she got to the steep place it was too slick and down she came, and would have hurt herself but for me.

Was she satisfied now? No. Nothing ever satisfies her but demonstration; untested theories are not in her line, and she won't have them. She was born scientific. It is the right spirit, I concede it; it attracts me; I feel the influence of it; if I were with her more I think I should take it up myself. Well, she had one theory remaining about this colossus: she thought that if we could tame him and make him friendly we could stand him in the river and use him for a bridge. It turned out that he was already plenty tame enough—at least as far as she was concerned—so she tried her theory, but it failed: every time she got him properly placed in the river and went ashore to cross over on him, he came out and followed her around like a pet mountain. Like the other animals. They all do that.

Tuesday—Wednesday—Thursday—and to-day: all without seeing him. It is a long time to be alone; still, it is better to be alone than unwelcome.

I *had* to have company—I was made for it, I think—so I made friends with the animals. They are just charming, and they have the kindest disposition and the politest ways; they never look sour, they never let you feel that you are intruding, they smile at you and wag their tail, if they've got one, and they are always ready for a romp or an excursion or anything you want to propose. I think they are perfect gentlemen. All these days we have had such good times, and it hasn't been lonesome for me, ever. Lonesome! No, I should say not. Why, there's always a swarm of them around—sometimes as much as four or five acres—you can't count them; and when you stand on a rock in the midst and look out over the furry expanse it is so mottled and splashed and gay with color and frisking sheen and sun-flash, and so rippled with stripes, that you might think it was a lake, only you know it isn't; and there's storms of sociable birds, and hurricanes of whirring wings; and when the sun strikes all that feathery commotion, you have a blazing up of all the colors you can think of, enough to put your eyes out.

We have made long excursions, and I have seen a great deal of the world; almost all of it, I think; and so I am the first traveller, and the only one. When we are on the march, it is an imposing sight—there's nothing like it anywhere. For comfort I ride a tiger or a leopard, because it is soft and has a round back that fits me, and because they are such pretty animals; but for long distance or for scenery I ride the elephant. He hoists me up with his trunk, but I can get off myself; when we are ready to camp, he sits and I slide down the back way.

The birds and animals are all friendly to each other, and there are no disputes about anything. They all talk, and they all talk to me, but it must be a foreign language, for I cannot make out a word they say; yet they often understand me when I talk back, particularly the dog and the elephant. It makes me ashamed. It shows that they are brighter than I am, and are therefore my superiors. It annoys me, for I want to be the principal Experiment myself—and I intend to be, too.

I have learned a number of things and am educated, now, but I wasn't at first. I was ignorant at first. At first it used to vex me because, with all my watching, I was never smart enough to be around when the water was running up-hill; but now I do not mind it. I have experimented and experimented until now I know it never does run up-hill, except in the dark. I know it does in the dark, because the pool never goes dry; which it would, of course, if the water didn't come back in the night. It is best to prove things by actual experiment; then you *know;* whereas if you depend on guessing and supposing and conjecturing, you will never get educated.

Some things you *can't* find out; but you will never know you can't by guessing and supposing: no, you have to be patient and go on experimenting until you find out that you can't find out. And it is delightful to have it that way, it makes the world so interesting. If there wasn't anything to find out, it would be dull. Even trying to find out and not finding out is just as interesting as trying to find out and finding out, and I don't know but more so. The secret of the water was a treasure until I *got* it; then the excitement all went away, and I recognized a sense of loss.

By experiment I know that wood swims, and dry leaves, and feathers, and plenty of other things; therefore by all that cumulative evidence you know that a rock will swim; but you have to put up with simply knowing it, for there isn't any way to prove it—up to now. But I shall find a way—then *that* excitement will go. Such things make me sad; because by-and-by when I have found out everything there won't be any more excitements, and I do love excitements so! The other night I couldn't sleep for thinking about it.

At first I couldn't make out what I was made for, but now I think it was to search out the secrets of this wonderful world and be happy and thank the Giver of it all for devising it. I think there are many things to learn yet—I hope so; and by economizing and not hurrying too fast I think they will last weeks and weeks. I hope so. When you cast up a feather it sails away on the air and goes out of sight; then you throw up a clod and it doesn't. It comes down, every time. I have tried it and tried it, and it is always so. I wonder why it is? Of course it *doesn't* come down, but why should it *seem* to? I suppose it is an optical illusion. I mean, one of them is. I don't know which one. It may be the feather, it may be the clod; I can't prove which it is, I can only demonstrate that one or the other is a fake, and let a person take his choice.

By watching, I know that the stars are not going to last. I have seen some of the best ones melt and run down the sky. Since one can melt, they can all melt; since they can all melt, they can all melt the same night. That sorrow will come—I know it. I mean to sit up every night and look at them as long as I can keep awake; and I will impress those sparkling fields on my memory, so that by-and-by when they are taken away I can by my fancy restore those lovely myriads to the black sky and make them sparkle again, and double them by the blur of my tears.

AFTER THE FALL

When I look back, the Garden is a dream to me. It was beautiful, surpassingly beautiful, enchantingly beautiful; and now it is lost, and I shall not see it any more.

The Garden is lost, but I have found *him*, and am content. He loves me as well as he can; I love him with all the strength of my passionate nature, and this, I think, is proper to my youth and sex. If I ask myself why I love him, I find I do not know, and do not really much care to know; so I suppose that this kind of love is not a product of reasoning and statistics, like one's love for other reptiles and animals. I think that this must be so. I love certain birds because of their song; but I do not love Adam on account of his singing—no, it is not that; the more he sings the more I do not get reconciled to it. Yet I ask him to sing, because I wish to learn to like everything he is interested in. I am sure I can learn, because at first I could not stand it, but now I can. It sours the milk, but it doesn't matter; I can get used to that kind of milk.

It is not on account of his brightness that I love him—no, it is not that. He is not to blame for his brightness, such as it is, for he did not make it himself; he is as God made him, and that is sufficient. There was a wise purpose in it, *that* I know. In time it will develop, though I think it will not be sudden; and besides, there is no hurry; he is well enough just as he is.

It is not on account of his gracious and considerate ways and his delicacy that I love him. No, he has lacks in these regards, but he is well enough just so, and is improving.

It is not on account of his industry that I love him—no, it is not that. I think he has it in him, and I do not know why he conceals it from me. It is my only pain. Otherwise he is frank and open with me, now. I am sure he keeps nothing from me but this. It grieves me that he should have a secret from me, and sometimes it spoils my sleep, thinking of it, but I will put it out of my mind; it shall not trouble my happiness, which is otherwise full to overflowing.

It is not on account of his education that I love him—no, it is not that. He is self-educated, and does really know a multitude of things, but they are not so.

It is not on account of his chivalry that I love him—no, it is not that. He told on me, but I do not blame him; it is a peculiarity of sex, I think, and he did not make his sex. Of course I would not have told on him, I would have perished first; but that is a peculiarity of sex, too, and I do not take credit for it, for I did not make my sex.

Then why is it that I love him? *Merely because he is masculine*, I think.

At bottom he is good, and I love him for that, but I could love him without it. If he should beat me and abuse me, I should go on loving him. I know it. It is a matter of sex, I think.

He is strong and handsome, and I love him for that, and I admire him and am proud of him, but I could love him without those qualities. If he were plain, I should love him; if he were a wreck, I should love him; and I would work for him, and slave over him, and pray for him, and watch by his bedside until I died.

Yes, I think I love him merely because he is *mine* and is *masculine*. There is no other reason, I suppose. And so I think it is as I first said: that this kind of love is not a product of reasonings and statistics. It just *comes*—none knows whence—and cannot explain itself. And doesn't need to.

It is what I think. But I am only a girl, and the first that has examined this matter, and it may turn out that in my ignorance and inexperience I have not got it right.

FORTY YEARS LATER

It is my prayer, it is my longing, that we may pass from this life together—a longing which shall never perish from the earth, but shall have place in the heart of every wife that loves, until the end of time; and it shall be called by my name.

But if one of us must go first, it is my prayer that it shall be I; for he is strong, I am weak, I am not so necessary to him as he is to me—life without him would not be life; how could I endure it? This prayer is also immortal, and will not cease from being offered up while my race continues. I am the first wife; and in the last wife I shall be repeated.

AT EVE'S GRAVE

ADAM: Wheresoever she was, *there* was Eden.

THE END

AUTOBIOGRAPHY OF EVE AND DIARIES ANTEDATING THE FLOOD

Although the public was introduced to Eve's own account of life in the Garden of Eden in "Eve's Diary" when it was published in *Harper's* in December 1905, that was not Mark Twain's first attempt to present Eve's record of her own experiences. In recording the fact that he had begun "Eve's Diary" on 12 July 1905, Twain's secretary Isabel Lyon noted that he had "tried Eve's Diary several times, but it never went right" (Lyon Journal, TS, p. 76, MTP). In fact, those earlier attempts began sometime in 1901 or 1902 with the "Autobiography of Eve." Perhaps the negotiations in January or February 1901 for republication of "Extracts from Adam's Diary" rekindled Twain's interest in Edenic times. Working notes and other details also point to connections with another project he was working on during that same February and March—"The Secret History of Eddypus," his burlesque history of civilization, which featured the fall of the Great Civilization, and the establishment of the Christian Science empire.

Mark Twain originally wrote some ninety-eight manuscript pages of the "Autobiography" with Eve as narrator. Subsequently, for reasons that must always remain speculative, he decided that the original approach was unsatisfactory for what he wanted to convey, then went back to page 68 and began assigning some of this material to other narrators and recasting it into new segments, several of which Bernard DeVoto later assembled under the rubric "Papers of the Adam Family" in *Letters from the Earth* (1962). In both his original effort and in extensive revisions, Twain's aim was to relate the narratives of Genesis 2–9 to the present and at the same time to demonstrate his cyclical theory of history. (Twain's original continuation of the "Autobiography of Eve," manuscript pages 68–98, is reprinted here in appendix 1. A full discussion of these manuscripts can be found in Baetzhold, McCullough, and Malcolm, 23–38.)

The manuscript shows that Twain first began writing the "Autobiography" simply as "Eve's Diary" with Eve recording her experiences as they happened—or shortly thereafter—much as she was to do in the later "Eve's Diary" of 1905. But very soon he decided to have her tell the story from a later perspective, for manuscript page 19 begins: "I still remember that time as if it were yesterday."† It was probably then that he went back to page one of his manuscript and added in the upper right-hand corner: "Autobiography of Eve" and under it, Roman numeral I, followed by "I will begin with a few extracts from my diary."† All that follows, then, is set at the time that Mark Twain later designated "Year of the World 1012." (Still later, near the very end of the manuscript, he would change 1012 to 920 in order to establish the fact that Adam, who presumably died in 930, was still alive.)

As Mark Twain first wrote it, the "Autobiography" continued through manuscript page 98, telling Eve's story by means of diary excerpts from both the earlier times and the present. The beginning portions (discarded by DeVoto) record her wonderings about her own identity and about her surroundings, her delight in nature, her enjoyment of the animals, her growing loneliness as she realizes that only she among the creatures has no mate. All of these—and especially her search for a companion, its many difficulties, her finding of Adam, and the growth of their affection—are treated both humorously and tenderly.

Eve then goes on to describe (at the point at which DeVoto picks up the text) the peace in the Garden during those early days and (largely humorously) the various "scientific" discoveries made by herself and Adam. In this peaceful Eden there is only a hint of things to come when a Voice (the Lord of the Garden) warns Adam and Eve about eating the fruit of the tree of the knowledge of good and evil. Having no idea what good and evil—and death—actually are, they decide that the only way to find out is to *try* the fruit. But just at that moment, a strange creature, which turns out to be a pterodactyl, "flounders" by, and their scientific curiosity impels them to chase it. Hence the Fall is postponed.

Then follows the account of Cain's birth about a year and a half or two years later, during one of Adam's absences, and much speculation as to what sort of creature "it" is before they determine that he is a human child. The next year Abel arrives, and then, during years five and six, daughters Gladys and Edwina. At that point the excerpt from Eve's early diary notes that after

Adam had "gotten the children scientifically classified," he came to love them dearly, "and from that time till now, the bliss of Eden is perfect."

Returning to the present, Eve remarks (in a passage later excised by Mark Twain but retained by DeVoto), "Ah, well, in that old simple, ignorant time it never entered our unthinking heads that we, humble, unknown and inconsequential little people, were cradling, nursing and watching over the most conspicuous and stupendous event which would happen in the universe for a thousand years—the founding of the human race" (*LE*, 89–90).

Eve then compares the solitude of the early days and the current "swarming hive of human life" and goes on to discuss the problems caused by the rapidly burgeoning population. But sometime later Mark Twain decided to include a few more episodes involving the early days of the family and introduced, among other details, Adam's and the children's efforts to compile a dictionary and to make flint-knives, arrowheads, and fossils. From here on, except for a few references to the past, the excerpts from Eve's diary are "contemporary" ones, which discuss the development of civilization and its present problems, most of which parallel those that Mark Twain saw pertinent to his own times. In this early version there was no mention of the Fall, even though that event had obviously occurred long before.

As originally written, the discussion in "Extract from an Article in 'The Radical,' January 916" was a more personal continuation of Eve's own diary account of the threats of overpopulation. In the course of explaining how a famine and pestilence in the year 508 had helped to ease the problem, she described the loss at that time of her own eldest daughter Gladys. Here Eve's reminiscences clearly formed a link between the conclusion of the earlier sections—the memories of Eden and the immediate post-Eden setting—and the beginning of passages that describe the chaotic conditions of the first civilization just prior to its destruction by the Flood.

After an account of Gladys's death and its aftermath—the outpouring of condolences, the tributes that followed, and the family's initial appreciation thereof, Eve's story continued with her reception of Reginald Selkirk, popularly called the Mad Philosopher, or Mad Prophet, whose professorship in mathematics Eve had been influential in obtaining some years earlier. Eve herself considered the epithet "Mad" undeserving, since Selkirk dealt in prognostications rather than prophecies, using history and statistics to forecast probabilities. Yet, in the popular mind, Selkirk's interests were sufficiently esoteric and his predictions seemingly far-fetched enough to warrant the appellation.

Reading the continuation of Eve's story as originally written, one sees that in these passages Mark Twain had successfully created certain key aspects of Eve's personality, some of which he manipulated from behind the first-person narrative for comic effect. When the "Diary of a Lady of the Blood," for example, is read as Eve's words, the reader sees Twain sometimes almost mocking his own protagonist. Eve here appears as a dowager, rather proud of her position and her ability to exert influence on behalf of the Mad Prophet—and a bit forgetful. What becomes clear in the continuation of that conversation, however, is that Mark Twain was finding difficulty in sustaining Eve's place at the center of the action. The session with Selkirk begins as a means of setting the backdrop for the revelation that Noah is building the Ark. But it quickly turns into a virtual monologue by the Mad Philosopher on the faults of the present civilization. Eve is reduced to a horrified onlooker, though at the end of that segment (in a passage later deleted) we do get a sense of her despair at the appalling news that the Ark is already under construction and the Flood is imminent.

At this point, though he had succeeded in tying Eden and the Flood together as a historical cycle, Mark Twain was nearing a narrative impasse. The cyclical effect that he had attempted to achieve became literally circular in the narrative. And in the final segment of the original manuscript, there came several pages (later incorporated into "Passage from a Lecture") which discuss the "Law of Periodical Repetition" and the "Law of Intellectual Averages" and end with a reference to the occasional emergence of a prodigy like the one Selkirk had discussed earlier. Originally (in another deleted portion) Eve tries to find some reassurance that there will be no more floods after the imminent one, and is further appalled when the Philosopher declares that by the Law of Periodical Repetitions the Flood, like all other events, will recur again and again.

Finally, however, the well evidently ran dry for Twain, for the manuscript ends with a cryptic new paragraph: "And so forth & so-on." Both the ending of the original story, as it circled back into the past, and additional planning notes show Mark Twain attempting to illustrate the workings of an eternally cyclical history without recourse to historical materials adequate to the task. Perhaps it was this specific deficiency that later prompted him to tear apart his original effort and recast it as a documentary account of the events and forces at work just prior to the first civilization's demise.

Toward the end of the original story, or perhaps when he next decided to try again, Twain apparently realized that he had taken the play away from Eve by concentrating so much on the Mad Philosopher. He may then have decided that he could show the state of the post-Edenic world and highlight the "Laws of the Intellectual Average and Periodical Repetition" and the parallels to his own time more effectively by recasting the material as documents recorded by several different narrators. At some point, too, he no doubt considered the fact that he had not treated the symbolic cause of it all—the original sin and the Fall.

To remedy that lack he wrote "Passage from Satan's Diary" and "Passage from Eve's Diary" (the pieces that Paine published as "That Day in Eden" and "Eve Speaks" in *Europe and Elsewhere* [1923]). In the first, Satan's account amplified Eve's earlier reference to the Voice's warning about the forbidden tree by recording Adam and Eve's further questioning of the meaning of good, evil, and death, and their discussion of these matters with Satan, the eating of the apple, and their resulting shame at their nakedness. In the second, Eve reports the expulsion from Eden, remarks upon the unfairness of the judgment, their consequent experience for the first time of cold, hunger, pain, and grief, and their later acquaintance with all the unadmirable qualities of human nature. Finally they experience death, when they discover Abel lying bloody in his field and cannot wake him. To conclude the episode an excerpt from Satan's diary announces that "Death has entered the world" and adds, "The Family think ill of Death—they will change their mind."

Though it is impossible to say just when Mark Twain decided to introduce the different narrators, notations on the manuscripts provide a good indication of the order he intended. Sometime after writing the above pieces, he wrote an "A" at the top of the "Satan's Diary" and next to it, "Passages from Diaries Antedating the Flood." At the top of Eve's account of the Fall he wrote "B?" Despite the question mark, which suggests that he was not quite sure of the placement, the material obviously relates to and expands the discussion in "A." These passages were almost certainly meant to follow the new pages 68–72 which marked the first revision of the original manuscript. Then, when Twain decided to introduce the "Passages from Diaries Antedating the Flood," he selected the original page 68, crossed out the page number, and wrote a new title, "Passage from Eve's Diary. / Year of the World 1012." At the same time he also wrote in the upper left corner of the page that this was "To follow Abel's death." Original pages 68–78 (with some revisions and deletions) were then recast to incorporate part of Selkirk's original discussion about the problems of overpopulation as "Extracts from an Article in 'The

Radical.'" Its suggestion that death through famine, pestilence, or war could be considered a blessing now serves to illustrate Satan's comment that the Family would not continue to "think ill of death."

Twain then set about recasting the original material by introducing multiple narrators or augmenting material in the original manuscript. For example, in "Year of the World, 920. Passage from Diary of the Mad Philosopher," Selkirk describes the grandeur and opulence of the palace the Family has occupied for many centuries, the splendor of Eve's robes, and the brilliant spectacle in general. His enthusiasm is sneered at by Nanga Parbat, the disreputable "Scion of the First Blood"—Eve's grandson—who scorns the "airs" now put on by the members of the First Family, whose beginning after all had been most simple.

Voicing opinions very like Mark Twain's, Parbat also scoffs at Selkirk's unwillingness to hear such criticisms of those in power, and accuses him of patriotism, which he defines as "groveling." He then embarks on a diatribe against loyalty to a government totally unworthy of that devotion and to those whose "accident of birth" alone had raised them to an elevated rank. Warming to his task, he blasts the rampant nepotism in the palace, where positions can be held only by "the First Three Grades of the Blood" and where even the scullery maids must be at least of the Third Grade.

Selkirk later remarks that he had not seen Eve since "the first year of the new century" when she conducted the first state ceremony she had ever performed alone. This was at the point that Mark Twain decided to change the date to 920 to indicate that Adam had not yet died. Deleting several references to Eve's widowhood, he named her "Acting Head," rather than "Head" of the Human Race, and noted that Adam had been under the care of physicians for some eighty years.

That decision then apparently prompted Twain to revise his subsequent attack upon the practices of physicians, which Selkirk had voiced in describing Adam's demise. Now he presented it in the form of a "Passage from Diary of ———." Finally, after the discussion of how physicians took advantage of "doctor-sickness" by exaggerating illnesses so as to be able to report substantial recoveries, and how they even manipulated the stock market by means of their periodic bulletins concerning the health of a prominent patient, the diarist's last two sentences exclaim: "One can see by this what value a bulletin is, where the patient has doctor-sickness. Well, it's a [word illegible] of a world!" It was at this point that Mark Twain abandoned the work that originally began as the "Autobiography of Eve."

What Twain was probably seeking by the new scheme was a broader scope, a documentary view of the doomed civilization. But just as it had been in the original intent, that vision was simply too large to handle, and the project was never brought to a successful conclusion. Even so, the importance of Eve as a narrator and a character in the revised and reassembled texts is almost as central as the original "Autobiography of Eve" and its continuation. And the inclusion of "Passage from Satan's Diary" and "Passage from Eve's Diary," which feature the expulsion from Eden and Abel's death, enhances the theme that the first civilization was doomed from the start, that the inevitable cycle of recurrence was set in motion with the Fall and the creation of history. The Fall and Abel's death usher in the unavoidable facts of human frailty, facts that no mortal, whether he is First Man or "Prodigy," can alter. The "Passage from Eve's Diary," describing the aftermath of the Fall and Abel's death, accomplishes the link between Eden and the Flood, a connection that Mark Twain saw as both a moral and a historical continuum, as well as a symbol of the fate of humanity in the years to come.

Here, then, published for the first time, are the fully reassembled "Autobiography of Eve" and "Diaries Antedating the Flood," ordered according to Mark Twain's "final" intentions. For the original continuation of the "Autobiography of Eve," also here first published, see appendix 1.

AUTOBIOGRAPHY OF EVE.†

I.

I will begin with a few extracts from my Diary.

Eve's Diary.

Monday, January 8, year 1. Who am I? What am I? Where am I?

Monday After. Those questions remain unanswered. It is no matter; let them go.

A Fortnight Later. It is lonely. Monotonous. Tedious, in fact. The birds and tigers and things are pleasant company, and they love me and I love them; but here lately they seem somehow insufficient. I lack something, I don't know what it is.

If only they could see how pretty I am, and how rounded and smooth, and how daintily formed are my limbs. Possibly they do; sometimes I think they do; but at most they only look it, they do not *say* it—at least in any language that I can understand.

I begin to feel sure that that is what I lack—to hear it *said.*

Wednesday. Nothing can be more beautiful than the reflection of my slender white body in the pool, when I stand in the edge of it and bend over and let my yellow hair hang down. Yesterday the leopard gazed like one rapt, and I blushed with pleasure and my eyes burned with humid fires, and I could have hugged him—but he did not *say* his admiration. And I was so longing for it!

Then he turned and saw the other leopard, and his eyes flashed welcome, and he said something which I did not understand, and then he strode eagerly forward and the two went away side by side into the forest, caressing each other. It made me cry for spite to have him act so. I will club that other leopard.

Friday. There is surely something wrong—at least a departure from the usual; it may be design, it may be only accidental—but anyway, there stands the fact: all the other creatures have mates, I have none. I am the only one that is alone. There are two leopards, two mastodons, two megatheriums, two pterodactyls, two tigers, two lions, two elephants, two of everything—and I am by myself. This cannot be natural; surely this was not intended. For, what have I done? I have done nothing. I have not deserved this sorrow, this shame, this embarrassment.

Saturday. For it *is* an embarrassment. It was not so before, but since those thinkings of yesterday I feel as if all eyes are upon me furtively, questioningly, and it makes me shy, and unhappy.

And foolish, too. For it was foolish to talk *at* the creatures, while talking to myself, this morning, saying, "Dear me, I did not know it was so late; here I am, idling about, and my mate likely to arrive at any moment from his long journey and be *so* disappointed if I am not there to welcome him." It was foolish, but I could not help it, I so longed to have them think I had a mate and was like other animals, and not a freak. But of course they did not understand me, and my effort went for nothing. I had half persuaded myself that one or two of the animals might catch my meaning and tell the rest, but it was not so. They all stood around me, where I sat, and gazed and listened, but indicated nothing. Presently a gentle little stranger, soft-eyed and pretty, and quite new to me—the Gazelle, I will call it—came up and laid its head in the hollow of my arm, and I hugged it gratefully to my breast, believing it understood; and said "You *do* understand, don't you, dear?—*say* you understand, and will help me find my lost mate."

But it did not know what I said; and so my hope was all gone, and I rose and went away crying, some of the creatures following from habit, the others tarrying, indifferent.

Three Months Later. May. There have been such changes! It is no longer couples, it is families, now. With every couple there are the dearest little cubs and kitties, and so cunning and graceful and sweet and pretty. They romp with me all the day long, and sleep all over me at night, and drive away my loneliness and give me peace. And all the flying creatures have nests, and broods of little folk, and the woods are filled with the charm of their singing.

So I am happier than I was. I try to put away from me that thought—the thought of a mate—and in the day I succeed, and am content, and do not feel my pain. But at night I dream—and dream.

II.

May 19. There is a colt, now, and so that pair of horses are happy. The colt is the size of a puppy, the parents the size of a hound. Five-toed, they are, which does not seem the correct thing for a horse, but they do not seem to mind it.

At first I considered the big hairy spider an ugly animal, and unpleasant to have about, but his patience and good temper have quite won me. The flies and the coleoptera pester him all day long, buzzing and fluttering around him when he is trying to sleep; and they plunge into his beautiful web and tug and struggle there trying to get loose; and instead of getting angry he severs their bonds and sets them free, then puts in whole hours mending the holes in his web where they have torn it, and never shows any resentment. He gets no time to go out and seek for food, and I marvel that he keeps well and fat; he sucks the dew-beads, but I have never seen him eat anything. All the other creatures eat.

The lion eats turnips; the tiger eats tomatoes; the hyena lives on strawberries; the fox eats apples; the otter eats cherries; the vulture eats oranges; the buzzard eats bananas; the chicken-hawk lives on peaches; but if the spider eats anything I cannot find it out.

All the animals play together, grouped according to size: the sheep and lambs and horses and deer and wolves and dogs, and others of similar size in one group; the camels and calves and cows and lions and tigers and leopards and so-on in another; the elephant, the mastodon, the megatherium, the rhinoceros, the sloth that is as big as a tree-trunk, the giant frog that is nine feet high as he sits, in another; and the mighty saurians in still another group. And these monsters, how they do gambol and cavort when the spirit of play is upon them! When they make a rush the ground quakes under them and when they come together you can hear the concussion a mile, and see the big ones toss the smaller fry, such as the elephant and the hippopotamus, high in the air, just as I would toss a clod; and it is all good-humored, and great fun; and I always run to see it, and it is *such* good sport, and makes me laugh till the tears come.

And those vast lizards—my! When they sweep their tails around, the smaller trees go down like weeds. But what they mainly like is wrestling. Yesterday the big ichthyosaurus, who is ninety feet long, wrestled with his mate, who is eighty-seven feet, and they rose in the air forty feet, struggling in each other's arms, and roaring like the hurricane; and it was grand to see.

It seems such a pity that I have no mate to enjoy these good times with me.

III.

May 25. I have company. That beautiful parrot which I have been petting, talks! I was never so astonished. This morning he straddled sideways along his limb, in his awkward way, till he got to me, then canted his head to one side so cunning, and said—

"Nice Eve, p'ty Eve! Polly want a cracker."

He said it just as plainly. I snatched him to my heart, and hugged him for joy, saying—

"Oh, you darling! Are you my mate?"

But he only shouted, in his shrill voice, along with explosions of fiendish laughter—

"Cracker! cracker! P'ty Polly! Polly wants a cracker! Hurry, Satan!"

Oh, it was rapture to hear my mother tongue! "It *must* be that you are my lost mate—say it, I beseech you!"

It was a foolish thought, but I was crazed by my longings. He has a mate—I already knew that. She comes every day, and they go off gathering persimmons and radishes for their young to eat. She came first then, and took him away, although he kept storming that strange word "cracker," and was greatly incensed and quite unwilling to go.

"*Eve.*" I wonder what that is? and Satan; and cracker. Polly is a name, that is clear—his own name. Who gave it him? No other animal has a name, so far as I know. I will have one for myself, if I can think of a pretty one.

June 3. Polly is getting to be very sociable and pleasant, now that he knows that I can talk. He is gay and happy and impudent, and talks and laughs and screeches all the time. But after all, he is something of a disappointment, he cares so little for elevated conversation, and his range of subjects is so limited. Another defect—he repeats himself too much. This is a vulgarity. It indicates a low order of mentality, also indifferent cultivation. I would not judge him unjustly, yet in candor I am forced to say I believe he lacks spirituality. It sounds unkind, but I think it is true; indeed I know it is. He is not soulful; he has hardly a vestige of sentiment; the movements of his spirit are earthy; if I try to lead him to high planes of thought, he looks tired, and says "Cheese it;" and yesterday when I spoke with strong emotion, and said "How majestic is the universe, how noble the design, how spacious, how impressive, how . . . ." he broke in with a hoarse shriek, followed by his odious laugh, then stormed out a string of strange words which instinct told me were not nice, and demanded a cracker.

I was deeply hurt, and changed the subject. I had hoped so much from him—and now that dream is over. He cannot supply the higher needs of my nature; my longings in these regards must remain unsatisfied, my starved spirit unappeased. It is a bitter awakening.

But where got he his English? Not from his mate; she speaks no tongue but her own. Sometimes the conviction comes upon me that he must have met my mate—seen him face to face—heard him speak! Then the world swims about me, and I almost swoon with the adorable ecstasy of the thought.

At these times I beg him to tell me; I beseech him, I implore him, I go on my knees to him, with the tears running down my face—but to no purpose; for all answer, he only wants a cracker. I would I knew what a cracker is, that I might satisfy his desire and get a rest from that weary theme. He has been used to low company, and unintellectual; his talk shows it. Could it indeed have been my mate? The thought is a pleasure, but mixed with a pain. I would like my mate to be noble, gracious, refined; and oh, surely he is! I will not believe otherwise.

June 7. It dawns upon me at last that Eve is a name—and *my* name! Who gave it me? Polly? No—poor muddle-headed thing, he can originate nothing. Then was it my mate? I do believe it; I will not allow myself to doubt it. He knows of my existence, I am sure of it; is seeking me, mourning for me, longing for me—perhaps is thinking of me at this moment—and breathing my name! Oh, I could faint for happiness! Oh, my Satan, my darling!

But that may not be the one. Satan is a name—I have satisfied myself of that; but of late there is another: Adam. For a time it seemed to mean a species; next it seemed to mean an individual of a species; but latterly it has sometimes seemed to stand for the *name* of an individual—a something to address that particular individual by. It is no matter; so I find my mate, I care nothing for names. Oh, let me but see him! And let me know beforehand; so that I can comb my hair and look my best.

IV.

June 9. Those same teasing questions continue to run in my head much of the time. What am I? Whence came I? What am I for? And there is no answer. Polly cannot tell me; at any rate he does not try; the matter does not interest him, and he will not talk about it. His mind is frivolous, and he cares only for frivolous things. It is pathetic to note with what embarrassed haste he gets away from any topic that is serious. I think he suspects his limitations, and is ashamed of them. If urged, he forgets decorum, and breaks into profanity. This is another evidence that he has had commerce with one who speaks my tongue and is of my kind, for he did not invent these phrases—he is not capable of it. Does he know Satan? Does he know Adam? I would it were my privilege. Satan is a pretty name. I wonder if he would like me with a wreath of radiant orchids around my head? I think so. I am wearing it.

It is very lonely. Not always, but sometimes. Never, in the daytime, for I am very busy, then, naming and classifying the creatures and plants and trees and flowers and things, from eight until noon, and from two till six, for these are my office hours. And when I please—which is somewhat often—I take a little holiday, and play with the animals; also, with some frequency, I sit on the elephant's head and make long excursions through the wooded hills and the flowery valleys, camping where the night overtakes me. And there is plenty of company, for the animals come along in droves, and the birds in flocks. Thousands! They never get tired, but romp and race all the time, and it is a beautiful spectacle, all that life and grace and animation, and sun-smitten flash and sparkle of rich color, every velvet back and every brilliant wing furnishing its separate contribution to the general effect.

But at night, when the creatures are asleep, I am lonely at times. I lie on a bank of flowers, with nothing to do but look at the moon sailing in the sky and turning the woods and the plains to silver. And then it is so profoundly still! Not a sound—for there are no night-animals. There ought to be some, I think. I tried to train the owl and the fox to range at night, but they were not interested, and would not take to it. They will not eat anything but oranges and pine apples, and there is no occasion to sit up nights to get those.

So I lie and look at the moon or the stars, and think over that mystery, that problem: Who am I? what am I? whence came I? what am I for? Am I an accident? did I just happen, or was I intentional? And where is Satan? where is Adam? In my excursions I have traveled so many, many leagues, and have found no trace of them. Nor any end to the land. Is there no end to it? I know I have traveled more than two hundred miles in a straight line, yet have not found the end—always there is more land. The very vastness of it is awful, and oppresses my spirit.

I still remember that time as if it were yesterday. I was a blithe young thing, and all alive with the splendid enthusiasms of youth; travel was my delight; every mile of my journey revealed new things and new aspects to me, and every novelty brought its own special pleasure; every day I moved through a new world, new wonders, new combinations of beauty and majesty and sublimity, and every night I dreamed the day's enchantments and lived them again. This was the longest journey I had yet made; I had never been so far from home before. I was climbing high into the mountains, now—a fresh experience.

DIARY. It was observable that the weather was growing colder, yet there was no rain. This was strange. Always before, coolness came only with the rain. There was no accounting for this new thing. The coolness grew—grew steadily. I closely examined the earth and the rocks, but they were of the usual sort—the change of temperature could not be charged to their influence. I was troubled. There was something eerie and uncanny about this causeless coolness.

I quieted myself for a while with the reflection that this unnatural condition of things could last but a little while longer, for with patience and perseverance we should by and by be so high up toward the sun that the coolness could not stand out against his rays at such close quarters, and then we should cease to shiver and begin to roast. But, miracle of miracles, the reverse happened. The higher we climbed toward the source of all heat, the colder it got. This is the actual truth. It is a mystery which will probably never be explained.

Before night it was bitter cold, biting cold; and the wind, instead of softly caressing my unprotected body as was its wont, cut me cruelly. My hair, which I was wearing in two long plaits down my back, and which had gathered dampness from the atmosphere, became hard and stiff, and my cheeks and my nose ached so that the tears came.

Then all of a sudden we arrived upon a lofty precipice, and there, far away below us, lay an enchanted valley of unimaginable glory and beauty, sleeping in the golden sunlight. Such meads, such meadows, such groves, such glades, such prodigality of flowers, such softness, such richness, such flush and glow, such rhapsodies of color—it was a dream! Through it poured four shining rivers, pictured with reflections, which wound hither and thither down the mellow distances of that heaven of solitude and peace, and faded out in the dim remoteness where earth and sky melted together and became one.

My poor home, which had seemed so beautiful before—

How to reach that happy valley! That was my thought. I would descend into it, and live there always. "There I shall find Satan, there I shall find Adam," I said; "there I shall not be lonely any more."

But I could find no opening in the precipice. I wandered eagerly up and down, seeking, but there was no way. And all the time the sun was sinking. At last the darkness closed down, and through my tears I saw that land of my longing fade and disappear. I am but a slip of a girl, and I sat down and cried. But the animals came and comforted me, and tried to tell me I had friends, and not to grieve; and I rose up and went with them, seeking a bed-place.

We lay down, and they snuggled about me, and their furs warmed me and I fell asleep. I woke at dawn, and a strange thing was happening. A white powder was sifting down from above, and where it fell upon my skin it turned to water. I was frightened, and climbed to my place on the elephant, and cared not whither he went, so he got me away from this strange invasion from the skies.

I named it snow—and that is indeed what it was. The elephant carried me down the mountain; then for two weeks we skirted the base of the highlands, trying to find where those rivers came out, so that I could enter the Happy Valley; but we never found any trace of them, and at last we went back home in sorrow, for I had come to think that the Valley must have been only a vision, not a reality.

I was not contented for long. Daily and nightly the vision rose before me in its dreamy loveliness, and tormented me with unappeasable longings to see it again. My surroundings had lost their charm; they seemed commonplace and poor; I no longer took pleasure in them.

And so, in September I went forth again, with my great following, and again I searched day after day for the rivers, but I did not find them; then I climbed the mountains, for I was even willing to face the dreaded snow if once more I might see the vision.

I saw it! I stood in the snow and in the bitter wind, and through rents in the storm-driven sleet and snow I caught glimpses of the magic valley again.

After that, I haunted the place. I camped at the mountain's base, and rode up every day and fed my spirit with the vision, then searched for a way down the precipice.

Diary. To-day, up there, I got the most stupendous shock of my life. In the fresh snow I came upon a large *human footprint.*

My head swam, and I almost swooned. My limbs trembled under me with weakness—or with overpowering gratitude, perhaps. I stood a moment gazing upon the footprint in a delicious delirium of happiness, then sank down and kissed it. Kissed it a dozen times, then sprang up and was hoisted to the elephant's head and said "Follow where the tracks lead!"

I remember it so well. I followed the tracks some fifteen or twenty miles around the curving precipice, and then downward by a hardly noticeable path which was too narrow for the elephant. I left him where he was, along with the other big animals, and hurried down on foot, followed by the tigers and lions, monkeys, Irish elks, cave bears and the other small creatures, hundreds and thousands, and by birds a plenty.

Soon I was in the Valley. The glory, the splendor, the beauty of the reality, surpassed the vision; and the fragrance was intoxicating. But the tracks were gone; they vanished where the velvet sod began. There was a plenty of creatures, and they welcomed us with caresses; but among them was no mate of mine.

It was a sad day—indeed, the first poignantly sad one that had come into my young life. I am old, now: bent, broken, withered, widowed, my head is white with unnumbered sorrows, I have been familiar with grief for a thousand years, but that day stands out clear in my memory, for it is a land-mark: it brought me my first real misery, my first real heartbreak. This faded manuscript is blurred by the tears which fell upon it then, and after ten centuries I am crying over it again. Crying over it for pity of that poor child; and from this far distance it seems to be not me, but a child that I have lost—*my* child. Other mothers have felt something akin to this in recalling, not their former selves, (as in my case), but the little figures which represent sons and daughters of theirs which have since grown to the gravity and stature of full age. Sometimes, for a moment, these poor mothers have a vision of those little creatures romping by, and they recognise the voices and the laughter—gone silent long ago!—and they have a pain at the heart, as knowing that *those* children are lost to them for always, in the flesh, although their grown-up selves are still present in life and still precious. The loved and lost! *They* know—the mothers! They know what the grown-ups are, and what they *were*—that the "are" and the "were" are the same, yet not the same; that the "are" remain, but that the "were" have gone out from their mothers' lives to return no more but in visions.

Yes, across the mouldering centuries I still see that silken little creature, just as she was, the fairest thing in that fair Eden; and in my old heart, leathery as it is, I feel again the pang of that day's disappointment.

Diary. It is weeks that I have been wandering here. I have searched leagues and leagues in all directions, and have found no trace of him. The Valley is so cruelly vast! Early I had a happy thought, and took the bloodhound up to the snow and showed him the tracks, and was full of hope, not doubting he would hunt him down in an hour. But it was another disappointment; he took no interest. It seemed to indicate that the track gave out no smell. I made a test. I dodged out of the hound's sight in the woods and hid. He was never able to find me, but would sniff the ground all around, within ten steps of me, and then go sniffing off elsewhere. So it is plain that our breed give off no smell. This may indicate superiority—even primacy. And it may not. This question can be left to another time.

Year 2, Jan. 6. My birthday. I am a year old. And on this day, of all days, I found him! He was lying on a mossy bank, under a spreading tree, asleep. My heart was near to bursting with joy. Tongue cannot tell how beautiful he was: as young and fresh and blooming as I am, but taller, more muscular and more sinewy, but not so broad in the hips; Curly brown hair, tumbling negligently about his shoulders—oh, *so* handsome! And such a smooth whity-pinky face, and lovely to the touch, like mine. I stroked it to my content, and played with his hair, and kissed his eyes and his lips, and was never, never so happy in this whole long year since I was born. Such a bewitching boy—and all mine! I cooed, and murmured, and cooed again, and said softly, "Satan—dear Satan!" not to wake him, but only to hear the name, and feel the thrill of it.

At last he suddenly woke, and sat straight up, staring at me. I could not hold myself, but threw my arms around his neck, and pressed him close and kissed him on the mouth—one, two, three, six times. Which frightened him, and he flung me off and jumped to his feet, his eyes flashing anger and astonishment, his nostrils swelling and subsiding like a horse's, and his knees quaking.

How could he use me so? What had I done? I had not meant any harm. I was glad to be with him, I only wanted to express it and I knew no other way; I am young and have had no one to teach me, and if I made a mistake was it so great a one that I deserved such humiliation? I could hardly believe it had happened. I had never been treated so before; the animals always gave me love for love, and never thought to hurt my body or shame my pride. It was so strange—this that had happened.

I turned and went away, with my face in my hands, sobbing; my dream was spoiled, he was not what I had thought he would be, I did not wish to see him any more.

I did not look back.

I am in my home again. It is rainy and dark. I wish I had a mother. The others have. I have not missed her before.

A Month Later. The hurt stayed with me, and I would not go near that place. I was resolved I would absorb myself in work, and forget him. I did the work, but the old pleasure in it was somehow gone; I did not care for it any more. I made a lot of fossils, but they were not good ones, for my heart was not in it. Some of them were tolerable, but mainly they were crude and inartistic; they lacked finish. I wanted them for the Quaternary, but they were not good enough for that, and I was obliged, to my regret, to set them back and stick them in the Primary, where of course they are apochryphal and foolish, and don't belong, and can't belong, and will give Science the blind staggers some day; but what am I to do? Waste them? It is not likely. As inventions, some of them are not bad, I think. I have put up a hydrocephalous plantigrade with fused reptilian and molluscous characters and an evolutionary disposition toward feathers, which will attract attention in the remote by and by when they find it. It may turn out a help in reconciling Science and the Scriptures, but the more I look at it the more I am persuaded that there will have to be considerable concessions on both sides before that happens.

Those long days, those desolate days—how they dragged! In spite of me I began secretly to wish—never mind what it was I wished. I was ashamed of it, and resisted it. One day, in the smooth white sand of the lake shore I found these words written:

"I am sorry. I repent. Forgive!"

And there were his footprints, also. For a moment the responsive blood went leaping through my veins, and I—

Then I remembered that day, and the bitterness came back. I effaced the words, and went away and hid.

The next day I went there, implacable, resentful, to efface them again. To my surprise, there were none to efface. I was deeply offended. It was another affront. I said to myself, he is a person of no stability of character; now I *am* done with him; this is final.

The next day it was the very same—nothing to efface. I was ashamed of myself for coming, and said this was the last—I would never come again.

And I kept my word. I did go, the next day, but not to look for the words: I was not aware that I was there till I was there. Then I looked for other things.

In this there was no harm, and I went every day and looked for other things. But I never found any of those things. At last, one day, mechanically, and without noticing what I was doing, I wrote some words myself:

"Come back."

When I saw what I had done I was ashamed of myself, and obliterated the words. Thus:

~~COME BACK.~~

The next day, there they were. And nothing else. At least nothing except some footprints. And for three days there they were—and nothing else. Except footprints. I cried—though there was nothing to cry about—and obliterated the words utterly. By and by, in an absent mood, I wrote them again; and again my pride rose against me, and I partially scratched them out:

~~COME BACK.~~

And there they were, next day. Also the footprints. Also a flower—if one may call a weed by that name; it was a dandelion. It gave me a thrill, but I threw it away, for it was an impertinence for him to leave it there. I went back in the night and got it; I did not know why—it was just an impulse—for I do not care for dandelions.

Next day, the words, the footprints, and a *marigold.* I kept the flower, though my first impulse was to throw it away. I was very miserable, and in my distress I obliterated the words, and then wrote them again, and forgot to make any erasure:

COME BACK.

In the dewy morning I flew to the lake, my heart beating as it had never beaten before, and there— The *words*—only the words, and nothing more! The tears came, and a weakness quivered through my limbs, and I fell—into his arms!

It was a blessed day. "Come home," he said, "this poor weather-worried land is no fit place for my Eve;" and he kissed me, and I said—

"All lands are fit where my Satan is."

Then he laughed, and patted me on the cheek, and said—

"You dear little simpleton!"

"Why?"

So he told me who he was, and who Satan was, and we laughed and cackled over it like the giddy children we were. Oh, careless Youth! oh, golden Youth! oh, only precious thing in this weary life, how lightly we prize you when we have you, how we mourn you when we have lost you!

Daily we walked the glades of Eden with our arms about each other, and over and over again he told the same tale, and it was always fresh and always new, and always a joy to my enchanted ears: how he grieved, that tragic day, and followed me at a distance, hoping I would look back; and how he lived near me all that long time, afterward, never returning to his Eden; and had me always in his sight; and was afraid to let me see him, thinking I hated him. And often I broke into the tale, to make him say things again which he had said a hundred times before:

"And when did you find out I loved you, dear?"

"When you wrote the words."

"Were you glad, Adam?"

He stopped my mouth, for answer. But not with his hand.

"But I scratched out the words."

"Oh, yes; oh, certainly. One could almost notice it."

It seemed *such* a good joke, the cunning way he said it. So we laughed and laughed.

"Well, then, since you could read it, why didn't you *come* back?"

"Because I was so sure of you?"

"Sure of me?"

"Yes. I said, 'She wants me, but tries to pretend she is indifferent. I will wait. She shall write it again—and plainer. And yet again. She shall keep writing it till she leaves the scratches all off. And *that's* frank, straight, unblushing confession!' "

"How naughty of you!"

"Yes, but very pleasant."

"Pleasant! Ah, it wasn't for me. How could you endure all that waiting?"

"It *was* hard, but I had to make you confess. And then there were modifying circumstances—they made it easier for me."

"How do you mean?"

"Why, I had your company. All the day long I followed you and fed upon the sight of you. Often I was so near you that I could have touched you. Sometimes I *did*."

"Actually touched me?"

"One might call it so. Kissed you while you slept."

"Oh, if I could have known it! But it was better so. It was very indelicate."

"Criminal, too; it was robbery. Put up your mouth—I will give them back."

It was done.

"Adam, if you loved me so, why did you give me such a poor thing as that dandelion?"

"That was only to test you, dear. I said, if she keeps that, I'll *know* she loves me."

"The test failed! I threw it away."

"Yes, I saw you."

"Poor boy, I am sorry I did it, now. How did it make you feel?"

"Badly—very badly."

"Well, you shan't grieve about it any more. I will tell you a secret: I went back and got it."

"Yes, I remember it. I was there."

Then I boxed his ears, and we laughed and laughed at the foolish trifle as if there was never going to be such a thing as grief and heartbreak in the world.

. . . . Love, peace, comfort, measureless contentment—that was life in the Garden. It was a joy to be alive. Pain there was none, nor infirmity, nor any physical signs to mark the flight of time; disease, care, sorrow—one might feel these outside the pale, but not in Eden. There they had no place, there they never came. All days were alike, and all a dream of delight.

Interests were abundant; for we were children, and ignorant; ignorant beyond the conception of the present day. We knew *nothing*—nothing whatever. We were starting at the very bottom of things—at the very beginning; we had to learn the a b c of things. To-day the child of four years knows things which we were still ignorant of at thirty. For we were children without nurses and without instructors. There was no one to tell us anything. There was no dictionary, and we could not know whether we used our words correctly or not; we liked large ones, and I know now that we often employed them for their sound and dignity, while quite ignorant of their meaning; and as to our spelling, it was profligate. But we cared not a straw for these trifles; so that we accumulated a large and showy vocabulary, we cared nothing for the means and the methods.

But studying, learning, inquiring into the cause and nature and purpose of everything we came across, were passions with us, and this research filled our days with brilliant and absorbing interest. Adam was by constitution and proclivity a scientist; I may justly say I was the same, and we loved to call ourselves by that great name. Each was ambitious to beat the other in scientific discovery, and this incentive added a spur to our friendly rivalry, and effectively protected us against falling into idle and unprofitable ways and frivolous pleasure-seeking.

Our first memorable scientific discovery was the law that water and like fluids run down-hill, not up. It was Adam that found this out. Days and days he conducted his experiments secretly, saying nothing to me about it; for he wanted to make perfectly sure before he spoke. I knew something of prime importance was disturbing his great intellect, for his repose was troubled and he thrashed about in his sleep a good deal. But at last he was sure, and then he told me. I could not believe it, it seemed so strange, so impossible. My astonishment was his triumph, his reward. He took me from rill to rill—dozens of them—saying always, "There—you see it runs down-hill—in every case it runs down-hill, never up. My theory was right; it is proven, it is established, nothing can controvert it." And it was a pure delight to see his exultation in his great discovery.

In the present day no child wonders to see the water run down and not up, but it was an amazing thing then, and as hard to believe as any fact I have ever encountered. You see, that simple matter had been under my eyes from the day I was made, but I had never happened to notice it. It took me some time to accept it and adjust myself to it, and for a long time I could not see a running stream without voluntarily or involuntarily taking note of the dip of the surface, half expecting to see Adam's law violated; but at last I was convinced, and remained so; and from that day forth I should have been startled and perplexed to see a waterfall going up the wrong way. Knowledge has to be acquired by hard work; none of it is flung at our heads gratis.

That law was Adam's first great contribution to science; and for more than two centuries it went by his name—Adam's Law of Fluidic Precipitation. Anybody could get on the soft side of him by dropping a casual compliment or two about it in his hearing. He was a good deal inflated—I will not try to conceal it—but not spoiled. Nothing ever spoiled him, he was so good and dear and right-hearted. He always put it by with a deprecating gesture, and said it was no great thing, some other scientist would have discovered it by and by; but all the same, if a visiting stranger had audience of him and was tactless enough to forget to mention it it was noticeable that that stranger was not invited to call again. After a couple of centuries, the discovery of the Law got into dispute, and was wrangled over by scientific bodies for as much as a century, the credit being finally given to a more recent person. It was a cruel blow. Adam was never the same man afterward. He carried that sorrow in his heart for six hundred years, and I have always believed that it shortened his life. Of course throughout his days he took precedence of kings and of all the race as First Man, and had the honors due to that great rank, but these distinctions could not compensate him for that lamented ravishment, for he was a true scientist and the First; and he confided to me, more than once, that if he could have kept the glory of Discoverer of the Law of Fluidic Precipitation he would have been content to pass as his own son and Second Man. I did what I could to comfort him. I said that as First Man his fame was secure; and that a time would come when the name of the pretended discoverer of the law that water runs down-hill would fade and perish and be forgotten in the earth. And I believe that. I have never ceased to believe it. That day will surely come.

I scored the next great triumph for science myself: to-wit, how the milk gets into the cow. Both of us had marveled over that mystery a long time. We had followed the cows around for years—that is, in the daytime—but had never caught them drinking a fluid of that color. And so, at last we said they undoubtedly procured it at night. Then we took turns and watched them by night. The result was the same—the puzzle remained unsolved. These proceedings were of a sort to be expected in beginners, but one perceives, now, that they were unscientific. A time came when experience had taught us better methods. One night as I lay musing, and looking at the stars, a grand idea flashed through my head, and I saw my way! My first impulse was to wake Adam and tell him, but I resisted it and kept my secret. I slept no wink the rest of the night. The moment the first pale streak of dawn appeared I flitted stealthily away; and deep in the woods I chose a small grassy spot and wattled it in, making a secure pen; then I enclosed a cow in it. I milked her dry, then left her there, a prisoner. There was nothing there to drink—she must get milk by her secret alchemy, or stay dry.

All day I was in a fidget, and could not talk connectedly I was so preoccupied; but Adam was busy trying to invent a multiplication table, and did not notice. Toward sunset he had got as far as 6 times 9 are 27, and while he was drunk with the joy of his achievement and dead to my presence and all things else, I stole away to my cow. My hand shook so with excitement and with dread of failure that for some moments I could not get a grip on a teat; then I succeeded, and the milk came! Two gallons. Two gallons, and nothing to make it out of. I knew at once the explanation: *the milk was not taken in by the mouth, it was condensed from the atmosphere* through the cow's hair. I ran and told Adam, and his happiness was as great as mine, and his pride in me inexpressible.

Presently he said—

"Do you know, you have not made merely one weighty and far-reaching contribution to science, but two."

And that was true. By a series of experiments we had long ago arrived at the conclusion that atmospheric air consisted of water in invisible suspension; also, that the components of water were hydrogen and oxygen, in the proportion of two parts of the former to one of the latter, and expressible by the symbol H_2O. My discovery revealed the fact that there was still another ingredient—milk. We enlarged the symbol to H_2O,M.

DIARY. Another discovery. One day I noticed that William McKinley was not looking well. He is the original first lion, and has been a pet of mine from the beginning. I examined him, to see what was the matter with him, and found that a cabbage which he had not chewed, had stuck in his throat. I was unable to pull it out, so I took the broomstick and rammed it home. This relieved him. In the course of my labors I had made him spread his jaws, so that I could look in, and I noticed that there was something peculiar about his teeth. I now subjected the teeth to careful and scientific examination, and the result was a consuming surprise: the lion is not a vegetarian, he is carnivorous, a flesh-eater! Intended for one, anyway.

I ran to Adam and told him, but of course he scoffed, saying—

"Where would he find flesh?"

I had to grant that I didn't know.

"Very well, then, you see, yourself, that the idea is apochryphal. Flesh was not intended to be eaten, or it would have been provided. No flesh having been provided, it follows, of a necessity, that no carnivora have been intruded into the scheme of things. Is this a logical deduction, or isn't it?"

"It is."

"Is there a weak place in it anywhere?"

"No."

"Very well, then, what have you to say?"

"That there is something better than logic."

"Indeed? What is it?"

"Fact."

I called a lion, and made him open his mouth.

"Look at this larboard upper jaw," I said. "Isn't this long forward tooth a canine?"

He was astonished, and said impressively—

"By my halidome it is!"

"What are these four, to rearward of it?"

"Premolars, or my reason totters!"

"What are these two at the back?"

"Molars, if I know a molar from a past participle when I see it. I have no more to say. Statistics cannot lie; this beast is not graminivorous."

He is always like that—never petty, never jealous, always just, always magnanimous; prove a thing to him and he yields at once and with a noble grace. I wonder if I am worthy of this marvelous boy, this beautiful creature, this generous spirit?

It was a week ago. We examined animal after animal, then, and found the estate rich in thitherto unsuspected carnivora. Somehow it is very affecting, now, to see a stately Bengal tiger stuffing himself with strawberries and onions; it seems so out of character, though I never felt so about it before.

To-day, in a wood, we heard a Voice.

We hunted for it, but could not find it. Adam said he had heard it before, but had never seen it, though he had been quite close to it. So he was sure it was like the air, and could not be seen. I asked him to tell me all he knew about the Voice, but he knew very little. It was Lord of the Garden, he said, and had told him to dress the Garden and keep it; and it had said we must not eat of the fruit of a certain tree and that if we ate of it we should surely die. Our death would be certain. That was all he knew. I wanted to see the tree, so we had a pleasant long walk to where it stood alone in a secluded and lovely spot, and there we sat down and looked long at it with interest, and talked. Adam said it was the tree of the knowledge of good and evil.

"Good and evil?"

"Yes."

"What is that?"

"What is what?"

"Why, those things. What is good?"

"I do not know. How should I know?"

"Well, then, what is evil?"

"I suppose it is the name of something, but I do not know what."

"But Adam, you must have *some* idea of what it is."

"*Why* should I have some idea? I have never seen the thing, how am I to form any conception of it? What is your own notion of it?"

Of course I had none, and it was unreasonable of me to require him to have one. There was no way for either of us to guess what it might be. It was a new word, like the other; we had not heard them before, and they meant nothing to us. My mind kept running on the matter, and presently I said—

"Adam, there are those other new words—die, and death. What do *they* mean?"

"I have no idea."

"Well, then, what do you *think* they mean?"

"My child, cannot you see that it is impossible for me to make even a plausible *guess* concerning a matter about which I am absolutely ignorant? A person can't *think*, when he has no material to think *with*. Isn't that true?"

"Yes—I know it; but how vexatious it is. Just because I can't know, I all the more *want* to know."

We sat silent a while turning the puzzle over in our minds; then all at once I saw how to find out, and was surprised that we had not thought of it in the beginning, it was so simple. I sprang up and said—

"How stupid we are! Let us eat of it; we shall die, and then we shall know what it is, and not have any more bother about it."

Adam saw that it was the right idea, and he rose at once and was reaching for an apple when a most curious creature came floundering by, of a kind which we had never seen before, and of course we dropped a matter which was of no special scientific interest, to rush after one that *was*.

Miles and miles over hill and dale we chased that lumbering, scrambling, fluttering goblin till we were away down the western side of the Valley where the pillared great banyan tree is, and there we caught him. What a joy, what a triumph: he is a pterodactyl! Oh, he is a love, he is so ugly! And has such a temper, and such an odious cry. We called a couple of tigers and rode home, and fetched him along, and now I have him by me, and it is late, but I can't bear to go to bed, he is such a fascinating fiend and such a royal contribution to science. I know I shan't sleep for thinking of him and longing for morning to come, so that I can explore him and scrutinize him, and search out the secret of his birth, and determine how much of him is bird and how much is reptile, and see if he is a survival of the fittest; which we think is doubtful, by the look of him. Oh, Science, where thou art, all other interests fade and vanish away!

Adam wakes up. Asks me not to forget to set down those four new words. It shows he has forgotten them. But I have not. For his sake I am always watching. They are down. It is he that is building the Dictionary—as *he* thinks—but I have noticed that it is I who do the work. But it is no matter, I like to do anything that he wants me to do; and in the case of the Dictionary I take special pleasure in the labor, because it saves him a humiliation, poor boy. His spelling is unscientific. He spells cat with a *k*, and catastrophe with a *c*, although both are from the same root.

Three days later. We have named him Terry, for short, and oh, he *is* a love! All these three days we have been wholly absorbed in him. Adam wonders how science ever got along without him till now, and I feel the same. The cat took a chance in him, seeing that he was a stranger, but has regretted it. Terry fetched Thomas a rake fore and aft which left much to be desired in the way of fur, and Thomas retired with the air of a person who had been intending to confer a surprise, and was now of a mind to go and think it over and see how it happened to go the other way. Terry is just grand—there's no other creature like him. Adam has examined him thoroughly, and feels sure he is a survival of the fittest. I think Thomas thinks otherwise.

DIARY. *Year* 3. Early in July, Adam noticed that a fish in the pond was developing legs—a fish of the whale family, though not a true whale itself, it being in a state of arrested development. It was a tadpole. We watched it with great interest, for if the legs did really mature and become usable, it was our purpose to develop them in other fishes, so that they could come out and walk around and have more liberty. We had often been troubled about those poor creatures, always wet and uncomfortable, and always restricted to the water whilst the others were free to play amongst the flowers and have a pleasant time. Soon the legs were perfected, sure enough, and then the whale was a frog. It came ashore and hopped about and sang joyously, particularly in the evenings, and its gratitude was without bounds. Others followed rapidly, and soon we had abundant music, nights, which was a great improvement on the stillness which had prevailed before.

We brought various kinds of fishes ashore and turned them loose in the meadows, but in all cases they were a disappointment—no legs came. It was strange; we could not understand it. Within a week they had all wandered back to the water, and seemed better satisfied there than they had been on land. We took this as evidence that fishes as a rule do not care for the land, and that none of them took any strong interest in it but the whales. There were some large whales in a considerable lake three hundred miles up the valley, and Adam went up there with the idea of developing them and increasing their enjoyment.

When he had been gone a week, little Cain was born. It was a great surprise to me, I was not aware that anything was going to happen. But it was just as Adam is always saying: "It is the unexpected that happens."

I did not know what to make of it at first. I took it for an animal. But it hardly seemed to be that, upon examination, for it had no teeth and hardly any fur, and was a singularly helpless mite. Some of its details were human, but there were not enough of them to justify me in scientifically classifying it under that head. Thus it started as a *lusus naturae*—a freak—and it was necessary to let it go at that, for the time being, and wait for developments.

However, I soon began to take an interest in it, and this interest grew day by day; presently this interest took a warmer cast and became affection, then love, then idolatry, and all my soul went out to the creature and I was consumed with a passion of gratitude and happiness. Life was become a bliss, a rapture, an ecstasy, and I longed, day by day, hour by hour, minute by minute for Adam to return and share my almost unendurable joy with me.

Year 4–5. At last he came, but he did not think it was a child. He meant well, and was dear and lovely, but he was a scientist first and man afterward—it was his nature—and he could accept of nothing until it was scientifically proven. The alarms I passed through, during the next twelvemonth, with that student's experiments, are quite beyond description. He exposed the child to every discomfort and inconvenience he could imagine, in order to determine what kind of bird or reptile or quadruped it was, and what it was for, and so I had to follow him about, day and night, in weariness and despair to appease its poor little sorrows and help it to bear them the best it could. He believed I had found it in the woods, and I was glad and grateful to let him think so, because the idea beguiled him to go away at times and hunt for another, and this gave the child and me blessed seasons of respite and peace. No one can ever know the relief I felt whenever he ceased from his distressful experiments and gathered his traps and bait together and started for the woods. As soon as he was out of sight I hugged my precious to my heart and smothered it with kisses, and cried for thankfulness. The poor little thing seemed to realize that something fortunate for us had happened, and it would kick and crow, and spread its gummy mouth and smile the happy smile of childhood all the way down to its brains—or whatever those things are that are down in there.

* * * *

Year 10. Next came our little Abel. I think we were a year and a half or two years old when Cain was born, and about three or three and a half when Abel was added. By this time Adam was getting to understand. Gradually his experiments grew less and less troublesome, and finally, within a year after the birth of Gladys and Edwina—years 5 and 6—ceased altogether. He came to love the children fondly, after he had gotten them scientifically classified, and from that time till now the bliss of Eden is perfect.

We have nine children, now—half boys and half girls.

Cain and Abel are beginning to learn. Already Cain can add as well as I can, and multiply and subtract a little. Abel is not as quick as his brother, mentally, but he has persistence, and that seems to answer in the place of quickness. Abel learns about as much in three hours as Cain does, but Cain gets a couple of hours out of it for play. So, Abel is a long time on the road, but, as Adam says, he "arrives on schedule, just the same." Adam has concluded that persistence is one of the talents, and has classified it under that head in his dictionary. Spelling is a gift, too, I am sure of it. With all Cain's brightness he cannot learn to spell. Now that is like his father, who is the brightest of us all, and yet whose orthography is just a calamity. I can spell, and so can Abel. These several facts prove nothing, for one cannot deduce a principle from so few examples, but they do at least indicate that the ability to learn to spell correctly is a gift; that it is born in a person, and is a sign of intellectual inferiority. By parity of reasoning, its absence is a sign of great mental power. Sometimes, when Adam has worked a good large word like Ratiocination through his mill and is standing over the wreck mopping away his sweat, I could worship him he seems so intellectually grand and awful and sublime. He can spell Phthysic in more different ways than there are.

Cain and Abel are dear little chaps, and they take very nice care of their little brothers and sisters. The four eldest of the flock go wandering everywhere, according to their desire, and often we see nothing of them for two or three days together. Once they lost Gladys, and came back without her. They could not remember just where or when it was that they missed her. It was far away, they said, but they did not know how far; it was a new region for them. It was rich in berries of the plant which we call the deadly nightshade—for what reason we do not know. It hasn't any meaning, but it utilizes one of the words which we long ago got of the Voice, and we like to employ new words whenever a chance offers, and so make them workable and handy. They are fond of those berries, and they long wandered about, eating them; by and by when they were ready to go somewhere else, they missed Gladys, and she did not answer to her name.

Next day she did not come. Nor the next day, nor the day after that. Then three more days, and still she did not come. It was very strange; nothing quite the match of this had ever happened before. Our curiosity began to be excited. Adam was of the opinion that if she did not come next day, or at furthest the day after, we ought to send Cain and Abel to look.

So we did that. They were gone three days, but they found her. She had had adventures. In the dark, the first night, she fell in the river and was washed down a long distance, she did not know how far, and was finally flung upon a sandbar. After that, she lived with a kangaroo's family, and was hospitably entertained, and there was much sociability. The mama-kangaroo was very sweet and motherly, and would take her babies out of her pocket and go foraging among the hills and dales and fetch home a pocketful of the choicest fruits and nuts; and nearly every night there was company—bears and rabbits and buzzards and chickens and foxes and hyenas and polecats and other creatures—and gay romping and grand times. The animals seemed to pity the child because she had no fur; for always when she slept they covered her with leaves and moss to protect her dainty flesh, and she was covered like that when the boys found her. She had been homesick the first days, but had gotten over it.

That was her word—homesick. We have put it in the dictionary, and will presently settle upon a meaning for it. It is made of two words which we already had, and which have clear meanings when by themselves, though apparently none when combined. Building a dictionary is exceedingly interesting work, but tough; as Adam says.

* * * *

Year 15. The children promise well. Edwina makes quite creditable dolls, out of forked carrots, with a straw thrust through the body for arms, and a radish for a head. Gladys helps her father engrave outline-elephants and mastodons on bone, and Abel helps him make flint knives and arrow-heads for the kitchen-middens. Cain is the cleverest of all. He is really an expert at making the simpler kinds of fossils, and will soon be taking the most of that work off our hands, I think. And he has invented one fossil, all by himself.

DIARIES ANTEDATING THE FLOOD

PASSAGE FROM SATAN'S DIARY

Long ago I was in the bushes near the Tree of Knowledge when the Man and the Woman came there and had a conversation. I was present, now, when they came again after all these years. They were as before—mere boy and girl; trim, rounded, slender, flexible—snow images lightly flushed with the pink of the skies, innocently unconscious of their nakedness, lovely to look upon, beautiful beyond words.

I listened again. Again as in that former time, they puzzled over those words, Good, Evil, Death, and tried to reason out their meaning; but of course they were not able to do it. Adam said—

"Come, maybe we can find Satan. He might know these things."

Then I came forth, still gazing upon Eve and admiring, and said to her—

"You have not seen me before, sweet creature, but I have seen you. I have seen all the animals, but in beauty none of them equals you. Your hair, your eyes, your face, your flesh-tints, your form, the tapering grace of your white limbs—all are beautiful, adorable, perfect."

It gave her pleasure, and she looked herself over, putting out a foot and a hand and admiring them; then she naively said—

"It is a joy to be so beautiful. And Adam—he is the same."

She turned him about, this way and that, to show him off, with such guileless pride in her blue eyes, and he—he took it all as just matter of course, and was innocently happy in it, and said, "When I have flowers on my head it is better still."

Eve said, "It is true—you shall see," and she flitted hither and thither like a butterfly and plucked flowers, and in a moment laced their stems together in a glowing wreath and set it upon his head; then tip-toed and gave it a pat here and there with her nimble fingers, with each pat enhancing its grace and shape, none knows how, or why it should so result, but in it there is a law somewhere, though the delicate art and mystery of it is her secret alone, and not learnable by another; and when at last it was to her mind she clapped her hands for pleasure, then reached up and kissed him—as pretty a sight, taken altogether, as in my experience I have seen.

Presently, to the matter at hand. The meaning of these words—would I tell her?

Certainly none could be more willing, but how was I to do it? I could think of no way to make her understand, and I said so. I said—

"I will try, but it is hardly of use. For instance—what is pain?"

"Pain? I do not know."

"Certainly. How should you? Pain is not of your world; pain is impossible to you; you have never experienced a physical pain. Reduce that to a formula, a principle, and what have we?"

"What have we?"

"This: Things which are outside our orbit—our own particular world—things which by our constitution and equipment we are unable to see, or feel, or otherwise experience—*cannot be made comprehensible to us in words.* There you have the whole thing in a nutshell. It is a principle, it is axiomatic, it is a *law.* Now do you understand?"

The gentle creature looked dazed, and for all result she was delivered of this vacant remark:

"What is axiomatic?"

She had missed the point. Necessarily she would. Yet her effort was success for me, for it was a vivid confirmation of the truth of what I had been saying. Axiomatic was for the present a thing outside of the world of her experience, therefore it had no meaning for her. I ignored her question, and continued:

"What is fear?"

"Fear? I do not know."

"Naturally. Why should you? You have not felt it, you cannot feel it, it does not belong in your world. With a hundred thousand words I should not be able to make you understand what fear is. How then am I to explain Death to you? You have never seen it, it is foreign to your world, it is impossible to make the word mean anything to you, so far as I can see. In a way, it is a sleep—"

"Oh, I know what that is!"

"But it is a sleep only in a way, as I said. It is more than a sleep."

"Sleep is pleasant, sleep is lovely!"

"But Death is a *long* sleep—*very* long."

"Oh, all the lovelier. Therefore I think nothing could be better than Death."

I said to myself, "Poor child, some day you may know what a pathetic truth you have spoken; some day you may say, out of a broken heart, 'Come to me, oh, Death, the compassionate! steep me in thy merciful oblivion, oh refuge of the sorrowful, friend of the forsaken and the desolate!' " Then I said aloud, "But this sleep is eternal."

The word went over her head. Necessarily it would.

"Eternal? What is eternal?"

"Ah, that also is outside your world, as yet. There is no way to make you understand it."

It was a hopeless case. Words referring to things outside her experience were a foreign language to her, and meaningless. She was like a little baby whose mother says to it, "Don't put your finger in the candle-flame, it will burn you." Burn—it is a foreign word to the baby, and will have no terrors for it until experience shall have revealed its meaning. It is not worth while for mamma to make the remark, the baby will goo-goo cheerfully, and put its finger in the pretty flame—*once*. After these private reflections I said again that I did not think there was any way to make her understand the meaning of the word eternal. She was silent a while, turning these deep matters over in the unworn machinery of her mind; then she gave up the puzzle and shifted her ground, saying—

"Well, there are those other words. What is good? and what is evil?"

"It is another difficulty. They, again, are outside your world. They have place in the moral kingdom only. You have no morals."

"What are morals?"

"A system of law which distinguishes between right and wrong, good morals and bad. These things do not exist for you. I cannot make it clear, you would not understand."

"But try."

"Well, obedience to constituted authority is a moral law. Suppose Adam should forbid you to put your child in the river and leave it there over night—would you put the child there?"

She answered with a darling simplicity and guilelessness—

"Why, yes, if I wanted to."

"There, it is just as I said—you would not know any better; you have no idea of duty, command, obedience, they have no meaning for you. In your present estate you are in no possible way responsible for anything you do or say or think. It is impossible for you to do wrong, for you have no more notion of right and wrong than the other animals have. You and they can only do right; whatever you and they do is right and innocent. It is a divine estate, the loftiest and purest attainable in heaven and in earth. It is the angel-gift. The angels are wholly pure and sinless, for they do not know right from wrong, and all the acts of such are blameless. No one can do wrong without knowing how to distinguish *between* right and wrong."

"Is it an advantage to know?"

"Most certainly not! That knowledge would remove all that is divine, all that is angelic, from the angels, and immeasurably degrade them."

"Are there any persons that know right from wrong?"

"Not in—well, not in heaven."

"What gives that knowledge?"

"The Moral Sense."

"What is that?"

"Well—no matter. Be thankful you lack it."

"Why?"

"Because it is a degradation, a disaster. Without it one *cannot* do wrong; with it, one can. Therefore it has but one office, only one—to teach how to do wrong. It can teach no other thing—no other thing whatever. It is the *creator* of wrong; wrong cannot exist until the Moral Sense brings it into being."

"How can one acquire the Moral Sense?"

"By eating of the fruit of the Tree, here. But why do you wish to know? Would you like to have the Moral Sense?"

She turned wistfully to Adam:

"Would you like to have it?"

He showed no particular interest, and only said:

"I am indifferent. I have not understood any of this talk, but if you like we will eat it, for I cannot see that there is any objection to it."

Poor ignorant things, the command to refrain had meant nothing to them, they were but children, and could not understand untried things and verbal abstractions which stood for matters outside of their little world and their narrow experience. Eve reached for an apple!—oh, farewell, Eden, and your sinless joys, come poverty and pain, hunger and cold and heartbreak, bereavement, tears and shame, envy, strife, malice and dishonor, age, weariness, remorse; then desperation and the prayer for the release of death, indifferent that the gates of hell yawn beyond it!

She tasted—the fruit fell from her hand.

It was pitiful. She was like one who wakens slow and confusedly out of a sleep. She gazed half-vacantly at me, then at Adam, holding her curtaining fleece of golden hair back with her hand, then her wandering glance fell upon her naked person. The red blood mounted to her cheek, and she sprang behind a bush and stood there crying, and saying—

"Oh, my modesty is lost to me—my unoffending form is become a shame to me—my mind was pure and clean; for the first time it is soiled with a filthy thought!" She moaned and muttered in her pain, and drooped her head, saying, "I am degraded—I have fallen, oh so low, and I shall never rise again."

Adam's eyes were fixed upon her in a dreamy amazement, he could not understand what had happened, it being outside his world as yet, and her words having no meaning for one void of the Moral Sense. And now his wonder grew: for, unknown to Eve, her hundred years rose upon her, and faded the heaven of her eyes and the tints of her young flesh, and touched her hair with gray, and traced faint sprays of wrinkles about her mouth and eyes, and shrunk her form, and dulled the satin lustre of her skin.

All this the fair boy saw: then loyally and bravely he took the apple and tasted it, saying nothing.

The change came upon him also. Then he gathered boughs for both and clothed their nakedness, and they turned and went their way, hand in hand and bent with age, and so passed from sight.

PASSAGE FROM EVE'S DIARY

I.

They drove us from the Garden with their swords of flame, the fierce Cherubim. And what had we done? We meant no harm. We were ignorant, and did as any other children might do. We could not know it was wrong to disobey the command, for the words were strange to us and we did not understand them. We did not know right from wrong—how should we know? We could not, without the Moral Sense; it was not possible. If we had been given the Moral Sense first—ah, that would have been fairer, that would have been kinder: then we should be to blame if we disobeyed. But to say to us poor ignorant children words which we could not understand, and then punish us because we did not do as we were told—ah, how can that be justified? We knew no more than this littlest child of mine knows now with its four years—oh, not so much, I think. Would I say to it, "If thou touchest this bread I will overwhelm thee with unimaginable disaster, even to the dissolution of thy corporeal elements," and when it took the bread and smiled up in my face, thinking no harm, as not understanding those strange words, would I take advantage of its innocence and strike it down with the mother-hand it trusted? Whoso knoweth the mother-heart, let him judge if I would do that thing. Adam says my brain is turned by my troubles, and that I am become wicked. I am as I am; I did not make myself.

They drove us out. Drove us out into this harsh wilderness, and shut the gates against us. We that had meant no harm. It is three months. We were ignorant then, we are rich in learning, now—ah, how rich! We know hunger, thirst and cold; we know pain, disease and grief; we know hate, rebellion and deceit; we know remorse, the conscience that persecutes guilt and innocence alike, making no distinction; we know weariness of body and spirit, the unrefreshing sleep, the rest which rests not, the dreams which restore Eden, and banish it again with the waking; we know misery, we know torture, and the heartbreak; we know humiliation and insult; we know indecency, immodesty, and the soiled mind; we know the scorn that attaches to the transmitted image of God exposed unclothed to the day; we know fear; we know vanity, folly, envy, hypocrisy; we know irreverence, we know blasphemy; we know Right from Wrong, and how to avoid the one and do the other; we know all the rich product of the Moral Sense, and it is our possession. Would we could sell it for one hour of Eden and white purity, would we could degrade the animals with it!

We have it all—that treasure. All but Death. Death.....Death. What may that be?

Adam comes.

"Well?"

"He still sleeps."

That is our second-born—our Abel.

"He has slept enough for his good, and his garden suffers for his care. Wake him."

"I have tried, and cannot."

"Then he is very tired. Let him sleep on."

"I think it is his hurt that makes him sleep so long."

I answer—"It may be so. Then we will let him rest; no doubt the sleep is healing it."

II.

It is a day and a night, now, that he has slept. We found him lying by his altar in his field, that morning, with his head crushed and his face and body drenched in blood. He said his eldest brother struck him down. Then he spoke no more, and fell asleep. We laid him in his bed and washed the blood away, and were glad to know that the hurt was light and that he had no pain; for if he had had pain he would not have slept.

It was in the early morning that we found him. All day he slept that sweet reposeful sleep, lying on his back, and never moving, never turning. It showed how tired he was, poor thing. He is so good, and works so hard, rising with the dawn and laboring till the dark. And now he is overworked; it will be best that he tax himself less, after this, and I will ask him; he will do anything I wish.

All the day he slept. I know, for I was always near, and made dishes for him and kept them warm against his waking. Often I crept in softly, and fed my eyes upon his gentle face, and was thankful for that blessed sleep. And still he slept on—slept with his eyes wide; a strange thing, and made me think he was awake at first, but it was not so, for I spoke and he did not answer. He always answers when I speak. Cain has moods and will not answer, but not Abel.

I have sat by him all the night, being afraid he might wake and want his food. His face was very white; and it changed, and he came to look as he had looked when he was a little child in Eden long ago, so sweet and good and dear. It carried me back, over the abyss of years, and I was lost in dreams and tears—oh, hours, I think. Then I came to myself; and thinking he stirred, I kissed his cheek to wake him, but he slumbered on and I was disappointed. His cheek was cold. I brought sacks of wool and the down of birds and covered him, but he was still cold, and I brought more. Adam has come again, and says he is not yet warm. I do not understand it.

III.

We cannot wake him! With my arms clinging about him I have looked into his eyes, through the veil of my tears, and begged for one little word, and he will not answer. Oh, is it that long sleep—is it Death? And will he wake no more?

Death has entered the world, the creatures are perishing, one of the Family is fallen; the product of the Moral Sense is complete. The Family think ill of Death—they will change their mind.

PASSAGE FROM EVE'S DIARY.

Year of the World, 920.

It is true that the world was a solitude in the first days, but the solitude was soon modified. When we were 30 years old we had 30 children, and our children had 300; in 20 years more the population was 6,000; by the end of the second century it was become millions. For we are a long-lived race, and not many died. More than half of my children are still alive. I did not cease to bear until I was approaching middle age. As a rule, such of my children as survived the perils of childhood have continued to live, and this has been the case with the other families. Our race now numbers billions.

Extracts from Article in "The Radical,"
Jan., 916.

* * * * When the population reached five billions the earth was heavily burdened to support it. But wars, pestilences and famines brought relief, from time to time, and in some degree reduced the prodigious pressure. The memorable benefaction of the year 508, which was a famine reinforced by a pestilence, swept away sixteen hundred millions of people in nine months.

It was not much, but it was something. The same is all that can be said of its successors of later periods: The burden of population grew heavier and heavier and more and more formidable, century by century, and the gravity of the situation created by it was steadily and proportionately increased. After the age of infancy, few died. The average of life was 600 years. The cradles were filling, filling, filling—always, always, always; the cemeteries stood comparatively idle, the undertakers had but little traffic, they could hardly support their families. The death-rate was 2250 in the 1,000,000. To the thoughtful this was portentous; to the light-witted it was matter for brag! These latter were always comparing the population of one decade with that of the previous one and hurrahing over the mighty increase—as if that were an advantage to the world; a world that could hardly scratch enough out of the earth to keep itself from starving.

And yet, worse was to come! Necessarily our true hope did not and could not lie in spasmodic famine and pestilence, whose effects could be only temporary, but in war and the physicians, whose help is constant. Now, then, let us note what has been happening. In the past fifty years science has reduced the doctor's effectiveness by half. He uses but one deadly drug now, where formerly he used ten. Improved sanitation has made whole regions healthy which were previously not so. It has been discovered that the majority of the most useful and fatal diseases are caused by microbes of various breeds; very well, they have learned how to render the effects of these microbes innocuous. As a result, yellow fever, black plague, cholera, diphtheria, and nearly every valuable distemper we had are become but entertainments for the idle hour, and are of no more value to the State than is the stomach-ache. Marvelous advances in surgery have been added to our disasters. They remove a diseased stomach, now, and the man gets along better and cheaper than he did before. If a man loses a faculty, they bore into his skull and restore it. They take off his legs and arms, and refurnish him from the mechanical junk-shop, and he is as good as new. They give him a new nose if he needs it; new entrails; new bones; new teeth; glass eyes; silver tubes to swallow through; in a word, they take him to pieces and make him over again, and he can stand twice as much wear and tear as he could before. They do these things by help of antiseptics and anaesthesia, and there is no gangrene and no pain. Thus war has become nearly valueless; out of a hundred wounded that would formerly have died, ninety-nine are back in the ranks again in a month.

What, then, is the grand result of all this microbing and sanitation and surgery? This—which is appalling: the death-rate has been reduced to *twenty-two in the million.* And foolish people rejoice at it and boast about it! It is a serious matter. It promises to double the globe's population every twelve months. In time there will not be room in the world for the people to stand, let alone sit down.

Remedy? I know of none. The span of life is too long, the death-rate is too trifling. The span should be 35 years—a mere moment of time—the death-rate should be 20 or 30 in the *thousand*, not million. And even then the population would double in 35 years, and by and by even this would be a burden again and make the support of life difficult.

Honor to whom honor is due: the physician failed us, war has saved us. Not that the killed and wounded amount to anything as a relief, for they do not; but the poverty and desolation caused by war sweep myriads away and make space for immigrants. War is a rude friend, but a kind one. It keeps us down to 60,000,000,000 and saves the hard-grubbing world alive. It is all that the globe can support. * * *

FROM DIARY OF A LADY OF THE BLOOD, THIRD GRADE.

Received the Mad Prophet to-day.

He is a good man, and I think his intellect is better than its reputation. He got his nickname long ago, and did not deserve it; for he merely builds prognostications, not prophecies. He pretends to nothing more. Builds them out of history and statistics, using the facts of the past to forecast the probabilities of the future. It is merely applied science. An astronomer foretells an eclipse, yet is not obnoxious to the charge of pretending to be a prophet. Noah is a prophet; and certainly no one has more reverence for him and for his sacred office than has this modest dealer in probabilities and prognostications.

I have known the Mad Prophet—or the Mad Philosopher, for he has both names—ever since he was a student in college, in the beginning of the third century. He was nineteen or twenty, then. I have always had a kindly feeling for him; partly, of course, because he was a relative, (though distant), but mainly, I am sure, because of the good qualities of his head and heart. He married when he was 24, and when neither he nor the girl was properly situated to marry, for they were poor and belonged to families which had the same defect. Both families were respectable enough, and in a far-away fashion were allied to the nobility; but as Adam always said, "Respectability butters no parsnips," and it was not just the right capital to marry on. I advised them to wait a while, and of course they did it, since advice from a Personage of the Blood was—and is—law, by courtesy and custom of the race; but they were an impatient little pair and dreadfully in love with each other, and they only waited long enough to cover the bare necessities of etiquette. My influence got the lad a small mathematics-professorship in his university and kept him in possession of it, and he worked hard and saved faithfully. Poor things, they endured the suspension of life, as they called it, as long as they could; they waited sixty years, then they got married. She was a lovely little rat, and sweetly captivating: slender, lissom, brown-eyed, dimpled, complexioned like a peach-blossom, frisky, frolicsome, graceful—just a picture, she was, just a poem. She was of foreign extraction; her little drop of nobility had trickled down to her, in the lapse of time, from a great lord whose habitat was in a remote land many meridians of longitude away, the Duke of Washoe. He was descended from me through—I forget the name now—but the source was my daughter Regina's branch, I mean the one proceeding from Regina's second marriage. He was second cousin to—but I have forgotten that name, too. The little bride's name was Red Cloud, and was as foreign as her extraction. It was a kind of inheritance.

The couple remained poor, and are poor yet, but as happy as many that are richer. They have always had enough for their needs, for my influence has kept him in his post, and has also augmented his salary a little, more than once. Their tranquil life has suffered one blight, one heavy sorrow, which fell upon them toward the end of the first century of their union, and whose shadow lies upon their hearts yet. They lost sixteen children in a railway accident.

* * * *

Before he came, to-day, the Philosopher had been examining the mobile which is propelled by the wonderful new force, liquified thought. He was profoundly impressed. He said he could see no reason why this force should not displace steam and electricity, since it is much more powerful than those agents, occupies almost no space, and costs next to nothing. That is, the cost to the Trust that owns the patent is next to nothing. It is the same trust that owns the globe's railways and ships—the globe's transportation, in a word.

"Five years ago," said he, "this new force was laughed at by the ignorant, and discounted by the wise—a thing which always happens when there is a new invention. It happened with the Liograph, it happened with the Hellograph, it happened with the Mumble'n'screechograph, and it will go on happening with new inventions to the end of time. Why cannot people learn to wait for developments before they commit themselves? Surely experience has given them warnings enough. Almost as a rule the apparently insane invention turns out well by and by, through the discovery and application to it of improvements of one kind and another. Five years ago liquified thought had no value but as an Imperial-Academy-show on Ladies' Night. The cost of production was prohibitory, as far as business and commerce were concerned, for at that stage of development the only raw material which would answer had to be taken from statesmen, judges, scientists, poets, philosophers, editors, sculptors, painters, generals, admirals, inventors, engineers, and such like, but now—as [ ] says—you can get it from politicians and idiots; adding, in his unpleasant way, 'But that is tautology; Politician and idiot are synonymous terms.'

"I am of the opinion that the development of this mysterious new force has not yet proceeded beyond the infancy stage. I think we know but little about it now, compared with what we shall know a few decades hence. Why, it may turn out to be the renowned and lamented Lost Force of old tradition! And it isn't mere tradition, there is history for it. You know the tradition yourself, gracious Excellency—like the rest of the world—but you do not know the history. It has just been deciphered from the clay archives of an exhumed city of the Double Continent; and when it is published the nations will perceive that when the amazing man called 'the Prodigy,' who rose out of obscurity in the middle of the fifth century and in a few years conquered the world and brought all its kingdoms under his imperial sceptre, where they still abide under the sceptre of his son to-day, had formidable help in his stupendous work from a source outside of his colossal genius for war, statesmanship and administration, unrivaled and unapproachable as these confessedly were. That source was the agent known to tradition, romance and poetry as the Lost Force. It is true that that humble young shoemaker did sweep the Double Continent from end to end with fire and sword without that help, and establish his autocratic sway over all its monarchies by merely the faculties that were born in him, and that he handled a billion men in the field under a million generals trained by himself and subject to his sole will unhampered by meddling ministries and legislatures, and left mountains of dead and wounded upon his battle fields, but he subdued the rest of the globe without spilling blood, except in a single instance.

"That mystery is explained, now, by the clay records. It came to his knowledge that one Napeer, an obscure person but learned in science, had stated in his will that he had discovered a means whereby he could sweep a whole army out of existence in an instant, but that he would not reveal his secret, since war was already terrible enough and he would not be party to the augmentation of its destructiveness.

"The shoemaker-emperor said, 'The man was foolish—his invention would abolish war altogether,' and commanded that all papers left behind by him should be brought to him. He found the formula, mastered its details, then destroyed it. He privately manufactured that tremendous agent, and went out alone against the sovereigns of the eastern world, with it in his pocket. Only one army ever came against him. It formed itself in battle array in a great plain, and at a distance of twelve miles he blew it into the air, leaving no vestige of it behind but a few rags and buttons.

"He claimed the sovereignty of the globe, and it was accorded him without an objecting voice. As you are aware, his reign of thirty years was a reign of peace; then, by accident, he blew himself up with his machine, along with one of his vice-regal capitals, and his formidable secret died with him. Then the dreadful wars began again, and for the world's sins they still continue. But the universal empire which he established was founded in wisdom and strength, and to-day his son sits as securely upon its throne as he did when he mounted it so many centuries ago."

It was quite interesting. He was just beginning to speak about his "Law of Periodical Repetition"—or perhaps it was about his "Law of Permanency of the Intellectual Average"—but was interrupted. He was to be received by her Grandeur, and was now called to that exalted privilege by an officer of the Household.

EXTRACT FROM THE DISCOURSE OF REGINALD SELKIRK, THE MAD PHILOSOPHER, TO HER GRANDEUR THE ACTING HEAD OF THE HUMAN RACE

"Wonderful civilization? I will not object to the adjective—it rightly describes it—but I do object to the large and complacent admiration which it implies. By all accounts—yours in chief, Excellency—the pure and sweet and ignorant and unsordid civilization of Eden was worth a thousand millions of it. What *is* a civilization, rightly considered? Morally, it is the evil passions repressed, the level of conduct raised; spiritually, idols cast down, God enthroned; materially, bread and fair treatment for the greatest number. That is the common formula, the common definition; everybody accepts it and is satisfied with it.

"Our civilization is wonderful, in certain spectacular and meretricious ways; wonderful in scientific marvels and inventive miracles; wonderful in material inflation, which it calls advancement, progress, and other pet names; wonderful in its spying-out of the deep secrets of Nature—and its vanquishment of her stubborn laws; wonderful in its extraordinary financial and commercial achievements; wonderful in its hunger for money, and in its indifference as to how it is acquired; wonderful in the hitherto undreamed of magnitude of its private fortunes and the prodigal fashion in which they are given away to institutions devoted to the public culture; wonderful in its exhibitions of poverty; wonderful in the surprises which it gets out of that great new birth, ORGANIZATION, the latest and most potent creation and miracle-worker of the commercialized intellect, as applied in transportation-systems, in manufactures, in systems of communication, in news-gathering, book-publishing, journalism; in protecting labor; in oppressing labor; in herding the national parties and keeping the sheep docile and usable; in closing the public service against brains and character; in electing purchaseable legislatures, blatherskite Congresses, and city governments which rob the town and sell municipal protection to gamblers, thieves, prostitutes and professional seducers for cash. It is a civilization which has destroyed the simplicity and repose of life; replaced its contentment, its poetry, its soft romance-dreams and visions with the money-fever, sordid ideals, vulgar ambitions, and the sleep which does not refresh; it has invented a thousand useless luxuries, and turned them into necessities, it has created a thousand vicious appetites and satisfies none of them; it has dethroned God and set up a shekel in His place.

"Religion has removed from the heart to the mouth. You have the word of Noah for it. Time was, when two sects, divided but by a single hair of doctrine, would fight for that hair, would kill, torture, persecute for it, suffer for it, starve for it, die for it. *That* religion was in the heart; it was vital, it was a living thing, it was the very man himself. Who fights for his religion now, but with the mouth? Your civilization has brought the flood. Noah has said it, and he is preparing."

PASSAGE FROM A LECTURE.

The monthly meeting of the Imperial Institute took place on the 18th. With but two exceptions the seats of the Forty Immortals were occupied. The lecturer of the evening was the distinguished Professor of the Science of Historical Forecast. A part of his subject concerned two of the Laws of Angina Pectoris, commonly called the Mad Philosopher; namely, the "Law of Intellectual Averages" and the "Law of Periodical Repetition." After a consideration, at some length, of cognate matters, he said—

"I regard these Laws as established. By the terms of the Law of Periodical Repetition nothing whatever can happen in a single time only: everything happens again, and yet again, and still again—monotonously. Nature has no originality—I mean, no large ability in the matter of inventing new things, new ideas, new stage-effects. She has a superb and amazing and infinitely varied equipment of old ones, but she never adds to them. She repeats—repeats—repeats—repeats. Examine your memory and your experience, you will find it is true. When she puts together a man, and is satisfied with him, she is loyal to him, she stands by him through thick and thin forevermore, she repeats him by billions and billions of examples; and physically and mentally the *average* remains exactly the same, it doesn't vary a hair between the first batch, the middle batch and the last batch. If you ask—"

"But really—do you think all men are alike?" I reply—

"I said the *average* does not vary."

"But you will have to admit that some individuals do far overtop the average—intellectually, at least."

Yes, I answer, and Nature repeats *those*. There is nothing that she doesn't repeat. If I may use a figure, she has established the general intellectual level of the race at say, six feet. Take a billion men and stand them in a mass, and their head-tops will make a floor—a floor as level as a table. That floor represents the intellectual altitude of the masses—and it never changes. Here and there, miles apart, a head will project above it a matter of one intellectual inch, so to speak—men of mark in science, law, war, commerce, etc; in a spread of five thousand miles you will find three heads that project still an inch higher—men of national fame—and *one* that is higher than *those* by two inches, maybe three—a man of (temporarily) world-wide renown; and finally, somewhere around the circumference of the globe, you will find, once in five centuries of waiting, one majestic head which overtops the highest of all the others—an author, a teacher, an artist, a martyr, a conqueror, whose fame towers to the stars, and whose name will never perish, never fade, while time shall last; some colossus supreme above all the human herd, some unmated and unmateable prodigy like him who, by magic of the forces born in him, turned his shoe-hammer into the sceptre of universal dominion. Now in that view you have the ordinary man of all nations; you have the here-and-there man that is larger-brained and becomes distinguished; you have the still rarer man of still wider and more lasting distinction; and in that final head rising solitary out of the stretch of the ages, you have the limit of Nature's output.

Will she change this program? Not while time lasts. Will she repeat it forever? Yes. Forever and ever she will do those grades over and over again, always in the same proportions, and always with the regularity of a machine. In each million of people, just so many inch-superiorities; in each billion, just so many 2-inch superiorities—and so on; and always that recurrent solitary star once in an age, never oftener, never two of them at a time.

Nature, when pleased with an idea, never tires of applying it. She makes plains; she makes hills; she makes mountains; raises a conspicuous peak at wide intervals; then loftier and rarer ones, continents apart; and finally a supreme one six miles high. She uses this grading process in horses: she turns out myriads of them that are all of one common dull gait; with here and there a faster one; at enormous intervals a conspicuously faster one; and once in a half century a celebrity that does a mile in two minutes. She will repeat that horse every fifty years to the end of time.

By the Law of Periodical Repetition, everything which has happened once must happen again and again and again—and not capriciously, but at regular periods, and each thing in its own period, not another's, and each obeying its own law. The eclipse of the sun, the occultation of Venus, the arrival and departure of the comets, the annual shower of stars—all these things hint to us that the same Nature which delights in periodical repetition in the skies is the Nature which orders the affairs of the earth. Let us not underrate the value of that hint.

Are there any ingenuities whereby you can discredit the law of suicide? No. It is established. If there was such and such a number in such and such a town last year, that number, substantially, will be repeated this year. That number will keep step, arbitrarily, with the increase in population, year after year. Given the population a century hence, you can determine the crop of suicides that will be harvested in that distant year.

Will this wonderful civilization of to-day perish? Yes, everything perishes. Will it rise and exist again? It will—for nothing can happen that will not happen again. And again, and still again, forever. It took more than eight centuries to prepare this civilization—then it suddenly began to grow, and in less than a century it is become a bewildering marvel. In time, it will pass away and be forgotten. Ages will elapse, then it will come again; and not incomplete, but complete; not an invention nor discovery nor any smallest detail of it missing. Again it will pass away, and after ages will rise and dazzle the world again as it dazzles it now—perfect in all its parts once more. It is the Law of Periodical Repetition.

It is even possible that the mere *names* of things will be reproduced. Did not the Science of Health rise, in the old time, and did it not pass into oblivion, and has it not latterly come again and brought with it its forgotten name? Will it perish once more? Many times, I think, as the ages drift on; and still come again and again. And the forgotten book, Science and Health, With Key to the Scriptures—is it not with us once more, revised, corrected, and its orgies of style and construction tamed by an educated disciple? Will it not yet die, once, twice, a dozen times, and still at vast intervals rise again and successfully challenge the mind of man to understand it? We may not doubt it. By the Law of Periodical Repetition it must happen.

Year of the World, 920.

PASSAGE FROM THE DIARY OF THE MAD PHILOSOPHER.

Received in audience by the Most Illustrious, Most Powerful, Most Gracious, Most Reverend, her Grandeur the Acting Head of the Human Race, whom I addressed by these her official titles, and humbly thanked her, kneeling; then by permission indicated by a gesture, rose and stood before the Throne. It was in the Hall of Sovereigns in the same palace which she and the Family have occupied I do not know how many centuries, and which they prefer to any other. It is still the most gorgeous—and I think the most beautiful, too—in the Empire. Its gilded masses cover miles of space, and blaze like a fallen sun. Its interior parks and gardens and forests stretch away into the mellow distances, an apparently limitless paradise. A hundred thousand persons, not counting the brigades and divisions of Household Troops, serve the Parents and certain Eden-born families of their immediate descendants in this place. Yet the palace takes up no inordinate room in this monster capital, whose population almost defies figures, and which contains many streets that are upwards of two hundred miles long without a break.

The Hall of Sovereigns is a glittering vast rotunda which the ancient masters of all the arts wrought into a vision of glory and beauty with sculptured marbles and incrusted gems and costly gold-work and sunset splendors of color, and there the monarchs of all the globe have assembled every fifty years, with their officers of state, to do homage to the Parents of the Race. Spaciousness is requisite, and there is no lack of it. It must be a fine sight to see that multitude of black kings and white, yellow kings and brown, all in their dazzle of rich outlandish costumes; and it must be a bank holiday for interpreters, too. But the place was only sparsely peopled, now—guards, chamberlains, pages, and their sort, with a proper showing of secretaries ready and prepared to do nothing, and doing it.

Her Grandeur was clothed as the Arctic skies are clothed when the northern lights flood them with their trembling waves of purple and crimson and golden flame, and through this shifting and changing dream of rich colors the flash of innumerable jewels went chasing and turning, gleaming and expiring like trains of sparks through burnt paper. Afterward I spoke with enthusiasm of this brilliant spectacle to Nanga Parbat, that soured and dissolute Eden-born Scion of the First Blood whose bad heart banishment from the Presence long ago filled with malice and hate and envy, and he smiled a vinegar smile and said with scorn—

"Pah! These airs! I've seen the day when the Family hadn't a shirt amongst them."

I could not resent this; one of my degree is not permitted to talk back to an Eden-born, even if one were so disposed, which is a thought that could exist only a passionate moment or two in a loyal breast, but I begged him to spare me such words about the Powers That Be, it being improper that I should hear them.

"Oh, of course!" he scoffed. "You are a patriot—you and your sort. And what is a Patriot, pray? It's one who grovels to the Family, and shouts for the Emperor and the Government, be they in the right or in the wrong—and especially when they are in the wrong; and that they call 'standing by the *Country*.' Patriotism—oh, Laura! that sham, that perversion, that silver-gilt nursery-bauble wherewith this combination of land-grabbers, Constitution-tinkers, imbeciles and hypocrites called the Imperial Government beguiles and captures those confiding children the People. Oh, it's a sweet thing, is Patriotism. Adam used to call it 'the last refuge of a scoundrel.' Do you know, I've been called a patriot myself, by the ignorant and thoughtless. Alas and alas, in this world one is never safe from insult. Come and take something?"

It was an odiously embarrassing position, people passing and staring all the time, wondering to see a Scion of the First Blood and wearing the sacred uniform of his Order (noticeably the worse for wear, by the way,) familiarly button-holing one of my estate, just as if I were an equal. And he could hardly fail to be overheard, for he *would* talk in a frank free voice, (being "under the influence," as the saying is,) do what I might to quiet him. In order to get away from observation I went into the Eden Arms with him, and of course found respite and peace, the customers respectfully vacating the place and filing out uncovered.

"Slaves!" he snarled; "look at them! They abase themselves before clothes and the accident of birth—silver-gilt nursery-baubles again—lord, it sizes-up the quality of the human race!" and he rasped out a sardonic chuckle. "The human race, that has such a fine opinion of itself." He inspected his sacred uniform, detached a hanging rag of gold lace from it, musingly turned it this way and that in his fingers, then threw it to a dog, who sniffed at it hopefully a moment, then left it lying and slouched away disappointed. "Now *there's* a rational creature, a respect-worthy creature—I do him homage!" He passed his fingers through his thatch of snow, and said with a sigh, "Ah, well, we were once as wise as he, and as sane—I have seen that day."

Soon he broke into a tirade again—this time about nepotism. He did not go quite so far as to mention names, but it was plain enough that his target was the Acting Head of the Human Race, his Grandmother. It made the flesh crawl to hear him.

"There isn't a place of value in that place," he said, "that goes by merit; not a rich sinecure but is encumbered by some incapable dotard whose only qualification is that he belongs by accident of birth in one or another of the First Three Grades of the Blood. Everything worth having is saved for the Three Orders—and how they do hang on, those jibbering senilities! Adam used to sigh and say, 'They seldom die, and never resign.' Nepotism? it's just a buzzard's nest of it. She—why dear me she can't endure the touch or smell of plebian flesh, the very scullery-maids must be of the Family—Third Grade, Herald's Office certificate, no Bar Sinister in the line, 'no Irish need apply,' as the saying is. Oh, the sarcasm of it—why, she was never married, herself!"

I ventured to rebuke him, saying—

"She was born married."

"Huh!" he scoffed, and snapped his fingers; "tell it to the marines."

Then he went on and on about nepotism, and there was nothing too bitter for him to say. I could have reminded him, if it had been meet for one of my condition to say such a thing, that if the system was evil none had gotten more advantage out of it than himself; for, through no merit but his Blood alone, he had served in the palace a couple of centuries, in a descending scale of offices sacred to the Third Degree, discrediting and degrading each in turn until he got down to boot-polisher; and not until it was found that he was even able to bring dishonor upon that was he at last given up in despair and forbidden the premises.

He attacked in turn everything that one respects and reveres, and I was obliged to stay and listen, for he is a capricious in his humors and might have taken mortal offence if I had asked for my dismissal. But finally, without preliminary or circumlocution he suddenly said he was tired of my monotonous gabble, and waved his hand toward the door. It was unjust, for it was he that had done the talking, I had said hardly a word; but I backed immediately out of the presence without protest, being glad to go on any terms. Almost immediately he himself emerged and marched down the street, the people falling apart before him and bowing and scraping as he passed, he taking no notice of them. As disagreeable a scamp as I know—of that I am certain.

In spirit, in speech and in looks he was a sorrowful contrast to his noble grandam. Long ago she was rebellious, it is said, and would not be appeased; but trouble and the burden of the ages have chastened her heart and restored it to the charity and gentleness that were its birthright, and their grace is in her face, which is beautiful. It was a privilege to see her again. I had not seen her since the first year of the new century, when she drove in state and showed herself to the people, in the glare of the illuminations, and formally inaugurated the Epoch, in accordance with antique custom—always an impressive function, but peculiarly and movingly so on this occasion, it being the first time she had ever performed it alone. No eye fell unmoistened upon the vacant place at her side, a place not likely ever to be occupied again.

Eighty years ago, owing to failing health, his Serene Supremacy the Head of the Race resigned his functions into the hands of his Consort—though not his Authority—and since then has taken no active part in the administration of the Family's affairs, except that fifty-five years ago he received the Emperor of the World in private audience upon an occasion of urgency, and was persuaded to do the like again thirty-one years later. He has lived continuously in retirement in the hands of his physicians during the past three-quarters of a century, and by help of the advancing efficiency of medical science year by year for the past half-century has been mercifully enabled to retain his frail hold upon life. It is truly wonderful what the physicians have done; it is hardly too much to call it miraculous. It has made immense fame for them throughout the world, and prosperity as well.

PASSAGE FROM THE DIARY OF ______

* * * * His exact condition has at no time been revealed to the public—certainly not by the physicians' bulletins. The sophisticated among us know how to discount those, it being quite understood that it is reputation in a physician's pocket to multiply an illustrious patient's danger by 16 or 20 from time to time and then acquire the world's astonished admiration and reverence—and business—by pulling him up again to where he can take spoon victuals, and smile a sappy smile, and do some taffy about "my beloved peoples" to be cabled around the earth and sniveled about in the papers and utilized by the pulpit to mellow-up the congregations and enable it to take another go at the contribution-pump. In all these decades he has never had anything really the matter with him but doctor-sickness—the understudy of one of the professional nurses told me so. Such of us as are not asses know what that disease is for, and who creates it, and how it is worked, and the money that is in it, and the reputation. Strictly select, strictly aristocratic, confined to the rich and the renowned, is doctor-sickness; and for steady lastingness can give points to immortality.

To my certain knowledge, privately acquired from the understudy, the doctors have worked the stock market on this case from the start, selling bulletins to the brokers a week in advance—sometimes to such as were long on danger, sometimes to such as were short. Once, with consols at 102, they secretly treated both parties, offering to send the market up to 108 in the one case and down to 94 in the other, according to the best bid. It is a fact; the understudy told me so. The bulls got it; she told me that, too. In innumerable other cases they have sold for a rise or a fall, though she did not know the figures. One can see by this what value a bulletin is, where the patient has doctor-sickness. Well, it's a [word illegible] of a world!

DOCUMENTS RELATED TO "DIARIES ANTEDATING THE FLOOD"

Sometime after Mark Twain abandoned the work that originally began as the "Autobiography of Eve" and was expanded to include "Diaries Antedating the Flood," he wrote two brief related items which he titled "Passage from 'Glances at History' (suppressed.)" and "Passage from 'Outlines of History' (suppressed.)" in order to present further documents describing the nature of the pre-Deluge civilizations, with even more direct references to his own times.

The "Glances," originally titled "First Fall of the Great Republic," develops some of the conditions leading up to that demise and clearly reflects Mark Twain's loathing of American military actions in the Philippines, the reactions of the American public to those events, and the patriotic fervor that the war engendered. Here Twain argues that through the abuse of patriotism, "citizens of the Great Republic" can be stampeded into supporting an unjust war and men of principle can be branded as traitors by "a silly phrase—Our Country, right or wrong."

The segment from "Outlines" offers an alternate nightmarish fantasy of the fall of the Great Republic to the one detailed in "The Secret History of Eddypus." Here Twain provides a prophecy of the aftermath of the Great Republic's "lust of conquest" and describes its "drift toward monarchy" and the eventual triumph of "the Prodigy," who ultimately establishes an oppressive military dictatorship controlled by the "money-changers."

Mark Twain was not alone in fearing the effects of the alliance between the trusts, the politicians, and the military. In a speech made before the 1901 annual meeting of the New England Anti-Imperialist League, the Reverend A. A. Berle summarized many of the same ideas stated in "Outlines" when he argued that "the huge combinations of capital and their almost uniform adhesion to the forces that seek imperialist development tends [*sic*] to make even the bravest fear that the conscience has gone down before the dollar" (quoted in Zwick, 70).

Although it is not clear precisely when these pieces were written, the references in "Outlines" to the buying of votes through increasing the numbers eligible for military pensions could suggest that this essay may have been written as late as 1904, for in April of that year Theodore Roosevelt and the Republican Party endeavored to assure Roosevelt's reelection by just such a move. But, since Mark Twain was very much concerned about the injustices of the Philippine War in 1901 and 1902, and the matter of pensions was obviously on his mind as early as 1901, it is more likely that Twain wrote them earlier. One of his blasts at imperialism, "The Stupendous Procession" (written in January 1901), for example, cites the potential problems resulting from enlarged pension rolls. In "The Secret History of Eddypus," too, at one point in the portion written in February or March 1901, the notation "Pensions" at the top of a page (ms., Book II, 58) shows that he was then thinking of discussing the burden of military pensions as a factor in the fall of the "Great Civilization." Moreover, the reference to the shoemaker-Prodigy links this passage to Reginald Selkirk's account and to other references in the "Autobiography of Eve" and "Diaries Antedating the Flood." And the name "Popoatahualpacatapetl," as well as the inclusion of "Prodigy," connects the Prodigy with Planning Notes that Twain made for the "Autobiography of Eve." Also the ninth-century date, if indeed this is the ninth century A.C. (After Creation), would provide yet another link with the "Autobiography of Eve."

Accordingly, then, since both of these pieces are thematically linked to the "Autobiography of Eve" and "Diaries Antedating the Flood," as well as to "The Secret History of Eddypus" (written in February and March 1901 and a later portion during the same period in 1902), they probably also date from 1901 or 1902.

PASSAGE FROM "GLANCES AT HISTORY" (suppressed.)

Date, 9th century.

* * * In a speech which he made more than 500 years ago, and which has come down to us intact, he said:

We, free citizens of the Great Republic, feel an honest pride in her greatness, her strength, her just and gentle government, her wide liberties, her honored name, her stainless history, her unsmirched flag, her hands clean from oppression of the weak and from malicious conquest, her hospitable door that stands open to the hunted and the persecuted of all nations; we are proud of the judicious respect in which she is held by the monarchies which hem her in on every side, and proudest of all of that lofty patriotism which we inherited from our fathers, which we have kept pure, and which won our liberties in the beginning and has preserved them unto this day. While that patriotism endures the Republic is safe, her greatness is secure, and against them the powers of the earth cannot prevail.

I pray you to pause and consider. Against our traditions we are now entering upon an unjust and trivial war, a war against a helpless people, and for a base object—robbery. At first our citizens spoke out against this thing, by an impulse natural to their training. To-day they have turned, and their voice is the other way. What caused the change? Merely a politician's trick—a high-sounding phrase, a blood-stirring phrase which turned their uncritical heads: *Our Country, right or wrong!* An empty phrase, a silly phrase. It was shouted by every newspaper, it was thundered from the pulpit, the Superintendent of Public Instruction placarded it in every school-house in the land, the War Department inscribed it upon the flag. And every man who failed to shout it or who was silent, was proclaimed a traitor—none but those others were patriots. To be a patriot, one had to say, and keep on saying, "Our Country, right or wrong," and urge on the little war. Have you not perceived that that phrase is an insult to the nation?

For in a republic, who *is* "the country?" Is it the Government which is for the moment in the saddle? Why, the Government is merely a *servant*—merely a temporary servant; it cannot be its prerogative to determine what is right and what is wrong, and decide who is a patriot and who isn't. Its function is to obey orders, not originate them. Who, then, is "the country?" Is it the newspaper? is it the pulpit? is it the school-superintendent? Why, these are mere parts of the country, not the whole of it; they have not command, they have only their little share in the command. They are but one in the thousand; it is in the thousand that command is lodged; *they* must determine what is right and what is wrong; they must decide who is a patriot and who isn't.

Who are the thousand—that is to say, who are "the country?" In a monarchy, the king and his family are the country; in a republic it is the common voice of the people. Each of you, for himself, by himself and on his own responsibility, must speak. And it is a solemn and weighty responsibility, and not lightly to be flung aside at the bullying of pulpit, press, government, or the empty catch-phrases of politicians. Each must for himself alone decide what is right and what is wrong, and which course is patriotic and which isn't. You cannot shirk this and be a man. To decide it against your convictions is to be an unqualified and inexcusable traitor, both to yourself and to your country, let men label you as they may. If you alone of all the nation shall decide one way, and that way be the right way according to your convictions of the right, you have done your duty by yourself and by your country—hold up your head! you have nothing to be ashamed of.

Only when a republic's *life* is in danger should a man uphold his government when it is in the wrong. There is no other time.

This republic's life is not in peril. The nation has sold its honor for a phrase. It has swung itself loose from its safe anchorage and is drifting, its helm is in pirate hands. The stupid phrase needed help, and it got another one: "Even if the war be wrong we are in it and must fight it out: *we cannot retire from it without dishonor.*" Why, not even a burglar could have said it better. We cannot withdraw from this sordid raid because to grant peace to those little people upon their terms—independence—would dishonor us. You have flung away Adam's phrase—you should take it up and examine it again. He said, "*An inglorious peace is better than a dishonorable war.*"

You have planted a seed, and it will grow.

PASSAGE FROM "OUTLINES OF HISTORY" (suppressed.)

Date, 9th century.

* * * But it was impossible to save the Great Republic. She was rotten to the heart. Lust of conquest had long ago done its work; trampling upon the helpless abroad had taught her, by a natural process, to endure with apathy the like at home; multitudes who had applauded the crushing of other people's liberties, lived to suffer for their mistake in their own persons. The government was irrevocably in the hands of the prodigiously rich and their hangers-on, the suffrage was become a mere machine, which they used as they chose. There was no principle but commercialism, no patriotism but of the pocket. From showily and sumptuously entertaining neighboring titled aristocracies, and from trading their daughters to them, the plutocrats came in the course of time to hunger for titles and heredities themselves. The drift toward monarchy, in some form or other, began; it was spoken of in whispers at first, later in a bolder voice.

It was now that that portent called "The Prodigy" rose in the far South. Army after army, sovereignty after sovereignty went down under the mighty tread of the shoemaker, and still he held his conquering way—North always North. The sleeping republic awoke at last, but too late. It drove the money-changers from the temple, and put the government into clean hands—but all to no purpose. To keep the power in their own hands, the money-changers had long before bought up half the country with soldier-pensions and turned a measure which had originally been a righteous one into a machine for the manufacture of bond-slaves—a machine which was at the same time an irremovable instrument of tyranny—for every pensioner had a vote, and every man and woman who had ever been acquainted with a soldier was a pensioner; pensions were dated back to the Fall, and hordes of men who had never handled a weapon in their lives came forward and drew three hundred years' back-pay. The country's conquests, so far from being profitable to the Treasury, had been an intolerable burden from the beginning. The pensions, the conquests, and corruption together, had brought bankruptcy in spite of the maddest taxation, the government's credit was gone, the arsenals were empty, the country unprepared for war. The military and naval schools, and all commissioned offices in the army and navy, were the preserve of the money-changers; and the standing army—the creation of the conquest-days—was their property.

The army and navy refused to serve the new Congress and the new Administration, and said ironically, "What are you going to do about it?" A difficult question to answer. Landsmen manned such ships as were not abroad watching the conquests—and sunk them all, in honest attempts to do their duty. A civilian army, officered by civilians, rose brimming with the patriotism of an old forgotten day and rushed multitudinously to the front, armed with sporting-guns and pitchforks—and the standing army swept it into space. For the money-changers had privately sold out to the shoemaker. He conferred titles of nobility upon the money-changers, and mounted the republic's throne without firing a shot.

It was thus that Popoatahualpacatapetl became our master; whose mastership descended in a little while to the Second of that name, who still holds it by his Viceroy this day.

TWO ADDITIONAL PRE-DELUGE DIARISTS

The following passages from the diaries of Methuselah and Shem are all that remain of a much larger project which Mark Twain conceived in the late 1860s. Toward the end of July 1866 he recorded the initial idea in his notebook: "Conversation between the carpenters of Noah's Ark, laughing at him for an old visionary—his money as good as anybody's though going to bust himself on this crazy enterprise" (*N&J1*, 147). Sometime thereafter he expanded the notion into a seventy- or eighty-page manuscript, which he then left with his sister Pamela for safekeeping. On 20 August 1869, however, he wrote to her from Buffalo, asking her to find "my account of the Deluge (it is a diary kept by Shem)," and send it to him. Though it was of "no account now," he hoped to make a "telling article" of it (*Letters 3*, 312).

During the next several months his enthusiasm for the project led him to plan a full-length book. "I mean to take plenty of time and pains with the Noah's Ark book," he wrote to his publisher Elisha Bliss on 22 January 1870, "—maybe it will be several years before it is *all* written—but it will be a perfect lightning-striker when it *is* done" (*MTLP*, 29). And he assured the publisher that he would be given first refusal of the volume.

The following December he sent an extract from that work for a volume of sketches that Bliss was preparing, and in a postscript to his letter of transmittal (the only portion still extant) suggested that "the curious beasts & great contrasts in this Pre-deluge article offer a gorgeous chance for the artist's fancy & ingenuity, I think" (*ET&S*, 1: 574–75). Unfortunately, that sketchbook was never published, and neither the extract—listed in a preliminary table of contents as "Pre-flood show"—nor any of the other early portions of the "Noah's Ark book" have survived, unless the earlier of the two fragments from "Shem's Diary" that remain in the Mark Twain Papers was among them.

Two years later, however, Mark Twain's fascination with antediluvian times led him to attempt another diary—that of Methuselah, which he began in Edinburgh during his British trip in 1873. Actually, the diaries of Shem and that of Methuselah were so closely related in his mind that in later years he seems to have mixed them up. Speaking about unfinished literary projects in August 1890, for instance, he told an interviewer from the New York *World* that he had written the first six chapters of "The Diary of Shem in the Ark" in Edinburgh "seventeen years ago" (i.e., in 1873), at the time "when the idea of it occurred to me" (Budd, 47). Though he had, of course, conceived the idea much earlier, the early fragment of "Shem's Diary," which does deal to some extent with the building of the Ark, *could* have been written in Edinburgh. But the segment consists of only seven pages plus three lines on an eighth. Mark Twain, therefore, was almost certainly remembering his first attempt at "Methuselah's Diary," though that journal involved Noah and the Ark only through indirect references to the diarist's scoffing at prophecies of the Flood. Moreover, though there are no chapter divisions in this manuscript, on one page among his planning notes, Mark Twain doodled the word "Edinburgh" four times (see appendix 4, group 2-A).

The fact that Methuselah's style in this first segment reflects one of Mark Twain's current literary enthusiasms also supports the argument for the 1873 date. On 29 June, just a month before the late July visit to Edinburgh, Mark Twain informed his minister friend Joe Twichell, in a special postscript, that he was currently "luxuriating in glorious old Pepy's [*sic*] Diary . . ." (*MTL*, 1:207, 9 June, corrected to 29 June in *N&J1*, 528, n. 4). It may even have been his interest in Pepys's journal that led him to another try at a biblical diary. The styles are indeed similar. Both, of course, were strongly influenced by biblical rhythms and constructions, but they resemble each other more closely than either resembles the Bible, even to the extent that Methuselah occasionally echoes several of Pepys's frequent and presumably favorite ejaculations, such as "But Lord" and "I pray God."

A number of the planning notes for Methuselah's journal also reflect some of Twain's current concerns in 1873. Fresh from the composition of *The Gilded Age*, a satire of political and social abuses in America written the preceding winter and spring in collaboration with his Hartford neighbor Charles Dudley Warner, Mark Twain had become increasingly disturbed with governmental and other forms of corruption, especially by what he saw as misuse of the suffrage by the ignorant and incompetent.

These earliest planning notes then, besides projecting a triumphal visit of Adam and conflicts that were to arise from family plans to marry off Methuselah, proposed that the diarist should travel to "Enoch and other strange cities" and record "manners, customs, literature, laws and religion." He would describe the worshippers of Baal, their "many sects, with trivial differences like Christians," public entertainments, and the arrival of a tribe of "Wandering Jabals" who "scalp and paint faces in war." More seriously, perhaps, he would consider "women's rights," "the slave mart," and "Slavery in full—Ex 21," the Baalish Missionary Society "for propagating religion in foreign parts," demagogue politicians, elective judgeships and the suffrage, as well as various customs, and laws and their penalties (see appendix 4, group 1-A–J).

Mark Twain first began his story with Methuselah still a child, at age sixty, enjoying "divers toys & things wherewith to play,"† and went on to outline the diarist's genealogy. After only five manuscript pages, however, he decided that such an approach would not do and began again with Methuselah still at sixty, but uneasy now about his family's urgings that he marry. And before subsequent travel plans interrupted Twain's work, he finished some forty-one pages, in which Methuselah described several of the entertainments mentioned in the planning notes, introduced the theme of slavery, with the complications arising from his desire to free his slave Zuar, and recorded the diarist's less than complimentary opinions of his intended bride, the princess Sarah; his attraction to Zillah, his tutor's "comely" daughter; and, finally, the arrival of the Jabalites. But then Mark Twain put the project aside for some two and a half years.

In July 1877, anticipating a brief trip from Quarry Farm to Hartford, Mark Twain reminded himself to "get Methuselah," along with some source material for the novel that was eventually to be *The Prince and the Pauper* (1882). But the diary still remained on a "to do" list as late as 23 November (*N&J2*, 39, 50).

When he took up the story again, probably early in December after he finished the farcical "Loves of Alonzo Fitz Clarence and Rosannah Ethelton" (*Atlantic Monthly*, March 1878), he first oriented himself by compiling a two-page list of the incidents he had already included. Coming to the Jabalites, he labeled them "savages, dwellers in tents" and added a contemporary note: "Give them Sitting-Bull names."† The last item on the list, unless he had destroyed part of the earlier manuscript, carried the story one item beyond what he had already written, namely a mention of "Meth's first child—foolish fondnesses"† (see appendix 4, groups 3-A, 3-B).

When he began to write he numbered the first page 42 but soon decided to postpone the account of the Jabalites on 33–41. He then changed his initial page number to 34 and added a note on the original page 41: "Take this up again under brief republican form of govt. when Meth about 300 or 400 old, and put in Custer and Howard and the Peace Commissioners (Quakers) and the Modoc Lava Beds &c & satirize freely." And on another line: "The Jabalites are descended from Cain."†

Mark Twain's plans for the diary obviously had expanded considerably. He now envisioned a wide-ranging satire of contemporary events. The Modoc War, characterized by astounding military ineptness and Indian fortitude, had provided sensational news stories in late 1872 and the first half of 1873 (see notes for further details). But mention of Custer and Howard moved the note's frame of reference forward several years. Custer's war against the Sioux in 1876 had culminated in the Little Big Horn massacre on 22 June. The linking of the two generals suggests, however, that Mark Twain was specifically inspired by events in 1877. That spring and fall newspapers carried stories of Custer's defeat at Little Big Horn as told by Sioux chieftains Red Horse and Kill Evil. And on 15 November appeared the account by the famous Sitting Bull himself. These reports may well have inspired the idea to give the Jabalites "Sitting-Bull names."

As for "Howard," during that same summer and fall of 1877 Gen. Otis Oliver Howard was conducting an often fruitless military operation against the Nez Percé tribe in the Pacific Northwest. Again the papers closely followed the campaign and the efforts of a peace commission to bring about a settlement. Discussions of the war and injustices done to the Nez Percés continued through October and November, with General Howard's own report carried by the New York *Times* of 28 November. Because of the several juxtapositions it seems that Mark Twain's note almost certainly dates from late November 1877.

By 1877 Mark Twain's disillusionment with the processes of government in his own country was at a peak. Reflected in such works as "The Curious Republic of Gondour" (*Atlantic Monthly*, October 1875) and in the irony of Pap Finn's diatribe against the "govment" in chapter six (written in 1876) of *Huckleberry Finn*, as well as in personal letters and comments, that bitterness would surely have dominated Methuselah's account of the "brief republican form of govt." (For a fuller account of Mark Twain's political and social views during these years, see Baetzhold, 1970, chapter 2).

The diary never did get around to dealing with the major evils indicated in the above note and others. In this new session Mark Twain immediately introduced another contemporary element, the current enthusiasm for baseball. Methuselah here notes that only two years earlier "an ancient game, played with a ball" had been revived "yet already are all mouths filled with the phrases that describe its parts and movement."† And with Methuselah's further commentary, Mark Twain presented a parody of baseball jargon.

Mark Twain himself loved baseball and doubtless followed closely the fortunes of the Hartford "Blue Stockings," one of the original members of the National League, which was formed in February 1876 (see notes), very close to the "two years gone" when Methuselah's game "came up again." And Twain never did get back to the Jabalites. From baseball he turned to news of Adam's forthcoming visit, a description of the great museum that housed relics of the Garden and the Fall, a comment on the present degeneration of music, and the commencement of preparations for Adam's reception.

At that point the narrative closes, but in a note that he added to the final page of Methuselah's account, Mark Twain envisioned an even broader satire of contemporary civilization. After projecting a "great battle" involving an army of ten thousand, and taking another swipe at drama critics who traditionally sneer at any new play (probably reflecting his annoyance at the poor reviews in the summer of 1877 of *Ah Sin!*, the play he had written with Bret Harte), he wrote: "Just satirize America straight through after once beginning. Satirize Russia Turkey England and a wee German principality separately."

Other planning notes show that Mark Twain also intended to expand some of the original notes for the first segment. One describes how Methuselah's adoption of "scientific religion" was to weaken his traditional faith until he became "a regular free-thinker," who "bothers over the foolish prophecies of a flood; and ends, through his love for Zillah, in becoming an idolater (it is only *hinted*) since he did not sail in the Ark."† Other notes suggest that Mark Twain intended to follow the biblical account of events leading up to the time of Noah and the Flood, pointing out some of the ridiculousness of the old laws, restrictions, and rituals, and to satirize the unreasoning perpetuation of old codes (see appendix 4).

But the humorist never saw fit to develop Methuselah's story any further. Perhaps he grew tired of it or, more probably, decided that the concept was too nebulous, too broad. Possibly his distress at the failure of his speech at the

Whittier Birthday Dinner on 17 December 1877 played a part in the interruption. And when he began to write again in late December he turned his primary attention to *The Prince and the Pauper.* Still, the idea of providing diaries of our biblical ancestors, and in some cases criticizing contemporary civilization through them, obviously remained with him and ultimately resulted in the diaries of Adam and Eve, Eve's "Autobiography," the other diaries "antedating the flood," and the passages from "Glances at History (suppressed.)" and "Outlines of History (suppressed.)" contained in this volume. And he would also attempt "The Secret History of Eddypus" (unfinished) and other pieces collected by John Tuckey in *Fables of Man* under the rubric "The Nightmare of History" (315–402).

As for Shem's Diary, the early fragment that has survived dates from the 1870s, the later from 1908 or early 1909. In the first Mark Twain has Shem mention Noah's six hundredth birthday, a strike by the workers of the Ark, Methuselah's criticisms, and his treating of Noah's sons as children. Shem also describes Methuselah's grieving over an early lost love, and, briefly, the resumption of work on the Ark and the bustle and confusion that ensued. The piece closes with the observation that the Ark should have been completed "a month ago."

In an April 1909 addition to an earlier unsent letter to Jeannette Gilder, editor of the *Critic*, after repeating his possibly mistaken idea that he had first begun Shem's Diary in Edinburgh in 1873, Mark Twain wrote: "I began it again several months ago, but only for recreation; I hadn't any intention of carrying it to a finish—or even to the end of the first chapter, in fact" (*MTL*, 2:488).

This time he was accurate. The later fragment, though complete with a rather elaborate title page (see notes), is only seven pages long. But in it Mark Twain added important details to the earlier piece, describing the carousing of the populace and their scoffing at the Ark and the idea of a deluge. Here Shem's account also fixes on Methuselah's enjoyment of the attention he receives because of his great age and, again, on Shem's own annoyance at Methuselah's scornful refusal to treat him as an adult, even though he was now one hundred years old.

Though it was never carried out, it is remarkable that this project lingered in the author's mind for more than forty years.

PASSAGES FROM METHUSELAH'S DIARY

The First Day of the Fourth Month of the Year 747 from the Beginning of the World.—This day am I sixty years old, I being born in the year 687 from the beginning of the world. Came certain of the family to me praying that I would marry, so that heirs fail not. I am but young to take upon me such cares, albeit I am minded that my father Enoch, my grandfather Jared, my great-grandfather Mahalaleel, and my great-great-grandfather Cainan did each and all take wives at an age like to that which I am now arrived at. All these have spoken their minds concerning me, and do concur in desiring that I marry, I being eldest son of my father and heir of this princely house in due succession, and ultimate possessor of the cities, principalities and dignities unto it pertaining, when it shall please the gods to call hence those heirs and elder brethren that live and still stand between me and these high honors.

Tenth Day—Dismissed the several wise men and their servants, with presents and sent them upon their way to their several countries, I not requiring tutors more, having finished my youth and stepped upon the threshold of manhood. With the sage Uz, that dwelleth in the far land of Nod, in that old city called Enoch, I did send a centurion and many stout men of war out of my own body guard to protect him and his caravan from the children of Jabal that infest the desert places by the way. His great-great-grand-daughter Zillah tarrieth yet in the house of their kinsman Habakkuk, she being content to extend her visit, and they to have her. A comely maid and modest.

Eighteenth Day—The anniversary of the building of the city—prosperity abide with Aumrath and all that dwell within her gates! My great-grandfather, Mahalaleel, that did lay the corner stone three hundred years ago, sat in state in the high place of the temple and received the chiefs of the city, praising the greatness thereof, and the strength and power and the splendor of her belongings; saying he had seen the first house builded and watched the growth from that small beginning till this day that it covereth the five hills and the valleys between and possesseth a population that no man is able to number. And indeed it is a goodly city, with temples and palaces, strong walls, and streets that have no end, and not one house but is stone. The house that was the first one is fallen to ruin, but many visit it with reverence and none are allowed to injure it, though many foolish persons, wanderers from other parts, have the vain fashion of graving their names and the obscure places whence they come, upon its stones, which is silly, and marketh the doer for a fool.

Twenty-fourth Day—This day performed before my father's court certain mountebanks, whereof one did eat fire, placing living coals within his mouth and crushing them with his teeth and swallowing them; also drinking naphtha while it flamed, yet betraying no inconvenience from it, but only relish and content.

Then another, placing a child under a basket, drove a sword down through it and drew it forth dripping blood, the child shrieking meanwhile. The basket being turned, the child was nowhere to be seen, nor yet its blood. But these be aged tricks, and little worth.

One swallowed a crooked sword above an arm's length long. This was a soft-spoken, gentle varlet, yet did I wish it might rend his bowels and so end these entertainments since I nor any might sit in my father's presence or depart whilst he remained. But he was charmed, and marveled much; which comes of holding himself in retirement and study and seeing little that doth transpire abroad. Verily these threadbare vagaries did stir his admiration to that degree that no louting clown new come from out the country could surpass it.

Then went he to the theatre in state, the court attending, all in brave attire. This new actor Luz, whose fame filleth the land of late, so wrought upon the multitude in the great part of Adam in the classic, venerable and noble play of the Driving Forth From Eden (there being nothing comparable to it written in these modern times,) that they wept aloud and many times rose up shouting and so stood till it seemed they would never give over. Yet in the midst cometh in Jebel, that never-failing half-brother of my great-great-great-great grandfather Enos, and did raise his brows and turn him this way and that, looking with compassion upon the people, as who should say, "In sooth, call they *this* acting?" So always does he, being never satisfied with anything except it be something ancient and stupid which he hath seen and others have not; decrying all that is modern as being trivial and weak, neither enjoying anything himself nor permitting others that would. Then discoursed he long and loud with much inflated speech and pompous air, concerning what the stage had been in other times before this degenerate day, saying, "When the great Uzziel lived, lo, *there* was an Adam! Please God, when we that have seen true acting, look back and remind us what the stage was four and five hundred years ago—" and then would he work himself up to such an anguish of grief and boasting and most hardy and prodigious lying, that one could be content he were back among his vanished idols and God be thanked that it was so. How tiresome these people be, soured and toothless and old, that go on living for no end, it seemeth, but to keep flinging in one's face the over-rated marvels of an age that is forgot and that none regret but they themselves. Old age hath its charms, but this fashion is not of them. I had told him so, indeed, if such language might become my meagre years and downy head.

Twenty-seventh Day—This day, Zuar, a slave of mine, did prostrate himself before me, humbly reminding me that it is now six years since I bought him of his father. Calling my steward, he shewed me that it was so. Wherefore, the man being a Hebrew, I might not longer hold him, so told him he was free from bondage. Then bowed he again to the earth, saying, "My Lord, I have a wife and children." Then would I, not thinking, have said, "Take them also," but that my steward, falling upon his knees, cried, "O Prince, I must not fail my duty, albeit it is hard: they came not with him when he was bought; Your Grace did give him his wife, and his children were born in servitude." Whereat I was troubled, as not knowing my own matter, I having no experience of a like case before, but said, "Well, if it be so, let it be so—give him money and clothing and let him depart from his house alone; but be kind to his wife and babes, they shall not be sold, neither suffered to want."

Then Zuar rose up and saluting, went out bowed as one that is stricken with a great sorrow. I was not easy in my mind, though fulfilling the law. I wished it might be otherwise. I went out to see, forbidding the guards to come, and found them locked in each other's arms, but not speaking, their faces turned to stone, and not a tear, the babes prattling about their knees, contending for a butterfly that one had caught. I drew back to my place, the pleasure of life gone out of me, which was strange, these being only slaves, dust under my feet. I must give this thing some further thought.

Twenty-eighth Day—Came these poor creatures to me, and Zuar, with a despondent face that belied his words, said, "My Lord, in the form and according to the usage of the law, I am come to declare that I love my lord, and my wife and my children, and do refuse to go out free; therefore, let my ear be bored with an awl before the judges, and I and mine by this token be returned to slavery forever, since that or even death itself is better than that I be parted from these that are more to me than bread and sunshine and the breath that giveth life."

I know not if I did right, but there was no finding it in my heart to suffer this; so I said, "It is a hard law and cruel; go forth free, all of ye, that my conscience may trouble me no more." These were servants of price, but I pray God I shall not repent me of it, since my state is so great and opulent it is but casting away a farthing in any wise.

Fifth Month, Third Day—I cannot abide the Princess Sarah, grand-daughter of my kinsman Eliah, rich and great, and old as that house is, nor will I marry her unless my father force me. Came she again, with a great train of nobles and lesser servants, three days since, to visit at my father's palace, which is over against my new one and no great space away. This girl is near my own age, though a trifle older, which is less pleasant than if she were a trifle younger, she being just turned sixty-one. But Lord, whilst at her age she should be blooming and gay, she apeth the gravity of a matron and hath a mature look and a dull complexion. She affects to be wise and learned, and goeth about with her nose in the air, lost in lofty contemplation. Pray God she hitch it not upon the bough of a tree and so hang herself, for it hath a hook that might serve for it. After the fashion of the time, she hath more hair upon her head that cometh from the bazaar than nature hath provided of her own to keep it company. It were as sensible to add to the proportions of the nose God's grace hath given us—then what, I marvel, would this woman do? Whithersoever she goeth, she draggeth a woolly and insufferable dog by a string and taketh it in her lap and comforteth it when she sits, and in chill weather covereth its body with a red embroidered cloth lest it be taken of a cold or a fever and the world mourn. Cursed be the day that I fall heir to its place and the affliction of the affections of its mistress. Amen.

Fifth Day—Came Zuar and his wife Mahlah, as I walked in the Court of Fountains and fell upon their faces before me to make a petition; and when the guards would have dealt roughly by them for intruding upon my privacy and my meditations, I would not suffer it; for since I was lately merciful to these there hath sprung up within me a consideration for them. Their petition being that I would attach them to my service. I did so, albeit it was odd simplicity in creatures of their degree to prefer a prayer in person to one of my quality; and did appoint Mahlah to serve in the apartment of the women, and Zuar to be near me and be the Master of the Pages, with good wages for both, whereat they were very grateful, not expecting or aspiring to such high fortune.

About noon saw the girl Zillah pass by the great gate of the palace, with but a single servant following, for these are people of mere civilian degree and of no estate. Uz, her great-grandfather hath great learning, but cometh of ancestry of no quality. They be idolaters, worshipers of Baal, and so suffer certain restraints and curtailments of privilege under the law. This girl is very beautiful—more so, indeed, than I had before observed.

Tenth Day—All the whole city did flock to the streets, the walls, the housetops and all places of vantage, to get sight of the savages new come to town from the famous tribe of the Jabalites that live not in houses, but in tents, and wander in lawless hordes through the length and breadth of the great deserts in the far North-east that lie toward the land of Nod. These came to the number of twenty, greater and lesser chiefs, with many servants, all upon camels and dromedaries, with a fantastic sort of barbaric pomp, to make submission to my father and enter into a covenant of peace, they receiving goods and trinkets and implements of husbandry, and undertaking to make the right of way secure and not molest our caravans and merchants.

A visit like to this they make to us as often as once in fifty or sixty years, and then go away and break the covenant and make trouble again. But they are not always to blame. They covenant to go apart and abide upon lands set apart for them, and subsist by the arts of peace; but the agents sent out to govern them do cheat them and maltreat them, removing them to other stations not so good and stealing from them their fertile lands and hunting districts, and abusing them with blows when they resist—a thing they will not abide; and so they rise by night and slaughter all that fall into their hands, revenging the agents' treachery and oppression as best they can. Then go our armies forth to try to carry desolation to their hearthstones but succeed not. These that came to-day went about the city viewing the wonders of it, yet never exclaiming, nor betraying admiration in any way. At the audience many loving speeches were made upon both sides, and they were feasted and sent away with store of presents, mainly implements of husbandry, the which they will fashion into weapons and go out against their persecutors again. They were a wild spectacle, and fierce of countenance, a goodly show; but they and the other tribes of their sort are a sore problem to my father and his council.

They worship no god; and if we in goodness of heart do send a missionary to show them the way of life, they listen with respect to all he hath to say, and then they eat him. This doth tend to hinder the spread of light.

Take this up again under brief republican form of govt, when Meth about 300 or 400 old, and put in Custer and Howard and the Peace Commissioners (Quakers) and the Modoc Lava Beds, etc. and satirize freely.†

Methuselah's Diary, Later Passage

Tenth Day—It taketh but short space to craze men of indifferent understanding with a new thing. Behold 'tis now but two years gone that a certain ancient game, played with a ball, hath come up again, yet already are all mouths filled with the phrases that describe its parts and movement; insomuch, indeed, that the ears of the sober and such as would busy themselves with weightier matters are racked with the clack of the same till they do ache with anguish. If a man deceive his neighbor with a shrewd trick that doth advantage himself to his neighbor's hurt, the vulgar say of the sufferer that he was Caught out on a Foul. If one accomplisheth a great and sudden triumph of any sort soever, 'tis said of him that he hath Made a Three-base Hit. If one fail utterly in an enterprise of pith and moment, you shall hear this said concerning him: **Hashbat-kakolath.* Thus hath this vile deformity of speech entered with familiar insolence into the very warp and woof of the language, and made ugly that which before was shapely and beautiful. To-day, by command of my father, was this game contested in the great court of his palace after the manner of the playing of it three centuries gone by. Nine men that had their calves clothed in red did strive against other nine that had blue hose upon their calves. Certain of those in blue stood at distances, one from another, stooping, each with his palms upon his knees, watching; these they called Basemen and Fielders—wherefore, God knoweth. It concerneth me not to know, neither to care. One with red legs stood wagging a club about his head, which from time to time he struck upon the ground, then wagged he it again. Behind him bent one with blue legs that did spit much upon his hands, and was called a Catcher. Beside him bent one called Umpire, clothed in the common fashion of the time, who marked upon the ground with a stick, yet

*This is not translatable into English; but it is about equivalent to "Lo, he is *whitewashed.*"—[The Editor.]

accomplished nothing by it that I could make out. Saith this one, Low Ball. Whereat one with blue legs did deliver a ball with vicious force straight at him that bore the club, but failed to bring him down, through some blemish of his aim. At once did all that are called Basemen and Fielders spit upon their hands and stoop and watch again. He that bore the club did suffer the ball to be flung at him divers times, but did always bend in his body or bend it out and so save himself, whilst the others spat upon their hands, he at the same instant endeavoring to destroy the Umpire with his bludgeon, yet not succeeding, through grievous awkwardness. But in the fulness of time was he more fortunate, and did lay the Umpire dead, which mightily pleased me, yet fell himself, he failing to avoid the ball, which this time cracked his skull, to my deep gratitude and satisfaction. Conceiving this to be the end, I did crave my father's leave to go, and got it, though all beside me did remain, to see the rest disabled. Yet I had seen a sufficiency, and shall visit this sport no more, forasmuch as the successful hits come too laggingly, wherefore the game doth lack excitement. Moreover was Jebel there, windy with scorn of these modern players, and boastful of certain mighty Nines he knew three hundred years gone by—dead, now, and rotten, praise God, who doeth all things well.

Twelfth Day—The rumor that has been steadily gathering strength these twenty years, that the head of our princely house, the father of the nations of the earth, the most noble, most august and venerable ADAM (on whom be peace!) willeth to visit my father in this his capital city, is rumor no more, but verity. The embassage approacheth with the tidings. Exceeding great is the tumult of the city for joy and thanksgiving. My father commandeth his chief ministers to make due preparation.

Thirteenth Day—Came men of trust this day, that report the embassage as tarrying by the oasis Balka, eighteen days journey hence, toward the south.

Fourteenth day—There is no talk but of the great news and of the embassage. At the rising of the sun went my father's envoys forth in gorgeous state, to take the road, they bearing presents of gold and precious stones, spices and robes of honor. With banners and with sound of martial music went they, a glittering host, marching past until I wearied of the numbers and the noise. The multitudes that massed themselves upon the house-tops or followed shouting were beyond the power of man to estimate. 'Tis a great day.

Fifteenth Day—My father hath commanded that the Palace of the Palms be new garnished for the ambassador that cometh, and his following. Eight hundred artisans and artists will set to work, with all dispatch to paint and gild and renovate.

Sixteenth Day—To the museum, to see the raiments of fig leaves and of strange untanned skins of beasts our parents wore in Eden, in the olden time. Likewise the Flaming Sword the which the Angel bore. Now that the city is so wrought upon by the growing excitement, 'tis said the museum cannot accommodate more than some few thousands of the hosts that now daily clamor for admittance to the relics. That I might see as the simple see, and hear as the simple hear, and not be myself a show and plagued with the attentions due my state and dignity, went I disguised as a mere mohac,* not even clogged with a servant. Some hundreds of guides walked the prodigious ranges of apartments, with eager troops of people following, and made explanation of the gathered marvels. I perceived that these touched not upon their wares at random, but in rigid sequence, and that their speech by old habit had formed itself into an unchangeable sequence of words, hard, inflexionless, and void of all heart and expression as if a machine had made it. He whom I did follow, had held his post four hundred years, clacking the same speech, day in, day out, through all that weary time, till now was he no more master of his jaws; once they set themselves a-wagging, only God could stop them before the speech was done. The foolish rhetoric and flourish of it, that once had had a sort of showy sound, mayhap, was now like to make one laugh for derision or cry for pity, so flat and lifeless was it. Poor old withered ass, thrice did I interrupt, to test him. 'Twas as I had conceived; it threw him out, and he was forced to go back and begin again at the beginning. It was on this wise: Saith he, Lo, this dread weapon, grim memorial of that awful day; flaming with consuming fires that o'er the darkening fields of Eden cast their lurid ray—. I, interrupting, did inquire about a huge thing that bore the legend, The Similitude and Likeness of the Key of the Garden, the Original whereof lieth in the Treasure House of Cain in the far City of Enoch. The aged guide was sore troubled with this, and did try to answer me, but failing once and yet again, did then endeavour to find the place whereat he had late left off in his wretched speech; but not succeeding, went he back again and rasped out as formerly: Lo, this dread weapon, grim memorial of that awful day; flaming with consuming fires that o'er the darkening fields of Eden cast their lurid ray—. I, interrupting yet twice again, each time returned he to his accursed Lo, this dread weapon. Then suddenly being wroth, perceiving by signs of merriment among the crowd that he was being played upon, turned he upon me, saying, Though I be of mean estate and lowly calling, it ill becometh one of but *mohac* degree and graceless youth

*Untranslatable. It means something better than a professional man, and not so good as an artist. Thus fine were the caste distinctions of the time.—[Editor.]

to shame mine age with scorn. Being angered, I never having known insult before, I was near to saying, By the law, whoso offends any of the royal house his head is forfeit. But I remembered myself in time and spake not, purposing at another season to have him crucified, together with his family.

I saw no curiosity that riveted the people's gaze like to the Fig Leaves. Yet they are not leaves, in truth, but only the skeletons thereof, instead, the fabric all decayed and gone save only the ribs or veinings. There be cavilers that say we shall not lack for the original garments of the Garden whilst fig trees grow and beasts remain to renew these sacred treasures withal. As for me, I say nothing, since that is most discreet. Yet am I pained to remember that there exists at this day in each of Seven cities, the Only True and Original Flaming Sword of Expulsion. This moveth one to doubt.

Presently came the sweet idolater by, and was swallowed up and lost in the crowd. Straightway began I to dream and muse, and so, losing zest for the marvels treasured about me, betook me home.

Twentieth Day—God send that embassage come soon, else cannot the people contain themselves. There is naught but talk of this great thing, and preparation for it. Still, many days must yet elapse before these expectations bring their fruit.

Twenty-seventh Day—Perish the generation of Jubal! Let the hand wither that ceased not with contriving the noble organ and the charming harp, but must shut up an unappeasable devil in the bowels of a box, with privilege to vagrants to grind anguish out of him with a crank and name it Music. This new thing, being not yet a century invented, has yet spread to all parts like to a pestilence; so that at this day, in every city shall you see vagabonds from strange lands grinding these dread boxes, in the company and companionship of a monkey. 'Twere endurable, were there variety in the Music; but alack, they seem all to play but the one tune—the new one that did come into favor some thirty years agone and seems not like to go out again before the world shall drown in that silly deluge whereof over-pious fools with ill digestion do prate and prophesy from time to time. 'Tis said the new excitement hath increased our horde of grinders mightily, so that there be in the city now full eighty thousand, which do all grind, without ceasing, that one tearful ditty, "O, Kiss Haggag for His Mother." Verily is this tune waxing intolerable to me. Though Haggag were damned, yet could I not be content, so sore is my rage that he was ever born, since without him this infliction had not come upon us.

Second Day of the Sixth Month of the Year 747—Yesterday arrived my father's envoys, bringing the august embassage; whom my father received in mighty state at the city gates. Vast was the procession, and curious the garbs, and everything very fine and noble to see. The city was mad with exultation. Nothing like to this noise and confusion have I seen before. Every house and street and all the palaces were blazing with light all the night; and such as stood upon the distant eastward mountains said the city had the seeming of a far-off plain frosted thick with cut gems that glowed and winked with a bewitching soft radiance.

The ambassador hath delivered his tidings, and now there is not any more doubt. Adam indeed will come, the time is set: the year 787 or the year that followeth it. Public proclamation was made and all the city is clamorous with delight. My father's orders have gone forth to set in train the preparations due to so majestic an event.

Now will begin the games and other pleasures meet for the entertainment of the ambassadors, so my father has commanded public holiday during the two months which this must last.

[Here Mark Twain penciled in additional notes, as follows:]

Army of 10,000 men—great battle
The asinine newspaper (vellum MS) scribe says of every new play, plot is thin and meagre and nothing original in it.†

Just satirize America straight through after once beginning. Satirize Russia, Turkey, England and a wee German principality separately.†

PASSAGES FROM SHEM'S DIARY†

Friday. Papa's birthday. He is six hundred years old. We celebrated it in the big black tent. Principal men of the tribe present. Afterward they were shown over the Ark, which was looking desolate and empty and dreary, on account of the misunderstanding with the workmen about wages. Methuselah was as free with his criticisms as usual, and as voluble. And familiar. Which I and my brothers do not like; for we are past our hundredth year and married. He still calls me Shemmy, just as he did when I was a child of sixty. I am still but a youth, it is true, but youth has its feelings, and I do not like this. The way he acts, one would think there was no valuable commodity in this world but age and that he possessed a monopoly of it. Why, there is a plenty of men who are several centuries older than he is, but they are not in the patriarchal succession. Therefore they attract no attention. If I ever get to be as old as Methuselah, I will not allow myself to regard youth as a crime; I will remember that it exists not by its own fault, and so is excusable; and I will also try to find some better excuse for old age than Methuselah's ways furnishes. Not even his nine hundred and sixty-eight years can cover up the fact that his biting tongue is a defect. If he were not a relative I would hint as much to him. It cannot be denied that he has a sagacious mind and a clever use of words, but neither can it be denied that he makes a poor use of these great gifts, as a rule. He had a disappointment in love in the morning of his life, and the bitterness of this misfortune had remained in his heart all these weary centuries. Much must be excused to a man so loyal as this, and who has suffered so much and so long. It is said that over the dim far stretch of nine centuries he still sees that young girl in his dreams and is heard to talk with her and call her by endearing names in his sleep. She has been dead all that time.

So it is true, as I have said—one must forgive much to such a man. But it is hard to keep enough charity in stock to meet the demands which he makes upon it—especially in these latter days. Privately, I do not think very much of the Ark myself; but he—why he speaks straight out and is unsparingly candid. Sometime I'll set down some of the things he said.

Saturday. Keeping the Sabbath.

Sunday. Papa has yielded the advance, and everybody is hard at work; the shipyard so crowded that the men hinder each other; everybody hurrying or being hurried; the rush and confusion and shouting and wrangling are astonishing to people like our family, who have always been used to a quiet country life. Hundreds and hundreds of new men have been put on, this morning, for time is pressing us cruelly. The Ark ought to have been done fully a month ago—oh, yes, two months ago—but first one thing and then another delayed us; mainly the scarcity of gopher wood; and secondarily the strike.†

Shem's Diary, Later Passage

Sabbath Day. As usual—nobody keeping it. Nobody but our family. Multitudes of the wicked swarming everywhere, and carousing. Drinking, fighting, dancing, gambling, laughing, shouting, singing—men, women, girls, youths, all at it. And at other infamies besides—infamies not to be set down in words. And the noise! Blowing of horns, banging on pots and kettles, blaring of brazen instruments, boom and clatter of drums—it is enough to burst a person's ears. And this is the Sabbath—think of it! Father says it was not like this in the earlier times. When he was a boy everybody kept the Day, and there was no wickedness, no pleasuring, no noise; there was peace, silence, tranquillity; there was divine service several times a day and in the evening. This was near six hundred years ago. Think of that time and this! One can hardly believe such a change could come in so little a while that men not yet old can remember it.

These horrible creatures have come in even greater crowds than usual, to-day, to look at the Ark, and prowl over it and make fun of it. They ask questions, and when they are told it is a boat, they laugh, and ask where the water is, out here in the dry plain. When we say the Lord is going to send the water from heaven and drown all the world, they mock again, and say, "Tell it to the marines."

Methuselah was here again to-day. While he isn't the oldest person in the world, he is the oldest distinguished person in it, and because of that peculiar supremacy, he is regarded with awe by everybody; and wherever he appears the riotings cease and silence falls upon the multitude, and they uncover and salute him with slavish reverence as he passes by, murmuring to each other, "Look at him—there he goes—most a thousand years old—used to know Adam, they say." He is a vain old creature, and anybody can see how it gratifies him, though he dodders along with his nose in the air and a simpering cake-walk gait, pretending to be pondering some great matter profoundly, and letting on that he doesn't know anything is happening.

I know, from certain things I have noticed, that he is of a jealous disposition; envious, too. Perhaps I ought not to say this, for I am related to him by marriage, my wife being his great-great-great-great-great-great-great-great-great-great-great-great-great-great-great grandaughter, or somewhere along there, and indeed I wouldn't say it in public, but I think there can be no harm in my saying it in the privacy of my Diary, which is merely the same as saying it to myself. He is jealous about this Ark, I am quite sure of it. Jealous because he wasn't asked to build it instead of father. The Ark is such a wonder to all the nations around that it has raised father from obscurity to world-wide fame, and Methuselah is jealous of that. At first, people used to say, "Noah?—pray who is Noah?"—but now they come miles to get his autograph. It makes Methuselah tired.

He doesn't have to sit up nights doing autographs, but we do. All of us—the whole eight; for father can't do them all, nor even a tenth of them, his hand being old and stiff. Methuselah has a most unpleasant disposition. I think he is never happy except when he is making other people uncomfortable. He always speaks of my brothers and me and our wives as "the children." He does it because he sees that it hurts our feelings. One day Japheth timidly ventured to remind him that we were men and women. You could have heard him scoff a mile! And he closed his eyes in a kind of ecstasy of scorn, and puckered his withered lips, exposing his yellow fangs and the gaps between them, and hacked out a dry odious laugh with an asthmatic cough mixed with it, and said—

"*Men and women!*—the likes of *you!* Pray how old are you venerable relics?"

"Our wives are nearly eighty; and of *us* I am the youngest and I was a hundred last spring."

"Eighty, dear me! a hundred, *dear* me! And *married!* dear, dear, dear! You cradle-rubbish! you rag dolls! Married! In my young days nobody would ever have thought of such a thing as children getting married. It's monstrous!"

I started to remind him that more than one of the patriarchs had married in early youth, but he wouldn't listen. That is just his way; if you catch him out with an argument that he can't answer, he raises his voice and shouts you down, and the only thing you can do is to shut your mouth and drop the matter. It won't do to dispute with him, it would be considered a scandal and irreverent. At least it would not do for us boys to talk back. Neither us nor anybody else. Except the surgeon. The surgeon isn't afraid of him, and hasn't any reverence, anyway. The surgeon says a man is just a man, and his being a thousand years old doesn't make him any more than a man.

ADAM'S EXPULSION

Sometime in October 1877 Mark Twain's active conscience caused him to dream up a novel apology for one of his sins of omission. As he explains in the preface to "Adam's Expulsion," he had visited Lake Seneca, one of the New York Finger Lakes, and had promised to write a description of that visit for a woman friend. But he had "put it off so long that he forgot what the lake looked like, and what State it was in; wherefore he could only excuse himself and explain as below." What followed that explanation became a description of what had occurred when Adam's children began asking him to write about "the marvels and loveliness of the Garden, and of the delight and the charm and the splendor . . . of the enchanted life which thou and our mother Eve did lead there." † Here, his humor relied heavily for its effects on garbled quotations from Scripture and other sources.

This story was Mark Twain's first attempt to present Adam as a narrator and hence was an important forerunner of the later diaries of Adam and Eve. Just what brought Adam to Twain's attention in 1877 cannot now be ascertained, but the incident that prompted the later apology may well have been a family visit the summer before to Ithaca, New York, on Lake Cayuga. On 6 August the humorist told Mollie Fairbanks, the daughter of his Cleveland friend, that "we run over to Ithaca tomorrow for a two-day visit" (*MTMF*, 205). When he wrote his introduction, he either forgot the name of the lake or, if he was contemplating publication of the piece, changed it to neighboring Lake Seneca in order to disguise the location.

In any event, on 28 October he made a copy of his original pencil manuscript, probably for the "lady friend" whom he had promised the account of the visit. And sometime in 1881, while going over manuscripts for inclusion in *The Stolen White Elephant* (1882), he would dig out his original manuscript, provide a title, the brief introduction explaining the procrastination that had produced the piece, and the following note: "The author afterward offered this Oration or Essay for the Twenty-Dollar Prize at the Great National Sunday-School Reunion at Chautauqua Lake, August, 1881. Now first published."† And at the end of the manuscript, a footnote proclaimed, "Did not take the prize."

The announcement of publication proved to be premature, for when Twain submitted his batch of manuscripts to his friend William Dean Howells for comment and approval in 1882, "Adam's Expulsion" was one of the ten items that Howells advised omitting from the book (JRO to SLC, 8 April 1882, MTP). Hence, after still more delay, it is here that "Adam's Expulsion" is "now first published."

ADAM'S EXPULSION†

[The author visited Seneca Lake, and promised a lady friend a description of it, but put it off so long that he forgot what the lake looked like, and what State it was in; wherefore he could only excuse himself and explain, as below. The author afterward offered this Oration or Essay for the Twenty-Dollar Prize at the great National Sunday-School Reunion at Chautauqua Lake, August, 1881. Now first published.]*

After Adam was expelled from Eden, children were born to him, and when they had achieved the age of inquiry they said, "Father, take thou a pen and write of the marvels and the loveliness of the Garden, and of the delight and the charm and the splendor and the bewitchment of the enchanted life which thou and our mother Eve did lead there, that we may read it—and so it shall come to pass that we also shall enjoy it, albeit we see it not, save only through thine eyes and thy memory." And Adam answering, said, "Lo, wait ye but a little time, and I will do it."

But Adam procrastinated.

The years waxed and waned, and the grandchildren of Adam lifted up their voices and said, "Grandfather, take thou a pen and write of the marvels and the loveliness of the Garden, and of the delight and the charm and the splendor and the bewitchment of the enchanted life which thou and our mother Eve did lead there, that we may read it—and so it shall come to pass that we also shall enjoy it, albeit we see it not, save only through thine eyes and thy memory." And Adam answering, said, "Lo, wait ye but a little time and I will do it."

But Adam procrastinated—for behold, men may be made each after his

*Did not take the prize.

kind, and Adam was of the kind which put not off until the morrow that which may be done to-day, but do even put it off until the next week, yea even unto the middle thereof, yet do it not then, nevertheless, but again neglect it. Therefore, whosoever is without guile, let him lie down with the lion and the lamb and be not ashamed of his nakedness; for they shall put a ring upon his hand and shoes upon his feet; and all that was his father's shall be his, and also all that his mother and his sister hath, and likewise the mote that is in his brother's eye. For it is easier for a rich man to go through the eye of a camel than for another man to break the Sabbath day and keep it holy.

So the years waxed and waned, and the great-grandchildren of Adam lifted up their voices and cried with a mighty tumult, saying, "*Write!*" even as the generations that had gone before. Wherefore did Adam promise yet once again.

And again did he procrastinate, as in the days of old, he loving his ease the more as the winters did gather upon his head and other the signs and symbols of age accumulate about him. For even so is the estate of man: one day he cometh up as a flower, fair to look upon; but the next day is he cut down and trampled under foot of men and cast into outer darkness, where the grasshopper is a burden and thieves break through and steal and he hath naught of raiment but camel's hair and ashes, and a leathern girdle about his loins.

So the years waxed and waned, and generations passed, and three centuries came and went, and the fourth was far spent. And behold all the seed of Adam had made the welkin of the drifting ages ring with that petition which they had come to know by heart, and Adam had magnified the clamor with his ancient promise, yet had he still procrastinated, as in that old day when the world was young and Eden a dream of yesterday. Now came forth all the host of his posterity, a mighty and exceeding multitude that no man might number, and did lift up their voices and did utter as it were in quaking thunders, the saying, "Father of the nations and peoples of the earth here gathered in thy presence from the four winds and the uttermost parts beyond the great seas, take thy pen and write of the glories and the joys of Eden, that we may see with thine eyes and be blest in the contemplation of it."

Then did Adam answering say, "Lo, ages have rolled their waves of care and sorrow over me, and regret for the divine Eden hath grown with my years, until it hath come to pass that now am I no longer able to bring back the memory of that gracious time, so wasted and obliterated is it with these centuries of picturing in my mind *that woful day that saw me banished thence.*"

Then went that great multitude forth unto the far regions whence they came, saying one to another, "Lo, this old man hath beguiled us to our hurt. Therefore, when it shall come to pass that another Adam departeth out of another Eden, let it be the law that he shall write that which he hath seen whilst yet it basketh in the gold and purple crimson of the morning of his memory, ere the clouds and the night of age close down and hide it away and it be lost forever. Then shall he be clothed in sack-cloth and fine linen, and men shall bow down and worship him, even as did the children the fatted calf in the plain, what time the floods came and the winds blew, and beat upon it, yet it fell not, for it was founded upon a rock; and an exceeding great fear came upon all that saw it, and their legs quaked and their limbs clove to the roof of their mouth and they fled away to the mountains, crying "Hold the fort for I am coming."

Read, mark, and inwardly digest this parable, for it describes the state of one who enjoyed the lake and the cottage and the people that tarried there, yet wrote not concerning these things at the time, but procrastinated.

ADAM'S SOLILOQUY

After his return from Europe following Livy's death in June 1904 and a brief time in Elmira, Mark Twain spent a relatively quiet summer and early fall in the Berkshires. In November the household, minus daughter Clara, moved into 21 Fifth Avenue in New York City, where, beginning in late January, Twain began a remarkable period of literary production, one that would last through 1906. His immediate efforts produced no fewer than three "soliloquies," featuring the Russian czar, King Leopold of Belgium, and Adam, respectively. The first, "The Czar's Soliloquy," dated "February 2, 1905" at the end, was perhaps inspired by reports of the "Bloody Sunday" massacre of 22 January (mentioned in the piece as "my massacre of the unoffending innocents the other day"), when the czar's troops fired on the crowd assembled before the Winter Palace in St. Petersburg to petition the czar for political and economic reforms. In his soliloquy the monarch, while contemplating his naked reflection in a mirror and musing that his power obviously depended on "clothes," titles, and other trappings of monarchy, describes his many tyrannical atrocities, and accepts responsibility for them.

Evidently impressed with Isabel Lyon's enthusiastic praise of the piece, and that of Col. George Harvey, editor of the *North American Review* (which published "The Czar's Soliloquy" in the March issue), Twain then turned to a similar exposé of King Leopold and his alleged enslavement, mutilation, and murder of the natives of the Congo. Colonel Harvey obviously thought this piece too strong for some of his readers, however, for the *North American Review* turned it down. The Congo Reform Association, to which Mark Twain then offered it, was by no means as reluctant, and published the Belgian king's diatribe in September 1905 as a pamphlet with the ironic title *King Leopold's Soliloquy: A Defence of his Congo Rule.*

Though Mark Twain delighted in attacking these tyrants, he may well have felt weighted down with the horrors perpetrated by these "fathers" of their countries and wished to try a lighter vein. The very day after finishing Leopold's "defence," he turned away from current political subjects and caustic satire to take up the musings of another father—the father of mankind—in "Adam's Soliloquy."

In this return to his interest in Adam's story, Twain further developed his difficulty in accepting the biblical explanations of life in Eden, the Fall, and the Flood, especially as they conflicted with evolution and the extinction of species. Here he presented Adam as visiting present-day New York City and pondering the restored skeleton of a dinosaur in the American Museum of Natural History, puzzling over why Noah's "cargo list" had not included this creature but had included insects, rats, and cholera germs, and indirectly discrediting the biblical account of the Flood—a theme he had treated more fully in the "Autobiography of Eve," and one to which he would return in "Letters from the Earth." The treatment of Noah also expands on the brief portraits of the patriarch in Shem's and Methuselah's diaries.

This first portion of "Adam's Soliloquy" obviously was inspired by a widely publicized exhibit of a brontosaurus skeleton at the American Museum of Natural History in February 1905, while Twain was working on "King Leopold's Soliloquy." To display the creature, which had been undergoing restoration for most of the decade following its discovery in Wyoming in 1894, the museum established a new fossil hall. The grand opening of the hall on 16 February, which was celebrated by a "Dinosaur Tea" for some five hundred select guests, cosponsored by J. P. Morgan, received extensive coverage in the New York *Times* and *Tribune* in articles, poems, and cartoons.

The second section of Adam's musings moves to Central Park, and presents his astonishment at the numbers of people, his pleasurable realization that he is related to all of them, and his largely comic confrontation with a mother and infant. Under the humor, however, runs a strong sentimental strain and sense of the eternal presence of maternal love, which Twain would also emphasize the following summer in "Eve's Diary," when Adam notes how the young mother's eyes reflect the worship of her child: "It is the very look that used to shine in Eve's. To think—that so subtle and intangible a thing as a *look* could flit and flash from face to face down a procession three hundred thousand years long and remain the same, without shade of change! Yet here it is, lighting this young creature's face just as it lighted Eve's in the long ago—the newest thing I have seen in the earth, and the oldest."

ADAM'S SOLILOQUY

[*Inspecting the Dinosaur at the Museum of Natural History.*] It is strange. . . . very strange. *I* do not remember this creature. [After gazing long and admiringly.] Well, it is wonderful! The mere *skeleton* 57 feet long and 16 feet high! Thus far, it seems, they've found only this sample—without doubt a merely medium-sized one; a person could not step out here into the Park and happen by luck upon the largest horse in America; no, he would happen upon one that would look small alongside of the biggest Normandy. It is quite likely that the biggest Dinosaur was 90 feet long and 25 feet high. It would be five times as long as an elephant; an elephant would be to it what a calf is to an elephant. The bulk of the creature! The weight of him! As long as the longest whale, and twice the substance in him. And all good wholesome pork, most likely; meat enough to last a village a year. . . . Think of a hundred of them in line, draped in shining cloth of gold!—a majestic thing for a coronation procession. But expensive, for he would eat much; only kings and millionaires could afford him.

I have no recollection of him; neither Eve nor I had heard of him until yesterday. We spoke to Noah about him; he colored and changed the subject. Being brought back to it—and pressed a little—he confessed that in the matter of stocking the Ark the stipulations had not been carried out with absolute strictness—that is, in minor details, unessentials. There were some irregularities. He said the boys were to blame for this—the boys mainly, his own fatherly indulgence partly. They were in the giddy heydey of their youth at the time, the happy springtime of life, their hundred years sat upon them lightly, and—well, he had been a boy himself, and he had not the heart to be too exacting with them. And so—well, they did things they shouldn't have done, and he—to be candid, he winked. But on the whole they did pretty faithful work, considering their age. They collected and stowed a good share of the really useful animals; and also, when Noah was not watching, a multitude of useless ones, such as flies, mosquitoes, snakes, and so on, but they did certainly leave ashore a good many creatures which might possibly have had value some time or other in the course of time. Mainly these were vast saurians a hundred feet long, and monstrous mammals, such as the megatherium and that sort, and there was really some excuse for leaving them behind, for two reasons: (1) it was manifest that some time or other they would be needed as fossils for museums; and (2) there had been a miscalculation, the Ark was smaller than it should have been, and so there wasn't room for those creatures. There was actually fossil-material enough all by itself to freight twenty-five Arks like that one. As for the Dinosaur, Noah's conscience was easy; it was not named in his cargo-list and the boys were not aware that there was such a creature. He said he could not blame himself for not knowing about the Dinosaur, because it was an American animal, and America had not then been discovered.

Noah went on to say, "I did reproach the boys for not making the most of the room we had, by discarding trashy animals and substituting beasts like the mastodon which could be useful to man in doing heavy work such as the elephant performs, but they said those great creatures would have increased our labors beyond our strength, in the matter of feeding and watering them, we being short-handed. There was something in that. We had no pump; there was but one window; we had to let down a bucket from that, and haul it up a good fifty feet, which was very tiresome; then we had to carry the water down stairs—fifty feet again, in cases where it was for the elephants and their kind, for we kept them in the hold to serve for ballast. As it was, we lost many animals; choice animals that would have been valuable in menageries—different breeds of lions, tigers, hyenas, wolves, and so on; for they wouldn't drink the water after the salt seawater got mixed with the fresh. But we never lost a locust, nor a grasshopper, nor a weevil, nor a rat, nor a cholera-germ, nor any of that sort of beings. On the whole, I think we did very well, everything considered. We were shepherds and farmers, we had never been to sea before, we were ignorant of naval matters, and I know this, for certain, that there is more difference between agriculture and navigation than a person would think. It is my opinion that the two trades do not belong together. Shem thinks the same, so does Japheth. As for what Ham thinks, it is not important. Ham is biased; you find me a Presbyterian that isn't, if you think you can."

He said it aggressively; it had in it the spirit of a challenge. I avoided argument by changing the subject. With Noah, arguing is a passion, a disease, and it is growing upon him; has been growing upon him for thirty thousand years and more; it makes him unpopular, unpleasant; many of his oldest friends dread to meet him. Even the strangers soon get to avoiding him, although at first they are glad to meet him and gaze at him, on account of his celebrated adventure. For a time they are proud of his notice, because he is so distinguished; but he argues them to rags, and before long they begin to wish, like the rest, that something had happened to the Ark.

II

[On a bench in the Park, mid-afternoon, dreamily noting the drift of the species back and forth.] To think—this multitude is but a wee little fraction of the earth's population! And all blood-kin to me, every one! Eve ought to have come with me; this would excite her affectionate heart, she was never able to keep her composure when she came upon a relative; she would try to kiss every one of these people, black and white and all. [A baby-wagon passes.] How little change one can notice—none at all, in fact. I remember the first child well—let me see. . . . it is three hundred thousand years ago come Tuesday; this one is just like it. So between the first one and the last one there is really nothing to choose. The same insufficiency of hair, the same absence of teeth, the same feebleness of body and apparent vacancy of mind, the same general unattractiveness all around. Yet Eve worshiped that early one, and it was pretty to see her with it. This latest one's mother worships *it;* it shows in her eyes—it is the very look that used to shine in Eve's. To think—that so subtle and intangible a thing as a *look* could flit and flash from face to face down a procession three hundred thousand years long and remain the same, without shade of change! Yet here it is, lighting this young creature's face just as it lighted Eve's in the long ago—the newest thing I have seen in the earth, and the oldest. Of course, the Dinosaur—but that is in another class.

She drew the baby-wagon to the bench and sat down and began to shove it softly back and forth with one hand while she held up a newspaper with the other and absorbed herself in its contents. Presently, "My!" she exclaimed; which startled me, and I ventured to ask her, modestly and respectfully, what was the matter. She courteously passed the paper to me and said—pointing with her finger—

"There—it reads like fact, but I don't know."

It was very embarrassing. I tried to look at my ease, and nonchalantly turned the paper this and that and the other way, but her eye was upon me and I felt that I was not succeeding. Pretty soon she asked, hesitantly—

"Can't—can't you—read?"

I had to confess that I couldn't. It filled her with wonder. But it had one pleasant effect—it interested her in me, and I was thankful, for I was getting lonesome for some one to talk to and listen to. The young fellow who was showing me around—on his own motion, I did not invite him—had missed his appointment at the museum, and I was feeling disappointed, for he was good company. When I told the young woman I could not read, she asked me another embarrassing question—

"Where are you from?"

I skirmished—to gain time and position. I said—

"Make a guess. See how near you can come."

She brightened, and exclaimed—

"I shall dearly like it, sir, if you don't mind. If I guess right will you tell me?"

"Yes."

"Honor bright?"

"Honor bright?—what is that?"

She laughed delightedly, and said—

"That's a good start! I was *sure* that that phrase would catch you. I know one thing now, all right. I know—"

"What do you know?"

"That you are not an American. And you aren't, *are* you?"

"No, you are right. I'm not—honor bright, as you say."

She looked immensely pleased with herself, and said—

"I reckon I'm not always smart, but *that* was smart, anyway. But not so *very*, after all, because I already knew—believed I knew—that you were a foreigner, by another sign."

"What was that?"

"Your accent."

She was an accurate observer; I do speak English with a heavenly accent, and she had detected the foreign twang in it. She ran charmingly on, most naïvely and engagingly pleased with her triumph—

"The minute you said 'See 'ow near you can come to it' I said to myself 'Two to one he is a foreigner, and ten to one he's English.' Now that *is* your nationality, *isn't* it?"

I was sorry to spoil her victory, but I had to do it—

"Ah—you'll have to guess again."

"What—you are not an Englishman?"

"No—honor bright."

She looked me searchingly over, evidently communing with herself—adding up my points, then she said—

"Well, you don't *look* like an Englishman, and that is true." After a little she added, "The fact is, you don't look like *any* foreigner—nor quite like. . . . like *anybody* I've seen before. I will guess some more."

She guessed every country whose name she could think of, and grew gradually discouraged. Finally she said—

"You must be the Man Without a Country—the one the story tells about. You don't seem to have any nationality at all. How did you come to come to America? Have you any kinfolks here?"

"Yes—several."

"Oh, then you came to see *them.*"

"Partly—yes."

She sat a while, thinking; then—

"Well, I'm not going to give up quite yet. Where do you live when you are at home—in a city, or in the country?"

"Which do you think?"

"Well, I don't quite know. You *do* look a little countrified, if you don't mind my saying it; but you look a little citified, too—not much, but a little, although you can't read, which is very curious, and you are not used to newspapers. Now *my* guess is, that you live mainly in the country when you are at home, and not very much in the city. Is that right?"

"Yes, quite right."

"Oh, good! Now I'll take a fresh start."

Then she wore herself to the bone, naming cities. No success. Next she wanted me to help her a little with some "pointers," as she phrased it. Was my city large? Yes. Was it very large? Yes. Did they have mobiles there? No. Electric light? No. Railroads, hospitals, colleges, cops? No.

"Why, then, it's not civilized! Where *can* that place be? Be good and tell me just one peculiarity of it—then maybe I can guess."

"Well then, just one: it has gates of pearl."

"Oh, go along! That's the New Jerusalem. It isn't fair to joke. Never mind, I'll guess it yet—it will come into my head pretty soon, just when I'm not expecting it. Oh, I've got an idea! Please talk a little in your own language—that'll be a good pointer." I accommodated her with a sentence or two. She shook her head despondently.

"No," she said, "it doesn't sound—human. I mean, it doesn't sound like any of these other foreigners. It's pretty enough—it's quite pretty, I think—

but I'm sure I've not heard it before. Maybe if you were to pronounce your name—what *is* your name, if you'll be so good?"

"Adam."

"Adam?"

"Yes."

"But Adam *what?*"

"That is all—just Adam."

"Nothing at all but just that?"

"Yes, nothing but that."

"Why, how curious! There's plenty of Adams; how can they tell you from the rest?"

"Oh, that is no trouble; I'm the only one there is, there where I'm from."

"Upon my word! Well, it beats the band! It reminds a person of the old original. That was his name, too, and he hadn't any but that—just like you." Then archly, "You've heard of him, I suppose?"

"Oh, yes. Do you know him? Have you ever seen him?"

"*Seen* him? Seen *Adam?* Thanks to goodness, no! It would scare me into fits."

"I don't see why."

"You don't?"

"No."

"*Why* don't you see why?"

"Because there is no sense in a person being scared of his kin."

"*Kin?*"

"Yes. Isn't he a distant relative of yours?"

She thought it was prodigiously funny, and said it was perfectly true, but *she* never would have been bright enough to think of it. I find it a new and most pleasant sensation to have my wit admired, and was about to try to do some more when that young fellow came. He planted himself on the other side of the young woman and began a vapid remark about the weather, but she gave him a look that withered him, and got stiffly up and wheeled the baby away.

Heaven

CAPTAIN STORMFIELD'S VISIT TO HEAVEN

Obviously an appropriate beginning for this section, "Captain Stormfield's Visit to Heaven" bears an additional distinction. Among the works published during Mark Twain's lifetime, it holds the record for the longest period between gestation and publication—almost forty years. Even then, parts of it remained unpublished until much later, and one substantial last-minute deletion is published here for the first time (see appendix 5b).

Stormfield's story was born of a meeting in July 1868 with the colorful Captain Edgar "Ned" Wakeman, with whom Clemens had sailed from San Francisco to Nicaragua in December 1866 aboard the steamer *America*. At that time the humorist was on his way from California to New York and eventually to Europe and the Holy Land on the voyage that engendered *The Innocents Abroad* (1869). The captain's vivid tales enchanted him and a number of them later found their way into his own works. In the 1866 *Alta California* letters Wakeman reappeared both as himself and as "Captain Waxman"; in chapter 50 of *Roughing It* (1872), he became "Captain Ned Blakely," and in "Some Rambling Notes of an Idle Excursion" (*Atlantic*, November 1877) he was "Captain 'Hurricane Jones.'" Some of Wakeman's qualities would also appear later in other characters.

Now in Panama City, on the first leg of his journey home from San Francisco with a draft of *The Innocents Abroad* in his baggage, Clemens was delighted to see Wakeman again. And it was on a late-night visit to the captain's ship at anchor in the harbor that, among other anecdotes, "the old gentleman told his remarkable dream." Though Mark Twain's own version of that dream would not see print for many years, Wakeman's story made a profound impression.

Establishing the exact course of composition of "Stormfield" is difficult, especially since for the period between August 1868 and May 1877 none of Mark Twain's notebooks have survived, except for a fairly brief stenographer's notebook for June and July 1873 during one of his trips to England. Moreover, his own accounts of the beginnings and the progress of the story in letters and autobiographical dictations are somewhat contradictory.

Possibly the most nearly accurate version, because it was closest to the time of composition, occurs in a letter to his brother Orion on 23 March 1878. There, in discussing his own literary methods, Twain noted that he had "mapped out" his "Journey in Heaven" nine years earlier (i.e., in 1869), and went on: "I gave it a deal of thought, from time to time. After a year or more, I wrote it up. It was not a success. Five years ago I wrote it again, altering the plan. That MS is at my elbow now. It was a considerable improvement on the first attempt, but still it wouldn't do—last year and year before I talked frequently with Howells about the subject, and he kept urging me to do it again."

Finally he found what he thought was the right plan, he said, and again discussed the entire story with Howells, who assured him that this time he had "got it."

In later years, Mark Twain several times noted that the early version of "Stormfield" had turned into a satire on Elizabeth Stuart Phelps's immensely popular *The Gates Ajar* (1868). In an autobiographical dictation of 29 August 1906, for instance, after mentioning Wakeman's tale, he said: "I kept it in my mind, and a month or two later I put it on paper—this was the first quarter of 1868, I think. It made a small book of about forty thousand words. . . . Five or six years afterward I showed the manuscript to Howells and he said 'Publish it.'" Twain had resisted his friend's urging, however, because, as he put it: "I had turned it into a burlesque of 'The Gates Ajar,' a book which had imagined a mean little ten-cent heaven about the size of Rhode Island."

If his earliest version of the story had indeed intended to satirize *The Gates Ajar*, Mark Twain's memory was somewhat faulty, for Phelps's book was not entered for copyright until November 1868 and not issued until early in 1869. Moreover, though Phelps's heaven was by no means as immense as that described in "Stormfield," it had far greater dimensions than Mark Twain's derogatory description would suggest. And whether or not his early version did contain other satirical jibes at Phelps's sentimental but rational picture of heaven, the extant version makes fun of some of the same elements satirized in *The Gates Ajar*—closely enough, in fact, to suggest actual borrowing.

Mark Twain's interest in the story, or at least in Captain Wakeman, was sparked anew while he was writing up the trip to Bermuda in May 1877 with his Hartford minister friend Joseph Twichell for the *Atlantic Monthly.* In the second of four installments of "Some Rambling Notes of an Idle Excursion," he embellished his account of shipboard conversations with Ned Wakeman's inimitable interpretation of a biblical event, "Isaac and the Prophets of Baal," a tale the captain had told to Twichell during a voyage in 1874. Here Twain commemorated the captain, who had died in May 1875, by crediting the story to "Old Hurricane Jones of the Pacific Ocean—peace to his ashes!" Twichell himself is represented in the sketch as "the Reverend Mr. Peters."

When Mark Twain began his revision of "Stormfield," he kept the name "Hurricane Jones" for his protagonist all the way through his first section of the manuscript (1–62). Moreover, he also presented Jones as telling this tale to "Peters," and sometime later, after changing his hero's name to Stormfield, he drafted a title page that read: "The Travels / of / Capt. Eli Stormfield, Mariner / in Heaven. / Taken down from his own lips / by / Rev. George H. Peters / of Marysville, California."

In the meantime, in late June and early July 1877, besides reading proof for the Bermuda articles, he had focused his attention on a play featuring "Cap'n" Simon Wheeler as an amateur detective. Working almost feverishly, he completed his drama in little more than two weeks, and enthusiastically sought a producer.

Those efforts having proven unsuccessful, the next October he followed Howells's advice to turn the play into a novel and, in doing so, to make Wheeler as much like Captain Wakeman as possible. In the novel Wheeler does emulate some of Wakeman's hearty ebullience, though in some respects he also resembles Clemens's brother Orion. More important, however, near the end of the tale Twain had the captain tell the story of his own dream journey and entrance into heaven in a version probably quite close to the 1873 draft of the story (see "Captain Simon Wheeler's Dream Visit to Heaven," which follows "Stormfield").

Although Mark Twain lost interest in the novel shortly after writing that episode—probably in February 1878—his inclusion of the dream may well have led to the discussion with Howells which he described in the letter to Orion that March and to Twain's decision to rework the entire Wakeman/Stormfield story.

Whenever the earlier drafts were written, Mark Twain's major work on the story (present chapters 3–4) occurred between March 1878 and the fall of 1881. He was obviously considering new episodes for the tale just a day or two before he wrote to Orion. At that time he jotted a number of reminders into his notebook, still clearly identifying his project with Ned Wakeman. Besides suggesting that "an awkward new arrival" was to brush "Wakeman in the eye with his wing," he laid the groundwork for Stormfield's arrival at the wrong gate of heaven, but more especially for the final episode of the 1878–81 manuscript:

> Have all sorts of heavens—have a gate for each sort. One gate where they receive a barkeeper with artillery salutes, swarms of angels in the sky & a noble torch-light procession. *He* thinks he is *the* lion of Heaven. Procession over, he drops at once into awful obscurity ⟨,⟩ ⟨& thinks this⟩ But the roughest part of it is, that he has to do 30 weeks penance—day & night he must carry a torch, & shout himself hoarse, to do honor to some poor scrub whom he wishes had gone to hell.

Following this item, Twain added ideas for two further episodes that he did not ultimately develop, the second of which once more suggests his own sense of the immensity of the universe: "Wakeman visits these various heavens" and "W. is years & years in darkness *between* solar systems."

Enthusiastic as he was about his plan, he might well have begun work this time on the initial episode, which featured "Hurricane Jones" hurtling through space some thirty years after his death. But Twain probably did not get very far with the story, for the family's preparation for an extended trip to Europe soon interrupted any literary work. On 11 April, after a farewell visit to Elmira, the Clemenses sailed for Hamburg aboard the *Holsatia* on a voyage that would take them to Germany, Italy, France, and England before they returned to America in September 1879.

During that voyage Mark Twain was thinking of "Stormfield" and jotted down two further notes. The first envisioned the necessity for language study in heaven: "Wakeman comes across Ollendorff & proceeds to learn the language of a near-lying district of Heaven—people of Jupiter?" The second suggested a concept of heaven's political structure which he would later develop: "Have some people ⟨an⟩ dissatisfied because Heaven is an absolute monarchy, with many viceroys, when they expected a leatherheaded Republic with the damnation of unrestricted suffrage."

From Heidelberg late in June, however, when William Dean Howells asked for news "about Capt. Wakeman in Heaven, and all your other enterprises," he almost lamented: "I wish I was writing that Wakeman book, but I suppose I shan't get at it again before next year."

The book remained very much on his mind, nevertheless. In Munich, where the family settled from early November 1878 through February 1879, besides his work on *A Tramp Abroad*, he found time to read the new seventh edition of Amédée Guillemin's *The Heavens* (1868), which he purchased that December, and he jotted further ideas for "Wakeman's" story in its margins.

Although he did not eventually develop any of those notes, one passage must at least have provided support for the idea of Stormfield's race with the comet. On the top of a page which featured a drawing of the "Great Comet of 1811" (252) he noted: "Let Wakeman meet it,"† and a few pages later he marked a passage describing the comet's head as 108,000 miles in diameter, and its tail as 108,000,000 miles long. Of course Stormfield's comet was much larger even than this "Great Comet of 1811."

As time went by, Mark Twain became increasingly frustrated by his slow progress with *A Tramp Abroad*, and possibly by his inability to do much work on "Stormfield." He was still evidently intending to get to the latter, for on 15 December 1878 Olivia wrote to her sister-in-law Mollie Clemens that he hoped to have "one and perhaps two books ready" when they returned home. And toward the end of the stay in Munich, after describing some of his problems with *A Tramp Abroad*, he vowed to Howells that as soon as that book was off his hands, he would "take up Wakeman & Heaven at once." But *A Tramp Abroad* would not be off his hands for a long time.

From Munich the Clemenses went to Paris, where they remained from March until early July 1879. Then after a nine-day tour of Belgium and Holland and a month in England, they sailed from Liverpool on 23 August. Arriving in New York on 3 September they went immediately to Elmira where they stayed until about 21 October. In the months following their return to Hartford on October 24 or 25, Twain several times thought he had finished *A Tramp Abroad*, but it was not until 8 January 1880 that he could write to Howells: "I am soary (& flighty) as a rocket, to-day, with the unutterable joy of getting that Old Man of the Sea off my back."

Exactly how much of "Stormfield" had been finished prior to this time cannot be ascertained, but by the middle of the following June, Mark Twain's manuscript pile contained all of present chapter 3, which took him to the episode in which the angel Sandy discusses the presence of pain and its relationship to happiness in heaven, and also the final segment describing the reception for the bartender at the end of present chapter 4.

Just when Mark Twain decided to rename his narrator Stormfield is also uncertain. But probably when he resumed work on the story in 1880, he went back and in the first segment of his manuscript substituted "Eli Stormfield," "Cap'n," and "Stormfield" in the three instances where "Hurricane Jones" or "Jones" had appeared.

Twain did not finish filling in (or possibly revising) the episodes that precede the bartender's reception in present chapter 4 until the following year. The best conjecture is that he completed these passages, and hence his major work on the story, sometime soon after 15 October 1881 when he wrote to tell Howells that he was again "hard at work on Capt. Ned Wakeman's adventures in heaven—merely for the love of it."

Still concerned that the piece was radical enough to injure his reputation, he added: "For laws bless you, it can't ever be published. At least not unless I trim it like everything & then father it upon some good man—say Osgood. This is my purpose at present."

Shortly thereafter, then, he finished the segment containing Sandy's several additional explanations of the real nature of heaven, Stormfield's complicated struggles in learning to control his wings, and Sandy's discussion of preparations for reception of the bartender.

Although Twain obviously never carried out his plan to attribute his story to someone else so as to avoid the opprobrium that its "shocking" views might bring, his mind returned to "Stormfield" many times over the years that followed. Occasionally he jotted down notebook ideas for additional episodes or incidents. In January 1890, speaking of his work methods to an interviewer from the New York *World*, Mark Twain revealed a slightly different point of view concerning his story. Indicating the pigeonholed manuscript, and again somewhat incorrectly identifying it as "a book that I began in 1867," he said: "It could have been finished any time in the last twenty years by an addition of a chapter. I suppose it could be published as it is; but I'm not satisfied with it yet. Once in awhile I take the manuscript out and look at it. There's no hurry for its publication. The time isn't ripe for it. I expect to finish the book if I live long enough."

Though he still would remain dissatisfied with the tale for many years, he sometimes did regret not having finished it. From New York, during a business trip in February 1894, he wrote to Livy in France describing his success in entertaining C. A. Dana's dinner guests with a reading from "Stormfield." That the story had never been published was "a raging pity," he said. But he then consoled himself somewhat with the thought that the tale was a sure-fire "dinner-table yarn." †

Some three years later he was thinking about the story again, and in January 1897, while making notes for a tribute to his daughter Susy, who had died the preceding August, he asked himself: "What was her opinion of Capt. Stormfield's visit to Heaven (begun in the winter of 1867–8 as a ⟨bur⟩ satire upon the 'Gates Ajar' & still in MS.) & 'The Reception of Rev. Sam Jones in Heaven' (written in Berlin in 1891 & still in MS.)" At various other times, too, he listed "Stormfield" as a possibility for readings or for eventual inclusion in his autobiography. But except for those instances and several other notebook reminders that he must rewrite the tale, the manuscript remained pigeonholed until October 1902, when Clemens asked his lawyer, Franklin Whitmore, to retrieve it from the "manuscript trunk" in Hartford, and send it to him in Riverdale, New York, where the family was then living.

The Clemenses needed money at the time, since Olivia wished to build an extensive addition on a house that they had recently purchased in Tarrytown, New York, and Clemens was doubtless thinking that publishing the story could provide the funds. But when he and Livy decided not to live in the Tarrytown house, the manuscript went back into its pigeonhole.

Sometime after mid 1905 and probably during the early months of 1906 Mark Twain finally began his long-projected expansion of Stormfield's saga. This time he wrote a brief introductory note beginning, "I knew Captain Stormfield well," in which he described the captain in much the same terms as he would use in picturing Ned Wakeman in the autobiographical dictation of 29 August 1906, mentioned earlier, and again noted the captain's dream as the source of the tale. This he followed with two new beginning chapters, detailing Stormfield's death and a number of his early experiences on the journey to heaven. Here, perhaps momentarily forgetting the name he had used earlier, Mark Twain called the captain *Ben* Stormfield, rather than Eli. And he ultimately provided two new chapters—"Captain Stormfield Resumes," which also contained "A Journey to the Asterisk," and "From Captain Stormfield's Reminiscences," which expanded Stormfield's experiences and dealt with several moral and philosophical problems that were troubling the author during these years.

In the first of the two later chapters Stormfield's angel friend Sandy astounds the captain by introducing him to the vast distances envisioned in the concept of the light-year, and noting that even that unit is not really adequate for measuring the immensity of heaven. In the "Reminiscences," Sandy relates his friend Slattery's account of the creation of human beings and how the vagaries of human nature actually came about, and, in doing so, discusses the difference between earthly time and heavenly time. Both of these elements

Mark Twain would later dramatize in the creation myth at the beginning of "Letters from the Earth."

If not before, he had almost certainly completed these passages by mid May, when he went to Dublin, New Hampshire, where he would spend the summer. That June, Mark Twain was working on the latter portions of "The Refuge of the Derelicts," a short novel begun the year before, which featured still another incarnation of Ned Wakeman—Admiral Abner Stormfield—who had established his home, the Anchor Watch, as a refuge for indigent sailors. At one point Twain had also considered introducing the dream visit to heaven into this piece, for he mentions "Ned Wakeman's Dream of heaven" in his working notes.

These notes in turn may well have caused Twain to unearth his "Stormfield" manuscript once more. On 13 June, as Isabel Lyon reported in her journal, he delighted his listeners by reading passages from the old manuscript, which Lyon pronounced clearly publishable. The following evening he read "the most readable part of the second part," which she again pronounced "delightful." Whether the "second part" referred to the latest segments is not clear, but Lyon's added notation that during the same morning Twain had read her "an unpublishable bit from the same ms." further suggests that they had been written by this time.

The favorable responses of his listeners no doubt encouraged him. Though he still felt that the story was too controversial to publish, he told his friend Howells on June 17 that he decided to include it in his autobiographical dictations among other "pigeon-holed things of the years gone by, which I or editors didn't das't to print. . . . It reads quite to suit me without altering a word, now that it isn't to see print until I am dead."

He evidently then had the manuscript typed and ultimately made it a part of his dictation for 29 August 1906. Following his reminiscences about Ned Wakeman, and the somewhat erroneous account of the genesis of the story, he noted: "I mean to put it into the Autobiography now."

Interestingly enough, in his original typescript, following the quoted phrase, Twain inked in a circled footnote number "2," and at the bottom of the page entered: "*Three hours later.* I have just burned the closing two thirds of it."

If he actually destroyed anything, it could have been the typescripts of the later fragments—though by no means two-thirds of the whole—for the extant typescript includes only present chapters 3 and 4. And if he did so, he did not destroy the manuscripts of these segments, or of the new beginning.

But he probably did not destroy any of the material, for at the beginning of the following day's dictation, in a passage that he ultimately marked for omission, he wrote:

"I was never willing to destroy 'Captain Stormfield's Visit to Heaven.' Now and then, in the past thirty years, I have overhauled my literary stock and transferred some of it to the fire, but 'Stormfield's Visit' always escaped. I am obliged to suspect that the hand of Providence was in it." Sometime later he lined out that last sentence and in its place inserted "Secretly & privately I liked it. I couldn't help it."

Despite his continued scruples about publishing the iconoclastic tale, when Col. George Harvey asked for a story for the *Harper's* Christmas edition early in September, he removed the typed pages from the autobiographical dictations and sent them, or a copy, to the publisher. Perhaps he was becoming concerned over the mounting construction costs of the new home he was building in Redding, Connecticut, ultimately to be named "Stormfield" in honor of the part the story would play in its financing.

At this time, however, Colonel Harvey's scruples were greater than his own. The captain's tale seemed "exact, truthful and, as you say, godly," he said, but added "—too damn godly for a secular paper like the Magazine." And then, "I'm sure it wouldn't do to print it now, and I guess you're sure, too, if you'll tell the truth." In her subsequent letter asking him to return the manuscript, Isabel Lyon wrote: "Mr. Clemens is crying but he's going to bear it for your sake's & the magazines [*sic*]."

But even though Harvey suddenly changed his mind, and wrote on 11 September that he had "formulated a scheme" for publishing the story, and would discuss his plans when the author came "next week," nothing came of that meeting. And the following February, at Clemens's request, Frederick Duneka of *Harper's* returned the "original copy" of the manuscript.

The next August, when Duneka again asked for a contribution for the 1907 Christmas issue, Mark Twain first sent "Wapping Alice," another story culled from his autobiographical dictations. Given his reservations about publishing "Stormfield," it is strange that he was willing to publish the strange story of "Alice," which ended with the revelation that "she" was actually a male transvestite. Not surprisingly, the Harper editors turned that story down—almost immediately. But since they badly wanted a Mark Twain piece for the Christmas number, they and he evidently decided that "Stormfield" now would do.

On 9 August, then, the author sent Isabel Lyon off on a dual mission: to accompany Dorothy Quick (one of the members of Mark Twain's Aquarium Club of young girls) to New York after a visit to Clemens at Tuxedo Park,

New York, where he spent that summer, and to deliver the Stormfield copy to *Harper's*. During the journey, Lyon followed Twain's instructions to count the words in the story to be sure that he would receive the agreed-upon thirty cents per word for the original, even though some passages might later be deleted.

Even then Mark Twain still worried about having agreed to publish the piece. On 15 September, therefore, he decided to try it out on his guests of the evening, and Lyon was pleased to report that the comments were wholly positive.

When the *Harper's* proofs arrived on the first or second of October, Twain decided his account of Stormfield's difficulties in learning to manage his angelic wings was far too long so cut out all but a few paragraphs. With that and other minor revisions, the story was finally ready, and "Extract from Captain Stormfield's Visit to Heaven" appeared in *Harper's Monthly* for December 1907, with a second installment to follow in January 1908.

But Mark Twain was not through tinkering with the story. In April 1909 he agreed to *Harper's* plan to issue "Stormfield" in book form. This time when he received the proofs early in July, besides minor revisions, he decided to introduce a condensed version of a much longer episode he had earlier deleted from his typescript—an extremely sentimental one, perhaps originally inspired by his own family's grief at the loss of their daughter Susy in 1896. In the original, a mother, Mrs. Rushmore, arrives in heaven expecting to find her infant daughter the same age as when she had died, and there follows a long and involved description of her sorrow at finding the daughter grown and with children of her own, and her ultimate adjustment to the situation (see appendix 5a).

This time, Twain struck out the final three paragraphs of the December 1907 installment, in which Sandy emphasized the fact that heaven was for "all kinds" of people, and inserted a highly abridged version of the Rushmore incident, though without using the woman's name.

If Mark Twain had indeed drafted his first version of Captain Wakeman's dream story in 1869, this final revision in 1909 stretched the tale's course of composition to *exactly* forty years.

And though he did not publish the new beginning and the later chapters at the time, he borrowed concepts discussed in "Captain Stormfield Resumes" and "From Captain Stormfield's Reminiscences" to help him formulate the creation myth at the beginning of "Letters from the Earth," which he wrote in 1909, the year the book version of "Stormfield" appeared.

CAPTAIN STORMFIELD'S VISIT TO HEAVEN

NOTE. I knew Captain Stormfield well. I made three long sea-voyages with him in his ship. He was a rugged, weather-tanned sailor, with a picked-up education, a sterling good heart, an iron will, abundant pluck, unshakable beliefs and convictions, and a confidence in himself which had no discoverable limits. He was open, frank, communicative, affectionate, and as honest, simple and genuine as a dog. He was deeply religious, by nature and by the training of his mother, and a fluent and desolating swearer by the training of his father and by the necessities of his occupation. He was born in his father's ship, he had spent his entire life at sea, had seen the edges of all lands and the interiors of none, and when I first knew him he was sixty-five years old and his glossy black hair and whiskers were beginning to show threads of gray; but there was no trace of age in his body, yet, nor in his determined spirit, and the fires that burned in his eyes were the fires of youth. He was a lovable man when people pleased him, but a tough person to deal with when the case was otherwise.

He had a good deal of imagination, and it probably colored his statements of fact; but if this was so, he was not aware of it. He made no statement which he did not believe to be true. When he told me about his strange and uncanny adventures in the Devil's Race-Track—a vast area in the solitudes of the South Pacific where the needle of the compass is powerless to exercise its office and whizzes madly and continuously around—I spared him the hurt of suggesting that he had dreamed the tale, for I saw that he was in earnest; but in secret I believed it was only a vision, a dream. Privately I think his visit to the Other World was a dream, also, but I did not wound him with the expression of the thought. He believed that the visit was an actual experience; I accepted it on those terms, listened to it attentively, took down the details of each day's revelations in short-hand, by his permission, then afterward reduced the result to long-hand. I have polished some of the ruggednesses out of his grammar and construction, and in places I have cooled off his language a little; otherwise his tale stands here as he told it.

Mark Twain

CHAPTER 1

I was dying, and I knew it. I was making gasps, with long spaces between, and they were standing around the bed, quiet and still, waiting for me to go. Now and then they spoke; and what they said got dimmer and dimmer, and further and further away. I heard it all, though. The mate said—

"He's going out with the tide."

Chips the carpenter said—

"How do you know? No tide out here in the middle of the ocean."

"Yes there is. And anyway, they always do."

It was still again, a while—only the heaving and creaking, and the dull lanterns swinging this way and that, and the wind wheezing and piping, far off. Then I heard a voice, away off—

"Eight bells, sir."

"Make it so," said the mate.

"Aye-aye, sir."

Another voice—

"Freshening up, sir—coming on to blow."

"Sheet home," says the mate. "Reef tops'ls and sky-scrapers, and stand by."

"Aye-aye, sir."

By the by the mate says—

"How's it now?"

"He's cold, up to his ribs," says the doctor. "Give him ten minutes."

"Everything ready, Chips?"

"Canvas, cannon balls and all, sir."

"Bible and burial service?"

"All handy, sir."

Quiet again, for a while—wind so vague it sounded like dream-wind. Then the doctor's voice—

"Is he prepared for the change, do you think?"

"To hell? Oh, I guess so."

"I reckon there ain't any doubt."

It was Chips said it; kind of mournful, too.

"Doubt?" said the mate. "Hadn't any himself, if that's any sign."

"No," says Chips, "he always said he judged he was booked for there."

Long, long stillness. Then the doctor's voice, so far off and dim it sounded like it was down a deep well—

"There—it's over! Just at 12:14!"

Dark? Oh, pitch dark—all in a second! I was dead, and I knew it.

I felt myself make a plunge, and recognised that I was flashing through the air like a bird. I had a quick, dim glimpse of the sea and the ship, then everything was black darkness, and nothing visible, and I went whizzing through it. I said to myself, "I'm all here, clothes and all, nothing missing; they'll sink a counterfeit in the sea; it's not me, I'm all here."

Next, it began to get light, and straight off I plunged into a whole universe of blinding fire, and straight through it. It was 12:22 by my watch.

Do you know where I was? In the sun. That was my guess, and it turned out afterwards that I was right. Eight minutes out from port. It gave me my gait—exactly the speed of light, 186,000 miles a second. Ninety-three million miles in eight minutes by the watch. There wasn't ever a prouder ghost. I was as pleased as a child, and wished I had something to race with.

Before I was done thinking these things I was out on the other side and the sun shriveling up to a luminous wad behind me. It was less than a million miles in diameter, and I was through before I had time to get warm. I was in the dark again, now. In the dark; but I myself wasn't dark. My body gave out a soft and ghostly glow and I felt like a lightning bug. I couldn't make out the why of this, but I could read my watch by it, and that was more to the point.

Presently I noticed a glow like my own a little way off, and was glad, and made a trumpet of my hands and hailed it—

"Shipmate ahoy!"

"Same to you!"

"Where from?"

"Chatham street."

"Whither bound?"

"I vish I knew—aind it?"

"I reckon you're going my way. Name?"

"Solomon Goldstein. Yours?"

"Captain Ben Stormfield, late of Fairhaven and 'Frisco. Come alongside, friend."

He did it. It was a great improvement, having company. I was born sociable, and never could stand solitude. I was trained to a prejudice against Jews—Christians always are, you know—but such of it as I had was in my head, there wasn't any in my heart. But if I had been full of it it would have disappeared then, I was so lonesome and so anxious for company. Dear me, when you are going to—to—where I was going—you are humble-mindeder than you used to be, and thankful for whatever you can get, never mind the quality of it.

We spun along together, and talked, and got acquainted and had a good time. I thought it would be a kindness to Solomon to dissipate his doubts, so that he would have a quiet mind. I could never be comfortable in a state of doubt myself. So I reasoned the thing out, and showed him that his being pointed the same as me was proof of where he was bound for. It cost him a good deal of distress, but in the end he was reconciled and said it was probably best the way it was, he wouldn't be suitable company for angels and they would turn him down if he tried to work in; he had been treated like that in New York, and he judged that the ways of high society were about the same everywhere. He wanted me not to desert him when we got to where we were going, but stay by him, for he would be a stranger and friendless. Poor fellow, I was touched; and promised—"to all eternity."

Then we were quiet a long time, and I let him alone, and let him think. It would do him good. Now and then he sighed, and by and by I found he was crying. You know, I was mad with him in a minute; and says to myself, "Just like a Jew! he has promised some hayseed or other a coat for four dollars, and now he has made up his mind that if he was back he could work off a worse one on him for five. They haven't any heart—that race—nor any principles."

He sobbed along to himself, and I got colder and colder and harder and harder towards him. At last I broke out and said—

"Cheese it! Damn the coat! Drop it out of your mind."

"Goat?"

"Yes. Find something else to cry about."

"Why, I vasn't crying apoud a goat."

"What then?"

"Oh, captain, I loss my little taughter, and now I never, never see her again any more. It break my heart!"

By God, it went through me like a knife! I wouldn't feel so mean again, and so grieved, not for a fleet of ships. And I spoke out and said what I felt; and went on damning myself for a hound till he was so distressed I had to stop; but I wasn't half through. He begged me not to talk so, and said I oughtn't to make so much of what I had done; he said it was only a mistake, and a mistake wasn't a crime.

There now—wasn't it magnanimous? I ask you—wasn't it? I think so. To my mind there was the stuff in him for a Christian; and I came out flat-footed and told him so. And if it hadn't been too late I would have reformed him and made him one, or died in the act.

We were good friends again, and he didn't need to keep his sorrows to himself any more, he could pour them right into my heart, which was wide open and ready; and he did; till it seemed to me I couldn't bear it. Lord, the misery of it! She was his pet, his playfellow, the apple of his eye; she was ten years old, and dead six months, and he was glad to die, himself, so he could have her in his arms again and be with her always—and now that dream was over. Why she was gone—*forever.* The word had a new meaning. It took my breath, it made me gasp. All our lives we believe we are going to see our lost friends again—we are not disturbed with doubts, we think we *know* it. It is what keeps us alive. And here, in this father's heart that hope was dead, I had never seen that before. This was the first time. And I—why it was I that had killed it. If I had only thought! If I had only kept still, and left him to find it out for himself. He let his tears run, and now and then his trouble wrung a groan out of him, and his lips quivered and he said—

"Poor little Minnie—and poor me."

And to myself I said the same—

"Poor little Minnie—and poor me."

That feeling stayed by me, and never left me. And many's the time, when I was thinking of that poor Jew's disaster, I have said in my thoughts, "I wish I was bound for heaven, and could trade places with him, so he could see his child, damned if I wouldn't do it." If ever you are situated like that, you will understand the feeling.

CHAPTER 2

We talked late, and fell asleep pretty tired, about two in the morning; had a sound sleep, and woke refreshed and fine towards noon. Pitch dark, still. We were not hungry, but I could have smoked with a relish, if I had had the things. Also, I could have enjoyed a drink.

We had to stop and think a minute, when we woke, before we came fully to ourselves and realized our situation, for we thought we had been dreaming. In fact it was hard to get rid of the idea that it was all a dream. But we had to get rid of it, and we did. Then a ghastly cold shock went through us—we remembered where we were pointed for. Next, we were astonished. Astonished because we hadn't arrived. Astonished and glad. Glad we hadn't arrived. Hopeful that we might not arrive for some little time yet.

"How far is it that ve haf come, Captain Sthormfilt?"

"Eleven or twelve hundred million miles."

"Ach Gott, it is a speed!"

"Right you are. There isn't anything that can pass us but thought. It would take the lightning express twenty-four or twenty-five days to fly around the globe; we could do it four times in a second—yes, sir, and do it easy. Solomon, I wish we had something to race with."

Along in the afternoon we saw a soft blur of light a little way off, north-east-by-east-half-east, about two points off the weather bow, and hailed it. It closed up on us, and turned out to be a corpse by the name of Bailey, from Oshkosh, that had died at 7:10 the night before. A good creature, but mooney and reflective. Republican in politics, and had the idea that nothing could save civilization but that party. He was melancholy, and we got him to talk, so as to cheer him up; and along by spells, as he got to feeling better, his private matters got to leaking out—among others, the fact that he had committed suicide. You know, we had suspected it; he had a hole through his forehead that you couldn't have plugged with a marlin-spike.

By and by his spirits sagged again. Then the cause came out. He was delicate and sensitive in his morals, and he had been doing something in politics, the last thing, which he was wondering if it was exactly straight. There was an election to fill a vacancy in his town government, and it was such a close fit that his one vote would decide it. He wasn't going to be there to vote—he was going to be up here, with us. But if he could keep a democrat from voting that would answer just as well, and the republican candidate would pull through. So, when he was ready for suicide he went to a rigidly honorable friend who was a democrat, and got him to pair off with him. The republican ticket was safe, then, and he killed himself. So he was a little troubled about it, and uncertain; afraid that maybe he hadn't played quite fair, for a Presbyterian.

But Solomon admired him, and thought it was an amazingly smart idea, and just gloated over him with envy, and grinned that Jew grin of intense satisfaction, you know, and slapped his thigh and said—

"Py Chorge, Pailey, almost thou persuadest me to pe a Ghristian."

It was about his girl that he killed himself—Candace Miller. He couldn't ever quite get her to say she loved him, though she seemed to, and he had good hopes. But the thing that decided him was a note from her, in which she told him she loved him as a friend, and hoped they would always be friends, but she found her heart belonged to another. Poor Bailey, he broke down, there and cried.

Curious! Just then we sighted a blue light a little astern, and hailed it, and when it ranged up alongside Bailey shouted—

"Why Tom Wilson! what a happy surprise; what ever brought you here, comrade?"

Wilson gave him an appealing look that was sort of heartbreaking to see, and said—

"Don't welcome me like that, George, I'm not worthy. I'm a low-down dog, and not fit for any clean man's company."

"Don't," said Bailey. "Don't talk like that. What is it?"

"George, I did a treacherous thing. To think I could do it to an old playfellow like you, that I was born and raised with! But it was only a silly practical joke, and I never dreamed that any harm could come of it. *I* wrote that letter. She loved you, George."

"My God!"

"Yes, she did. She was the first one to the house; and when she saw you lying dead in your blood and the letter by you, signed with her name, she read it and knew! She flung herself on your corpse, and kissed your face and your eyes, and poured out her love and her grief and despair, and I saw it. I had murdered you, I had broken her heart, I couldn't bear it—and I am here."

Another suicide, you see. Bailey—well, he couldn't go back, you know, and it was pitiful to see him, he was so frantic over what he had lost by killing himself before ever stopping to find out whether she wrote the letter or not. He kept on regretting and lamenting and wishing he had waited and been more rational, and arranging over and over again in different ways, how he ought to have acted, and how he would act now, if he could only have the chance over again. All no good, of course, and made us miserable to hear it, for he couldn't ever have his chance again forever—we realized that, and the whole ghastliness of the situation. Some people think you are at rest when you die. Let them wait, they'll see.

Solomon took Bailey aside to comfort him—a good idea; people that carry griefs in their hearts know how to comfort others' griefs.

We whizzed along about a week before we picked up another straggler. This time it was a nigger. He was about thirty-eight or forty, and had been a slave nearly half of his life. Named Sam. A cheerful, good-natured cuss, and likable. As I learned later, a pick-up is a depressing influence upon the company for some time, because he is full of thinkings about his people at home and their grief over losing him; and so his talk is all about that, and he wants sympathy, and cries a good deal, and tells you how dear and good his wife was, or his poor old mother, or his sisters and brothers; and of course in common kindness you have to listen, and it keeps the company feeling desolate and wretched for days and days together, and starts up their own sorrows over their own loss of family and friends; but when the pick-up is a young person that has lost a sweetheart, that is the worst. There isn't any end to their talk, and their sorrow and their tears. And dear, dear, that one tiresome everlasting question that they keep on asking till you are worn to the bone with it: *don't* we think he (or she) will die soon and come? What can you say? There's only one thing: *yes*, we hope he will. And when you have said it a couple of thousand times, you lose patience and wish you hadn't died. But dead people are people, just the same, and they bring their habits with them, which is natural. On the earth, when you arrive in a city—any city on the globe—the people peck at you with the same old regular questions—

"First time you have visited our city?"

"How does it impress you?"

"When did you arrive?"

"How long are you going to stay?"

Sometimes you have to leave next day, to get a rest. We arranged differently with the lovers, by and by: we bunched them together to themselves and made them burn their own smoke. And it was no harm: they liked it best that way. There was plenty of sympathy and sentiment, and that was what they wanted.

Sam had pipe, tobacco and matches; I cannot tell you how glad I was. But only for a little moment; then there was a sharp disappointment: the matches wouldn't light. Bailey explained it: there was no atmosphere there in space, and the match couldn't burn without oxygen. I said we would keep the things—we might strike through the atmosphere of a planet or a sun, some time or other, and if it was a big one we might have time for one whiff, anyway. But he said no, it wasn't in the cards.

"Ours are spiritualized bodies and spiritualized clothes and things," he said, "otherwise they would have been consumed in a flash when we first darted through the earth's atmosphere. This is spiritualized tobacco, and fire-proof."

It was very annoying. But I said we would keep it, just the same—

"It will burn in hell, anyway."

When the nigger found that that was where I was going, it filled him with distress, and he hoped I was mistaken, and did his best to persuade me I was; but I hadn't any doubts, and so he had to give in. He was as grieved about it as my best friend could be, and tried his best to believe it wouldn't be as hot there as people said, and hoped and believed I would get used to it after a while, and not mind it. His kindly talk won me completely; and when he gave me the pipe and tobacco, and begged me to think of him sometimes when I was smoking, I was a good deal moved. He was a good chap, and like his race: I have seen but few niggers that hadn't their hearts in the right place.

As week after week slipped along by, we picked up a straggler at intervals, and at the end of the first year our herd numbered 36. It looked like a flock of glow-worms, and was a quite pretty sight. We could have had a regiment if we had kept all we came across, but the speeds were various and that was an interference. The slowest ship makes the pace for the fleet, of course. I raised our gait a little, as an accommodation, and established it at 200,000 miles a second. Some wanted to get on faster, on account of wanting to join lost friends, so we let them go. I was not in a particular hurry, myself—my business would keep. Some that had been consumptives and such like, were rickety and slow, and they dropped behind and disappeared. Some that were troublesome and disagreeable, and always raising Cain over any little thing that didn't suit them, I ordered off the course, with a competent cursing and a warning to stand clear. We had all sorts left, young and old, and on the whole they were satisfactory enough, though a few of them were not up to standard, I will admit.

CHAPTER 3

Well, when I had been dead about thirty years, I begun to get a little anxious. Mind you, I had been whizzing through space all that time, like a comet. —*Like* a comet! Why, Peters, I laid over the lot of them! Of course there warn't any of them going my way, as a steady thing, you know, because they travel in a long circle like the loop of a lasso, whereas I was pointed as straight as a dart for the Hereafter; but I happened on one every now and then that was going my way for an hour or so, and then we had a bit of a brush together. But it was generally pretty one-sided, because I sailed by them the same as if they were standing still. An ordinary comet don't make more than about 200,000 miles a minute. Of course when I came across one of that sort—like Encke's and Halley's comets, for instance—it warn't anything but a flash of light and a vanish, you see, you couldn't rightly call it a race. It was as if the comet was a gravel-train and I was a telegraph dispatch. But after I got outside of our astronomical system, I used to flush a comet occasionally that was something *like! We* haven't got any such comets—ours don't begin. One night I was swinging along at a good round gait, everything taut and trim, and the wind in my favor—I judged I was going about a million miles a minute—it might have been more, it couldn't have been less—when I flushed a most uncommon big one about three points off my starboard bow. By his stern-lights I judged he was bearing about north-east-and-by-north-half-east. Well, it was so near my course that I wouldn't throw away the chance; so I fell off a point, steadied my helm, and went for him. You should have heard me whiz, and seen the electric fur fly! In about a minute and a half I was fringed-out with an electrical nimbus that flamed around for miles and miles and lit up all space like broad day. The comet was burning blue in the distance, like a sickly torch, when I first sighted him, but he begun to grow bigger and bigger as I crept up on him. I slipped up on him so fast that when I had gone about 150,000,000 miles I was close enough to be swallowed up in the phosphorescent glory of his wake, and I couldn't see anything for the glare. Thinks I, it won't do to run into him, so I shunted to one side and tore along. By and by I closed up abreast of his tail. Do you know what it was like? It was like a gnat closing up on the continent of America. I forged along. By and by I had sailed along his coast for a little upwards of a hundred and fifty million miles, and then I could see by the shape of him that I hadn't even got up to his waistband yet. Why, Peters, *we* don't know anything about comets, down here. If you want to see comets that *are* comets, you've got to go outside of our system—where there's room for them, you understand! My friend, I've seen comets out there that couldn't even lay down inside the *orbits* of our nobbiest comets without their tails hanging over.

Well, I boomed along another hundred and fifty million miles, and got up abreast his shoulder, as you may say. I was feeling pretty fine, I tell you; but just then I noticed the officer of the deck come to the side and hoist his glass in my direction. Straight off I heard him sing out—

"Below there, ahoy! Shake her up, shake her up! Heave on a hundred million billion tons of brimstone!"

"Aye-aye, sir!"

"Pipe the stabboard watch! All hands on deck!"

"Aye-aye, sir!"

"Send two hundred thousand million men aloft to shake out royals and sky-scrapers!"

"Aye-aye, sir!"

"Hand the stuns'ls! Hang out every rag you've got! Clothe her from stem to rudder-post!"

"Aye-aye, sir!"

In about a second I begun to see I'd woke up a pretty ugly customer, Peters. In less than ten seconds that comet was just a blazing cloud of red-hot canvas. It was piled up into the heavens clean out of sight—the old thing seemed to swell out and occupy all space; the sulphur-smoke from the furnaces—oh, well, nobody can describe the way it rolled and tumbled up into the skies, and nobody can half describe the way it smelt. Neither can anybody begin to describe the way that monstrous craft begun to crash along. And such another pow-wow—thousands of bo's'n's whistles screaming at once, and a crew like the population of a hundred thousand worlds like ours all swearing at once. Well, *I* never heard the like of it before.

We roared and thundered along side by side, both doing our level best, because I'd never struck a comet before that could lay over me, and so I was bound to beat this one or break something. I judged I had some reputation in space, and I calculated to keep it. I noticed I wasn't gaining as fast, now, as I was before, but still I was gaining. There was a power of excitement on board the comet. Upwards of a hundred billion passengers swarmed up from below and rushed to the side and begun to bet on the race. Of course this careened her and damaged her speed. My, but wasn't the mate mad! He jumped at that crowd, with his trumpet in his hand, and sung out—

"Amidships, amidships, ——— * you, or I'll brain the last idiot of you!"

Well, sir, I gained and gained, little by little, till at last I went skimming sweetly by the magnificent old conflagration's nose. By this time the captain of the comet had been rousted out, and he stood there in the red glare for'ard, by the mate, in his shirt-sleeves and slippers, his hair all rat's-nests and one suspender hanging; and how sick those two men did look!

I just simply couldn't help putting my thumb to my nose, as I glided away, and singing out—

"Ta-ta! ta-ta! Any word to send to your family?"

Peters, that was a mistake. Yes, sir, I've often regretted that—it was a mistake. You see, the captain had given up the race, but that remark was too tedious for him—he couldn't stand it. He turned to the mate, and says he—

"Have we got brimstone enough of our own to make the trip?"

* The captain could not remember what this word was. He said it was in a foreign tongue.

"Yes, sir."

"Sure?"

"Yes, sir—more than enough."

"How much have we got in cargo for Satan?"

"Eighteen hundred thousand billion quintillions of kazarks."

"Very well, then, let his boarders freeze till the next comet comes. Lighten ship! Lively, now, lively, men! Heave the whole cargo overboard!"

"Peters, look me in the eye and be calm. I found out, over there, that a kazark is exactly the bulk of *a hundred and sixty-nine worlds like ours!* They hove all that load overboard. When it fell it wiped out a considerable raft of stars just as clean as if they'd been candles and somebody blow'd them out. As for the race, *that* was at an end. The minute she was lightened, the comet swung along by me the same as if I was anchored. The captain stood on the stern, by the after-davits, and put his thumb to his nose and sung out—

"Ta-ta! ta-ta! Maybe *you've* got some message to send to your friends in the Everlasting Tropics!"

Then he hove up his other suspender and started for'ard, and inside of three quarters of an hour his craft was only a pale torch again in the distance. Yes, it was a mistake, Peters—that remark of mine. I don't reckon I'll ever get over being sorry about it. I'd 'a' beat the bully of the firmament if I'd kept my mouth shut.

But I've wandered a little off the track of my tale; I'll get back on my course again. Now you can see what kind of speed I was making. So, as I said, when I had been tearing along this way about thirty years, I begun to get uneasy. Oh, it was pleasant enough, with a good deal to be seen and a good deal to find out, but then it was kind of lonesome, you know. Besides, I wanted to get somewhere. I hadn't shipped with the idea of cruising forever. First off, I liked the delay, because I judged I was going to fetch up in pretty warm quarters when I got through; but towards the last I begun to feel that I'd rather go to—to—well, most any place, so as to finish up the uncertainty.

Well, one night—it was always night, except when I was rushing by some star that was occupying the whole universe with its fire and its glare—light enough then, of course, but I necessarily left it behind in a minute or two and plunged into a solid week of darkness again. The stars ain't so close together as they look to be. Where was I? Oh, yes; one night I was sailing along, when I discovered a tremendous long row of blinking lights away in the horizon ahead. As I approached, they begun to tower and swell, and look like mighty furnaces. Says I to myself—"By George, I've arrived at last—and at the wrong place, just as I expected!"

Then I fainted. I don't know how long I was insensible, but it must have been a good while, for when I came to, the darkness was all gone and there was the loveliest sunshine and the balmiest, fragrantest air in its place. And there was such a marvelous world spread out before me—such a glowing, beautiful, bewitching country! The things I took for furnaces were gates, miles high, made all of flashing jewels, and they pierced a wall of solid gold that you couldn't see the top of, nor yet the end of, in either direction. I was pointed straight for one of these gates and a-coming like a house afire. Now I noticed that the skies were black with millions of people pointed for those gates. What a roar they made, rushing through the air! The ground was as thick as ants with people, too—billions of them, I judge.

I lit. I drifted up to a gate with a swarm of people, and when it was my turn the head clerk says, in a business-like way—

"Well, quick! Where are you from?"

"San Francisco," says I.

"San fran- *what?*" says he.

"San Francisco."

He scratched his head and looked puzzled, then he says—

"Is it a planet?"

By George, Peters, think of it! "*Planet*," says I, "it's a city. And moreover, it's one of the biggest, and finest and—"

"There, there!" says he, "no time here for conversation. We don't deal in cities here. Where are you from in a *general* way?"

"Oh," I says, "I beg pardon. Put me down for California."

I had him *again*, Peters. He puzzled a second, then he says, sharp and irritable—

"I don't know any such planet—is it a constellation?"

"Oh, my goodness!" says I. "Constellation, says you? No—it's a State."

"Man, we don't deal in States here. *Will* you tell me where you are from *in general*—AT LARGE, don't you understand?"

"O, now I get your idea," I says. "I'm from America—the United States of America."

Peters, do you know I had him *again?* If I didn't I'm a clam. His face was as blank as a target after a militia shooting-match. He turned to an under-clerk and says—

"Where is America? *What* is America?"

The under-clerk answered up prompt and says—

"There ain't any such orb."

"*Orb*," says I. "Why, what are you talking about, young man? It ain't an orb; it's a country; it's a continent. Columbus discovered it; I reckon likely you've heard of *him*, anyway. America—why, sir, America—"

"Silence!" says the head clerk. "Once for all, where—are—you—*from?*"

"Well," says I, "I don't know anything more to say—unless I lump things, and just say I'm from the world."

"Ah," says he brightening up, "now that's something like. *What* world?"

Peters, he had *me*, that time. I looked at him, puzzled, he looked at me worried. Then he burst out—

"Come, come, what world?"

Says I, "Why, *the* world, of course."

"*The* world!" he says. "Hm! There's billions of them! ..... Next!"

That meant for me to stand aside. I did so, and a sky-blue man with seven heads and only one leg hopped into my place. I took a walk. It just occurred to me, then, that all the myriads I had seen swarming to that gate, up to this time, were just like that creature. I tried to run across somebody I was acquainted with, but they were out of acquaintances of mine just then. So I thought the thing all over and finally sidled back there pretty meek and feeling rather stumped, as you may say.

"Well?" says the head clerk.

"Well, sir," I says, pretty humble, "I don't seem to make out which world it is I'm from. But you may know it from this—it's the one the Savior saved."

He bent his head at the Name. Then he says, gently—

"The worlds He has saved are like to the gates of heaven in number—none can count them. What astronomical system is your world in?—perhaps that may assist."

"It's the one that has the sun in it—and the moon—and Mars"—he shook his head at each name—hadn't ever heard of them, you see—"and Neptune—and Uranus—and Jupiter—"

"Hold on!" says he, "hold on a minute. Jupiter..... Jupiter..... seems to me we had a man from there eight or nine hundred years ago—but people from that system very seldom enter by this gate." All of a sudden he begun to look me so straight in the eye that I thought he was going to bore through me. Then he says, very deliberate, "Did you come *straight here* from your system?"

"Yes, sir," I says—but I blushed the least little bit in the world when I said it.

He looked at me very stern, and says—

"That is not true; and this is not the place for prevarication. You wandered from your course. How did that happen?"

Says I, blushing again—

"I'm sorry, and I take back what I said, and confess. I raced with a comet one day—only just the least little bit—only the tiniest lit—"

"So-so," says he—and without any sugar in his voice, to speak of.

I went on, and says—

"But I only fell off just a bare point, and I went right back on my course again the minute the race was over."

"No matter—that divergence has made all this trouble. It has brought you to a gate that is billions of leagues from the right one. If you had gone to your own gate they would have known all about your world at once and there would have been no delay. But we will try to accommodate you." He turned to an under-clerk and says—

"What system is Jupiter in?"

"I don't remember sir, but I think there is such a planet in one of the little new systems away out in one of the thinly-worlded corners of the universe. I will see."

He got a balloon and sailed up and up and up, in front of a map that was as big as Rhode Island. He went on up till he was out of sight, and by and by he came down and got something to eat; and went up again. To cut a long story short, he kept on doing this for a day or two, and finally he came down and said he thought he had found that solar system, but it might be fly-specks. So he got a microscope and went back. It turned out better than he feared. He had rousted out our system, sure enough. He got me to describe our planet and its distance from our sun, and then he says to his chief—

"Oh, I know the one he means, now, sir. It is on the map. It is called the Wart."

Says I to myself, "Young man, it wouldn't be wholesome for you to go down *there* and call it the Wart."

Well, they let me in, then, and told me I was safe forever and wouldn't have any more troubles.

Then they turned from me and went on with their work the same as if they considered my case all complete and shipshape. I was a good deal surprised at this, but I was diffident about speaking up and reminding them. I did so hate to do it, you know; it seemed a pity to bother them, they had so much on their hands. Twice I thought I would give up and let the thing go; so twice I started to leave, but immediately I thought what a figure I should cut stepping out amongst the redeemed in such a rig, and that made me hang back and come to anchor again. People got to eyeing me—clerks, you know—wondering why I didn't get under weigh. I couldn't stand this long—it was too uncomfortable. So at last I plucked up courage and tipped the head clerk a signal. He says—

"What, you here yet? What's wanting?"

Says I, in a low voice and very confidential, making a trumpet with my hands at his ear—

"I beg pardon, and you mustn't mind my reminding you, and seeming to meddle, but hain't you forgot something?"

He studied a second, and says—

"Forgot something?...... No, not that I know of."

"Think," says I.

He thought. Then he says—

"No, I can't seem to have forgot anything. What is it?"

"Look at me," say I; "look me all over."

He done it.

"Well?" says he.

"Well," says I, "you don't notice anything? If I branched out amongst the elect looking like this, wouldn't I attract considerable attention?—wouldn't I be a little conspicuous?"

"Well," he says, "I don't see anything the matter. What do you lack?"

"Lack! Why I lack my harp, and my wreath, and my halo, and my hymn-book, and my palm branch—I lack everything that a body naturally requires up here, my friend."

Puzzled? Peters, he was the worst puzzled man you ever saw. Finally he says—

"Well, you seem to be a curiosity every way a body takes you. I never heard of these things before."

I looked at that man a while in solid astonishment; then I says—

"Now I hope you won't take it as an offense, for I don't mean any, but really, for a man that has been in the Kingdom as long as I reckon you have, you do seem to know powerful little about its customs."

"Its customs!" says he. "Heaven is a large place, good friend. Large empires have many and diverse customs. Even small dominions have, as you doubtless know by what you have seen of the matter on a small scale in the Wart. How can you imagine if I could ever learn the varied customs of the countless kingdoms of heaven? It makes my head ache to think of it. I know the customs that prevail in those portions inhabited by peoples that are appointed to enter by my own gate—and harkye, that is quite enough knowledge for one individual to try to pack into his head in the thirty-seven millions of years I have devoted night and day to that study. But the idea of learning the customs of the whole appalling expanse of heaven—O man, how insanely you talk! Now I don't doubt that this odd costume you talk about is the fashion in that district of heaven you belong to, but you won't be conspicuous in this section without it."

I felt all right, if that was the case, so I bade him good day and left. All day I walked toward the far end of a prodigious hall of the office, hoping to come out into heaven any moment, but it was a mistake. That hall was built on the general heavenly plan—it naturally couldn't be small. At last I got so tired I couldn't go any farther; so I sat down to rest, and begun to tackle the queerest sort of strangers and ask for information; but I didn't get any; they couldn't understand my language, and I could not understand theirs. I got dreadfully lonesome. I was so down-hearted and homesick I wished a hundred times I never had died. I turned back, of course. About noon next day I got back at last and I was on hand at the booking office once more. Says I to the head-clerk—

"I begin to see that a man's got to be in his own heaven to be happy."

"Perfectly correct," says he. "Did you imagine the same heaven would suit all sorts of men?"

"Well I had that idea—but I see the foolishness of it. Which way am I to go to get to my district?"

He called the under-clerk that had examined the map, and he gave me the general directions. I thanked him and started; but he says—

"Wait a minute; it is millions of leagues from here. Go outside and stand on that red wishing-carpet; shut your eyes, hold your breath, and wish yourself there."

"I'm much obliged," says I, "why didn't you dart me through when I first arrived?"

"We have a good deal to think of here; it was your place to think of it and ask for it. Good-bye, we probably shan't see you in this region again for a thousand centuries or so."

"In that case, *o revoor*," says I.

I hopped onto the carpet and held my breath and shut my eyes and wished I was in the booking-office of my own section. The very next instant a voice I knew sung out in a business kind of a way—

"A harp and a hymn-book, pair of wings and a halo, size No. 13, for Cap'n Eli Stormfield of San Francisco!—make him out a clean bill of health, and let him in."

I opened my eyes. Sure enough, it was a Pi Ute Injun I used to know in Tulare county; mighty good fellow—I remembered being at his funeral, which consisted of him being burnt and the other Injuns gauming their faces with his ashes and howling like wild-cats. He was powerful glad to see me, and you can make up your mind I was just as glad to see him, and feel that I was in the right kind of a heaven at last.

Just as far as your eye could reach, there was swarms of clerks, running and bustling around, tricking out thousands of Yanks, and Mexicans, and English, and A-rabs, and all sorts of people, in their new outfits; and when they gave me my kit and I put on my halo and took a look in the glass, I could have jumped over a house for joy I was so happy. "Now *this* is something like!" says I. "Now," says I, "I'm all right—show me a cloud."

Inside of fifteen minutes I was a mile on my way toward the cloud-banks, and about a million people along with me. Most of us tried to fly, but some got crippled and nobody made a success of it. So we concluded to walk, for the present, till we had had some wing-practice.

We begun to meet swarms of folks who were coming back. Some had harps and nothing else; some had hymn-books and nothing else; some had nothing at all; all of them looked meek and uncomfortable; one young fellow hadn't anything left but his halo, and he was carrying that in his hand; all of a sudden he offered it to me and says—

"Will you hold it for me a minute?"

Then he disappeared in the crowd. I went on. A woman asked me to hold her palm branch, and then *she* disappeared. A girl got me to hold her harp for her, and by George, *she* disappeared; and so on and so on, till I was about loaded down to the guards. Then comes a smiling old gentleman and asked me to hold *his* things. I swabbed off the perspiration, and says I, pretty tart—

"I'll have to get you to excuse me, my friend—*I* ain't no hat-rack."

About this time I begun to run across piles of those traps, laying in the road. I just quietly dumped my extra cargo along with them. I looked around, and Peters, that whole nation that was following me were loaded down, same as I'd been. The return crowd had got them to hold their things a minute, you see. They all dumped their loads, too, and we went on.

When I found myself perched on a cloud with a million other people, I never felt so good in my life. Says I, "Now this is according to the promises; I've been having my doubts, but now I *am* in heaven, sure enough." I gave my palm branch a wave or two, for luck, and then I tautened up my harp-strings and struck in. Well, Peters, you can't imagine anything like the row we made.

It was grand to listen to, and made a body thrill all over, but there was considerable many tunes going at once, and that was a drawback to the harmony, you understand; and then there was a lot of Injun tribes and they kept up such another war-whooping that they kind of took the tuck out of the music. By and by I quit performing, and judged I'd take a rest. There was quite a nice mild old gentleman sitting next me, and I noticed he didn't take a hand; I encouraged him, but he said he was naturally bashful, and was afraid to try before so many people. By and by the old gentleman said he never could seem to enjoy music, somehow. The fact was, I was beginning to feel the same way; but I didn't say anything. Him and I had a considerable long silence, then, but of course it warn't noticeable in that place. After about sixteen or seventeen hours, during which I played and sung a little, now and then—always the same tune, because I didn't know any other—I laid down my harp and begun to fan myself with my palm branch. Then we both got to sighing, pretty regular. Finally, says he—

"Don't you know any tune but the one you've been pegging at all day?"

"Not another blessed one," says I.

"Don't you reckon you could learn another one?" says he.

"Never," says I; "I've tried to, but I couldn't manage it."

"It's a long time to hang to the one—eternity, you know."

"Don't break my heart," says I; "I'm getting low-spirited enough already."

After another long silence, says he—

"Are you glad to be here?"

Says I, "Old man, I'll be frank with you. This *ain't* just as near my idea of bliss as I thought it was going to be, when I used to go to church."

Says he, "What do you say to knocking off and calling it half a day?"

"That's me," says I; "I never wanted to get off watch so bad in my life."

So we started. Millions were coming to the cloud-bank all the time, happy and hosannahing, millions were leaving it all the time, looking mighty quiet I tell you. We laid for the newcomers, and pretty soon I'd got them to hold all my things a minute, and then I was a free man again and most outrageously happy. Just then I ran across old Sam Bartlett, who had been dead a long time, and stopped to have a talk with him. Says I—

"Now tell me—is this to go on forever? Ain't there anything else for a change?"

Says he—

"I'll set you right on that point very quick. People take the figurative language of the Bible and the allegorists for literal, and the first thing they ask for when they get here is a halo and a harp, and so on. Nothing that's harmless and reasonable is refused a body here, if he asks it in the right spirit. So they are outfitted with these things without a word. They go and sing and play just about one day, and that's the last you'll ever see them in the choir. They don't need anybody to tell them that that sort of thing wouldn't make a heaven—at least not a heaven that a sane man could stand a week and remain sane. That cloud-bank is placed where the noise can't disturb the old inhabitants, and so there ain't any harm in letting everybody get up there and cure himself as soon as he comes.

"Now you just remember this—heaven is as blissful and lovely as it can be; but it's just the busiest place you ever heard of. There ain't any idle people here—after the first day. Singing hymns and waving palm branches through all eternity is mighty pretty when you hear about it in the pulpit, but it's as poor a way to put in valuable time as a body could contrive. It would just make a heaven of warbling ignoramuses, don't you see? Eternal Rest sounds mighty comforting in the pulpit, too. Well, you try it once, and see how heavy time will hang on your hands. Why Stormfield, a man like you, that had been active and stirring all his life, would go mad in six months in a heaven where he hadn't anything to do. Heaven is the very last place to come to to *rest* in!—and don't you be afraid to bet on that!"

Says I—

"Sam, I'm as glad to hear it as I thought I'd be sorry. I'm glad I come, now."

Says he—

"Cap'n, ain't you pretty physically tired?"

Says I—

"Sam, it ain't any name for it. Fiddling and singing all day on a damp cloud ain't rest, as I look at it. I'm dog-tired."

"Just so—just so. You've earned a good sleep, and you'll get it. You've earned a good appetite and you'll enjoy your dinner. It's the same here it is on earth—you've got to earn a thing, square and honest, before you enjoy it. You can't enjoy first and earn afterwards. But there's this difference, here: you can choose your own occupation, and all the powers of heaven will be put forth to help you make a success of it, if you do your level best. The shoemaker on earth that had the soul of a poet in him, won't have to make shoes here."

"Now that's all reasonable and right," says I. "Plenty of work, and the kind you hanker after; no more pain, no more suffering—"

"O, hold on; there's plenty of pain here—but it don't kill. There's plenty of suffering, here, but it don't last. You see, happiness ain't a *thing in itself*—it's only a *contrast* with something that ain't pleasant. That's all it is. There ain't a thing you can mention that is happiness in its own self—it's only so by contrast with the other thing. And mind you, as soon as the novelty is over and the force of the contrast dulled, it ain't happiness any longer, and you've got to get up something fresh. Well, there's plenty of pain and suffering in heaven—consequently there's plenty of contrasts, and just no end of happiness."

Says I, "It's the sensiblest heaven I ever heard of, Sam, though it's about as different from the one I was brought up on as a live princess is from her own wax-figger."

Along in the first months I knocked around about the Kingdom, making friends and looking at the country, and finally settled down in a pretty likely region, to have a rest before taking another start. I went on making acquaintances and gathering up information.

I had a good deal of talk with an old bald-headed angel by the name of Sandy McWilliams. He was from somewheres in New Jersey. I went about with him, considerable. We used to lay around, warm afternoons, in the shade of a rock, on some meadow-ground that was pretty high and out of the marshy slush of his cranberry farm, and there we used to talk about all kinds of things, and smoke pipes. One day, says I—

"About how old might you be, Sandy?"

"Seventy-two."

"I judged so. How long you been in heaven?"

"Twenty-seven years, come Christmas."

"How old was you when you come up?"

"Why seventy-two, of course."

"You can't mean it."

"Why can't I mean it?"

"Because, if you was seventy-two then, you are naturally ninety-nine, now."

"No, but I ain't. I stay the same age I was when I come."

"Well," says I, "come to think, there's something just there that I want to ask about. Down below, I always had an idea that in heaven we would all be young, and bright, and spry."

"Well, you *can* be young, if you want to. You've only got to wish."

"Well, then, why didn't you wish?"

"I did. They all do. You'll try it, some day, like enough; but you'll get tired of the change, pretty soon."

"Why?"

"Well, I'll tell you. Now you've always been a sailor; did you ever try some other business?"

"Yes, I tried keeping grocery, once, up in the mines; but I couldn't stand it; it was too dull—no stir, no storm, no life about it; it was like being part dead and part alive, both at the same time. I wanted to be one thing or t'other. I shut up shop pretty quick and went to sea."

"That's it. Grocery people like it, but you couldn't. You see, you wasn't used to it. Well, I wasn't used to being young, and I couldn't seem to take any interest in it. I was strong, and handsome, and had curly hair,—yes, and wings too!—gay wings like a butterfly. I went to picnics and dances and parties with the fellows, and tried to carry on and talk nonsense with the girls, but it wasn't any use, I couldn't take to it—fact is, it was an awful bore. What I wanted was early to bed and early to rise, and something to *do;* and when my work was done, I wanted to sit quiet, and smoke and think—not tear around with a parcel of giddy young kids. You can't think what I suffered whilst I was young."

"How long was you young?"

"Only two weeks. That was plenty for me. Laws, I was so lonesome! You see, I was full of the knowledge and experience of seventy-two years; the deepest subject those young folks could strike was only *a-b-c* to me. And to hear them argue—Oh, my! It would have been funny, if it hadn't been so pitiful. Well, I was so hungry for the ways and the sober talk I was used to, that I tried to ring in with the old people, but they wouldn't have it. They considered me a conceited young upstart, and gave me the cold shoulder. Two weeks was a plenty for me. I was glad to get back my bald head again, and my pipe, and my old drowsy reflections in the shade of a rock or a tree."

"Well," says I, "do you mean to say you're going to stand still at seventy-two, forever?"

"I don't know, and I ain't particular. But I ain't going to drop back to twenty-five any more—I know that, mighty well. I know a sight more than I did twenty-seven years ago, and I enjoy learning all the time, but I don't seem to get any older. That is, bodily—my mind gets older, and stronger, and better seasoned, and more satisfactory."

Says I, "If a man comes here at ninety, don't he ever set himself back?"

"Of course he does. He sets himself back to fourteen; tries it a couple of hours, and feels like a fool; sets himself forward to twenty; it ain't much improvement; tries thirty, fifty, eighty, and finally ninety—finds he is more at home and comfortable at the same old figure he is used to than any other way. Or, if his mind begun to fail him on earth at eighty, that's where he finally sticks, up here. He sticks at the place where his mind was last at its best, for there's where his enjoyment is best, and his ways most set and established."

"Does a chap of twenty-five stay always twenty-five, and look it?"

"If he is a fool, yes. But if he is bright, and ambitious and industrious, the knowledge he gains and the experiences he has, change his ways and thoughts and likings, and make him find his best pleasure in the company of people above that age; so he allows his body to take on the look of as many added years as he needs to make him comfortable and proper in that sort of society; he lets his body go on taking the look of age, according as he progresses, and by and by he will be bald and wrinkled outside, and wise and deep within."

"Babies the same?"

"Babies the same. Laws, what asses we used to be, on earth, about these things! We said we'd be always young, in heaven. We didn't say *how* young—we didn't think of that, perhaps—that is, we didn't all think alike, anyway. When I was a boy of seven, I suppose I thought we'd all be twelve, in heaven; when I was twelve, I suppose I thought we'd all be eighteen or twenty in heaven; when I was forty, I begun to go back; I remember I hoped we'd all be about *thirty* years old, in heaven. Neither a man nor a boy ever thinks the age he *has* is exactly the best one—he puts the *right* age a few years older or a few years younger than he is. Then he makes that ideal age the general age of the heavenly people. And he expects everybody *to stick* at that age—stand stock still—and expects them to enjoy it! Now just think of the idea of standing still in heaven! Think of a heaven made up entirely of hoop-rolling, marble-playing cubs of seven years!—or of awkward, diffident, sentimental immaturities of nineteen!—or of vigorous people of thirty, healthy-minded, brimming with ambition, but chained hand and foot to that one age and its limitations like so many helpless galley-slaves! Think of the dull sameness of a society made up of people all of one age and one set of looks, habits, tastes and feelings. Think how superior to it earth would be, with its variety of types and faces and ages, and the enlivening attrition of the myriad interests that come into pleasant collision in such a variegated society."

"Look here," says I, "do you know what you're doing?"

"Well, what am I doing?"

"You are making heaven pretty comfortable in one way, but you are playing the mischief with it in another."

"How do you mean?"

"Well," I says, "take a young mother that's lost her child, and— "

"Sh!" he says, "Look!"

It was a woman. Middle-aged, and had grizzled hair. She was walking slow, and her head was bent down, and her wings hanging limp and droopy; and she looked ever so tired, and was crying, poor thing. She passed along by, with her head down, that way, and the tears running down her face, and didn't see us. Then Sandy said, low and gentle and full of pity—

"*She's* hunting for her child! No, *found* it, I reckon. Lord, how she's changed. But I reconnized her in a minute, though it's twenty-seven years since I saw her. A young mother she was, about twenty-two or four, or along there; and blooming and lovely and sweet? oh, just a flower! And all her heart and all her soul was wrapped up in her child, her little girl, two years old. And it died, and she went wild with grief, just wild! Well, the only comfort she had, was that she'd see her child again, in heaven—'never more to part,' she said, and kept saying it over and over, 'never more to part.' And the words made her happy; yes they did, they made her joyful; and when I was dying, twenty-seven years ago, she told me to find her child the first thing, and say she was coming—'soon, soon, *very* soon, she hoped and believed!'"

"Why, it's pitiful, Sandy."

He didn't say anything for a while, but sat looking at the ground, thinking. Then he says, kind of mournful—

"And now she's come!"

"Well? Go on."

"Stormfield, maybe she hasn't found the child, but *I* think she has. Looks so to me. I've seen cases before. You see, she's kept that child in her head just the same as it was when she jounced it in her arms a little chubby thing. But here it didn't elect to *stay* a child. No, it elected to grow up, which it did. And in these twenty-seven years it has learned all the deep scientific learning there *is* to learn, and is studying and studying and learning and learning more and more, all the time, and don't give a damn for anything *but* learning; just learning, and discussing gigantic problems with people like herself."

"Well?"

"Stormfield, don't you see? Her mother knows *cranberries*, and how to tend them, and pick them, and put them up, and market them; and not another blamed thing! Her and her daughter can't be any more company for each other *now* than mud-turtle and bird o' paradise. Poor thing, she was looking for a baby to jounce; *I* think she's struck a disapp'intment."

"Sandy, what will they do—stay unhappy forever in heaven?"

"No, they'll come together and get adjusted by and by. But not this year and not next. By and by."

CHAPTER 4

I had been having considerable trouble with my wings. The day after I helped the choir, I made a dash or two with them, but I was not lucky. First-off, I flew thirty yards, and then fouled an Irishman and brought him down—brought us both down, in fact. Next, I had a collision with a Bishop—and bowled him down, of course. We had some sharp words, and I felt pretty cheap, to come banging into a grave old person like that, with a million strangers looking on and smiling to themselves.

I saw I hadn't got the hang of the steering, and so couldn't rightly tell where I was going to bring up when I started. I went afoot the rest of the day, and let my wings hang. Early next morning I went to a private place to have some practice. I got up on a pretty high rock, and got a good start, and went swooping down, aiming for a bush a little over three hundred yards off; but I couldn't seem to calculate for the wind, which was about two points abaft my beam. I could see I was going considerable to looard of the bush, so I worked my starboard wing slow and went ahead strong on the port one, but it wouldn't answer; I could see I was going to broach to, so I slowed down on both, and lit. I went back to the rock and took another chance at it. I aimed two or three points to starboard of the bush—yes, more than that—enough so as to make it nearly a head-wind. I done well enough, but made pretty poor time. I could see plain enough, that on a head-wind, wings was a mistake. I could see that a body could sail pretty close to the wind, but he couldn't go in the wind's eye. I could see that if I wanted to go a visiting any distance from home, and the wind was ahead, I might have to wait days, maybe, for a change; and I could see, too, that these things could not be any use at all in a gale; if you tried to run before the wind, you would make a mess of it, for there isn't any way to shorten sail—like reefing, you know—you have to take it *all* in—shut your feathers down flat to your sides. That would *land* you, of course. You could lay to, with your head to the wind—That is the best you could do, and right hard work you'd find it, too. If you tried any other game, you would founder, sure.

I judge it was about a couple of weeks or so after this, that I dropped old Sandy McWilliams a note one day—it was a Tuesday—and asked him to come over and take his manna and quails with me next day; and the first thing he did when he stepped in, was to twinkle his eye in a sly way, and say—

"Well, Cap., what you done with your wings?"

I saw in a minute that there was some sarcasm done up in that rag somewheres, but I never let on. I only says—

"Gone to the wash."

"Yes," he says, in a dry sort of way, "they mostly go to the wash—about this time—I've often noticed it. Fresh angels are powerful neat. When do you look for 'em back?"

"Day after to-morrow," says I.

He winked at me, and smiled.

Says I—

"Sandy, out with it. Come—no secrets among friends. I notice you don't ever wear wings—and plenty others don't. I've been making an ass of myself—is that it?"

"That is about the size of it. But it is no harm. We all do it—at first. It's perfectly natural. You see, on earth we jump to such foolish conclusions as to things up here. In the pictures we always saw the angels with wings on—and that was all right; but we jumped to the conclusion that that was their way of getting around—and that was all wrong. The wings ain't anything but a uniform, that's all. When they are in the field—so to speak—they always wear them; you never see an angel going with a message anywhere without his wings, any more than you would see a military officer presiding at a court martial without his uniform, or a postman delivering letters, or a policeman walking his beat, in plain clothes. But laws, they ain't to *fly* with! The wings are for show, not for use. Old experienced angels are like officers of the regular army—they dress plain, when they are off duty. New angels are like the militia—never shed the uniform—always fluttering and floundering around in their wings, butting people down, flapping here, and there, and everywhere, always showing off and always imagining they are attracting the admiring eye—well, they just think they are the very most important people in heaven. And when you see one of them come swooping sailing around with one wing tipped up and t'other down, you can make up your mind he is saying to himself, 'I wish Mary Ann in Arkansaw could see me now! I reckon she'd wish she hadn't shook me.' No, they're just for show, that's all—only just for show."

"I judge you've got it put up about right, Sandy," says I.

"Why, look at it yourself," says he. "*You* ain't built for wings—no man is. You know what a grist of years it took you to come here from the earth—and yet you were booming along faster than any cannon ball could go. Suppose you had had to fly that distance with your wings—wouldn't eternity have been over before you got here? Certainly. Well, angels have to go to the earth every day—millions of them—to appear in visions to dying children and good people, you know—it's the heft of their business. They appear with their wings, of course, because they are on official service, and because the dying persons wouldn't know they were angels if they hadn't wings—but do you reckon they fly with them? It stands to reason they don't. The wings would wear out before they got half way; even the pin-feathers would be gone; the wing-frames would be as bare as kite-sticks before the paper is pasted on. The distances in heaven are billions of times greater; angels have to go all over heaven every day; could they do it with their wings alone? No indeed; they wear the wings for style, but they travel any distance in an instant by *wishing*. The wishing-carpet of the Arabian Nights was a sensible idea—but our earthly idea of angels flying these awful distances with their clumsy wings was foolish.

"Our young saints, of both sexes, wear wings all the time—blazing red ones, and blue and green, and gold, and variegated, and rainbowed, and ring-streaked-and-striped ones—and nobody finds fault. It is suitable to their time of life. The things are beautiful, and they set the young people off. They are the most striking and lovely part of their outfit—a halo don't *begin*."

"Well," says I, "I've tucked mine away in the cupboard, and I allow to let them lay there till there's mud."

"Yes—or a reception."

"What's that?"

"Well, you can see one to-night if you want to. There's a barkeeper from Jersey City going to be received."

"Go on—tell me about it."

"This barkeeper got converted at a Moody and Sankey meeting, in New York, and started home on the ferry boat, and there was a collision and he got drowned. He is of a class that think all heaven goes wild with joy when a particularly hard lot like him is saved; they think all heaven turns out hosannahing to welcome them; they think there isn't anything talked about in the realms of the blest, but their case, for that day. This barkeeper thinks there hasn't been such another stir here in years, as his coming is going to raise. And I've always noticed this peculiarity about a dead barkeeper—he not only expects all hands to turn out when he arrives, but he expects to be received with a torchlight procession."

"I reckon he is disappointed, then."

"No he isn't. No man is allowed to be disappointed here. Whatever he wants when he comes—that is, any reasonable and unsacrilegious thing—he can have. There's always a few millions or billions of young folks around who don't want any better entertainment than to fill up their lungs and swarm out with their torches and have a high time over a barkeeper. It tickles the barkeeper till he can't rest, it makes a charming lark for the young folks, it don't do anybody any harm, it don't cost a rap, and it keeps up the place's reputation for making all comers happy and content."

"Very good. I'll be on hand and see them land the barkeeper."

"It is manners to go in full dress. You want to wear your wings, you know, and your other things."

"Which ones?"

"Halo, and harp, and palm branch, and all that."

"Well," says I, "I reckon I ought to be ashamed of myself, but the fact is I left them laying around that day I resigned from the choir. I haven't got a rag to wear but this robe and the wings."

"That's all right. You'll find they've been raked up and saved for you. Send for them."

"I'll do it, Sandy. But what was it you was saying about the unsacrilegious things, which people expect to get, and will be disappointed about?"

"O, there are a lot of such things that people expect and don't get. For instance, there's a Brooklyn preacher by the name of Talmage, who is laying up a considerable disappointment for himself. He says every now and then in his sermons, that the first thing he does when he gets to heaven, will be to fling his arms around Abraham, Isaac and Jacob, and kiss them and weep on them. There's millions of people down there on earth that are promising themselves the same thing. As many as sixty thousand people arrive here every single day, that want to run straight to Abraham, Isaac and Jacob, and hug them and weep on them. Now mind you, sixty thousand a day is a pretty heavy contract for those old people. If they were a mind to allow it, they wouldn't ever have anything to do, year in and year out, but stand up and be hugged and wept on thirty-two hours in the twenty-four. They would be tired out and as wet as muskrats all the time. What would heaven be, to *them?* It would be a mighty good place to get out of—you know that, yourself. Those are kind and gentle old Jews, but they ain't any fonder of kissing the emotional highlights of Brooklyn than you be. You mark my words, Mr. T.'s endearments are going to be declined, with thanks. There are limits to the privileges of the elect, even in heaven. Why, if Adam was to show himself to every new-comer that wants to call and gaze at him and strike him for his autograph, he would never have time to do anything else but just that. Talmage has said he is going to give Adam some of his attentions, as well as A., I., and J. But he will have to change his mind about that."

"Do you think Talmage will really come here?"

"Why certainly he will; but don't you be alarmed; he will run with his own kind, and there's plenty of them. That is the main charm of heaven—there's all kinds here—which wouldn't be the case if you let the preachers tell it. Anybody can find the sort he prefers here, and he just lets the others alone, and they let *him* alone. When the Deity builds a heaven, it is built right, and on a liberal plan."

Sandy sent home for his things, and I sent for mine, and about nine in the evening we begun to dress. Sandy says—

"This is going to be a grand time for you, Stormy. Like as not some of the patriarchs will turn out."

"No, but will they?"

"Like as not. Of course they are pretty exclusive. They hardly ever show themselves to the common public. I believe they never turn out except for an eleventh-hour convert. They wouldn't do it then, only earthly tradition makes a grand show pretty necessary on that kind of an occasion."

"Do they all turn out, Sandy?"

"Who?—all the patriarchs? Oh, no—hardly ever more than a couple. You will be here fifty thousand years—maybe more—before you get a glimpse of all the patriarchs and prophets. Since I have been here, Job has been to the front once, and once Ham and Jeremiah both at the same time. But the finest thing that has happened in my day was a year or so ago, that was Charles Peace's reception—him they called 'the Bannercross Murderer'—an Englishman. There were four patriarchs and two prophets on the Grand Stand that time—there hasn't been anything like it since Captain Kidd came; Abel was there—the first time in twelve hundred years. A report got around that Adam was coming; well, of course Abel was enough to bring a crowd, all by himself, but there is nobody that can draw like Adam. It was a false report, but it got around, anyway, as I say, and it will be a long day before I see the like of it again. The reception was in the English department, of course, which is eight hundred and eleven million miles from the New Jersey line. I went, along with a good many of my neighbors, and it was a sight to see, I can tell you. Flocks came from all the departments. I saw Esquimaux there, and Tartars, negroes, Chinamen—people from everywhere. You see a mixture like that in the Grand Choir, the first day you land here, but you hardly ever see it again. There were billions of people; when they were singing or hosannahing, the noise was wonderful; and even when their tongues were still, the drumming of the wings was nearly enough to burst your head, for all the sky was as thick as if it was snowing angels. Although Adam was not there, it was a great time anyway, because we had three Archangels on the Grand Stand—it is a seldom thing that even one comes out."

"What did they look like, Sandy?"

"Well, they had shining faces, and shining robes, and wonderful rainbow wings, and they stood eighteen feet high, and wore swords, and held their heads up in a noble way, and looked like soldiers."

"Did they have halos?"

"No—anyway, not the hoop kind. The archangels and the upper-class patriarchs wear a finer thing than that. It is a round, solid, splendid glory of gold, that is blinding to look at. You have often seen a patriarch in a picture, on earth, with that thing on—you remember it?—he looks as if he had his head in a brass platter. That don't give you the right idea of it at all—it is much more shining and beautiful."

"Did you talk with those archangels and patriarchs, Sandy?"

"Who—*I?* Why what can you be thinking about, Stormy? I ain't worthy to speak to such as they."

"Is Talmage?"

"Of course not. You have got the same mixed-up idea about these things that everybody has, down there. I had it once but I got over it. Down there they talk of the heavenly King—and that is right—but they go right on speaking as if this was a Republic and everybody was on a dead level with everybody else, and privileged to fling his arms around anybody he comes across, and be hail-fellow-well-met with all the elect, from the highest down. How tangled up and absurd that is! How are you going to have a republic under a king? How are you going to have a republic at all, where the head of the government is absolute, holds his place forever, and has no parliament, no council to meddle or make in his affairs, nobody voted for, nobody elected, nobody in the whole universe with a voice in the government, nobody asked to take a hand in its matters, and nobody *allowed* to do it? Fine republic, ain't it?"

"Well, yes—it *is* a little different from the idea I had—but I thought I might go around and get acquainted with the grandees, anyway—not exactly splice the main-brace with them, you know, but shake hands and pass the time of day."

"Could Tom, Dick, and Harry call on the Cabinet of Russia and do that?—on Prince Gortschakoff, for instance?"

"I reckon not, Sandy."

"Well, this is Russia—only more so. There's not the shadow of a republic about it anywhere. There are ranks, here. There are viceroys, princes, governors, sub-governors, sub-sub-governors, and a hundred orders of nobility, grading along down from grand-ducal archangels, stage by stage, till the general level is struck, where there ain't any titles. Do you know what a prince of the blood is, on earth?"

"No."

"Well, a prince of the blood don't belong to the royal family exactly, and he don't belong to the mere nobility of the kingdom; he is lower than the one, and higher than t'other. That's about the position of the patriarchs and prophets, here. There's some mighty high nobility here—people that you and I ain't worthy to polish sandals for—and *they* ain't worthy to polish sandals for the patriarchs and prophets. That gives you a kind of an idea of their rank, don't it? You begin to see how high up they are, don't you? Just to get a two-minute glimpse of one of them is a thing for a body to remember and tell about for a thousand years. Why Captain, just think of this: if Abraham was to set his foot down here by this door, there would be a railing set up around that foot-track right away, and a shelter put over it, and people would flock here from all over heaven, for hundreds and hundreds of years, to look at it. Abraham is one of the parties that Mr. Talmage, of Brooklyn, is going to embrace, and kiss, and weep on, when he comes. He wants to lay in a good stock of tears, you know, or five to one he will go dry before he gets a chance to do it."

"Sandy," says I, "I had an idea that *I* was going to be equals with everybody here, too, but I will let that drop. It don't matter, and I am plenty happy enough anyway."

"Captain, you are happier than you would be, the other way. These old patriarchs and prophets have got ages the start of you; they know more in two minutes than you know in a year. Did you ever try to have a sociable improving-time discussing winds, and currents, and variations of compass with an undertaker?"

"I get your idea, Sandy. He couldn't interest me. He would be an ignoramus in such things—he would bore me, and I would bore him."

"You have got it. You would bore the patriarchs when you talked, and when they talked they would shoot over your head. By and by you would say, 'Good morning, your Eminence, I will call again'—but you wouldn't. Did you ever ask the slush-boy to come up in the cabin and take dinner with you?"

"I get your drift again, Sandy. I wouldn't be used to such grand people as the patriarchs and prophets, and I would be sheepish and tongue-tied in their company, and mighty glad to get out of it. Sandy, which is the highest rank, patriarch, or prophet?"

"Oh, the prophets hold over the patriarchs. The newest prophet, even, is of a sight more consequence than the oldest patriarch. Yes, sir, Adam himself has to walk behind Shakspere."

"Was Shakspere a prophet?"

"Of course he was; and so was Homer, and heaps more. But Shakspere and the rest have to walk behind a common tailor from Tennessee, by the name of Billings; and behind a horse-doctor named Sakka, from Afghanistan. Jeremiah, and Billings and Buddha walk together, side by side, right behind a crowd from planets not in our astrononomy; next come a dozen or two from Jupiter and other worlds; next come Daniel, and Sakka and Confucius; next a lot from systems outside of ours; next come Ezekiel, Mahomet, Zoroaster, and a knife-grinder from ancient Egypt; then there is a long string, and after them, away down toward the bottom, come Shakspere and Homer and a shoemaker named Marais, from the back settlements of France."

"Have they really rung in Mahomet and all those other heathens?"

"Yes—they all had their message; and they all get their reward. The man who don't get his reward on earth, needn't bother—he will get it here, sure."

"But why did they throw off on Shakspere, that way, and put him away down there below those shoemakers and horse-doctors, and knife-grinders—a lot of people nobody ever heard of?"

"That is the heavenly justice of it—they warn't rewarded according to their deserts on earth, but here they get their rightful rank. That tailor Billings, from Tennessee, wrote poetry that Homer and Shakspere couldn't begin to come up to; but nobody would print it, nobody read it but his neighbors, an ignorant lot, and they laughed at it. Whenever the village had a drunken frolic and a dance, they would drag him in and crown him with cabbage leaves, and pretend to bow down to him; and one night when he was sick and nearly starved to death, they had him out and crowned him, and then they rode him on a rail about the village, and everybody followed along beating tin pans and yelling. Well, he died before morning. He wasn't ever expecting to go to heaven, much less that there was going to be any fuss made over him, so I reckon he was a good deal surprised when the reception broke on him."

"Was you there, Sandy?"

"Bless you, no!"

"Why? Didn't you know it was going to come off?"

"Well, I judge I did. It was the talk of these realms—not for a day, like this barkeeper business, but for twenty years before the man died."

"Why the mischief didn't you go, then?"

"Now, how you talk! The like of me go meddling around at the reception of a prophet? A mudsill like me trying to push in and help receive an awful grandee like Edward J. Billings? Why I should have been laughed at for a billion miles around. I shouldn't ever heard the last of it."

"Well, who did go, then?"

"Mighty few people that you and I will ever get a chance to see, Captain. Not a solitary commoner ever has the luck to see a reception of a prophet, I can tell you. All the nobility, and all the patriarchs and prophets—every last one of them—and all the archangels, and all the princes and governors and viceroys, were there,—and no small fry—not a single one. And mind you, I'm not talking about only the grandees from *our* world, but the princes and patriarchs and so-on from *all* the worlds that shine in our sky, and from billions more that belong in systems upon systems away outside of the one our sun is in. There were some prophets and patriarchs there that ours ain't a circumstance to, for rank and illustriousness and all that. Some were from Jupiter and other worlds in our own system, but the most celebrated were three poets, Saa, Bo, and Soof, from great planets in three different and very remote systems. These three names are common and familiar in every nook and corner of heaven, clear from one end of it to the other—fully as well known as the eighty Supreme Archangels, in fact—whereas our Moses, and Adam, and the rest, have not been heard of outside of our world's little corner of heaven, except by a few very learned men scattered here and there—and they always spell their names wrong, and get the performances of one mixed up with the doings of another, and they almost always locate them simply *in our solar system*, and think that is enough without going into little details such as naming the particular world they are from. It is like a learned Hindoo showing off how much he knows by saying Longfellow lives in the United States—as if he lived all over the United States, and as if the country was so small you couldn't throw a brick there without hitting him. Between you and me, it does gravel me, the cool way people from those monster worlds outside our system snub our little world, and even our system. Of course we think a good deal of Jupiter, because our world is only a potato to it, for size; but then there are worlds in other systems that Jupiter isn't even a mustard seed to—like the planet Goobra, for instance, which you couldn't squeeze inside the orbit of Halley's comet without straining the rivets. Tourists from Goobra (I mean parties that lived and died there—natives,) come here, now and then, and inquire about our world, and when they find out it is so little that a streak of lightning can flash clear around it in the eighth of a second, they have to lean up against something to laugh. Then they screw a glass into their eye and go to examining *us* as if we were a curious kind of foreign bug, or something of that sort. One of them asked me how long our day was; and when I told him it was twelve hours long, as a general thing, he asked me if people where I was from considered it worth while to get up and wash for such a day as that. That is the way with those Goobra people—they can't seem to let a chance go by to throw it in your face that their day is three hundred and twenty-two of our years long. This young snob was just of age—he was six or seven thousand of his days old—say two million of our years—and he had all the puppy airs that belong to that time of life—that turning point when a person has got over being a boy and yet ain't quite a man exactly. If it had been anywhere else but in heaven, I would have given him a piece of my mind. Well, anyway, Billings had the grandest reception that has been seen in thousands of centuries, and I think it will have a good effect. His name will be carried pretty far, and it will make our system talked about, and maybe our world, too, and raise us in the respect of the general public of heaven. Why look here—Shakspere walked backward before that tailor from Tennessee, and scattered flowers for him to walk on, and Homer stood behind his chair and waited on him at the banquet. Of course that didn't go for much *there*, amongst all those big foreigners from other systems, as they hadn't heard of Shakspere or Homer either, but it would amount to considerable down there on our little earth if they could know about it. I wish there was something *in* that miserable spiritualism, so we could send them word. That Tennessee village would set up a monument to Billings, then, and his autograph would outsell Satan's. Well, they had grand times at that reception—a small-fry noble from Hoboken told me all about it—Sir Richard Duffer, Baronet."

"What, Sandy, a nobleman from Hoboken? How is that?"

"Easy enough. Duffer kept a sausage shop, and never saved a cent in his life because he used to give all his spare meat to the poor, in a quiet way. Not tramps,—no, the other sort—the sort that will starve before they will beg—honest square people out of work. Dick used to watch hungry-looking men and women and children, and track them home, and find out all about them from the neighbors, and then feed them and find them work. As nobody ever *saw* him give anything to anybody, he had the reputation of being mean; he died with it, too, and everybody said it was a good riddance; but the minute he landed here, they made him a baronet, and the very first words Dick the sausage-maker of Hoboken heard when he stepped upon the heavenly shore, were, 'Welcome, Sir Richard Duffer!' It surprised him some, because he thought he had reasons to believe he was pointed for a warmer climate than this one."

All of a sudden the whole region fairly rocked under the crash of eleven hundred and one thunder-blasts, all let off at once, and Sandy says—

"There, that's for the barkeep."

I jumped up and says—

"Then let's be moving along, Sandy, we don't want to miss any of this thing, you know."

"Keep your seat," he says, "he is only just telegraphed, that is all."

"How?"

"That blast only means that he has been sighted from the signal station. He is off Sandy Hook. The committee will go down to meet him, now, and escort him in. There will be ceremonies and delays, they won't be coming up the Bay for a considerable time, yet. It is several billion miles away, anyway."

"*I* could have been a barkeeper and a hard lot just as well as not," says I, remembering the lonesome way I arrived, and how there wasn't any committee nor anything."

"I notice some regret in your voice," says Sandy, "and it is natural enough; but let bygones be bygones; you went according to your lights, and it is too late now to mend the thing."

"No, let it slide, Sandy, I don't mind. But you've got a Sandy Hook *here*, too, have you?"

"We've got everything here, just as it is below. All the States and Territories of the Union, and all the kingdoms of the earth and the islands of the sea are laid out here just as they are on the globe—all the same shape they are down there, and all graded to the relative sizes, only each State and realm and island is a good many billion times bigger here than it is below. There goes another blast."

"What is that one for?"

"That is only another fort answering the first one. They each fire eleven hundred and one thunder-claps at a single dash—it is the usual salute for an eleventh-hour guest; a hundred for each hour and an extra one for the guest's sex; if it was a woman we would know it by their leaving off the extra gun."

"How do we know there's eleven hundred and one, Sandy, when they all go off at once?—and yet we certainly do know."

"Our intellects are a good deal sharpened up, here, in some ways, and that is one of them. Numbers and sizes and distances are so great, here, that we have to be made so we can *feel* them—our old ways of counting and measuring and ciphering wouldn't ever give us an idea of them, but would only confuse us and oppress us and make our heads ache."

After some more talk about this, I says—

"Sandy, I notice that I hardly ever see a white angel; where I run across one white angel, I strike as many as a hundred million copper colored ones—people that can't speak English. How is that?"

"Well, you will find it the same in any State or Territory of the American corner of heaven you choose to go to. I have shot along a whole week on a stretch, and gone millions and millions of miles, through perfect swarms of angels, without ever seeing a single white one, or hearing a word I could understand. You see, America was occupied a billion years and more, by Injuns and Aztecs, and that sort of folks, before a white man ever set his foot in it. During the first three hundred years after Columbus's discovery, there wasn't ever more than one good lecture audience of white people, all put together, in America,—I mean the whole thing, British Possessions and all; in the beginning of our century there were only 6,000,000 or 7,000,000—say seven; 12,000,000 or 14,000,000 in 1825; say 23,000,000 in 1850; 40,000,000 in 1875. Our death rate has always been 20 in 1,000 per annum. Well, 140,000 died the first year of the century; 280,000 the twenty-fifth year; 500,000 the fiftieth year; about a million the seventy-fifth year. Now I am going to be liberal about this thing, and consider that fifty million whites have died in America, from the beginning up to to-day—make it sixty, if you want to; make it a hundred million—it's no difference about a few millions one way or t'other. Well, now, you can see, yourself, that when you come to spread a little dab of people like that over these hundreds of billions of miles of American territory here in heaven, it is like scattering a ten-cent box of homœopathic pills over the great Sahara and expecting to find them again. You can't expect us to amount to anything in heaven, and we *don't*—now that is the simple fact, and we have got to do the best we can with it. The learned men from other planets and other systems come here and hang around a while, when they are touring around the Kingdom and then go back to their own section of heaven and write a book of travels, and they give America about five lines in it. And what do they say about us? They say this wilderness is populated with a scattering few hundred thousand billions of red angels, with now and then a curiously complected *diseased* one. You see, they think we whites, and the occasional nigger, are Injuns that have been bleached out or blackened by some leprous disease or other—for some peculiarly rascally *sin*, mind you. It is a mighty sour pill for us all, my friend—even the modestest of us, let alone the other kind, that think they are going to be received like a long-lost government bond, and hug Abraham into the bargain. I haven't asked you any of the particulars, Captain, but I judge it goes without saying—if my experience is worth anything—that there wasn't much of a hooraw made over you when you arrived—now was there?"

"Don't mention it, Sandy," says I, coloring up a little, "I wouldn't have had the family see it for any amount you are a mind to name. Change the subject, Sandy, change the subject."

"Well, do you think of settling in the Californian department of bliss?"

"I don't know. I wasn't calculating on doing anything really definite in that direction till the family come. I thought I would just look around, meantime, in a quiet way, and make up my mind. Besides, I know a good many dead people, and I was calculating to hunt them up and swap a little gossip with them about friends, and old times, and one thing or another, and ask them how they like it here as far as they have got. I reckon my wife will want to camp in the Californian range, though, because most all her departed will be there, and she likes to be with folks she knows."

"Don't you let her. You see what the Jersey district of heaven is for whites; well, the Californian district is a thousand times worse. It swarms with a mean kind of leather-headed mud-colored angels—Digger Injuns, mainly—and your nearest white neighbor is likely to be a million miles away. *What a man mostly misses, in heaven, is company*—company of his own sort and color and language. I have come near settling in the European part of heaven once or twice on that account."

"Well, why didn't you, Sandy?"

"Oh, various reasons. For one thing, although you *see* plenty of whites there, you can't understand any of them, hardly, and so you go about as hungry for talk as you do here. I like to look at a Russian or a German or an Italian—I even like to look at a Frenchman if I ever have the luck to catch him engaged in anything that ain't indelicate—but *looking* don't cure the hunger—what you want is talk."

"Well, there's England, Sandy—the English district of heaven."

"Yes, but it is not so very much better than this end of the heavenly domain.

As long as you run across Englishmen born this side of three hundred years ago, you are all right; but the minute you get back of Elizabeth's time the language begins to fog up, and the further back you go the foggier it gets. I had some talk with one Langland and a man by the name of Chaucer—old-time poets—but it was no use, I couldn't quite understand them, and they couldn't quite understand me. I have had letters from them since, but it is such broken English I can't make it out. Back of those men's time the English are just simply foreigners, nothing more, nothing less; they talk Danish, German, Norman French, and sometimes a mixture of all of these; back of *them*, they talk Latin, and ancient British, Irish, and Gaelic; and then back of these comes billions and billions of pure savages that talk a gibberish that Satan himself couldn't understand. The fact is, where you strike one man in the English settlements that you can understand, you wade through awful swarms that talk something you can't make head nor tail of. You see, every country on earth has been overlaid so often, in the course of a billion years, with different kinds of people and different sorts of languages that this sort of mongrel business was bound to be the result in heaven."

"Sandy," says I, "did you see a good many of the great people history tells about?"

"Yes—plenty. I saw kings and all sorts of distinguished people."

"Do the kings rank just as they did below?"

"No; a body can't bring his rank up here with him. Divine right is a good enough earthly romance, but it don't go, here. Kings drop down to the general level as soon as they reach the realms of grace. I knew Charles the Second very well—one of the most popular comedians in the English section—draws first rate. There are better, of course—people that were never heard of on earth—but Charles is making a very good reputation indeed, and is considered a rising man. Richard the Lion-hearted is in the prize ring, and coming into considerable favor. Henry the Eighth is a tragedian, and the scenes where he kills people are done to the very life. Henry the Sixth keeps a religious-book stand."

"Did you ever see Napoleon, Sandy?"

"Often—sometimes in the Corsican range, sometimes in the French. He always hunts up a conspicuous place, and goes frowning around with his arms folded and his field glass under his arm, looking as grand, gloomy, and peculiar as his reputation calls for, and very much bothered because he don't stand as high here, for a soldier, as he expected to."

"Why, who stands higher?"

"Oh, a *lot* of people *we* never heard of before—the shoemaker and horse-doctor and knife-grinder kind, you know—clod-hoppers from goodness knows where, that never handled a sword or fired a shot in their lives—but the soldiership was in them, though they never had a chance to show it. But here they take their right place, and Caesar and Napoleon and Alexander have to take a back seat. The greatest military genius our world ever produced was a bricklayer from somewhere back of Boston—died during the Revolution—by the name of Absalom Jones. Wherever he goes, crowds flock to see him. You see, everybody knows that if he had had a chance he would have shown the world some generalship that would have made all generalship before look like child's-play and 'prentice-work. But he never got a chance; he tried heaps of times to enlist as a private, but he had lost both thumbs and a couple of front teeth, and the recruiting surgeon wouldn't pass him. However, as I say, everybody knows, now, what he *would* have been, and so they flock by the million to get a glimpse of him whenever they hear he is going to be anywhere. Caesar, and Hannibal, and Alexander, and Napoleon are all on his staff, and ever so many more great generals, but the public hardly care to look at *them* when *he* is around. Boom! There goes another salute. The barkeeper's off quarantine, now."

Sandy and I put on our things. Then we made a wish, and in a second we were at the reception-place. We stood on the edge of the ocean of space, and looked out over the dimness, but couldn't make out anything. Close by us was the Grand Stand. Tier on tier of dim thrones rising up toward the zenith. From each side of it spread away the tiers of seats for the general public. They spread away for leagues and leagues—you couldn't see the ends. They were empty and still, and hadn't a cheerful look, but looked dreary, like a theatre before anybody comes—gas turned down. Sandy says—

"We'll sit down here and wait. We'll see the head of the procession come in sight away off yonder pretty soon, now."

Says I—

"It's pretty lonesome, Sandy; I reckon there's a hitch somewheres. Nobody but just you and me—it ain't much of a display for the barkeeper."

"Don't you fret, it's all right. There'll be one more gun-fire—then you'll see."

In a little while we noticed a sort of a lightish flush away off on the horizon.

"Head of the torchlight procession," says Sandy.

It spread, and got lighter and brighter; soon it had a strong glare like a locomotive headlight; it kept on getting brighter and brighter till it was like the sun peeping above the horizon-line at sea—the big red rays shot high up into the sky.

"Keep your eyes on the Grand Stand and the miles of seats—sharp!" says Sandy, "and listen for the gun-fire."

Just then it burst out "Boom-boom-boom!" like a million thunderstorms in one, and made the whole heavens rock. Then there was a sudden and awful glare of light all about us, and in that very instant every one of the millions of seats was occupied, and as far as you could see, in both directions, was just a solid pack of people, and the place was all splendidly lit up! It was enough to take a body's breath away. Sandy says—

"That is the way we do it here. No time fooled away; nobody straggling in after the curtain's up. Wishing is quicker work than traveling. A matter of a second ago these folks were millions of miles from here. When they heard the last signal, all they had to do was to wish, and here they are."

The prodigious choir struck up—

"We long to hear thy voice,
To see thee face to face."

It was noble music but the uneducated chipped in and spoilt it, just as the congregations used to do on earth.

The head of the procession began to pass, now, and it was a wonderful sight. It swept along, thick and solid, five hundred thousand angels abreast, and every angel carrying a torch and singing—the whirring thunder of the wings made a body's head ache. You could follow the line of the procession back, and slanting upward into the sky, far away in a glittering snaky rope, till it was only a faint streak in the distance. The rush went on and on, for a long time, and at last, sure enough, along comes the barkeeper, and then everybody rose and a cheer went up that made the heavens shake, I tell you! He was all smiles, and had his halo tilted over one ear in a cocky way and was the most satisfied-looking saint I ever saw. While he marched up the steps of the Grand Stand, the choir struck up—

"The whole wide heaven groans,
And waits to hear that voice."

* * * * * * *

There were four gorgeous tents standing side by side in the place of honor, on a broad railed platform in the centre of the Grand Stand, with a shining guard of honor round about them. The tents had been shut up, all this time. As the barkeeper climbed along up, bowing and smirking to everybody, and at last got to the platform, these tents were jerked up aloft, all of a sudden, and we saw four noble thrones of gold, all caked with jewels, and in the two middle ones sat old white-whiskered men, and in the two others a couple of the most glorious and gaudy giants, with platter-halos and beautiful armor. All the millions went down on their knees, and stared, and looked glad, and burst out into a joyful kind of murmurs. They said—

"Two archangels!—that is splendid. Who can the others be?"

The archangels gave the barkeeper a stiff little military bow; the two old men rose; one of them said, "Moses and Esau welcome thee!" and then all the four vanished and the thrones were empty.

The barkeeper looked a little disappointed, for he was calculating to hug those old people, I judge; but it was the gladdest and proudest multitude you ever saw—because they had seen Moses and Esau. Everybody was saying, "Did you see them?—*I* did—Esau's side face was to me, but I saw Moses full in the face, just as plain as I see you this minute!"

The procession took up the barkeeper and moved on with him again, and the crowd broke up and scattered. As we went along home, Sandy said it was a great success, and the barkeeper would have a right to be proud of it forever. And he said *we* were in luck, too; said we might attend receptions for forty thousand years to come, and not have a chance to see a brace of such grand moguls as Moses and Esau. We found afterwards that we had come near seeing another patriarch, and likewise a genuine prophet besides, but at the last moment they sent regrets. Sandy said there would be a monument put up there, where Moses and Esau had stood, with the date and the circumstances, and all about the whole business, and travelers would come for thousands of years, and gawk at it, and climb over it, and scribble their names on it.

CHAPTER 5

Captain Stormfield Resumes

I

When I had been in heaven some time I begun to feel restless, the same as I used to on earth when I had been ashore a month, so I sejested to Sandy that we do some excursions. He said all right, and with that we started with a whiz—not that you could *hear* us go, but it was as if you ought to. On account of our going so fast, for you go by *thought.* If you went only as fast as light or electricity you would be forever getting to any place, heaven is so big. Even when you are traveling by thought it takes you days and days and days to cover the territory of any Christian State, and days and days and days to cover the uninhabited stretch between that State and the next one.

"You can't put it into miles," Sandy says.

"Why can't you?" says I.

"Becuz there ain't enough of them. If you had all the miles God ever made they wouldn't reach from the Catholic camp to the High Church Piscopalian—nor half way, for that matter; and yet they are the nearest together of any. Professor Higgins tries to work the miles on the measurements, on account of old earthly habit, and p'raps he gets a sort of grip on the distances out of the result, but you couldn't, and I can't."

"How do *you* know I couldn't, Sandy? Speak for yourself, hadn't you better? You just tell me his game, and wait till I look at my hand."

"Well, it's this. He used to be astronomical professor of astronomy at Harvard—"

"This was before he was dead?"

"Cert'nly. How could he be *after* he was dead?"

"Oh, well, it ain't important. But a *soldier* can be a soldier after he's dead. And he can breed, too. There's eleven million dead soldiers drawing pension at home, now—some that's been dead 125 years—and we've never had those millions on the pay-roll since the first Fourth of July. Go on, Sandy. Maybe it was before he was dead, maybe it wasn't; but it ain't important."

"Well, he was astronomical professor, and can't get rid of his habits. So he tries to figure out these heavenly distances by astronomical measurements. That is to say, he computes them in light-years."

"What is a light-year, Sandy?"

"He says light travels 186,000 miles a second, and—"

"How many?"

"186,000."

"In a *second,* Sandy—not a week?"

"No, in a second. He says the sun is 93,000,000 miles from the earth, and it takes light 8 minutes to cover the distance. Then he ciphers out how far the light would travel in a year of 365 days, at that gait, and he calls that distance a light-year."

"It's considerable, ain't it, Sandy?"

"Don't you doubt it!"

"How far is it, Sandy?"

"It's 63,280 times the distance from the earth to the sun."

"Land! Say it again, Sandy, and say it slow."

"63,280 times 93,000,000 miles."

"Sandy it beats the band. Do you think there's room for a straight stretch like that? Don't you reckon it would come to the edge and stick out over? What does a light-year foot up, Sandy, in a lump?"

"Six thousand million miles."

"Sandy, it is certainly a corker! Is there any known place as far off as a light-year?"

"Shucks, Stormy, *one* light-year is nothing. He says it's *four* light-years from our earth to the nearest star—and nothing between."

"*Nothing* between? Nothing but just emptiness?"

"That's it; nothing but emptiness. And he says there's not a star in the Milky Way nor anywhere else in the sky that's not *further* away from its nearest neighbor than that."

"Why, Sandy, if that is true, the sky is emptier than heaven."

"Oh, indeed, no! Far from it. In the Milky Way, the professor says, no star is more than six or seven light-years distant from its nearest neighbor, but there ain't any Christian sect in heaven that is nearer than 5,000 light years from the camp of the next sect. Oh, no, he says the sky *is* a howling wilderness, but it can't howl with heaven. No, sir, he says of all the lonesome places that ever was, give him heaven. Every now and then he gets so lonesome here that he makes an excursion amongst the stars, so's to have a sense of company."

"Why, Sandy, what have they made heaven so large, for?"

"So's to have room in the future. The redeemed will still be coming for billions and billions and billions and billions of years, but there'll always be room, you see. *This* heaven ain't built on any 'Gates Ajar' proportions."

. . . . Time drifted along. We went on excursioning amongst the colonies and over the monstrous spaces between, till at last I was so weighed down by the awful bigness of heaven that I said I'd got to see something small to get back my natural focus and lift off some of the load, I couldn't stand it any longer. Sandy says,

"Well, then, suppose we try an asterisk, or asteroid, or whatever the professor calls them. *They're* little enough to fit the case, I reckon."

II

Journey to the Asterisk

So we went, and it was quite interesting. It was a very nice little world, twenty-five or thirty miles in circumference; almost exactly a thousand times smaller than the earth, and just a miniature of it, in every way: little wee Atlantic oceans and Pacific oceans and Indian oceans, all in the right places; the same with the rivers, the same with the lakes; the same old familiar mountain ranges, the same continents and islands, the same Sahara—all in the right proportions and as exact as a photograph. We walked around it one afternoon, and waded the oceans, and had a most uncommon good time. We spent weeks and weeks walking around over it and getting acquainted with the nations and their ways.

Nice little dollies, they were, and not bigger than Gulliver's Lilliput people. Their ways were like ours. In their America they had a republic on our own plan, and in their Europe, their Asia and their Africa they had monarchies and established churches, and a pope and a czar, and all the rest of it. They were not afraid of us; in fact they held us in rather frank contempt, because we were giants. Giants have never been respected, in any world. These people had a quite good opinion of themselves, although they were no bigger than a banana, and many of them no bigger than a clothespin. In church it was a common thing for the preacher to look out over his congregation and speak of them as the noblest work of God—and never a clothes pin smiled! These little animals were having wars all the time, and raising armies and building navies, and striving after the approval of God every way they could. And wherever there was a savage country that needed civilizing, they went there and took it, and divided it up among the several enlightened monarchs, and civilized it—each monarch in his own way, but generally with Bibles and bullets and taxes. And the way they did whoop-up Morals, and Patriotism, and Religion, and the Brotherhood of Man was noble to see.

I couldn't see that they differed from us, except in size. It was like looking at ourselves through the wrong end of the spyglass. But Sandy said there was one difference, and a big one. It was this: each person could look right into every other person's mind and read what was in it, but he thought his own mind was concealed from everybody but himself!

CHAPTER 6

From Captain Stormfield's Reminiscences

One day, whilst I was there in Heaven, I says to Sandy—

"Sandy," I says, "You was telling me, a while back, that you knowed how the human race came to be created; and now, if you don't mind," I says, "I'd like you to pull off the narrative, for I reckon it's intresting."

So he done it. This is it.

—

Sandy's Narrative

=

Well, it was like this. I got it from Slattery. Slattery was there at the time, being an eye witness, you see; and so Slattery, he—

"Who's Slattery, Sandy?"

One of the originals.

"Original *which?*"

Original inventions. He used to be an angel, in the early times, two hunderd thousand years ago; and so, as it happened—

"Two hun—do you mean to say—"

Yes, I *do.* It was two hunderd thousand years ago. Slattery was born here in Heaven, and so time don't count. As I was a-telling you, he was an angel, first-off, but when Satan fell, he fell, too, becuz he was a connexion of Satan's, by marriage or blood or somehow or other, and it put him under suspicion, though they warn't able to prove anything on him. Still, they judged a little term down below in the fires would be a lesson to him and do him good, so they give him a thousand years down in them tropics, and—

"A *thousand*, Sandy?"

Cert'nly. It ain't anything to these people, Cap'n Stormfield. When you've been here as long as I have—but never mind about that. When he got back, he was different. The vacation done him good. You see, he had had experience, and it sharpened him up. And besides, he had traveled, and it made him important, which he warn't, before. Satan come near getting a thousand years himself, that time—

"But I thought he *did*, Sandy. I thought he went down for good and all."

No, sir, not that time.

"What saved him?"

Influence.

"M-m. So they have it here, too, do they?"

Oh, well, I sh'd *think!* Satan has fell a lot of times, but he hasn't ever been sent down permanent, yet—but only the small fry.

"Just the same it used to was, down on the earth, Sandy. Ain't it intresting? Go on. Slattery he got reinstated, as I understand it?"

Yes, so he did. And he was a considerable person by now, as I was a-saying, partly on accounts of his relative, and partly on accounts of him having been abroad, and all that, and affecting to talk with a foreign accent, which he picked up down below. So he was around when the first attempts was made. They had a mould for a man, and a mould for a woman, and they mixed up the materials and poured it in. They come out very handsome to look at, and everybody said it was a success. So they made some more, and kept on making them and setting them one side to dry, till they had about ten thousand. Then they blew in the breath, and put the dispositions in, and turned them loose in a pleasant piece of territory, and told them to go it.

"Put in the *dispositions?*"

Yes, The *Moral Qualities.* That's what makes disposition. They distributed 'em around perfectly fair and honorable. There was 28 of them, according to the plans and specifications, and the whole 28 went to each man and woman in equal measure, nobody getting more of a quality than anybody else, nor less. I'll give you the list, just as Slattery give it to me:

1. Magnanimity.	2. Meanness.
3. Moral courage—	4. Moral cowardice.
5. Physical courage.	6. Physical cowardice.
7. Honesty. . . .	8. Dishonesty.
9. Truthfulness. . .	10. Untruthfulness.
11. Love	12. Hate.
13. Chastity.	14. Unchastity.
15. Firmness. . . .	16. Unfirmness.
17. Diligence . . .	18. Indolence.
19. Selfishness . . .	20. Unselfishness.
21. Prodigality	22. Stinginess.
23. Reverence	24. Irreverence.
25. Intellectuality . . .	26. Unintellectuality.
27. Self-Conceit.	28. Humility.

"And a mighty good layout, Sandy. And all fair and square, too; and no favors to anybody. I like it. Looks to me elegant, and the way it had ought to be. Blamed if it ain't intresting. Go on."

Well, the new creatures settled in the territory that was app'inted for them, and begun to hatch, and multiply and replenish, and all that, and everything went along to the queen's taste, as the saying is. But by and by Slattery noticed something, and got Satan to go out there and take a look, which he done, and says,

"Well, something the matter, you think? What is it?"

"I'll show you," Slattery says. "Warn't they to be something fresh, something new and surprising?"

"Cert'nly," Satan says, "Ain't they?"

"Oh, well," says Slattery, "if you come right down to the fine shades, I ain't able to deny that they *are* new—but *how* new? That's the idea? Moreover, what I want to know is, what's now an *improvement?*"

"Go on," says Satan, a little impatient, "what's your point? Get at it!"

"Well, it's this. These new people don't differ from the angels. Except that they hain't got wings, and they don't get sick, and they don't die. Otherwise they're just angels—just the old usual thing. They're all the same size, they're all exactly alike—hair, eyes, noses, gait, everything—just the same as angels. Now, then, here's the point: The only solitary new thing about 'em is a new arrangement of their morals. It's the only fresh thing."

"Very well," says Satan, "ain't that enough? What are you complaining about?"

"No, it *ain't* enough, unless it's an improvement over the old regular arrangement."

"Come, get down to particulars!" says Satan, in that snappish way some people has.

"All right. Look at the old arrangement, and what do you find? Just this: the entire and complete and rounded-out sum of an angel's morals is *goodness*—plain, simple *goodness.* What's his equipment—a great long string of Moral Qualities with 28 specifications in it? No, there's only one—*Love.* It's the whole outfit. They can't hate, they don't know how, becuz they can't help loving everything and everybody. Just the same, they don't know anything about envy, or jealousy, or avarice, or meanness, or lying, or selfishness, or *any* of those things. And so they're never unhappy, there not being any way for them to *get* unhappy. It makes *character,* don't it? And A-1."

"Correct. Go on."

"Now then, look at these new creatures. They've got an immense layout in the way of Moral Qualities, and you'd think they'd have a stunning future in front of them—but it ain't so. For why? Because they've got Love *and* Hate, in the same proportions. The one neutralizes the other. They don't really love, and they don't really hate! They *can't*, you see. It's the same with the whole invoice: Honesty and Dishonesty, exactly the same quantity of each; selfishness and unselfishness; reverence and irreverence; courage and cowardice—and so on and so on. They are all exactly alike, inside and out, these new people—and *characterless*. They're ciphers, nothings, just wax-works. What do you say?"

"I see the point," says Satan. "The old arrangement was better."

Well, they got to talking around, and by and by others begun to see the point—and criticize. But not loud—only continuous. In about two hundred thousand years it got all around and come to be common talk everywheres. So at last it got to the Authorities.

"Would it take all that time, Sandy?"

"Here? Yes. It ain't long here, where a thousand years is as a day. It ain't six months, heavenly time. You've often noticed, in history, where the awful oppression of a nation has been going on eight or nine hundred years before Providence interferes, and everybody surprised at the delay. Providence *does* interfere, and mighty prompt, too, as you reconnize when you come to allow for the difference betwixt heavenly time and real time."

"By gracious I never thought of that before! I've been unfair to Providence a many and a many a time, but it was becuz I didn't think. Russia's a case in point; it looks like procasturation, but I see now, it ain't."

"Yes, you see, a thousand years earthly time, being exactly a day of heavenly time, then of course a year of earthly time is only just a shade over a minute of heavenly time; and if you don't keep these facts in mind you are naturally bound to think Providence is procrasturing when it's just the other way. It's on accounts of this ignorance that many and many a person has got the idea that prayer ain't ever answered, and stuck to it to his dying day; whereas, prayer is *always* answered. Take praying for rain, f'rinstance. The prayer comes up; Providence reflects a minute, judges it's all right, and says to the Secatry of State, "Turn it on." Down she comes, in a flood. But don't do any good of course, becuz it's a year late. Providence reflecting a minute has made all the trouble, you see. If people would only take the Bible at its word, and reconnize the difference betwixt heavenly time and earthly time, they'd pray for rain a year before they want it, and then they'd be all right. Prayer is always answered, but not inside of a year, becuz Providence has *got* to have a minute to reflect. Otherwise there'd be mistakes, on accounts of too much hurry."

"Why, Sandy, blamed if it don't make everything perfectly plain and understandable, which it never was before. Well, go on about what we was talking about."

"All right. The Authorities got wind of the talk, so They reckoned They would take a private view of them wax figures and see what was to be done. The end was, They concluded to start another Race, and do it better this time. Well, this was the Human Race."

"Wasn't the other the human race too, Sandy?"

"No. That one is neither one thing nor t'other. It ain't human because it's immortal; and it ain't any account, becuz everybody is just alike and hasn't any character. The Holy Doughnuts—that is what they're called, in private."

"Can we go and see them, some time, Sandy?" I says.

"Certn'ly. There's excursions every week-day. Well, the Authorities started out on the hypotheneuse that the thing to go for in the new race was *variety*. You see, that's where the Doughnuts failed. Now then, was the Human Race an easy job? Yes, sir, it was. They made rafts of moulds, this time, no two of them alike—so there's your *physical* differentiations, till you can't rest! Then all They had to do was to take the same old 28 Moral Qualities, and mix them up, helter-skelter, in all sorts of different proportions, and ladle them into the moulds—and there's your *dispositional* differentiations, b'George! *Variety?* Oh don't mention it! Slattery says to me, 'Sandy,' he says, 'this dreamy old quiet heaven of ourn has been asleep for ages, but if that Human Race didn't wake it up don't you believe *me* no more!'

"Wake it up? Oh, yes, that's what it done. Slattery says the Authorities was awful surprised when They come to examine that Human Race and see how careless They'd been in the distribution of them Qualities, and the results that was a-flowing from it.

"'Sandy,' he says, 'there wasn't any foreman to the job, nor any plan about the distributing. Anybody could help that wanted to; no instructions, only look out and provide *variety*. So these 'commodating volunteers would heave a dipperful of Hate into a mould and season it with a teaspoon of Love, and there's your *Murderer*, all ready for business. And into another mould they'd heave a teaspoonful of Chastity, and flavor it up with a dipperful of Unchastity—and so on and so on. A dipperful of Honesty and a spoonful of Dishonesty; a dipperful of Moral Courage and a spoonful of Moral Cowardice—

and there's your splendid man, ready to stand up for an unpopular cause and stake his life on it; in another mould they'd dump considerable Magnanimity, and then dilute it down with Meanness till there wasn't any strength left in it—and so on and so—the worst mixed-up mess of good and bad dispositions and half-good and half-bad ones a body could imagine—just a tagrag-and-bobtail Mob of nondescripts, and not worth propagating, of course; but what could the Authorities *do?* Not a thing. It was too late.' "

CAPTAIN SIMON WHEELER'S DREAM VISIT TO HEAVEN

During the summer of 1877, shortly after finishing with the proof of "Some Rambling Notes of an Idle Excursion," the story of his June trip to Bermuda with Joseph Twichell which included Ned Wakeman's story of "Isaac and the Prophets of Baal," Mark Twain plunged into a new project—a play entitled "Cap'n Simon Wheeler, The Amateur Detective." Immensely enthusiastic, he finished the piece in little more than two weeks. Unfortunately, however, he was never able to find a producer for his comic drama. Late in the following October, therefore, he followed William Dean Howells's suggestion that he turn the play into a novel.

At that time Howells also urged him to make the detective "as much like Capt. Wakeman as possible."

"Why not fairly and squarely retire an old sea-dog," he said, "and let him [take] to detecting in the ennui of the country. This is what you first tho't of doing, and I don't believe you can think of anything better" (*MTHL*, 1:207).

Though the Simon Wheeler in the unfinished novel resembles Clemens's brother Orion almost as much as he does Wakeman, he does emulate some of Wakeman's hearty ebullience. And, more important, his version of the dream visit to heaven near the end of the novel may well be closer to Wakeman's actual tale than Mark Twain's final rendering in "Captain Stormfield's Visit to Heaven." For, as Franklin Rogers has suggested (*S&B*, 432, n. 48), Mark Twain probably adapted Wheeler's account of his dream from the 1873 version of "Captain Stormfield's Visit to Heaven" mentioned in his letter to Orion of 23 March 1878 (see headnote to "Stormfield").

Here, then, is another description of a heavenly visit.

CAPTAIN SIMON WHEELER'S DREAM VISIT TO HEAVEN

The Captain had profound religious views, and their breadth equaled their profundity. He did not get his system from the pulpit, but thought it out for himself, after methods of his own. One may get an idea of it from a dream which he professed to have had once, and which he was very fond of telling about. Here it is, in *his* own language—

"I dreampt I died. I s'posed, of course, I was going to lay quiet when the rattle went out of my throat, and not know any more than if I was asleep. But it wasn't so. As I hove out the last gurgle, 'stead of settling down quiet, it was just as if I was shot off!—shot out of a gun, you understand! I whizzed along, head first, through the air, and when I looked back, in about a second, this earth was like a big, shining, brass ball, with maps engraved on it. But did it stay so? No sir! It shrunk together as fast as a soap bubble that is hanging to a pipe when you take your mouth away from the stem and let the air slip out. In another second it was nothing but a bright spark—and then it winked out! I went whizzing right along, millions of miles a minute. Dark? Dark ain't no name for it! There wasn't a thing to be seen. You can't imagine the awfulness of it. Says I to myself, 'Knowing what I know now, no friend of mine shall die with useless flowers in his hand if I can raise enough to buy him a lantern.' And cold? Nobody down here has any idea what real cold is.

"Well, pretty soon a great wave of gladness and gratitude went all through me because I glimpsed a little wee shiny speck away yonder in the blackness. But did it stay a speck? No, sir. It seemed to start straight for me, swelling as it came. In the time it took me to breathe three breaths it had swelled till it filled up the whole heavens and sent off prodigious red-hot wagon-wheel rays that stretched millions of miles beyond. And hot? People down here don't know what hot is. I shut my eyes—I couldn't stand the glare. Then I felt a great breath of wind and a sudden sound like *whoosh!* and I knew I'd passed her. I opened my eyes, and there she was, away yonder behind, withering up, paling down, cooling off—another second and she was a twinkling speck—one more instant and she was gone! Black again—black as ink—and I a-plowing along.

"Well, sir, I run across no end of these big suns—as many as half a million of them, I judge, with oceans of blackness between them, which shows you what a big scale things are got up there on—and I saw little specks sometimes that I didn't come near to, and every now and then a comet with a tail that I was as much as ten seconds passing—one as much as fifteen or twenty, I reckon—which shows you that we hain't ever seen any comets down here but seedlings, as you may say—sprouts—mere little pup-comets, so to speak. *You* won't ever know anything about what He can do till you have seen one of them grand old comets that's been finished and got its growth—one of them old long-handled fellows that he sweeps the cobwebs out of the far corners of His universe with.

"In the course of time—I should say it was about seven years—not short of seven, I know, and I think it was upwards of it—my speed begun to slacken up, and I came in sight of a white speck away off yonder. As it grew and grew, and spread itself all over everywhere and took up all the room, it turned out to be the loveliest land you can imagine. The most beautiful trees and lakes and rivers—nothing down here like them—nothing that begins with them at all. And the soft air! and the fragrance! and the music that came from you couldn't tell where! Ah that music!—you talk about music down here! It shows what you know about it.

"Well, I slacked up and slacked up, and by and by I landed. There was millions of people moving along—more different kinds of people, and more different kinds of clothes, and talking more different kinds of languages than I had ever heard of before. They were going toward a great high wall that you couldn't see the end of, away yonder in the plain. It was made of jewels, I reckon, because it dazzled you so you couldn't look steady at it. I joined in with these people and by and by we got to the wall. There was a glittering archway in it as much as a mile high, and under it was standing such a noble, beautiful Personage!—and with such a gentle face, when you could look at it. But you couldn't, much, because it shone so.

"I ranged up alongside the arch to watch and listen and find out what was agoing on, but I kept ruther shady, because I had old clothes on, but mainly because I was beginning to feel uneasy. Says I to myself, 'This is heaven, I judge, and what if I've been preparing myself on a wrong system all this time!' I listened, and my spirits begun to drop pretty fast.

"The people were filing in, all the time, mind you, and I a-watching with all my eyes. A mild-faced old man's turn came and he stepped forward. He had on a shad-belly coat. The Beautiful Personage looked at him ever so kindly, and in a low voice that was the sweetest music you ever heard, he says to him—

" 'Name, please?'

" 'Abel Hopkins,' says the old man.

" 'Where from, please?'

" 'Philadelphia,' says the old man.

" 'Denomination, please?'

("That word made me shiver, I can tell you. I felt my religious system caving from under me.)

" 'Quaker,' says the old man.

" 'Papers, please?' says the Beautiful Personage.

("I felt some more of my system cave from under me, and my spirits were lower than ever.)

"The Beautiful Personage took the papers and run his eye over them, and then says to the old man—

" 'Correct. Do you see that band of people away in yonder, gathered together? Go there and spend a blissful eternity with them, for you have been a good servant, and great is your reward. But do not wander from that place, which has been set apart forever for your people.'

"The Quaker passed in and I glanced my eye in and saw millions and millions of human beings gathered in monstrous masses as far as I could see—each denomination in a bunch by itself.

"A wild-looking, black-skinned man stepped up next, with a striped robe on, and a turban. Says the Beautiful Personage—

" 'Name, please?'

" 'Hassan Ben Ali.'

" 'Where from, please?'

" 'The deserts of Arabia.'

" 'Denomination, please?'

" 'Mohammedan.'

" 'Papers, please?'

"He examined the papers, and says—

" 'Correct. Do you see that vast company of people under the palm trees away yonder? Join them and be happy forever. But do not wander from them and trespass upon the domains of the other redeemed.'

"Next an English Bishop got in; then a Chinaman that said he was Bhuddist; then a Catholic priest from Spain and a Freewill Baptist from New Jersey, and next a Persian Fire-eater and after him a Scotch Presbyterian. Their papers were all right, and they were distributed around, where they belonged, and entered into their eternal rest.

"Not a soul had gone in on my system, yet. I had been a-hoping and hoping, feebler and feebler, but my heart was clear down and my hopes all gone, at last. I was feeling so mean and ashamed and low-spirited that I couldn't bear to look on at those people's good luck any longer; and I begun to be afraid I might be noticed and hauled up, presently, if I laid around there much longer. —So I slunk back and ducked my head and was just going to sneak off behind the crowd, when I couldn't help glancing back to get one more little glimpse of the Beautiful Personage so as to keep it in my memory always and be to me in the place of heaven—but I'd made a mistake. His eye was on me. His finger was up. I stopped in my tracks, and my legs trembled under me.—I was caught in the act. He beckoned with his finger, and I went forward—you see there wasn't any other way. The Beautiful Personage looked at me, a-trembling there, a moment or two, and then he says, low and sweet, the same as ever—

" 'Name please?'

" 'Simon Wheeler, your honor,' says I, and tried to bow, and dropped my hat.

" 'Where from?'—just as mild and gentle as ever.

" 'I—well, I ain't from any particular place, your honor—been knocked about a good deal, mostly in the show business, your honor—because, on account of hard luck I couldn't help it—but I am sorry, and if your honor will let me go, just this once, I—'

" 'Denomination, please?'

"He said it just as ca'm and sweet as ever, and I bowed—and bowed again—and tried to get my hat, but it rolled between my feet, and I says—scared most to death—I says—

" 'I didn't know any better, your honor, but I was ignorant and wicked, and I didn't know the right way, your honor, and I went a-blundering along and loving everybody just alike, niggers and Injuns and Presbyterians and Irish, and taking to them more and more the further and further I went in my evil ways—and so . . . so . . . if your honor would *only* let me go back just this one time, I—'

" 'Papers?' says he, just as soft and gentle as ever.

"I had got my hat, but my fingers shook so I couldn't hold onto it and it dropped again. The perspiration was rolling down my face, and it didn't seem to me I could get breath enough together to live. When that awful question come, I just gave up everything, and dropped on my knees and says—

" 'Have pity on a poor ignorant foolish man, your honor, that has come in his wicked blindness without a denomination, without one scrap of a paper, without'—

" 'Rise up, Simon Wheeler! The gates of heaven stand wide to welcome you! Range its barred commonwealths as free as the angels, brother and comrade of all its nations and peoples,—for the whole broad realm of the blest is your home!' "

Captain Wheeler had a voice like a man-o'-warsman, and he always brought out that closing passage with the roar and crash of a thunder-peal.

A SINGULAR EPISODE: THE RECEPTION OF REV. SAM JONES IN HEAVEN

Mark Twain probably wrote his account of this "Singular Episode" between sieges of rheumatism and other illnesses in Germany during the fall and winter of 1891. The most reliable direct evidence for the date of composition occurs in a note the author made while planning a eulogy for his daughter Susy, following her death in August 1896. Considering her reactions to certain of his literary efforts, he asked in part: "What was her opinion of Capt. Stormfield's Visit to Heaven? . . . . & 'The Reception of Rev. Sam Jones in Heaven' (written in Berlin in 1891 & still in MS.)" [Notebook 39, TS, p. 55, MTP].

He could have written the piece sometime between 16 October, when he braved the discomfort of his recurrent rheumatism to write Fred Hall—his arm was "howling," he said—and 8 November when he wrote again, complaining that writing only half a page gave him hours of pain (Clemens to Hall, *MTLP*, 285, 291). If not then, he probably squeezed it in sometime after mid November, between sessions devoted to completing several travel letters and to proofreading others for S. S. McClure's newspaper syndicate.

Early January saw the Clemenses off on a week's visit to Ilsenberg in the Hartz Mountains, and shortly after their return the author again took to his bed with "a mixture of influenza and congestion of the lungs," which incapacitated him until the family left for Menton, France, on the Riviera, about the first of March (*MTLP*, 301–7). Therefore, November or December 1891 seems the most likely time of composition. The first line of the story, "It was the year 1897," was added later, perhaps on one of the occasions when Clemens read the story to friends.

In later years Clemens said that the story of Sam Jones's reception in heaven was based on a dream that he himself had had (Sixty-seventh Birthday Dinner Speech, 28 November 1902, *MTS*, 455). Possibly, but not probably. A few years earlier, on 17 July 1895, Twain made a notation: "Ring in modification of Sam Jones in heaven—call it a dream" (Notebook 35, TS, p. 20, MTP). Very likely the stimulus for this story was closely related to his fondness for "Captain Stormfield's Visit to Heaven," as the linkage in his note of 1896 might suggest.

Though the story itself deals more with the results of "Mark Twain's" switching tickets with the Archbishop of Canterbury, the boorish boastings of "the Reverend Sam Jones" determine the final action. Here the inspiration was furnished by the career of Samuel Porter Jones (1847–1906), one of the most famous evangelists of his own or any other era. Alabama-born, Jones moved to Kentucky during the Civil War, set up as a lawyer, took to drink, and wound up a common day laborer. In 1872, having promised his dying father that he would reform, he was "converted," and became an itinerant preacher for the West Georgia Conference of the Methodist Episcopal Church, South. Soon his vigor, humor, and ability to talk with the common man on his own level won him a wide reputation. In January 1885 he was hired for a time for evangelical work in Brooklyn by T. DeWitt Talmage, another of Mark Twain's occasional targets (see *Captain Stormfield's Visit to Heaven;* "About Smells" in *WIM*, 48–50; and "The Second Advent" in *FM*, 50–68). From 1886 to 1900 he conducted crusades in almost all the major cities, often attracting crowds of more than ten thousand. As the *Dictionary of American Biography* notes, although his "exaggerations and crudities always offended the sensitive," so that the popular press often attacked him, he nevertheless remained extremely popular—"perhaps the foremost American public speaker of his generation."

Though Mark Twain was very fond of "A Singular Episode," it was not published during his lifetime. Olivia evidently put her foot down, probably deeming the sketch too disrespectful toward the Archbishop of Canterbury, among other features. On the top of the first page of the manuscript, the author himself wrote, at one point: "Not published—forbidden by Mrs. Clemens. SLC." Alfred Bigelow Paine contends that when Livy refused to allow publication, Mark Twain sought to avoid the injunction by laboriously translating the sketch into German, with the hope of publishing it surreptitiously. But his conscience apparently caused him to confess, whereupon even the German version, titled "Das Abenteuer des Hochwürdiger Sam Jones," was suppressed (*MTB*, 3:1, 430–31).

Although publication was banned, Clemens occasionally entertained friends and acquaintances with readings of the tale. In April 1895, on the way home from France, he told it at a shipboard gathering, and the next day reported the occasion to Henry H. Rogers. "Something prompted me to risk telling my dream about my trip to heaven and hell with Rev. Sam Jones and the Archbishop of Canterbury—and I did it. It was good fun—but just scandalous. When Mrs. Clemens finds out there will be a scalp lacking in the Clemens family" (Clemens to Rogers, 3 April 1895, *MTHHR*, 135). One wonders how much of the account of Livy's alleged horror was for show on this occasion, for a year earlier the humorist himself had reported to his wife that he had read "Rev. Sam Jones's Reception in Heaven" to a group of about twenty personal friends of Rogers's daughter Cara (Mrs. Bradford Duff) at the Oriental Hotel, Manhattan Beach, New York,—"& we had a gay time over it" (Clemens to Olivia, 22 July 1894, *LLMT*, 305). Livy's reaction is not recorded.

Besides summarizing the story again for his audience at his sixty-seventh birthday dinner in November 1902, he found an important occasion to refer to the piece again late in November 1907 when he concluded that "Sam Jones's Reception," by means of "mental telegraphy," may have inspired Bernard Shaw's idea for "Aerial Football," which had appeared in *Collier's Weekly* for 23 November (see "Mental Telegraphy?" in this volume). The fact that in "Mental Telegraphy?" Mark Twain refers to the piece as "The *Late* Rev. Sam Jones's Reception in Heaven" (italics ours) suggests that he knew of the great to-do that accompanied the evangelist's death in 1906. And perhaps the appearance of *The Life and Sayings of Sam P. Jones* (by the minister's wife) in 1907 helped stimulate the humorist's memory of having featured Sam in the visit to heaven "seventeen years ago."

A SINGULAR EPISODE: THE RECEPTION OF REV. SAM JONES IN HEAVEN

It was the year 1897.

It had been a long, weary journey, and even in my sleep I was conscious of being almost willing to have it come to an end. Of course not quite willing—considering the fate that was before me; that could not be expected. The long howl of the whistle bored its way into my drowsing ear, now, and as I came to myself the brakeman put his head in at the door and shouted the fatal words which so many of us had been daily expecting and dreading for many sad months:

"Noo-o-o Jer-roo-saLEM! Parties going through to Sheol please keep your seats, the rest step forward into the next car."

The misery in my heart was so heavy, so dull, so rayless, that the possibility of escape was an idea which could not have occurred to me. Yet escape was actually within my reach, as I perceived in the next moment! My former seatmate was gone, and in his place sat a stranger of a most noble and benignant mien, tranquilly sleeping—a stranger whom I recognized without difficulty, from his published portraits: it was the Archbishop of Canterbury. He was traveling on a pass—a special illuminated, gilt-edged personal pass—and had it in his hatband; for people with that kind of passes are easily tempted by the human nature in them to expose their high fortune to the view of the less fortunate. I had a pass too—also of a special and personal sort, but it was not the kind that one exhibits wantonly. With a feeling of humble and sincere gratitude I traded passes with the sleeper and moved into the forward car.

The train stopped, presently, and I stepped out onto the platform with the rest, but failed to get away in my turn, for a small person, clothed in a loud south-western costume, with a quid in his cheek and his wide-brimmed slouch hat tilted over his ear, elbowed me aside brusquely and went swaggering ashore whooping and screeching hosannahs like a demon.

But I was next, and glad I was to stand in the opaline glow of the pearly gates and realize that I was really there, though not expected. Only one person came from that other car. It was my substitute. I could not look him in the face, for at bottom I felt that my conduct had been doubtful. He stepped forward with a confidence which was pathetic to see, and turned his head about, this way and that, to let his pass be remarked—which it was, but the result was not reverence, but levity. That is, among the angels and other bystanders; St. Peter was not amused. To his mind this intrusion was a jest of poor quality and out of place. His manner was very cold. He said sternly to the Archbishop—

"Return to the train, sir. Professional humorists are not allowed here."

The unfortunate prelate was surprised and hurt. He drew himself up and said with some stiffness—

"It is evident that your Excellency does not recognize me. Permit me"—and he reached up for his pass and handed it to the offended saint with a barely perceptible bow. St. Peter made no motion to take it, but said with severity—

"Excuse me; although I do not recognize you, sir, I recognize your *nom de plume* with quite sufficient certainty, and must require you to make an end of this extraordinary impertinence and return at once to your train."

"My *nom de plume!* Pardon me; Archbishop of Canterbury is a title, not a *nom de plume.*" This with a frozen bow.

It was all that St. Peter could do to keep his hands off him.

"This is *too* much! That a person of your frivolous nature and profane instincts should conceive and carry out the daring jest of venturing across these sacred bounds was enough—quite enough; that you should add the affront of masquerading as an illustrious prelate whom all heaven is impatiently waiting for and expecting to arrive today is—is—water!—give me water, before I choke!"

These words did not merely astonish the Archbishop, they stupified him. He stood a moment or two like one in a dream, his eyes wandering vacantly about and resting nowhere; until at last they fell by chance upon the brimstone-tinted pass in his hand; then he murmured in a piteous voice, and as one distraught—

"Mark Twain?—Mark Twain? Alas, there has been some mistake."

Ah, he was humble, now, very humble, poor soul, and was about to plead with St. Peter to have pity on him and hear him try to account for the questionable situation he was in, but just at this point the riotous blatherskite from the south-west came hosannahing up and shouldered him out of the way, shrieking exultantly—

"Glory and amen, old Sam's *got* there!—hey, boys?" and he swept the circle of angels and elect with a joyous eye. To the Chief of the Apostles he exclaimed in his great voice, "*Know* me, hey?—I *bet* you do! Old Sam Jones—*Reverend* Sam Jones—old iron-bound brass-mounted copper-bellied hell-smiter and Satan's-terror from the wilds of Texas! Shake!"

St. Peter shuddered, and kept his hand to himself. He said in his chill official voice—

"Exhibit your credentials, sir."

The man got his railroad ticket out of his wallet, and the Apostle slowly and pains-takingly read the details on its back, reflected a good while, then read them again. He called an expert. The expert made a patient and particular examination and ended by pronouncing the ticket regular, also genuine. It was easy to see that St. Peter was disappointed and annoyed. He said to the expert—

"Can't you find *any* defect?"

"No, your Excellency; as far as the bald and sterile *letter* goes, it meets the requirements. There are several precedents; he will have to be accepted."

"Very well, then"—to the applicant—"you can enter. Wait—not here; go around the back way. And take off your arctics. Another thing: gag yourself until you are out of my hearing—this is not Texas. One of you go and show him where he can wash. Next!" He turned, and saw the Archbishop of Canterbury starting for the train; he was touched, and said, gently: "Wait, poor clown; come back and sit down. I will look into your case presently, and give you every chance; and if you can prove that a mistake has been made I will let you in."

The Archbishop turned about eagerly—then stopped, hesitated a moment and said, with some little embarrassment in his manner—

"You are very kind—and indeed I thank your Excellency; but is—is he—going to remain?"

"Who?"

"He. The—the person from Texas."

"Why—well—he—well, the fact is—but *you* see how we are situated."

"Yes, I am afraid I do, your Excellency. I believe I will not tarry. Adieu!"

The conductor shouted—

"All aboard for Sheol!" and the train went spinning away. All its other passengers were crying, but the Archbishop was calm. I heard St. Peter mutter, absently—

"That is no humorist, that is a man of a sound cold judgment. In my opinion there has been a mistake here somewhere. Come—just wait a moment, please. Who are *you?*" This to me, impatiently. It was a little sudden, and not altogether pleasant for me, for I was trying to glide in without verifying. I answered, with dignity, that I was the late Archbishop of Canterbury. That caught *him* a little sudden, but he used his miraculous powers and so nothing happened. *Others* laughed, though; that is, I suspected it was that at bottom, although to all outward appearances it was only a general outbreak of coughing. I have seen that kind of coughing before, and do not consider that there is anything either generous or polite about it. I was required to exhibit my credentials—my pass—and did it. There was a tedious long examination of it, and every effort made, as it seemed to me, to find something crooked about it. Meantime several angels talked me over in a quite free way, using the Chinese language, under the impression that I could not understand them. They spoke it very well, though with a slight foreign accent—a heavenly accent, and quite pretty. One said he would not have taken me for an Archbishop. Another said no, he wouldn't either—thought I looked pretty rocky. A third said it was a pity such unusual preparations had been made—they seemed hardly worth the candle. No. 1 said yes, the public were going to be disappointed in me, if he knew the tastes of the heavenly hosts, and he thought he did. No. 2 made a disparaging remark about the Texan rioter, coupling it with a like remark about me, and said it appeared to be a cold day for recruits. No. 3 said it was a grave mistake to let such characters in, it lowered the tone of the place *another* thirty or forty degrees. No. 2 thought the same; there had long been a growing complaint and dissatisfaction about this sort of thing; in the opinion of some, the society of the other place was already preferable in some respects to the society here, on account of the presence among us of Pope Alexander VI, and Torquemada, and Catherine de' Medici and a too liberal number of others like them—and *now!* why these two break the record! Yes, No. 1 said, there had been ominous mutterings this long time; in his opinion there would be open revolt now; indeed he should not be surprised to see the better classes emigrate. This embarrassing and ill-bred talk was still going on when the expert announced that my ticket was undeniably straight; whereupon St. Peter said to me with much unfriendliness in his tone—

"You can enter in, sir, I am not able to help it; but if I could have had my way I would have made short work of you and that Texan bandit."

I was there a week, and I pledge my word that I led a modest and inoffensive life and did the best I could to please the people; but they were prejudiced and said I had always been a light speaker and they could not abide such things. Now in sober truth I never had said anything half as bad as some ministers had been allowed to say and no fault found. But there was just the difference—I was a layman, you see, and not privileged to blaspheme; coarse speeches were permissible in some mouths, but not in all.

Sam Jones was preaching and exhorting and carrying on all the time, and in the sincerest and most heartfelt way, too, but it was in language that made the place fairly shudder; so the dissatisfaction was immediate and pronounced. Even the papal Borgias were revolted. The exodus began on the Monday morning early; there was a panic, and a universal break for the under-world. When the gates closed, Saturday night, the Texan had the place all to himself.

[signed] *Mark Twain*

MENTAL TELEGRAPHY?

At an evening gathering early in November 1907, Mark Twain heard one of the guests—probably either Robert Collier, son of the publisher of *Collier's Weekly*, or the magazine's editor Norman Hapgood—read George Bernard Shaw's story "Aerial Football: the New Game," soon to appear in *Collier's* (23 November 1907, 11–13). Both Collier and Hapgood were good friends with whom Mark Twain often exchanged dinner invitations. Twain also knew and admired Shaw, who was one of the first persons he met on arriving in England the previous June to receive his honorary D.Litt. degree from Oxford. Early in July, too, Shaw had entertained him at luncheon at the dramatist's flat in Adelphi Terrace.

Mark Twain had long been interested in the phenomena of thought transference. He often recorded personal experiences in his notebooks and in the 1890s included a number of them in two *Harper's Monthly* articles, "Mental Telegraphy" (December 1891) and "Mental Telegraphy Again" (September 1895). The very day after the reading, then, Twain looked to what is now called mental telepathy to account for the similarities to his own work that he saw in Shaw's story of the arrival in heaven of Mrs. Hairns, a dissipated charwoman, and her sometime employer, the rather haughty Bishop of St. Pancras.

Besides showing Mark Twain's continued interest in mental telepathy, as well as in Shaw himself, "Mental Telegraphy?" provides important information regarding the composition of both "Captain Stormfield's Visit to Heaven" and "A Singular Episode: The Reception of Rev. Sam Jones in Heaven."

"Mental Telegraphy?" was first published by Ray B. Browne in *Mark Twain's Quarrel with Heaven* (117–19) and reprinted, along with Shaw's "Aerial Football: the New Game," by Rodelle Weintraub, in " 'Mental Telegraphy?': Mark Twain on G.B.S.," *Shaw Review*, 17, no. 9 (May 1974): 68–77.

MENTAL TELEGRAPHY?

It really looks like it. Last night I listened with great and peculiar interest to the reading of a sketch by Bernard Shaw which is about to appear in Collier's Weekly. It was an account of the translation to heaven of a dissipated old woman of the hard-working class, and some of her experiences there.

Once I wrote an account of the translation to heaven of an uneducated and uncultivated old seaman, and certain of his experiences there. This was thirty or forty years ago. I began the article forty or forty-one years ago, as a good-natured satire upon "The Gates Ajar," a book which everybody was reading in those days, but I did not finish it. Twelve or fifteen years later I finished it and read it to Mr. Howells, who wanted it published, and said he believed Dean Stanley would shore it up with an introduction. But I pigeon-holed it. Now and then, as the years and decades drifted by, I took out the article and glanced through it with an eye to printing it, but always concluded to wait a while longer, and let it finish ripening.

Several months ago I examined it again. It seemed to be about ripe, so I sent it to Harper's Monthly for the Christmas number, labeling it "Captain Stormfield's Visit to Heaven." Three weeks ago I read and revised the proofs, and struck out one or two of the Captain's adventures, and by to-day the magazine is printed and waiting for delivery-day. Last night Mr. Shaw's article reminded me, several times, of my own, particularly in treatment—a flowing, free-handed treatment, not much embarrassed by shop-worn conventions. This resemblance, taken by itself, could not suggest mental-telegraphic origin, but there were several striking details that did strongly suggest it. So I said, "Mr. Shaw must have gotten those incidents out of my head when I was in England last summer, by thought-transference, for there was no talk of my article, and neither it nor any detail of it was mentioned to him."

But suppose those incidents were *not* in my article—what then? Upon reflection I found that that was indeed the case—they were not there, and to my sorrow the pleasant mental-telegraphy theory began to crumble to ruin. I say to my regret, because ever since a certain remarkable episode of about 1875 (recounted in one of my books), I have been a confirmed and stubborn believer in mental telegraphy—the unconscious transference of inventions, ideas, phrases, paragraphs, chapters, and even entire books, from mind to mind—so strong a believer in it, indeed, that I am now not able to believe that I often originate ideas in my mind but get almost all of them out of somebody else's by unconscious and uninvited thought-transference.

As I have said, there were incidents in Mr. Shaw's article which I recognized as mine, yet they were not in "Captain Stormfield's Visit to Heaven:" where, then, were they? The answer pleasantly dawned dimly above the horizon of my memory, then rose bright and clear: they were in a never-printed extravaganza which I wrote in Germany seventeen years ago, entitled "The Late Rev. Sam Jones's Reception in Heaven." And so my tottering mental-telegraphy edifice stiffened promptly up, from cellar to lightning-rod.

I was ever so fond of that "Reception" article, and dearly wanted to print it, but it was hilarious and extravagant to the very verge of impropriety, and I could not beguile my wife into consenting to its publication. In that day Sam Jones was sweeping the South like a cyclone with his revival meetings, and converting the unconverted here and there and everywhere with his thundering torrents of piety and slang. I represented him as approaching the New Jerusalem in the through express, and in the same pullman in which he and his feet together were occupying two chairs, sat his grace the late Archbishop of Canterbury (Mr. Tait), and I.

ETIQUETTE FOR THE AFTERLIFE: ADVICE TO PAINE

Early in April 1910, Albert Bigelow Paine, worried about reports of recurring bouts with severe chest pains—Clemens had been suffering periodically from *angina pectoris* for some time—went to Bermuda to accompany his ailing employer home. When Paine arrived, Clemens presented him with this advice for appropriate behavior in the afterlife, the last substantial bit of writing he would ever do. The pair left Bermuda on 12 April, arrived in New York on the fourteenth, and traveled directly to Redding, Connecticut, where Clemens died at Stormfield exactly a week later.

Though Paine included several paragraphs of this piece in the *Biography* (3:1, 566–67), this is the first appearance of the whole. By subject, and because it is presumably Mark Twain's last piece of writing, it forms a fitting close to the "Heaven" section of this volume. Some of its details reflect those in "Captain Stormfield's Visit to Heaven," notably the mother's loss of a daughter, and others echo the satire of "Letters from the Earth," written a year earlier. We have added the initial phrase of the title to clarify the content.

ETIQUETTE FOR THE AFTERLIFE:

ADVICE TO PAINE†

In hell it is not good form to refer, even unostentatiously, to your relatives in heaven, if persons are present who have none there.

Upon arrival in heaven do not speak to St. Peter until spoken to. It is not your place to begin.

Do not begin any remark with "*Say.*" It is vulgar. Call him "Hochwohlgeborene." To *start* with. After that, say "sir."

Wait patiently in the queue till it comes your turn to apply for a ticket. Do not look bored, and don't scratch your shin with your other foot.

When applying for a ticket, avoid trying to make conversation. St. Peter is hard-worked and has no time for conversation. If you *must* talk, let the weather alone. St. Peter cares not a damn for the weather. And don't ask him what time the 4:30 train goes; there aren't any trains in heaven, except the through-trains for the other place, and the less information you get about them, the better for you.

Don't tell him you used to have an uncle named after him, "maybe you have met him." He is tired of that.

You can ask him for his autograph—there is no harm in that—but be careful and don't remark that it is one of the penalties of greatness. He has heard *that* before.

Do not try to show off. St. Peter dislikes it. The simpler you are dressed, the better it will please him. He cannot abide showy costumes. Above all things, avoid *over*-dressing. A pair of spurs and a fig-leaf is a plenty.

Do not try to Kodak him. Hell is full of people who have made that mistake.

If you get in——If you get in—don't tip him. That is, publicly. Don't *hand* it to him, just leave a quarter on the bench by him, and let on you forgot it. If he bites it to see if it is good, you are not to seem to notice it.

Leave your dog outside. Heaven goes by favor. If it went by merit, you would stay out and the dog would go in.

Keep off the grass.

Always observe the forms of etiquette. Whenever you meet the redeemed, pay no heed unless they salute; but always when you meet angels, uncover and make a bow.

If you get seasick and feel you *must* go and lean over the bulwarks, don't *do* it, for those poor damned people down below have enough to bear without that.

When you meet a friend, don't volunteer to call on the rest of the family; it could be embarrassing. Just wait. If the man forgets to invite you, or casually remarks that the family are off on vacation, drop the matter right there, don't say a word. You can rely upon it the family are where they don't need any snowshoes.

Be always kind, always forgiving—let bygones be bygones. Send the Lyon-Ashcrofts a fan.

Explain to Helen why I don't come. If you can.

Sunday afternoons, when you go with the rest of the redeemed to lean over the balusters and see the little unbaptised Presbyterian and Roman Catholic children roasting in the red fires, don't *crowd;* remember, others want to see, as well as you. And you must rub your hands together, and laugh a little, and let on to enjoy it; otherwise people will suspect you are not as good a Christian as you look, and you will get talked about, and perhaps avoided. If a mother wants to look down and see her child, give her your place. When she remembers how she used to hug that little creature to her breast and smother it with kisses, she will have a great pain at her heart; and if it recognizes her and joyfully puts up its hands to her believing she will fly to its help, caring nothing for the flames of hell and all the devils if she can but rescue it, lay your hands quickly upon her or she will throw herself over the baluster to join her child; and once in hell she can get back to heaven no more. In fact she will not *want* to get back among any such human refuse.

You will be wanting to slip down at night and smuggle water to those poor little chaps, but don't you try it. You would be caught, and nobody in heaven would respect you after that.

Play no jokes—it isn't the place for humor. Once a joker surreptitiously placed this legend over the pearly gate: "Who enters here leaves his heart behind: but it doesn't matter, he won't have any use for it in *this* place." Ah, where is that joker now? Look over the balusters and you will see.

Be very careful about etiquette when invited to dinner. For evening dress, leave off your spurs.

Angels are in a class by themselves, and much higher than you. Do not try to look like an angel; it will not deceive.

By and by, if you behave, they will give you a halo. The most of them are flimsy and will not wear; but if you are good you will get one with a rubber tire.†

Letters from the Earth

LETTERS FROM THE EARTH

In a letter of 13 November 1909 to Elizabeth Wallace, a friend, from Stormfield, his home near Redding, Connecticut, Mark Twain revealed both his delight in and his concerns about a project that was to be his last substantial work:

> Dear Betsy,— .... I've been writing "Letters from the Earth," and if you will come here and see us I will—what? Put the MS in your hands, with the places to skip marked? No. I won't trust you quite that far. I'll read messages [*sic,* should read "passages"] to you. This book will never be published—in fact it couldn't be, because it would be felony to soil the mails with it, for it has much Holy Scripture in it of the kind that ... can't properly be read aloud, except from the pulpit and in family worship. Paine enjoys it, but Paine is going to be damned one of these days, I suppose (*MTL,* 2:833–34).

Though the "Letters" remained unfinished, they represent in many ways a summation or synthesis of Mark Twain's musings on the perplexing theological matters that he had been dabbling with for nearly forty years. The dramatic opening sequence presents a scathing creation myth, portraying God as an absent-minded scientist, Satan as a skeptic, and humanity as a botched experiment. And the work as a whole remains as Mark Twain's final word on God, the Bible, the world, human nature, and the paradoxical and contradictory religious beliefs of the human race.

The "Letters" thus contain the one common element missing from all of the earlier Genesis-based materials: a coherent account of creation that can provide more than the standard biblical account. The variability of time and the effects of perceiving time differently lead Twain toward the first key element in the development of a creation myth: the apprehension of an otherness with powers and forces beyond earthly dimensions. A result of such a different time perception is that the limitations imposed temporally on human existence do not affect the reasoning powers of "celestial beings." In the eyes of Twain's celestial beings, the human life span is absurdly brief, hardly sufficient to develop any kind of perspective on existence.

The second key element in the development of a coherent creation myth here is the sense of the moral foundation of the world being created. Twain's development of the moral dimension of the world is shaped precisely through the revelation of the distortions created by the temporal schism between heaven and earth. Morality is shaped by the creation of sin and the experience of death, and it is distorted, in Twain's eyes, by the impossibly immediate juxtaposition of these two elements.

Mark Twain had earlier introduced the notion of the different concepts of heavenly and earthly time in "Schoolhouse Hill," one of the so-called "Mysterious Stranger" manuscripts. There, Quarante-quatre, a son of Satan, explicitly defines the ratio of time between the two realms, though the mathematics involved are not quite accurate:

> "I was born before Adam's fall—"
>
> "Wh-at!"
>
> "It seems to surprise you. Why?"
>
> "Because it caught me unprepared, and because it is six thousand years ago, and you look to be only fifteen years old."
>
> "True—that is my age, within a fraction."
>
> "Only fifteen, and yet—"
>
> "Counting by *our* system of measurement, I mean—not yours."
>
> "How is that?"
>
> "A day with us is as a thousand years with you."
>
> Hotchkiss was awed. A seriousness which was near to solemnity settled upon his face. After a meditative pause he said—
>
> "Surely it cannot be that you really and not figuratively mean—"
>
> "Yes—really, not figuratively. A minute of our time is 41 $\frac{2}{3}$ years of yours. By our system of measurement I am fifteen years old; but by yours

I am five million, lacking twenty thousand years" (see appendix 6 for the full text of the relevant chapter 5 of "Schoolhouse Hill").

Twain had also suggested this notion in "From Captain Stormfield's Reminiscences," one of the late passages from "Stormfield" (written probably in 1906). The whole of "Captain Stormfield's Visit to Heaven" had posited a sense of illimitable space, so vast that the human imagination could not comprehend it. Now in that chapter Twain introduced a similar vast difference between earthly and heavenly time.

In introducing this concept into the "Creation of Man" sequence in "Letters from the Earth," then, Twain declared three centuries of celestial time to be the equivalent of a hundred million years of earthly time to account for the creative evolution from stars to planets to life forms. Thus, because of the differences between celestial time and earthly time, the Creator, interested in this new experiment with humans and animals, cannot be concerned with, or even understand, the limited perceptions resulting from the brief life span of human beings, especially as it involved their creation and the various elements of their nature.

But whereas the segment in "Stormfield" came about as just one of many episodes in Captain Stormfield's celestial adventure, in "Letters from the Earth" the concept became essential to the attempt to create a coherent creation myth. Here the Creator, from his lofty throne, envisions an experiment in which the universe would be governed by an immutable Law of Nature, the Law of God. In one flash he creates Man, who would be an amalgam of Moral Qualities, and good or bad according to which ones predominate. "Man is an experiment, the animals are another experiment. Time will show whether they were worth the trouble."

It should be remembered, however, that in the biblical tales before "Letters from the Earth" the creation of man was only a backdrop, an established condition. But here in the "Creation of Man" sequence, there appeared the development of a creation myth that provides the required elements to support Twain's view of the human condition.

The myth did not, however, emerge complete in "Letters from the Earth." In fact, its first consistent expression may be seen in the aforementioned fragment of the Stormfield saga, "From Captain Stormfield's Reminiscences." In that passage Stormfield's angel friend Sandy tells how "the Authorities" turned out handsome men and women from a mold for each sex, "blew in the breath, and put in the dispositions"—that is, the Moral Qualities, some twenty-eight vices and virtues all in equal proportion, so that, in effect, they canceled each other out; thus, instead of being "something new and surprising," the men and women were not really different from angels. Hence, after discussing the matter for about six months (two hundred thousand years of earthly time) "the Authorities" decided to create another race, the Human Race, which would have *variety;* and so, with multitudes of molds, they created physical differences and poured into them the Moral Qualities mixed up "helter-skelter" for the "*dispositional* differentiations." Later, though "the Authorities" were amazed at how careless they had been and at the dire results that followed, they decided that nothing further could be done.

In "Letters from the Earth," too, God mentions a similar distribution of the various moral qualities among beasts and men (here twenty-seven rather than twenty-eight). Moreover, the remoteness of heaven (and God) also leads to confusion and a set of problems on earth, which Satan (visiting earth during a spell of banishment) describes in a series of secret letters to the archangels Michael and Gabriel, though with different and more serious ramifications than the rather humorous discussion in "Stormfield." (See McCullough and Malcolm, 168–76, for a full discussion of the relationship of these texts.)

In another direction, Twain adapted the description of the Fall and the reasons for it from the "Passage from Satan's Diary" in "Diaries Antedating the Flood," again questioning the accepted orthodox belief in a just God and suggesting that the expulsion of Adam and Eve from Eden and the destruction of all humanity except Noah and his family in the Flood were clearly illogical and patently unjust and senseless. He also again puzzles over the creation of disease, and indicates that the existence of both disease and the housefly are among the beneficences for which people praise "an All-Just and All-Forgiving and All-Pitying Being who never answered a prayer."

Mark Twain, then, was expanding a belief that he had suggested as early as the 1870s in "God of the Bible vs. God of the Present Day," where he charged that God had been unfair to Adam: "He commanded Adam not to eat of the tree of the knowledge of good and evil; To disobey could not be a sin, because Adam could not comprehend a sin *until* the eating the fruit should reveal to him the difference between right and wrong. So he was unfair in punishing Adam for doing wrong when he could not know it was wrong"† (see appendix 7 for full text).

Finally, though some of Satan's early letters contain deft and even ribald humor, the later ones feature a scathing attack on God's injustice and, especially, on human stupidity. In the 1890s Twain had argued that a sublime and immense God could not be expected to be concerned about the sufferings of humankind, and should not be blamed for the various human tragedies any more than a scientist should be blamed for the deaths of millions of microbes boiled in a test tube during a scientific experiment. By the early 1900s however, and specifically in his autobiographical dictations in 1906, he had reached the conclusion that in establishing basic human temperament, and hence people's reactions to all "circumstances" they might meet, God was fundamentally to blame for all the sufferings, shams, hypocrisies, and pretenses of the human race. This position he amplified vividly in "Letters from the Earth."

But with it all, much humor remained, dark and sardonic though it sometimes became. And behind the piece as a whole lay Mark Twain's views of the irrationality of the Bible, a theme he had expounded in the early 1870s in "God of the Bible vs. God of the Present Day," and which continued to occupy his thoughts for the rest of his life.

LETTERS FROM THE EARTH

I

The Creator sat upon the throne, thinking. Behind Him stretched the illimitable continent of heaven, steeped in a glory of light and color; before Him rose the black night of Space, like a wall. His mighty bulk towered rugged and mountain-like into the zenith, and His divine head blazed there like a distant sun. At His feet stood three colossal figures, diminished to extinction, almost, by contrast—archangels—their heads level with His ancle-bone.

When the Creator had finished thinking, He said,

"I have thought. Behold!"

He lifted His hand, and from it burst a fountain-spray of fire, a million stupendous suns, which clove the blackness and soared, away and away and away, diminishing in magnitude and intensity as they pierced the far frontiers of Space, until at last they were but as diamond nail-heads sparkling under the domed vast roof of the universe.

At the end of an hour the Grand Council was dismissed.

II

They left the Presence impressed and thoughtful, and retired to a private place, where they might talk with freedom. None of the three seemed to want to begin, though all wanted somebody to do it. Each was burning to discuss the great event, but would prefer not to commit himself till he should know how the others regarded it. So there was some aimless and halting conversation about matters of no consequence, and this dragged tediously along, arriving nowhere, until at last the archangel Satan gathered his courage together—of which he had a very good supply—and broke ground. He said—

"We know what we are here to talk about, my lords, and we may as well put pretence aside, and begin. If this is the opinion of the Council—"

"It is, it is!" said Gabriel and Michael, gratefully interrupting.

"Very well, then, let us proceed. We have witnessed a wonderful thing; as to that, we are necessarily agreed. As to the value of it—if it has any—that is a matter which does not personally concern us. We can have as many opinions about it as we like, but that is our limit. We have no vote. I think Space was well enough, just as it was, and useful, too. Cold and dark—a restful place, now and then, after a season of the over-delicate climate and trying splendors of heaven. But these are details of no considerable moment; the new feature, the immense feature, is—what, gentlemen?"

"The invention and introduction of automatic, unsupervised, self-regulating *law* for the government of those myriads of whirling and racing suns and worlds!"

"That is it!" said Satan. "You perceive that it is a stupendous idea. Nothing approaching it has been evolved from the Master Intellect before. Law—*automatic* Law—exact and unvarying Law—requiring no watching, no correcting, no readjusting while the eternities endure! He said those countless vast bodies would plunge through the wastes of Space ages and ages, at unimaginable speed, around stupendous orbits, yet never collide, and never lengthen nor shorten their orbital periods by so much as the hundredth part of a second in two thousand years! That is the new miracle, and the greatest of all—*Automatic Law!* And He gave it a name—the LAW OF NATURE—and said Natural Law is the LAW OF GOD—interchangeable names for one and the same thing."

"Yes," said Michael, "and He said He would establish Natural Law—the Law of God—throughout His dominions, and its authority should be supreme and inviolable."

"Also," said Gabriel, "He said He would by and by create animals, and place them, likewise, under the authority of that Law."

"Yes," said Satan, "I heard Him, but did not understand. What *is* animals, Gabriel?"

"Ah, how should I know? How should any of us know? It is a new word."

[*Interval of three centuries, celestial time—the equivalent of a hundred million years, earthly time. Enter a messenger-Angel.*]

"My lords, He is making animals. Will it please you to come and see?"

They went, they saw, and were perplexed. Deeply perplexed-and the Creator noticed it, and said—

"Ask. I will answer."

"Divine One," said Satan, making obeisance, "what are they for?"

"They are an experiment in Morals and Conduct. Observe them, and be instructed."

There were thousands of them. They were full of activities. Busy, all busy—mainly in persecuting each other. Satan remarked—after examining one of them through a powerful microscope—

"This large beast is killing weaker animals, Divine One."

"The tiger—yes. The law of his nature is ferocity. The law of his nature is the law of God. He cannot disobey it."

"Then in obeying it he commits no offence, Divine One?"

"No, he is blameless."

"This other creature here, is timid, Divine One, and suffers death without resisting."

"The rabbit—yes. He is without courage. It is the law of his nature—the law of God. He must obey it."

"Then he cannot honorably be required to go counter to his nature and resist, Divine One?"

"No. No creature can be honorably required to go counter to the law of his nature—the law of God."

After a long time and many questions, Satan said—

"The spider kills the fly, and eats it; the bird kills the spider and eats it; the wildcat kills the goose; the—well, they all kill each other. It is murder all along the line. Here are countless multitudes of creatures, and they all kill, kill, kill, they are all murderers. And they are not to blame, Divine One?"

"They are not to blame. It is the law of their nature. And always the law of nature is the law of God. Now—observe—behold! A new creature-and the masterpiece—*Man!*"

Men, women, children, they came swarming in flocks, in droves, in millions.

"What shall you do with them, Divine One?"

"Put into each individual, in differing shades and degrees, all the various Moral Qualities, in mass, that have been distributed, a single distinguishing characteristic at a time, among the nonspeaking animal world—courage, cowardice, ferocity, gentleness, fairness, justice, cunning, treachery, magnanimity, cruelty, malice, malignity, lust, mercy, pity, purity, selfishness, sweetness, honor, love, hate, baseness, nobility, loyalty, falsity, veracity, untruthfulness—each human being shall have *all* of these in him, and they will constitute his nature. In some, there will be high and fine characteristics which will submerge the evil ones, and those will be called good men; in others the evil characteristics will have dominion, and those will be called bad men. Observe—behold—they vanish!"

"Whither are they gone, Divine One?"

"To the earth—they and all their fellow-animals."

"What is the earth?"

"A small globe I made, a time, two times and half a time ago. You saw it, but did not notice it in the explosion of worlds and suns that sprayed from my hand. Man is an experiment, the other animals are another experiment. Time will show whether they were worth the trouble. The exhibition is over; you may take your leave, my lords."

III

Several days passed by.

This stands for a long stretch of (our) time, since in heaven a day is as a thousand years.

Satan had been making admiring remarks about certain of the Creator's sparkling industries—remarks which, being read between the lines, were sarcasms. He had made them confidentially to his safe friends the other archangels, but they had been overheard by some ordinary angels and reported at Headquarters.

He was ordered into banishment for a day—the celestial day. It was a punishment he was used to, on account of his too flexible tongue. Formerly he had been deported into Space, there being nowhither else to send him, and had flapped tediously around, there, in the eternal night and the arctic chill; but now it occurred to him to push on and hunt up the Earth and see how the Human-Race experiment was coming along.

By and by he wrote home—very privately—to St. Michael and St. Gabriel about it.

Satan's Letter

This is a strange place, an extraordinary place, and interesting. There is nothing resembling it at home. The people are all insane, the other animals are all insane, the Earth is insane, Nature itself is insane. Man is a marvelous curiosity. When he is at his very very best he is a sort of low grade nickel-plated angel; at his worst he is unspeakable, unimaginable; and first and last and all the time he is a sarcasm. Yet he blandly and in all sincerity calls himself the "noblest work of God." This is the truth I am telling you. And this is not a new idea with him, he has talked it through all the ages, and believed it. Believed it, and found nobody among all his race to laugh at it.

Moreover—if I may put another strain upon you—he thinks he is the Creator's pet. He believes the Creator is proud of him; he even believes the Creator loves him; has a passion for him; sits up nights to admire him; yes, and watch over him and keep him out of trouble. He prays to Him, and thinks He listens. Isn't it a quaint idea? Fills his prayers with crude and bald and florid flatteries of Him, and thinks He sits and purrs over these extravagancies and enjoys them. He prays for help, and favor, and protection, every day; and does it with hopefulness and confidence, too, although no prayer of his has ever been answered. The daily affront, the daily defeat, do not discourage him, he goes on praying just the same. There is something almost fine about this perseverance. I must put one more strain upon you: he thinks he is going to heaven!

He has salaried teachers who tell him that. They also tell him there is a hell, of everlasting fire, and that he will go to it if he doesn't keep the Commandments. What are the Commandments? They are a curiosity. I will tell you about them by and by.

The salaried teacher tells them God is good. Good and merciful, and kind, and just, and generous, and patient, and loving. To whom? His "children." And who are His children? Why, these misbegotten creatures! They use that expression themselves. Speaking by and large, man is made up of ninety-

Letters from the Earth
Letter IV

I have told you nothing about man that is not true. You must pardon me if I repeat that remark now and then in these letters; I want you to take seriously the things I am telling you, and I feel that if I were in your place and you in mine, I should need that reminder from time to time, to keep my credulity from flagging.

For there is nothing about Man that is not strange to an Immortal. He looks at nothing as we look at it, his sense of proportion is quite different from ours, and his sense of values is so widely divergent from ours, that with all our large intellectual powers it is not likely that even the most gifted among us would ever be quite able to understand it.

For instance, take this sample: he has imagined a heaven, and has left entirely out of it the supremest of all his delights, the one ecstasy that stands first and foremost in the heart of every individual of his race—and of ours—sexual intercourse!

It is as if a lost and perishing person in a roasting desert should be told by a rescuer he might choose and have all longed-for things but one, and he should elect to leave out water!

His heaven is like himself: strange, interesting, astonishing, grotesque. I give you my word, it has not a single feature in it that he *actually values.* It consists—utterly and entirely—of diversions which he cares next to nothing about, here in the earth, yet is quite sure he will like in heaven. Isn't it curious? Isn't it interesting? You must not think I am exaggerating, for it is not so. I will give you details.

Most men do not sing, most men cannot sing, most men will not stay where others are singing if it be continued more than two hours. Note that.

Only about two men in a hundred can play upon a musical instrument, and not four in a hundred have any wish to learn how. Set that down.

Many men pray, not many of them like to do it. A few pray long, the others make a short cut.

More men go to church than want to.

To forty-nine men in fifty the Sabbath Day is a dreary, dreary bore.

Of all the men in a church on a Sunday, two-thirds are tired when the service is half over, and the rest before it is finished.

The gladdest moment for all of them is when the preacher uplifts his hands for the benediction. You can hear the soft rustle of relief that sweeps the house, and you recognize that it is eloquent with gratitude.

All nations look down upon all other nations.

All nations dislike all other nations.

All white nations despise all colored nations, of whatever hue, and oppress them when they can.

White men will not associate with "niggers," nor marry them.

They will not allow them in their schools and churches.

All the world hates the Jew, and will not endure him except when he is rich.

I ask you to note all those particulars.

Further. All sane people detest noise.

All sane people, sane or insane, like to have variety in their life. Monotony quickly wearies them.

Every man, according to the mental equipment that has fallen to his share, exercises his intellect constantly, ceaselessly, and this exercise makes up a vast and valued and essential part of his life. The lowest intellect, like the highest, possesses a skill of some kind and takes a keen pleasure in testing it, proving it, perfecting it. The urchin who is his comrade's superior in games is as diligent and as enthusiastic in his practice as are the sculptor, the painter, the pianist, the mathematician and the rest. Not one of them could be happy if his talent were put under an interdict.

Now then, you have the facts. You know what the human race enjoys, and what it doesn't enjoy. It has invented a heaven, out of its own head, all by itself: guess what it is like! In fifteen hundred eternities you couldn't do it. The ablest mind known to you or me in fifty million aeons couldn't do it. Very well, I will tell you about it.

II

1. First of all, I recall to your attention the extraordinary fact with which I began. To-wit, that the human being, like the immortals, naturally places sexual intercourse far and away above all other joys—yet he has left it out of his heaven! The very thought of it excites him; opportunity sets him wild; in this state he will risk life, reputation, everything—even his queer heaven itself—to make good that opportunity and ride it to the overwhelming climax. From youth to middle age all men and all women prize copulation above all other pleasures combined, yet it is actually as I have said: it is not in their heaven, prayer takes its place.

They prize it thus highly; yet, like all their so-called "boons," it is a poor thing. At its very best and longest the act is brief beyond imagination—the imagination of an immortal, I mean. In the matter of repetition the man is limited—oh, quite beyond immortal conception. We who continue the act *and* its supremest ecstasies unbroken and without withdrawal for centuries, will never be able to understand or adequately pity the awful poverty of these people in that rich gift which, possessed as we possess it, makes all other possessions trivial and not worth the trouble of invoicing.

2. In man's heaven *everybody sings!* There are no exceptions. The man who did not sing on earth, sings there; the man who could not sing on earth is able to do it there. This universal singing is not casual, not occasional, not relieved by intervals of quiet, it goes on, all day long, and every day, during a stretch of twelve hours. And *everybody stays;* whereas in the earth the place would be empty in two hours. The singing is of hymns alone. Nay, it is of *one* hymn alone. The words are always the same, in number they are only about a dozen,

there is no rhyme, there is no poetry: "Hosannah, hosannah, hosannah, Lord God of Sabaoth, 'rah! 'rah! 'rah!—ssht!—boom.....a-a-ah!"

3. Meantime, *every person* is playing on a harp—those millions and millions! whereas not more than twenty in the thousand of them could play an instrument in the earth, or ever *wanted* to.

Consider the deafening hurricane of sound—millions and millions of voices screaming at once, and millions and millions of harps gritting their teeth at the same time! I ask you—is it hideous, is it odious, is it horrible?

Consider further: it is a *praise* service; a service of compliment, of flattery, of adulation! Do you ask who it is that is willing to endure this strange compliment, this insane compliment; and who not only endures it but likes it, enjoys it, requires it, *commands* it? Hold your breath!

It is God! This race's God, I mean. He sits on his throne, attended by his four and twenty elders and some other dignitaries pertaining to his court, and looks out over his miles and miles of tempestuous worshippers, and smiles, and purrs, and nods his satisfaction northward, eastward, southward; as quaint and naif a spectacle as has yet been imagined in this universe, I take it.

It is easy to see that the inventor of the heaven did not originate the idea, but copied it from the show-ceremonies of some sorry little sovereign State up in the back settlements of the Orient somewhere.

All sane white people *hate noise;* yet they have tranquilly accepted this kind of a heaven—without thinking, without reflection, without examination—and they actually want to go to it! Profoundly devout old gray-headed men put in a large part of their time dreaming of the happy day when they will lay down the cares of this life and enter into the joys of that place. Yet you can see how unreal it is to them, and how little it takes a grip upon them as being *fact*, for they make no practical preparation for the great change: you never see one of them with a harp, you never hear one of them sing.

As you have seen, that singular show is a service of divine worship—a service of praise: praise by hymn, praise by instrumental ecstasies, praise by prostration. It takes the place of "church." Now then, in the earth these people cannot stand much church—an hour and a quarter is the limit, and they draw the line at once a week. That is to say, Sunday. One day in seven; and even then they do not look forward to it with longing. And so—consider what their heaven provides for them: "church" that lasts forever, and a *Sabbath that has no end!* They quickly weary of this brief hebdomadal Sabbath here, yet they long for that eternal one; they dream of it, they talk about it, they *think* they think they are going to enjoy it—with all their simple hearts they think they think they are going to be happy in it!

It is because they do not think *at all;* they only think they think. Whereas they can't think; not two human beings in ten thousand have anything to think with. And as to imagination—oh, well, look at their heaven! They accept it, they approve it, they admire it. That gives you their intellectual measure.

4. The inventor of their heaven empties into it all the nations of the earth, in one common jumble. All are on an equality absolute, no one of them ranking another; they have to be "brothers;" they have to mix together, pray together, harp together, hosannah together—whites, niggers, Jews, everybody—there's no distinction. Here in the earth all nations hate each other, every one of them hates the Jew. Yet every pious person adores that heaven and wants to get into it. He really does. And when he is in a holy rapture he thinks he thinks that if he were only there he would take all the populace to his heart, and hug, and hug, and hug!

He is a marvel—man is! I would I knew who invented him.

5. Every man in the earth possesses some share of intellect, large or small; and be it large or be it small he takes a pride in it. Also his heart swells at mention of the names of the majestic intellectual chiefs of his race, and he loves the tale of their splendid achievements. For he is of their blood, and in honoring themselves they have honored him. Lo, what the mind of man can do! he cries; and calls the roll of the illustrious of all the ages; and points to the imperishable literatures they have given to the world, and the mechanical wonders they have invented, and the glories wherewith they have clothed science and the arts; and to them he uncovers, as to kings, and gives to them the profoundest homage and the sincerest his exultant heart can furnish—his exalting intellect above all things else in his world, and enthroning it there under the arching skies in a supremacy unapproachable. And then he contrives a heaven that hasn't a rag of intellectuality in it anywhere!

Is it odd, is it curious, is it puzzling? It is exactly as I have said, incredible as it may sound. This sincere adorer of intellect and prodigal rewarder of its mighty services here in the earth has invented a religion and a heaven which pay no compliments to intellect, offer it no distinctions, fling to it no largess: in fact, never even mention it.

By this time you will have noticed that the human being's heaven has been thought out and constructed upon an absolutely definite plan; and that this plan is, that it shall contain, in labored detail, each and every imaginable thing that is repulsive to a man, and not a single thing he likes!

Very well, the further we proceed the more will this curious fact be apparent.

Make a note of it: in man's heaven there are no exercises for the intellect, nothing for it to live upon. It would rot there in a year—rot and stink. Rot and stink—and at that stage become holy. A blessed thing; for only the holy can stand the joys of that bedlam.

Letter V

You have noticed that the human being is a curiosity. In times past he has had (and worn out and flung away) hundreds and hundreds of religions; to-day he has hundreds and hundreds of religions, and launches not fewer than three new ones every year. I could enlarge that number and still be within the facts.

One of his principal religions is called the Christian. A sketch of it will interest you. It is set forth in detail in a book containing 2,000,000 words, called the Old and New Testaments. Also it has another name—The Word of God. For the Christian thinks every word of it was dictated by God—the one I have been speaking of.

It is full of interest. It has noble poetry in it; and some clever fables; and some blood-drenched history; and some good morals; and some execrable morals; and a wealth of obscenity; and upwards of a thousand lies.

This Bible is built mainly out of the fragments of older Bibles that had their day and crumbled to ruin. So it noticeably lacks in originality, necessarily. Its three or four most imposing and impressive events all happened in earlier Bibles; all its best precepts and rules of conduct come also from those Bibles; there are only two new things in it: hell, for one, and that singular heaven I have told you about.

What shall we do? If we believe, with these people, that their God invented these cruel things, we slander him; if we believe that these people invented them themselves, we slander *them.* It is an unpleasant dilemma in either case, for neither of these parties has done *us* any harm.

For the sake of tranquillity, let us take a side. Let us join forces with the people and put the whole ungracious burden upon *him*—heaven, hell, Bible and all. It does not seem right, it does not seem fair; and yet when you consider that heaven, and how crushingly charged it is with everything that is repulsive to a human being, how *can* we believe a human being invented it? And when I come to tell you about hell, the strain will be greater still, and you will be likely to say *No*, a man would not provide *that* place, for either himself or anybody else; he simply *couldn't*.

That innocent Bible tells about the Creation. Of what—the universe? Yes, the universe. In *six days!* God did it. He did not call it the universe—that name is modern. His whole attention was upon *this world*. He constructed it in five days—and then? It took him only *one* day to make *twenty million suns and eighty million planets!*

What were they for—according to his idea? To furnish light for this little toy-world. That was his whole purpose; he had no other. *One* of the 20,000,000 suns (the smallest one), was to light it in the day-time, the rest were to help *one* of the universe's countless moons modify the darkness of its nights.

It is quite manifest that he believed his fresh-made skies were diamond-sown with those myriads of twinkling stars the moment his first-day's sun sank below the horizon; whereas, in fact not a single star winked in that black vault until three years and a half after that memorable week's formidable industries had been completed.* Then one star appeared, all solitary and alone, and began to blink. Three years later another one appeared. The two blinked together for more than four years before a third joined them. At the end of the first hundred years there were not yet twenty-five stars twinkling in the wide wastes of those gloomy skies. At the end of a thousand years not enough stars were yet visible to make a show. At the end of a million years only half of the present array had sent their light over the telescopic frontiers, and it took another million for the rest to follow suit, as the vulgar phrase goes. There being at that time no telescope, their advent was not observed.

For three hundred years, now, the Christian astronomer has known that his Deity *didn't* make the stars in those tremendous six days; but the Christian astronomer does not enlarge upon that detail. Neither does the priest.

In his Book, God is eloquent in his praises of his mighty works, and calls them by the largest names he can find—thus indicating that he has a strong and just admiration of magnitudes; yet he made those millions of prodigious suns to light this wee little orb, instead of appointing this orb's little sun to

*It takes the light of the nearest star (61 Cygni) three and a half years to come to the earth, traveling at the rate of 186,000 miles per second. Arcturus had been shining 200 years before it was visible from the earth. Remoter stars gradually became visible after thousands and thousands of years.—[*Editor*].

dance attendance upon *them.* He mentions Arcturus in his Book—you remember Arcturus; we went there once. *It* is one of this earth's night-lamps!—that giant globe which is 50,000 times as large as this earth's sun, and compares with it as a melon compares with a cathedral.

However, the Sunday school still teaches the child that Arcturus was created to help light this earth, and the child grows up and continues to believe it long after he has found out that the probabilities are against its being so.

According to the Book and its servants the universe is only six thousand years old. It is only within the last hundred years that studious, inquiring minds have found out that it is nearer a hundred million.

During the Six Days, God created man and the other animals.

He made a man and a woman and placed them in a pleasant garden, along with the other creatures. They all lived together there in harmony and contentment and blooming youth for some time; then trouble came. God had warned the man and the woman that they must not eat of the fruit of a certain tree. And he added a most strange remark: he said that if they ate of it they should surely *die.* Strange, for the reason that inasmuch as they had never seen a sample of death they could not possibly know what he meant. Neither would he nor any other god have been able to make those ignorant children understand what was meant, without furnishing a sample. The mere *word* could have no meaning for them, any more than it would have for an infant of days.

Presently a serpent sought them out privately, and came to them walking upright, which was the way of serpents in those days. The serpent said the forbidden fruit would store their vacant minds with knowledge. So they ate it, which was quite natural, for man is so made that he eagerly *wants to know;* whereas the priest, like God, whose imitator and representative he is, has made it his business from the beginning to keep him *from* knowing any useful thing.

Adam and Eve ate the forbidden fruit, and at once a great light streamed into their dim heads. They had acquired knowledge. What knowledge—useful knowledge? No—merely knowledge that there was such a thing as good, and such a thing as evil, and how to *do* evil. They *couldn't* do it before, therefore all their acts up to this time had been without stain, without blame, without offence.

But *now* they could do evil—and suffer for it; *now* they had acquired what the Church calls an invaluable possession, the Moral Sense; that sense which differentiates man from the beast and sets him *above* the beast. Instead of *below* the beast—where one would suppose his proper place would be, since he is always foul-minded and guilty and the beast always clean-minded and innocent. It is like valuing a watch that *must* go wrong, above a watch that *can't.*

The Church still prizes the Moral Sense as man's noblest asset to-day, although the Church knows God had a distinctly poor opinion of it and did what he could in his clumsy way to keep his happy Children of the Garden from acquiring it.

Very well, Adam and Eve now knew what evil was, and how to do it. They knew how to do various kinds of wrong things, and among them one principal one—the one God had his mind on principally. That one was, the art and mystery of sexual intercourse. To them it was a magnificent discovery, and they stopped idling around and turned their entire attention to it, poor exultant young things!

In the midst of one of these celebrations they heard God walking among the bushes, which was an afternoon custom of his, and they were smitten with fright. Why? Because they were naked. They had not known it before. They had not minded it before, neither had God.

In that memorable moment *immodesty* was born; and some people have valued it ever since, though it would certainly puzzle them to explain why.

Adam and Eve entered the world naked and unashamed—naked and pure-minded; and no descendant of theirs has ever entered it otherwise. All have entered it naked, unashamed, and clean in mind. They have entered it *modest.* They had to *acquire* immodesty and the soiled mind, there was no other way to get it. A Christian mother's first duty is to soil her child's mind, and she does not neglect it. Her lad grows up to be a missionary, and goes to the innocent savage and to the civilized Japanese, and soils their minds. Whereupon they adopt immodesty, they conceal their bodies, they stop bathing naked together.

The convention miscalled Modesty has no standard, and cannot have one, because it is opposed to nature and reason, and is therefore an artificiality and subject to anybody's whim, anybody's diseased caprice. And so, in India the refined lady covers her face and breasts and leaves her legs naked from the hips down, while the refined European lady covers her legs and exposes her face and her breasts. In lands inhabited by the innocent savage the refined European lady soon gets used to full-grown native stark-nakedness, and ceases to be offended by it. A highly cultivated French count and countess—unrelated to each other—who were marooned in their night clothes, by shipwreck, upon an uninhabited island in the eighteenth century, were soon naked. Also ashamed—for a week. After that their nakedness did not trouble them, and they soon ceased to think about it.

You have never seen a person with clothes on. Oh, well, you haven't lost anything.

To proceed with the Biblical curiosities. Naturally you will think the threat to punish Adam and Eve for disobeying was of course not carried out, since they did not create themselves, nor their natures nor their impulses nor their weaknesses, and hence were not properly subject to any one's commands, and not responsible to anybody for their acts. It will surprise you to know that the threat *was* carried out. Adam and Eve were punished, and that crime finds apologists unto this day. *The sentence of death was executed.*

As you perceive, the only person responsible for the couple's offence escaped; and not only escaped but became the executioner of the innocent.

In your country and mine we should have the privilege of making fun of this kind of morality, but it would be unkind to do it here. Many of these people have the reasoning faculty, but no one uses it in religious matters.

The best minds will tell you that when a man has begotten a child he is morally bound to tenderly care for it, protect it from hurt, shield it from disease, clothe it, feed it, bear with its waywardness, lay no hand upon it save in kindness and for its own good, and never in any case inflict upon it a wanton cruelty. God's treatment of his earthly children, every day and every night, is the exact opposite of all that, yet those best minds warmly justify these crimes, condone them, excuse them, and indignantly refuse to regard them as crimes at all, when *he* commits them. Your country and mine is an interesting one, but there is nothing there that is half so interesting as the human mind.

Very well, God banished Adam and Eve from the Garden, and eventually assassinated them. All for disobeying a command which he had no right to utter. But he did not stop there, as you will see. He has one code of morals for himself, and quite another for his children. He requires his children to deal justly—and gently—with offenders, and forgive them seventy-and-seven times; whereas he deals neither justly nor gently with any one, and he did not forgive the ignorant and thoughtless first pair of juveniles even their first small offence and say "You may go free this time, I will give you another chance."

On the contrary! He elected to punish *their* children, all through the ages to the end of time, for a trifling offence committed by others before they were born. He is punishing them yet. In mild ways? No, in atrocious ones.

You would not suppose that this kind of a Being gets many compliments.

Undeceive yourself: the world calls him the All-Just, the All-Righteous, the All-Good, the All-Merciful, the All-Forgiving, the All-Truthful, the All-Loving, the Source of All Morality. These sarcasms are uttered daily, all over the world. But not as conscious sarcasms. No, they are meant seriously; they are uttered without a smile.

Letter . . .

So the First Pair went forth from the Garden under a curse—a permanent one. They had lost every pleasure they had possessed before "The Fall;" and yet they were rich, for they had gained one worth all the rest: they knew the Supreme Art.

They practised it diligently, and were filled with contentment. The Deity *ordered* them to practise it. They obeyed, this time. But it was just as well it was not forbidden, for they would have practised it anyhow, if a thousand Deities had forbidden it.

Results followed. By the name of Cain and Abel. And these had some sisters; and knew what to do with them. And so there were some more results: Cain and Abel begot some nephews and nieces. These, in their turn, begot some second-cousins. At this point classification of relationships began to get difficult, and the attempt to keep it up was abandoned.

The pleasant labor of populating the world went on from age to age, and with prime efficiency; for in those happy days the sexes were still competent for the Supreme Art when by rights they ought to have been dead eight hundred years. The sweeter sex, the dearer sex, the lovelier sex was manifestly at its very best, then, for it was even able to attract gods. Real gods. They came down out of heaven and had wonderful times with those hot young blossoms. The Bible tells about it.

By help of those visiting foreigners the population grew and grew until it numbered several millions. But it was a disappointment to the Deity. He was dissatisfied with its morals; which in some respects were not any better than his own. Indeed they were an unflatteringly close imitation of his own. They were a very bad people, and as he knew of no way to reform them, he wisely concluded to abolish them. This is the only really enlightened and superior idea his Bible has credited him with, and it would have made his reputation for all time if he could only have kept to it and carried it out. But he was always unstable—except in his advertisements—and his good resolution broke down. He took a pride in man; man was his finest invention; man was his pet, after the housefly, and he could not bear to lose him wholly; so he finally decided to save a sample of him and drown the rest.

Nothing could be more characteristic of him. He created all those infamous people, and he alone was responsible for their conduct. Not one of them deserved death, yet it was certainly good policy to extinguish them; especially since in creating them the master crime had already been committed, and to allow them to go on procreating would be a distinct *addition* to the crime. But at the same time there could be no justice, no fairness, in any favoritism—*all* should be drowned or none.

No, he would not have it so; he would save half a dozen and try the race over again. He was not able to foresee that it would go rotten again, for he is only the Far-Sighted One in his advertisements.

He saved out Noah and his family, and arranged to exterminate the rest. He planned an Ark, and Noah built it. Neither of them had ever built an Ark before, nor knew anything about Arks; and so something out of the common was to be expected. It happened. Noah was a farmer, and although he knew what was required of the Ark he was quite incompetent to say whether this one would be large enough to meet the requirements or not (which it wasn't), so he ventured no advice. The Deity did not know it wasn't large enough, but took the chances and made no adequate measurements. In the end the ship fell far short of the necessities, and to this day the world still suffers for it.

Noah built the Ark. He built it the best he could, but left out most of the essentials. It had no rudder, it had no sails, it had no compass, it had no pumps, it had no charts, no lead-lines, no anchors, no log, no light, no ventilation; and as for cargo-room—which was the main thing—the less said about that the better. It was to be at sea eleven months, and would need fresh water enough to fill two Arks of its size—yet the additional Ark was not provided. Water from outside could not be utilized: half of it would be salt water, and men and land-animals could not drink it.

For not only was a sample of man to be saved, but business-samples of the other animals, too. You must understand that when Adam ate the apple in the Garden and learned how to multiply and replenish, the other animals learned the Art, too, by watching Adam. It was cunning of them, it was neat; for they got all that was worth having out of the apple without tasting it and afflicting themselves with the disastrous Moral Sense, the parent of all the immoralities.

Noah began to collect animals. There was to be one couple of each and every sort of creature that walked or crawled, or swam or flew, in the world of animated nature. We have to guess at how long it took to collect the creatures and how much it cost, for there is no record of these details. When Symmachus made preparation to introduce his young son to grown-up life in imperial Rome, he sent men to Asia, Africa and everywhere to collect wild animals for the arena-fights. It took the men three years to accumulate the animals and fetch them to Rome. Merely quadrupeds and alligators, you understand—no birds, no snakes, no frogs, no worms, no lice, no rats, no fleas, no ticks, no caterpillars, no spiders, no houseflies, no mosquitoes,—nothing but just plain simple quadrupeds and alligators; and no quadrupeds except fighting ones. Yet it was as I have said: it took three years to collect them, and the cost of animals and transportation and the men's wages footed up $4,500,000.

How many animals? We do not know. But it was under 5,000, for that was the largest number *ever* gathered for those Roman shows, and it was Titus, not Symmachus, who made that collection. Those were mere baby-museums, compared to Noah's contract. Of birds and beasts and fresh-water creatures he had to collect 146,000 kinds; and of insects upwards of 2,000,000 species.

Thousands and thousands of those things are very difficult to catch, and if Noah had not given up and resigned, he would be on the job yet, as Leviticus used to say. However, I do not mean that he withdrew. No, he did not do that. He gathered as many creatures as he had room for, and then stopped.

If he had known all the requirements in the beginning, he would have been aware that what was needed was a fleet of Arks. But he did not know how many kinds of creatures there were, neither did his Chief. So he had no kangaroo, and no 'possum, and no Gila Monster, and no ornithorhynchus, and lacked a multitude of other indispensable blessings which a loving Creator had provided for man and forgotten about, they having long ago wandered to a side of his world which he had never seen and with whose affairs he was not acquainted. And so every one of them came within a hair of getting drowned.

They only escaped by an accident: there was not water enough to go around. Only enough was provided to flood one small corner of the globe—the rest of the globe was not then known, and was supposed to be non-existent.

However, the thing that really and finally and definitely determined Noah to stop with enough species for purely business purposes and let the rest become extinct, was an incident of the last days: an excited stranger arrived with some most alarming news. He said he had been camping among some mountains and valleys about six hundred miles away, and he had seen a wonderful thing there: he stood upon a precipice overlooking a wide valley, and up the valley he saw a billowy black sea of strange animal life coming. Presently the creatures passed by, struggling, fighting, scrambling, screeching, snorting—horrible vast masses of tumultuous flesh! Sloths as big as an elephant; frogs as big as a cow; a megatherium and his harem, huge beyond belief; saurians and saurians and saurians, group after group, family after family, species after species—a hundred feet long, thirty feet high, and twice as quarrelsome; one of them hit a perfectly blameless Durham bull a thump with its tail and sent it whizzing three hundred feet into the air and it fell at the man's feet with a sigh and was no more. The man said that these prodigious animals had heard about the Ark and were coming. Coming to get saved from the flood. And not coming in pairs, they were *all* coming: they did not know the passengers were restricted to pairs, the man said, and wouldn't care a rap for the regulations, anyway—they would sail in that Ark or know the reason why. The man said the Ark would not hold the half of them; and moreover they were coming hungry, and would eat up everything there was, including the menagerie and the family.

All these facts were suppressed, in the Biblical account. You find not a hint of them there. The whole thing is hushed up. Not even the names of those vast creatures are mentioned. It shows you that when people have left a reproachful vacancy in a contract they can be as shady about it in Bibles as elsewhere. Those powerful animals would be of inestimable value to man now, when transportation is so hard pressed and expensive, but they are all lost to him. All lost, and by Noah's fault. They all got drowned. Some of them as much as eight million years ago.

Very well, the stranger told his tale, and Noah saw that he must get away before the monsters arrived. He would have sailed at once, but the upholsterers and decorators of the housefly's drawing room still had some finishing touches to put on, and that lost him a day. Another day was lost in getting the flies aboard, there being sixty-eight billions of them and the Deity still afraid there might not be enough. Another day was lost in stowing 40 tons of selected filth for the fly's sustenance.

Then at last, Noah sailed; and none too soon, for the Ark was only just sinking out of sight on the horizon when the monsters arrived, and added their lamentations to those of the multitude of weeping fathers and mothers and frightened little children who were clinging to the wave-washed rocks in the pouring rain and lifting imploring prayers to an All-Just and All-Forgiving and All-Pitying Being who had never answered a prayer since those crags were builded, grain by grain out of the sands, and would still not have answered one when the ages should have crumbled them to sand again.

Letter VII

On the third day, about noon, it was found that a fly had been left behind. The return-voyage turned out to be long and difficult, on account of the lack of chart and compass, and because of the changed aspects of all coasts, the steadily rising water having submerged some of the lower landmarks and given to higher ones an unfamiliar look; but after sixteen days of earnest and faithful seeking, the fly was found at last, and received on board with hymns of praise and gratitude, the Family standing meanwhile uncovered, out of reverence for its divine origin. It was weary and worn, and had suffered somewhat from the weather, but was otherwise in good estate. Men and their families had died of hunger on barren mountain tops, but It had not lacked for food, the multitudinous corpses furnishing it in rank and rotten richness. Thus was the sacred bird providentially preserved.

Providentially. That is the word. For the fly had not been left behind by accident. No, the hand of Providence was in it. There are no accidents. All things that happen, happen for a purpose. They are foreseen from the beginning of time, they are ordained from the beginning of time. From the dawn of Creation the Lord had foreseen that Noah, being alarmed and confused by the invasion of the prodigious brevet Fossils, would prematurely fly to sea unprovided with a certain invaluable disease. He would have all the other diseases, and could distribute them among the new races of men as they appeared in the world, but he would lack one of the very best—typhoid fever; a malady which, when the circumstances are especially favorable, is able to utterly wreck a patient without killing him; for it can restore him to his feet with a long life in him, and yet deaf, dumb, blind, crippled and idiotic. The housefly is its main disseminator, and is more competent and more calamitously effective than all the other distributors of the dreaded scourge put together. And so, by foreordination from the beginning of time, this fly was left behind to seek out a typhoid corpse and feed upon its corruptions and gaum its legs with the germs and transmit them to the repeopled world for permanent business. From that one housefly, in the ages that have since elapsed, billions of sickbeds have been stocked, billions of wrecked bodies sent tottering about the earth, and billions of cemeteries recruited with the dead.

It is most difficult to understand the disposition of the Bible God, it is such a confusion of contradictions; of watery instabilities and iron firmnesses; of goody-goody abstract morals made out of words, and concreted hell-born ones made out of *acts;* of fleeting kindnesses repented of in permanent malignities.

However, when after much puzzling you get at the key to his disposition, you do at last arrive at a sort of understanding of it. With a most quaint and juvenile and astonishing frankness he has furnished that key himself. It is *jealousy!*

I expect that to take your breath away. You are aware—for I have already told you in an earlier letter—that among human beings jealousy ranks distinctly as a *weakness;* a trade-mark of small minds; a property of *all* small minds, yet a property which even the smallest is ashamed of; and when accused of its possession will lyingly deny it and resent the accusation as an insult.

Jealousy. Do not forget it, keep it in mind. It is the key. With it you will come to partly understand God as we go along; without it nobody can understand him. As I have said, he has openly held up this treasonous key himself, for all to see. He says, naïvely, outspokenly, and without suggestion of embarrassment,

"I the Lord thy God am a jealous God."

You see, it is only another way of saying,

"I the Lord thy God am a small God; a small God, and fretful about small things."

He was giving a warning: he could not bear the thought of any other God getting some of the Sunday compliments of this comical little human race—he wanted all of them for himself. He valued them. To him they were riches; just as tin money is to a Zulu.

But wait—I am not fair; I am misrepresenting him; prejudice is beguiling me into saying what is not true. He did not say he wanted all of the adulations; he said nothing about not being willing to share them with his fellow-gods; what he said was,

"Thou shalt have no other gods *before* me."

It is a quite different thing, and puts him in a much better light—I confess it. There was an abundance of gods, the woods were full of them, as the saying is, and all he demanded was, that he should be ranked as high as the others—not above any of them, but not below any of them. He was willing that they should fertilize earthly virgins, but not on any better terms than he could have for himself in his turn. He wanted to be held their equal. This he insisted upon, in the clearest language: he would have no other gods *before* him. They could march abreast with him, but none of them could head the procession, and he did not claim the right to head it himself.

Do you think he was able to stick to that upright and creditable position? No. He could keep to a bad resolution forever, but he couldn't keep to a good one a month. By and by he threw this one aside and calmly claimed to be the only God in the entire universe.

As I was saying, jealousy is the key; all through his history it is present and prominent. It is the blood and bone of his disposition, it is the basis of his character. How small a thing can wreck his composure and disorder his judgment if it touches the raw of his jealousy! And nothing warms up this trait so quickly and so surely and so exaggeratedly as a suspicion that some competition with the god-Trust is impending. The fear that if Adam and Eve ate of the fruit of the Tree of Knowledge they would "be as gods," so fired his jealousy that his reason was affected, and he could not treat those poor creatures either fairly or charitably, or even refrain from dealing cruelly and criminally with their blameless posterity.

To this day his reason has never recovered from that shock; a wild nightmare of vengefulness has possessed him ever since, and he has almost bankrupted his native ingenuities in inventing pains and miseries and humiliations and heartbreaks wherewith to embitter the brief lives of Adam's descendants. Think of the diseases he has contrived for them! They are multitudinous; no book can name them all. And each one is a trap, set for an innocent victim.

The human being is a machine. An automatic machine. It is composed of thousands of complex and delicate mechanisms, which perform their functions harmoniously and perfectly, in accordance with laws devised for their governance, and over which the man himself has no authority, no mastership, no control. For each one of these thousands of mechanisms the Creator has planned an enemy, whose office is to harass it, pester it, persecute it, damage it, afflict it with pains, and miseries, and ultimate destruction. Not one has been overlooked.

From cradle to grave these enemies are always at work, they know no rest, night nor day. They are an army; an organized army; a besieging army; an assaulting army; an army that is alert, watchful, eager, merciless; an army that never wearies, never relents, never grants a truce.

It moves by squad, by company, by battalion, by regiment, by brigade, by division, by army corps; upon occasion it masses its parts and moves upon mankind with its whole strength. It is the Creator's Grand Army, and he is the Commander in Chief. Along its battlefront its grisly banners wave their legends in the face of the sun: Disaster, Disease, and the rest.

Disease! that is the main force, the diligent force, the devastating force! It attacks the infant the moment it is born; it furnishes it one malady after another: croup, measles, mumps, bowel-troubles, teething-pains, scarlet fever, and other childhood specialties. It chases the child into youth and furnishes it some specialties for that time of life. It chases the youth into maturity; maturity into age, and age into the grave.

With these facts before you will you now try to guess man's chiefest pet name for this ferocious Commander in Chief? I will save you the trouble—but you must not laugh. It is Our Father in Heaven!

It is curious—the way the human mind works. The Christian begins with this straight proposition, this definite proposition, this inflexible and uncompromising proposition: *God is all-knowing, and all-powerful.*

This being the case, nothing can happen without his knowing beforehand that it is going to happen; nothing happens without his permission; nothing can happen that he chooses to prevent.

That is definite enough, isn't it? It makes the Creator distinctly responsible for everything that happens, doesn't it?

The Christian concedes it in that italicised sentence. Concedes it with feeling, with enthusiasm.

Then, having thus made the Creator responsible for all those pains and diseases and miseries above enumerated, and which he could have prevented, the gifted Christian blandly calls him Our Father!

It is as I tell you. He equips the Creator with every trait that goes to the making of a fiend, and then arrives at the conclusion that a fiend and a father are the same thing! Yet he would deny that a malevolent lunatic and a Sunday school superintendent are essentially the same. What do you think of the human mind? I mean, in case you think there is a human mind.

Letter . . .

Noah and his family were saved—if that could be called an advantage. I throw in the if for the reason that there has never been an intelligent person of the age of sixty who would consent to live his life over again. His or any one else's. The family were saved, yes, but they were not comfortable, for they were full of microbes. Full to the eyebrows; fat with them, obese with them; distended like balloons. It was a disagreeable condition, but it could not be helped, because enough microbes had to be saved to supply the future races of men with desolating diseases, and there were but eight persons on board to serve as hotels for them. The microbes were by far the most important part of the Ark's cargo, and the part the Creator was most anxious about and most infatuated with. They had to have good nourishment and pleasant accommodations. There were typhoid germs, and cholera germs, and hydrophobia germs, and lockjaw germs, and consumption germs, and black-plague germs, and some hundreds of other aristocrats, specially precious creations, golden bearers of God's love to man, blessed gifts of the infatuated Father to his children—all of which had to be sumptuously housed and richly entertained; these were located in the choicest places the interiors of the family could furnish: in the lungs, in the heart, in the brain, in the kidneys, in the blood, in the guts. In the guts particularly. The great intestine was the favorite resort. There they gathered, by countless billions, and worked, and fed, and squirmed, and sang hymns of praise and thanksgiving; and at night when it was quiet you could hear the soft murmur of it. The large intestine was in effect their heaven. They stuffed it solid; they made it as rigid as a coil of gaspipe. They took a pride in this. Their principal hymn made gratified reference to it:

"Constipation, O constipation,
    The joyful sound proclaim
Till man's remotest entrail
    Shall praise its makers' name."

The discomforts furnished by the Ark were many, and various. The family had to live right in the presence of the multitudinous animals, and breathe the distressing stench they made and be deafened day and night with the thunder-crash of noise their roarings and screechings produced; and in addition to these intolerable discomforts it was a peculiarly trying place for the ladies, for they could look in no direction without seeing some thousands of the creatures engaged in multiplying and replenishing. And then, there were the flies. They swarmed everywhere, and persecuted the family all day long. They were the first animals up, in the morning, and the last ones down, at night. But they must not be killed, they must not be injured, they were sacred, their origin was divine, they were the special pets of the Creator, his darlings.

By and by the other creatures would be distributed here and there about the earth—*scattered:* the tigers to India, the lion and the elephant to the vacant desert and the secret places of the jungle, the birds to the boundless regions of empty space, the insects to one or another climate, according to nature and requirement; but the fly? He is of no nationality; all the climates are his home, all the globe is his province, all creatures that breathe are his prey, and unto them all he is a scourge and a hell.

To man he is a divine ambassador, a minister plenipotentiary, the Creator's special representative. He infests him in his cradle; clings in bunches to his gummy eyelids; buzzes and bites and harries him, robbing him of his sleep and his weary mother of her strength in those long vigils which she devotes to protecting her child from this pest's persecutions. The fly harries the sick man in his home, in the hospital, even on his death-bed at his last gasp. Pesters him at his meals; previously hunts up patients suffering from loathsome and deadly diseases; wades in their sores, gaums its legs with a million death-dealing germs, then comes to that healthy man's table and wipes these things off on the butter and discharges a bowel-load of typhoid germs and excrement on his batter-cakes. The housefly wrecks more human constitutions and destroys more human lives than all God's multitude of misery-messengers and death-agents put together.

Shem was full of hookworms. It is wonderful, the thorough and comprehensive study which the Creator devoted to the great work of making man miserable. I have said he devised a special affliction-agent for each and every detail of man's structure, overlooking not a single one, and I said the truth. Many poor people have to go barefoot, because they cannot afford shoes. The Creator saw his opportunity. I will remark, in passing, that he always has his eye on the poor. Nine-tenths of his disease-inventions were intended for the poor, and they *get* them. The well-to-do get only what is left over. Do not suspect me of speaking unheedfully, for it is not so: the vast bulk of the Creator's affliction-inventions *are* specially designed for the persecution of the poor. You could guess this by the fact that one of the pulpit's finest and commonest names for the Creator is "The Friend of the Poor." Under no circumstances does the pulpit ever pay the Creator a compliment that has a vestige of truth in it. The poor's most implacable and unwearying enemy is their Father in Heaven. The poor's only real friend is their fellow man. He is sorry for them, he pities them, and he shows it by his deeds. He does much to relieve their distresses; and in every case their Father in Heaven gets the credit of it.

Just so with diseases. If science exterminates a disease which has been working for God, it is God that gets the credit, and all the pulpits break into grateful advertising-raptures and call attention to how good he is! Yes, *he* has done it. Perhaps he has waited a thousand years before doing it. That is nothing; the pulpit says he was thinking about it all the time. When exasperated men rise up and sweep away an age-long tyranny and set a nation free, the first thing the delighted pulpit does is to advertise it as God's work, and invite the people to get down on their knees and pour out their thanks to him for it. And the pulpit says with admiring emotion, "Let tyrants understand that the Eye that never sleeps is upon them; and let them remember that the Lord our God will not always be patient, but will loose the whirlwinds of his wrath upon them in his appointed day."

They forget to mention that he is the slowest mover in the universe; that his Eye that never sleeps, might as well, since it takes it a century to see what any other eye would see in a week; that in all history there is not an instance where he thought of a noble deed *first*, but always thought of it just a little after somebody else had thought of it and *done* it. He arrives then, and annexes the dividend.

Very well, six thousand years ago Shem was full of hookworms. Microscopic in size, invisible to the unaided eye. All of the Creator's specially-deadly disease-producers are invisible. It is an ingenious idea. For thousands of years it kept man from getting at the roots of his maladies, and defeated his attempts to master them. It is only very recently that science has succeeded in exposing some of these treacheries.

The very latest of these blessed triumphs of science is the discovery and identification of the ambuscaded assassin which goes by the name of the hookworm. Its special prey is the barefooted poor. It lies in wait in warm regions and sandy places and digs its way into their unprotected feet.

The hookworm was discovered two or three years ago by a physician, who had been patiently studying its victims for a long time. The disease induced by the hookworm had been doing its evil work here and there in the earth ever since Shem landed on Ararat, but it was never suspected to *be* a disease at all. The people who had it were merely supposed to be *lazy* and were therefore despised and made fun of, when they should have been pitied. The hookworm is a peculiarly sneaking and underhand invention, and has done its surreptitious work unmolested for ages; but that physician and his helpers will exterminate it now.

God is back of this. He has been thinking about it for six thousand years, and making up his mind. The idea of exterminating the hookworm was his. He came very near doing it before Dr. Charles Wardell Stiles did. But he is in time to get the credit of it. He always is.

It is going to cost a million dollars. He was probably just in the act of contributing that sum when a man pushed in ahead of him—as usual. Mr. Rockefeller. He furnishes the million, but the credit will go elsewhere—as usual. This morning's journals tell us something about the hookworm's operations:

> The hookworm parasites often so lower the vitality of those who are affected as to retard their physical and mental development, render them more susceptible to other diseases, make labor less efficient, and in the sections where the malady is most prevalent greatly increase the death rate from consumption, pneumonia, typhoid fever and malaria. It has been shown that the lowered vitality of multitudes, long attributed to malaria and climate and seriously affecting economic development, is in fact due in some districts to this parasite. The disease is by no means confined to any one class; it takes its toll of suffering and death from the highly intelligent and well to do as well as from the less fortunate. It is a conservative estimate that two millions of our people are affected by this parasite. The disease is more common and more serious in children of school age than in other persons.
>
> Widespread and serious as the infection is, there is still a most encouraging outlook. The disease can be easily recognized, readily and effectively treated and by simple and proper sanitary precautions successfully prevented, with God's help.

The poor little children are under the Eye that never sleeps, you see. They have had that ill luck in all the ages. They and "the Lord's poor"—as the sarcastic phrase goes—have never been able to get away from that Eye's attentions.

Yes, the poor, the humble, the ignorant—they are the ones that catch it. Take the "sleeping sickness," of Africa. This atrocious cruelty has for its victims a race of ignorant and unoffending blacks whom God placed in a remote wilderness, and bent his parental Eye upon them—the one that never sleeps when there is a chance to breed sorrow for somebody. He arranged for these people before the Flood. The chosen agent was a fly, related to the tzetze; the tzetze is a fly which has command of the Zambesi country and stings cattle and horses to death, thus rendering that region uninhabitable by man. The tzetze's awful relative deposits a microbe which produces the Sleeping Sickness. Ham was full of these microbes, and when the voyage was over he discharged them in Africa and the havoc began, never to find amelioration until six thousand years should go by and science should pry into the mystery and hunt out the cause of the disease. The pious nations are now thanking God, and praising him for coming to the rescue of his poor blacks. The pulpit says the praise is due to him, for the reason that the scientists got their inspiration from him. He is surely a curious Being. He commits a fearful crime, continues that crime unbroken for six thousand years, and is then entitled to praise because he suggests to somebody else to modify its severities. He is called patient, and he certainly must be patient, or he would have sunk the pulpit in perdition ages ago for the ghastly compliments it pays him.

Science has this to say about the Sleeping Sickness, otherwise called the Negro Lethargy.

> It is characterised by periods of sleep recurring at intervals. The disease lasts from four months to four years, and is always fatal. The victim appears at first languid, weak, pallid, and stupid. His eyelids become puffy, an eruption appears on his skin. He falls asleep while talking, eating, or working. As the disease progresses he is fed with difficulty and becomes much emaciated. The failure of nutrition and the appearance of bedsores are followed by convulsions and death. Some patients become insane.

It is he whom Church and people call Our Father in Heaven who has invented the fly and sent him to inflict this dreary long misery and melancholy and wretchedness, and decay of body and mind, upon a poor savage who has done the Great Criminal no harm. There isn't a man in the world who doesn't pity that poor black sufferer, and there isn't a man that wouldn't make him whole if he could. To find the one person who has no pity for him you must go to heaven; to find the one person who is able to heal him and couldn't be persuaded to do it, you must go to the same place. There is only one father cruel enough to afflict his child with that horrible disease—only one. Not all the eternities can produce another one. Do you like reproachful poetical indignations warmly expressed? Here is one, hot from the heart of a slave:

"*Man's* inhumanity to man
Makes countless thousands mourn!"

I will tell you a pleasant tale which has in it a touch of pathos. A man got religion, and asked the priest what he must do to be worthy of his new estate. The priest said, "Imitate our Father in Heaven, learn to be like him." The man studied his Bible diligently and thoroughly and understandingly, and then with prayers for heavenly guidance instituted his imitations. He tricked his wife into falling down stairs, and she broke her back and became a paralytic for life; he betrayed his brother into the hands of a sharper, who robbed him of his all and landed him in the almshouse; he inoculated one son with hookworms, another with the sleeping sickness, another with the gonorrhea, he furnished one daughter with scarlet fever and ushered her into her teens deaf dumb and blind for life; and after helping a rascal seduce the remaining one, he closed his doors against her and she died in a brothel cursing him. Then he reported to the priest, who said that *that* was no way to imitate his Father in

Heaven. The convert asked wherein he had failed, but the priest changed the subject and inquired what kind of weather he was having, up his way.

Letter . . .

Man is without any doubt the most interesting fool there is. Also the most eccentric. He hasn't a single written law, in his Bible or out of it, which has any but just one purpose and intention—to *limit or defeat a law of God.*

He can seldom take a plain fact and get any but a wrong meaning out of it. He cannot help this; it is the way the confusion he calls his mind is constructed. Consider the things he concedes, and the curious conclusions he draws from them.

For instance, he concedes that God made man. Made him without man's desire or privity.

This seems to plainly and indisputably make God, and God alone, responsible for man's acts. But man denies this.

He concedes that God has made angels perfect, without blemish, and immune from pain and death, and that he could have been similarly kind to man if he had wanted to, but denies that he was under any moral obligation to do it.

He concedes that man has no moral right to visit the child of his begetting with wanton cruelties, painful diseases and death, but refuses to limit God's privileges in this sort with the children of his begetting.

The Bible and man's statutes forbid murder, adultery, fornication, lying, treachery, robbery, oppression and other crimes, but contend that God is free of these laws and has a right to break them when he will.

He concedes that God gives to each man his temperament, his disposition, at birth; he concedes that man cannot by any process change this temperament, but must remain always under its dominion. Yet if it be full of dreadful passions, in one man's case, and barren of them in another man's, it is right and rational to punish the one for his crimes, and reward the other for abstaining from crime.

There—let us consider these curiosities.

Temperament (disposition.) Take two extremes of temperament—the goat and the tortoise.

Neither of these creatures makes its own temperament, but is born with it, like man, and can no more change it than can man.

Temperament is the *law of God*, written in the heart of every creature by

God's own hand, and *must* be obeyed, and *will* be obeyed, in spite of all restricting or forbidding statutes, let them emanate whence they may.

Very well, lust is the dominant feature of the goat's temperament, the law of God in its heart, and it must obey it and *will* obey it the whole day long in the rutting season; without stopping to eat or drink. If the Bible said to the goat "Thou shalt not fornicate, thou shalt not commit adultery," even man—sap-headed man—would recognize the foolishness of the prohibition, and would grant that the goat ought not to be punished for obeying the law of his make. Yet he thinks it right and just that man should be put under the prohibition. *All* men. All alike.

On its face this is stupid, for, by temperament, which is the *real* law of God, many men are *goats* and can't *help* committing adultery when they get a chance; whereas there are numbers of men who, by temperament, can keep their purity and let an opportunity go by if the woman lacks in attractiveness. But the Bible doesn't allow adultery *at all*, whether a person can help it or not. It allows no distinction between goat and tortoise—the excitable goat, the emotional goat, that *has* to have some adultery every day or fade and die; and the tortoise, that cold calm puritan, that takes a treat only once in two years and then goes to sleep in the midst of it and doesn't wake up for sixty days. No lady goat is safe from criminal assault, even on the Sabbath Day, when there is a gentleman goat within three miles to leeward of her and nothing in the way but a fence fourteen feet high, whereas neither the gentleman tortoise nor the lady tortoise is ever hungry enough for the solemn joys of fornication to be willing to break the Sabbath to get them. Now according to man's curious reasoning, the goat has earned punishment, and the tortoise praise.

"Thou shalt not commit adultery" is a command which makes no distinction between the following persons. They are all required to obey it:

Children at birth.

Children in the cradle.

School children.

Youths and maidens.

Fresh adults.

Older ones.

Men and women of 40.

Of 50.

Of 60.

Of 70.

Of 80.

Of 90.

Of 100.

The command does not distribute its burden equally, and cannot.

It is not hard upon the three sets of children.

It is hard—harder—still harder upon the next three sets—cruelly hard.

It is blessedly softened to the next three sets.

It has now done all the damage it can, and might as well be put out of commission.

Yet with comical imbecility it is continued, and the four remaining estates are put under its crushing ban. Poor old wrecks, they couldn't disobey if they tried. And think—because they holily refrain from adulterating each other, they get praise for it! Which is nonsense; for even the Bible knows enough to know that if the oldest veteran there could get his lost hey-day back again for an hour he would cast that commandment to the winds and ruin the first woman he came across, even though she were an entire stranger.

It is as I have said: every statute in the Bible and in the law books is an attempt to defeat a law of God—in other words an unalterable and indestructible law of nature. These people's God has shown them by a million acts that he respects none of the Bible's statutes. He breaks every one of them himself, adultery and all.

The law of God, as quite plainly expressed in woman's *construction* is this:

There shall be *no limit* put upon your intercourse with the other sex sexually, at any time of life.

The law of God, as quite plainly expressed in *man's* construction is this:

During your entire life you shall be under inflexible *limits and restrictions*, sexually.

During 27 days in every month (in the absence of pregnancy) from the time a woman is seven years old till she dies of old age, she is ready for action, and *competent*. As competent as the candlestick is to receive the candle. Competent every day, competent every night. Also, she *wants* that candle—yearns for it, longs for it, hankers after it, as commanded by the law of God in her heart.

But man is only briefly competent; and only then in the moderate measure applicable to the word in *his* sex's case. He is competent from the age of sixteen or seventeen thenceforward for thirty-five years. After 50 his performance is of poor quality, the intervals between are wide, and its satisfactions of no great value to either party; whereas his great-grandmother is as good as new. There is nothing the matter with her plant. Her candlestick is as firm as ever, whereas his candle is increasingly softened and weakened by the weather of age, as the years go by, until at last it can no longer stand, and is mournfully laid to rest in the hope of a blessed resurrection which is never to come.

By the woman's make, her plant has to be out of service three days in the month and during a part of her pregnancy. These are times of discomfort, often of suffering. For fair and just compensation she has the high privilege of unlimited adultery all the other days of her life.

That is the law of God, as revealed in her make. What becomes of this high privilege? Does she live in the free enjoyment of it? No. Nowhere in the whole world. She is robbed of it everywhere. Who does this? Man. Man's statutes—ordained against her without allowing her a vote. Also God's statutes—if the Bible is the Word of God.

Now there you have a sample of man's "reasoning powers," as he calls them. He observes certain facts. For instance, that in all his life he never sees the day that he can satisfy *one* woman; also, that no woman ever sees the day that she can't overwork, and defeat, and put out of commission any *ten* masculine plants that can be put to bed to her.* He puts those strikingly-suggestive and luminous facts together, and from them draws this astonishing conclusion:

The Creator intended the woman to be restricted to one man.

So he concretes that singular conclusion into a law, for good and all.

And he does it without consulting the woman, although she has a thousand times more at stake in the matter than he has. His procreative competency is limited to an average of a hundred exercises per year for 50 years, hers is good for 3,000 a year for that whole time—and as many years longer as she may live. Thus his life-interest in the matter is 5,000 refreshments, while hers is 150,000; yet instead of fairly and honorably leaving the making of the law to

*In the Sandwich Islands in 1866 a buxom royal princess died. Occupying a place of distinguished honor at her funeral were 36 splendidly built young native men. In a laudatory song which celebrated the various merits, achievements and accomplishments of the late princess those 36 stallions were called her *harem*, and the song said it had been her pride and her boast that she kept the whole of them busy, and that several times it had happened that more than one of them had been able to charge overtime.

the person who has an overwhelming interest at stake in it, this immeasurable hog, who has nothing at stake in it worth considering, makes it himself!

You have heretofore found out, by my teachings, that man is a fool; you are now aware that woman is a *damned* fool.

Now if you or any other really intelligent person were arranging the fairnesses and justices between man and woman, you would give the man a one-fiftieth interest in one woman, and the woman a *harem*. Now wouldn't you? Necessarily. I give you my word, this creature with the decrepit candle has arranged it exactly the other way. Solomon, who was one of the Deity's favorites, had a copulation-cabinet composed of 700 wives and 300 concubines. To save his life he could not have kept two of those young creatures satisfactorily refreshed, even if he had had fifteen experts to help him. Necessarily almost the entire thousand had to go hungry years and years on a stretch. Conceive of a man hard-hearted enough to look daily upon all that suffering and not be moved to mitigate it. He even wantonly *added* a sharp pang to that pathetic misery; for he kept within those women's sight, always, stalwart watchmen whose splendid masculine forms made the poor lassies' mouths water but who hadn't anything to solace a candlestick with, these gentry being eunuchs. A eunuch is a person whose candle has been put out. By art.*

From time to time, as I go along, I will take up a Biblical statute and show you that it always violates a law of God, and then is imported into the law books of the nations, where it continues its violations. But those things will keep; there is no hurry.

Letter . . .

The Ark continued its voyage, drifting around here and there and yonder, compassless and uncontrolled, the sport of the random winds and the swirling currents. And the rain, the rain, the rain! it kept on falling, pouring, drenching, flooding. No such rain had ever been seen before. Sixteen inches a day had been heard of, but that was nothing to this. This was a hundred and twenty inches a day—ten feet! At this incredible rate it rained forty days and forty nights, and submerged every hill that was 400 feet high. Then the heavens and even the angels went dry; no more water was to be had.

*I purpose publishing these Letters here in the world before I return to you. Two editions. One, unedited, for Bible readers and their children; the other, expurgated, for persons of refinement.

As a Universal Flood it was a disappointment, but there had been heaps of Universal Floods before, as is witnessed by all the Bibles of all the nations, and this was as good as the best one.

At last the Ark soared aloft and came to a rest on the top of Mount Ararat, 17,000 feet above the valley, and its living freight got out and went down the mountain.

Noah planted a vineyard, and drank of the wine and was overcome.

This person had been selected from all the populations because he was the best sample there was. He was to start the human race on a new basis. This was the new basis. The promise was bad. To go further with the experiment was to run a great and most unwise risk. Now was the time to do with these people what had been so judiciously done with the others—drown them. Anybody but the Creator would have seen this. But he didn't see it. That is, maybe he didn't. It is claimed that from the beginning of time he foresaw everything that would happen in the world. If that is true, he foresaw that Adam and Eve would eat the apple; that their posterity would be unendurable and have to be drowned; that Noah's posterity would in their turn be unendurable, and that by and by he would have to leave his throne in heaven and come down and be crucified to save that same tiresome human race again. The whole of it? No! A part of it? Yes. How much of it? In each generation, for hundreds and hundreds of generations, a billion would die and all go to perdition except perhaps ten thousand out of the billion. The ten thousand would have to come from the little body of Christians, and only one in the hundred of that little body would stand any chance. None of them at all except such Roman Catholics as should have the luck to have a priest handy to sandpaper their souls at the last gasp, and here and there a Presbyterian. No others saveable. All the others damned. By the million.

Shall you grant that he foresaw all this? The pulpit grants it. It is the same as granting that in the matter of intellect the Deity is the Head Pauper of the Universe, and that in the matter of morals and character he is away down on the level of David.

Letter . . .

The two Testaments are interesting, each in its own way. The Old one gives us a picture of these people's Deity as he was before he got religion, the other one gives us a picture of him as he appeared afterward. The Old Testament is interested mainly in blood and sensuality, the New one in salvation. Salvation by fire.

The first time the Deity came down to earth he brought life and death; when he came the second time, he brought hell.

Life was not a valuable gift, but death was. Life was a fever-dream made up of joys embittered by sorrows, pleasure poisoned by pain; a dream that was a nightmare-confusion of spasmodic and fleeting delights, ecstasies, exultations, happinesses, interspersed with long-drawn miseries, griefs, perils, horrors, disappointments, defeats, humiliations and despairs—the heaviest curse devisable by divine ingenuity; but death was sweet, death was gentle, death was kind, death healed the bruised spirit and the broken heart, and gave them rest and forgetfulness; death was man's best friend, his only friend; when man could endure life no longer, death came, and set him free.

In time, the Deity perceived that death was a mistake; a mistake, in that it was insufficient; insufficient, for the reason that while it was an admirable agent for the inflicting of misery upon the survivor, it allowed the dead person himself to escape from all further persecution in the blessed refuge of the grave. This was not satisfactory. A way must be contrived to pursue the dead beyond the tomb.

The Deity pondered this matter during four thousand years unsuccessfully, but as soon as he came down to earth and became a Christian his mind cleared and he knew what to do. *He invented hell*, and proclaimed it.

Now here is a curious thing. It is believed by everybody that while he was in heaven he was stern, hard, resentful, jealous, and cruel; but that when he came down to earth and assumed the name Jesus Christ, he became the opposite of what he was before: that is to say, he became sweet, and gentle, merciful, forgiving, and all harshness disappeared from his nature and a deep and yearning love for his poor human children took its place. Whereas it was as Jesus Christ that he devised hell and proclaimed it!

Which is to say, that as the meek and gentle Savior he was a thousand billion times crueler than ever he was in the Old Testament—oh, incomparably more atrocious than ever he was when he was at his very worst in those old days!

Meek and gentle? By and by we will examine this popular sarcasm by the light of the hell which he invented.

While it is true that the palm for malignity must be granted to Jesus, the inventor of hell, he was hard and ungentle enough for all godlike purposes even before he became a Christian. It does not appear that he ever stopped to reflect that *he* was to blame when a man went wrong, inasmuch as the man was merely acting in accordance with the disposition he had afflicted him with. No, he punished the man, instead of punishing himself. Moreover the punishment usually oversized the offence. Often, too, it fell, not upon the doer of a misdeed, but upon somebody else—a chief man, the head of a community, for instance.

And Israel abode in Shittim, and the people began to commit whoredom with the daughters of Moab.

And the Lord said unto Moses, Take *all the heads of the people*, and hang them up before the Lord against the sun, that the fierce anger of the Lord may be turned away from Israel.

Does that look fair to you? It does not appear that the "heads of the people" got any of the adultery, yet it is they that are hanged, instead of "the people."

If it was fair and right in that day it would be fair and right to-day, for the pulpit maintains that God's justice is eternal and unchangeable; also that he is the Fountain of Morals; and that his morals are eternal and unchangeable. Very well, then, we must believe that if the people of New York should begin to commit whoredom with the daughters of New Jersey, it would be fair and right to set up a gallows in front of the city hall and hang the mayor and the sheriff and the judges and the archbishop on it, although they did not get any of it. It does not look right to me.

Moreover, you may be quite sure of one thing: *it couldn't happen.* These people would not allow it. They are better than their Bible. *Nothing* would happen here, except some lawsuits, for damages, if the incident couldn't be hushed up; and even down South they would not proceed against persons who did not get any of it; they would get a rope and hunt for the corespondents; and if they couldn't find them they would lynch a nigger.

Things have greatly improved since the Almighty's time, let the pulpit say what it may.

Will you examine the Deity's morals and disposition and conduct a little further? And will you remember that in the Sunday school the little children are urged to love the Almighty, and honor him, and praise him, and make him their model and try to be as like him as they can? Read:

1 And the LORD spake unto Moses, saying,

2 Avenge the children of Israel of the Midianites: afterward shalt thou be gathered unto thy people.

7 And they warred against the Midianites, as the LORD commanded Moses; and they slew all the males.

8 And they slew the kings of Midian, besides the rest of them that were slain; *namely*, Evi, and Rekem, and Zur, and Hur, and Reba, five kings of Midian: Balaam also the son of Beor they slew with the sword.

9 And the children of Israel took *all* the women of Midian captives, and their little ones, and took the spoil of all their cattle, and all their flocks, and all their goods.

10 And they burnt all their cities wherein they dwelt, and all their goodly castles, with fire.

11 And they took all the spoil, and all the prey, *both* of men and of beasts.

12 And they brought the captives, and the prey, and the spoil unto Moses and Eleazar the priest, and unto the congregation of the children of Israel, unto the camp at the plains of Moab, which *are* by Jordan *near* Jericho.

13 And Moses, and Eleazar the priest, and all the princes of the congregation, went forth to meet them without the camp.

14 And Moses was wroth with the officers of the host, *with* the captains over thousands, and captains over hundreds, which came from the battle.

15 And Moses said unto them, Have ye saved all the women alive?

16 Behold, these caused the children of Israel, through the counsel of Balaam, to commit trespass against the LORD in the matter of Peor, and there was a plague among the congregation of the LORD.

17 Now therefore kill every male among the little ones, and kill every woman that hath known man by lying with him.

18 But all the women-children, that have not known a man by lying with him, keep alive for yourselves.

19 And do ye abide without the camp seven days: whosoever hath killed any person, and whosoever hath touched any slain, purify *both* yourselves and your captives on the third day, and on the seventh day.

20 And purify all *your* raiment, and all that is made of skins, and all work of goats' *hair*, and all things made of wood.

21 And Eleazar the priest said unto the men of war which went to the battle,

This *is* the ordinance of the law which the Lord commanded Moses.

25 And the Lord spake unto Moses, saying,

26 Take the sum of the prey that was taken, *both* of man and of beast, thou, and Eleazar the priest, and the chief fathers of the congregation:

27 And divide the prey into two parts; between them that took the war upon them, who went out to battle, and between all the congregation:

28 And levy a tribute unto the Lord of the men of war which went out to battle.

31 And Moses and Eleazar the priest did as the Lord commanded Moses.

32 And the booty, *being* the rest of the prey which the men of war had caught, was six hundred thousand, and seventy thousand, and five thousand sheep,

33 And threescore and twelve thousand beeves,

34 And threescore and one thousand asses,

35 And thirty and two thousand persons in all, of women that had not known man by lying with him.

40 And the persons *were* sixteen thousand, of which the Lord's tribute *was* thirty and two persons.

41 And Moses gave the tribute, *which was* was the Lord's heave-offering, unto *Eleazar* the priest; as the Lord commanded Moses.

47 Even of the children of Israel's half, Moses took one portion of fifty, *both* of man and of beast, and gave them unto the Levites, which kept the charge of the tabernacle of the Lord; as the Lord commanded Moses.

10 When thou comest nigh unto a city to fight against it, then proclaim peace unto it.

13 And when the Lord thy God hath delivered it into thine hands, thou shalt smite every male thereof with the edge of the sword:

14 But the women, and the little ones, and the cattle, and all that is in the city, *even* all the spoil thereof, shalt thou take unto thyself: and thou shalt eat the spoil of thine enemies, which the Lord thy God hath given thee.

15 Thus shalt thou do unto all the cities *which* are very far off from thee, which are not of the cities of these nations.

16 But of the cities of these people, which the Lord thy God doth give thee for an inheritance, *thou shalt save alive* NOTHING THAT BREATHETH.

The Biblical law says:
"*Thou shalt not kill.*"

The law of *God*, planted in the heart of man at his birth, says:

"Thou *shalt* kill."

The chapter I have quoted, shows you that the book-statute is once more a failure. It cannot set aside the more powerful law of nature.

According to the belief of these people, it was God himself who said:

"Thou shalt not kill."

Then it is plain that he cannot keep his own commandments.

He killed all those people—*every male.*

They had offended the Deity in some way. We know what the offence was, without looking; that is to say, we know it was a trifle; some small thing that no one but a god would attach any importance to. It is more than likely that a Midianite had been duplicating the conduct of one Onan, who was commanded to "go in unto his brother's wife"—which he did; but instead of finishing, "he spilled it on the ground." The Lord slew Onan for that, for the Lord could never abide indelicacy. The Lord slew Onan, and to this day the Christian world cannot understand why he stopped with Onan, instead of slaying all the inhabitants for three hundred miles around—they being innocent of offence, and therefore the very ones he would usually slay. For that had always been his idea of fair dealing. If he had had a motto, it would have read, "Let no innocent person escape." You remember what he did in the time of the flood. There were multitudes and multitudes of tiny little children, and he knew they had never done him any harm; but their *relations* had, and that was enough for him: he saw the waters rise toward their screaming lips, he saw the wild terror in their eyes, he saw that agony of appeal in the mothers' faces which would have touched any heart but his, but he was after the guiltless particularly, and he drowned those poor little chaps.

And you will remember that in the case of Adam's posterity *all* the billions are innocent—*none* of them had a share in his offence, but the Deity holds them guilty to this day. None gets off, except by acknowledging that guilt—no cheaper lie will answer.

Some Midianite must have repeated Onan's act, and brought that dire disaster upon his nation. If that was not the indelicacy that outraged the feelings of the Deity, then I know what it was: some Midianite had been *pissing against the wall.* I am sure of it, for that was an impropriety which the Source of all Etiquette *never* could stand. A person could piss against a tree, he could piss on his mother, he could piss his own breeches, and get off, but he must not piss against the wall—that would be going quite too far. The origin of the divine prejudice against this humble crime is not stated; but we know that the prejudice was very strong—so strong that nothing but a wholesale massacre of the people inhabiting the region where the wall was defiled could satisfy the Deity.

Take the case of Jeroboam. "I will cut off from Jeroboam him that pisseth against the wall." It was done. And not only was the man that did it cut off, but everybody else.

The same with the house of Baasha: everybody was exterminated, kinsfolks, friends, and all, leaving "not one that pisseth against a wall."

In the case of Jeroboam you have a striking instance of the Deity's custom of not limiting his punishments to the guilty; the innocent are included. Even the "remnant" of that unhappy house was removed, even "as a man taketh away dung, till it be all gone." That includes the women, the young maids, and the little girls. All innocent, for *they* couldn't piss against a wall. Nobody of that sex can. None but members of the other sex can achieve that feat.

A curious prejudice. And it still exists. Protestant parents still keep the Bible handy in the house, so that the children can study it; and one of the first things the little boys and girls learn is to be righteous and holy and not piss against the wall. They study those passages more than they study any others, except those which incite to masturbation. *Those* they hunt out and study in private. No Protestant child exists who does not masturbate. That art is the earliest accomplishment his religion confers upon him. Also the earliest *her* religion confers upon *her*.

The Bible has this advantage over all other books that teach refinement and good manners: that it goes to the child: it goes to the mind at its most impressible and receptive age—the others have to wait.

"Thou shalt have a paddle upon thy weapon: and it shall be, when thou wilt ease thyself abroad, thou shalt dig therewith, and shalt turn back and cover that which cometh from thee."

That rule was made in the old days because

"The Lord thy God walketh in the midst of thy camp."

It is probably not worth while to try to find out, for certain, why the Midianites were exterminated. We can only be sure that it was for no large offence; for the cases of Adam, and the Flood, and the defilers of the wall, teach us that much. A Midianite may have left his paddle at home and thus brought on the trouble. However, it is no matter. The main thing is the trouble itself, and the morals of one kind and another that it offers for the instruction and elevation of the Christian of to-day.

God wrote upon the tables of stone—

"Thou shalt not kill."

Also—

"Thou shalt not commit adultery."

Paul, speaking by the divine voice, advised against sexual intercourse *altogether.* A great change from the divine view as it existed at the time of the Midianite incident.

Letter . . .

Human history in all ages, is red with blood, and bitter with hate, and stained with cruelties; but not since Biblical times have these features been without a limit of some kind. Even the Church, which is credited with having spilt more innocent blood, since the beginning of its supremacy, than all the political wars put together have spilt, has observed a limit. A sort of limit. But you notice that when the Lord God of Heaven and Earth, adored Father of Man, goes to war, there is no limit. He is totally without mercy—he, who is called the Fountain of Mercy. He slays, slays, slays! all the men, all the beasts, all the boys, all the babies; also all the women and all the girls, except those that have not been deflowered.

He makes no distinction between innocent and guilty. The babies were innocent, the beasts were innocent, many of the men, many of the women, many of the boys, many of the girls, were innocent, yet they had to suffer with the guilty. What the insane Father required was blood and misery; he was indifferent as to who furnished it. The heaviest punishment of all was meted out to persons who could not by any possibility have deserved so horrible a fate—the 32,000 virgins. Their naked privacies were probed, to make sure that they still possessed the hymen unruptured; after this humiliation they were sent away from the land that had been their home, to be sold into slavery; the worst of slaveries and the shamefulest, the slavery of prostitution; bed-slavery, to excite lust, and satisfy it with their bodies; slavery to any buyer, be he gentleman or be he a coarse and filthy ruffian.

It was the Father that inflicted this ferocious and undeserved punishment upon those bereaved and friendless virgins, whose parents and kindred he had slaughtered before their eyes. And were they praying to him for pity and rescue, meantime? Without a doubt of it.

These virgins were "spoil," plunder, booty. He claimed his share and got it. What use had *he* for virgins? Examine his later history and you will know.

His priests got a share of the virgins, too. What use could priests make of virgins? The private history of the Roman Catholic confessional can answer that question for you. The confessional's chief amusement has been seduction—in all the ages of the Church. Père Hyacinth testifies that of 100 priests confessed by him, 99 had used the confessional effectively for the seduction of married women and young girls. One priest confessed that of 900 girls and women whom he had served as father confessor in his time, none had escaped his lecherous embrace but the elderly and the homely. The official list of questions which the priest is *required* to ask will overmasteringly excite any woman who is not a paralytic.

There is nothing in either savage or civilized history that is more utterly complete, more remorselessly sweeping than the Father of Mercy's campaign among the Midianites. The official report does not furnish incidents, episodes, and minor details, it deals only in information in masses: *all* the virgins, *all* the men, *all* the babies, *all* "creatures *that breathe*," *all* houses, *all* cities; it gives you just one vast picture, spread abroad here and there and yonder, as far as eye can reach, of charred ruin and storm-swept desolation; your imagination adds a brooding stillness, an aweful hush—the hush of death. But of course there *were* incidents. Where shall we get them?

Out of history of yesterday's date. Out of history made by the red Indian of America. He has duplicated God's work, and done it in the very spirit of God. In 1862 the Indians in Minnesota, having been deeply wronged and treacherously treated by the government of the United States, rose against the white settlers and massacred them; massacred all they could lay their hands upon, sparing neither age nor sex. Consider this incident:

Twelve Indians broke into a farm house at daybreak and captured the family. It consisted of the farmer and his wife and four daughters, the youngest aged fourteen and the eldest eighteen. They crucified the parents; that is to say, they stood them stark naked against the wall of the living room and nailed their hands to the wall. Then they stripped the daughters bare, stretched them upon the floor in front of their parents, and repeatedly ravished them. Finally they crucified the girls against the wall opposite the parents, and cut off their noses and their breasts. They also—but I will not go into that. There is a limit. There are indignities so atrocious that the pen cannot write them. One member of that poor crucified family—the father—was still alive when help came two days later.

Now you have *one* incident of the Minnesota massacre. I could give you fifty. They would cover all the different kinds of cruelty the brutal human talent has ever invented.

And now you know, by these sure indications, what happened under the personal direction of the Father of Mercies in his Midianite campaign. The Minnesota campaign was merely a duplicate of the Midianite raid. Nothing happened in the one that did not happen in the other.

No, that is not strictly true. The Indian was more merciful than was the Father of Mercies. He sold no virgins into slavery to minister to the lusts of the murderers of their kindred while their sad lives might last; he raped them, then charitably made their subsequent sufferings brief, ending them with the precious gift of death. He burned some of the houses, but not all of them. He carried off innocent dumb brutes, but he took the lives of none.

Would you expect this same conscienceless God, this moral bankrupt, to become a *teacher* of morals; of gentleness; of meekness; of righteousness; of purity? It looks impossible, extravagant; but listen to him. These are his own words:

Blessed are the poor in spirit, for theirs is the kingdom of heaven.

Blessed are they that mourn, for they shall be comforted.

Blessed are the meek, for they shall inherit the earth.

Blessed are they which do hunger and thirst after righteousness, for they shall be filled.

Blessed are the merciful, for they shall obtain mercy.

Blessed are the pure in heart, for they shall see God.

Blessed are the peace-makers, for they shall be called *the children of God.*

Blessed are they which are persecuted for righteousness' sake, for theirs is the kingdom of heaven.

Blessed are ye when men shall revile you and persecute you, and say all manner of evil against you falsely for my sake.

The mouth that uttered these immense sarcasms, these giant hypocrisies, is the very same that ordered the wholesale massacre of the Midianitish men and babies and cattle; the wholesale destruction of house and city; the wholesale banishment of the virgins into a filthy and unspeakable slavery. This is the same person who brought upon the Midianites the fiendish cruelties which were repeated by the red Indians, detail by detail, in Minnesota eighteen centuries later. The Midianite episode filled him with joy. So did the Minnesota one, or he would have prevented it.

The Beatitudes and the quoted chapters from Numbers and Deuteronomy ought always to be read from the pulpit *together;* then the congregation would get an all-around view of Our Father in Heaven. Yet not in a single instance have I ever known a clergyman to do this.

APPENDICES

APPENDIX 1

Original Continuation of "Autobiography of Eve"†

[Material deleted by Mark Twain during revision of the manuscript is inserted between angle brackets (⟨ ⟩) and printed in bold type.]

* * * *

Year 10. Next came our little Abel. I think we were a year and a half or two years old when Cain was born, and about three or three and a half when Abel was added. By this time Adam was getting to understand. Gradually his experiments grew less and less troublesome, and finally, within a year after the birth of Gladys and Edwina—years 5 and 6—ceased altogether. He came to love the children fondly, after he had gotten them scientifically classified, and from that time till now the bliss of Eden is perfect.

⟨**Ah, well, in that old simple, ignorant time it never entered our unthinking heads that we, humble, unknown and inconsequential little people, were cradling, nursing and watching over the most conspicuous and stupendous event which would happen in the universe for a thousand years—the founding of the human race!**

What a solitude the world was in those days, and what a swarming hive of human life it is now!⟩ The solitude was soon modified. When we were 30 years old we had 30 children, and our children had 300; in 20 years more the population was 6,000; by the end of the second century it was become millions. For we are a long-lived race, and not many died. More than half of my children are still alive. I did not cease to bear until I was approaching middle age. As a rule, such of my children as survived the perils of childhood have continued to live, and this has been the case with the other families. ⟨**When the population reached five billions the earth was heavily burdened to support it. But wars, physicians, pestilences and**⟩ famines brought relief, from time to time, and in some degree reduced the prodigious pressure. The memorable benefaction of the year 508, which was a famine reinforced by a pestilence, swept away sixteen hundred millions of people in nine months. **⟨My Gladys was a victim. She had never been strong since the shock of the Fall, she was of a sensitive and emotional nature, and her weakened constitution was not able to bear up under the horrors of the time. * * * * She was in the prime and glory of womanhood, poor thing, her sight was unimpaired, she had not a wrinkle nor a gray hair. Naturally her death was a stupendous event. No occurrence approaching it in importance had happened for centuries; nothing exceeding it in importance could have happened but Adam's death or mine. When the electric spark carried the word abroad that the First Daughter of the Race was dead, the news seemed to paralyze the world for the moment; the commotion which followed is not describable. From all the islands and from all the continents, from the obscurest corners of the globe as well as from its capital cities and centres of civilization, the grief of kings, emperors and nations was flashed back under the oceans and over the mountains and plains, and laid in sympathy and homage at our feet. These kindly words were precious to us; they could not heal our hurt, but they softened the pain and helped make it bearable. We read all we could of them; not the hundred thousandth part, but all we could; and we destroyed none of them, but kept them all; and they, and the like which came when Adam died I still keep in the vaults of the chief temple and shall leave them, with other memorials, when I die, to be treasured among the archives of the nations.**

The poetry which was sent from every part of the globe was marvelous for bulk and feeling, and was another testimony to the universality of the sorrow and distraction caused by my daughter's loss, but we did not preserve it. It was kindly meant, but in most cases was poor. The verses of the Poet Laureate had a universal currency, but that was mainly because they were official. The laureate was not expecting the event, and was taken unprepared, therefore the result seemed more or less labored, and suggested the pump rather than the fountain.

During the five years that the remains lay in state while the mausoleum was in course of construction, tributes, anecdotes, reminiscences, episodes, poured in a constant stream through the daily, hebdomadal and monthly periodicals, and it looked as if my daughter, as literary ma-

terial, would never be exhausted. Adam was happy in it for three years, then he began to get tired and wish for something fresh. He was politic, and spoke praisefully of it in public; but in private, toward the last he used to grind his teeth and say hard things about those people. To me he spoke out quite frankly and said that if Gladys had really been as good and gracious and magnanimous and just and liberal and benevolent and unselfish and wise and firm and great and grand and intellectual as these adulators made her out to be, she would have died earlier from pure lonesomeness, and she wouldn't find any society in heaven now that would be suitable for her, neither; and he said that if you boiled down the things written about Gladys you would find that if they had been written of an unknown person they would have pretty accurately described a commonplace one.

Next, the biographies began to appear. Always a copy was sent to the Family. With an inscription on the fly-leaf. Usually with a humble hope added that if one or the other of us would kindly give our opinion in a line or two, and thus help a struggling young author to etc., etc. Adam is gone from us, now; let us draw a veil over those scenes; they were not becoming to him.

Within a year after the funeral the biographies ceased, for lack of a market, and a year later the world had resumed its natural and customary ignorance and had forgotten everything about our poor Gladys except that she was dead.

The obsequies—

But I was speaking of the augmenting burden of population, and the increasing gravity of the situation created by it as the centuries accumulated.⟩ After the age of infancy, few died. The average of life was 600 years. The cradles were filling, filling, filling—always, always, always; the cemeteries stood comparatively idle, the undertakers had but little traffic, they could hardly support their families. The death-rate was 2250 in the 1,000,000. To the thoughtful this was portentous; to the light-witted it was matter for brag! These latter were always comparing the population of one decade with that of the previous one and hurrahing over the mighty increase—as if that were an advantage to the world; a world that could hardly scratch enough out of the earth to keep itself from starving.

And yet, worse was to come! ⟨The year 510 was a turning point. Only yesterday I was talking with Reginald Selkirk, the Mad Prophet, about

a conversation which we had had once, over the Report of the Imperial Academy for the fifty previous years. He had put his finger upon several items, and said—

"These mean disaster, Excellency. You know I have held that our true hope of relief did not lie⟩ in spasmodic famine and pestilence, whose effects could be only temporary, but in war and the physicians, whose help is constant. Now, then, let us note what has been happening. In the past fifty years science has reduced the doctor's effectiveness by half. He uses but one deadly drug now, where formerly he used ten. Improved sanitation has made whole regions healthy which were previously not so. It has been discovered that the majority of the most useful and fatal diseases are caused by microbes of various breeds; very well, they have learned how to render the efforts of those microbes innocuous. As a result, yellow fever, black plague, diphtheria, cholera, and nearly every valuable distemper we had are become but entertainments for the idle hour, and are of no more value to the State than is the stomach-ache. Marvelous advances in surgery have been added to our disasters. They remove a diseased stomach, now, and the man gets along better and cheaper than he did before. If a man loses a faculty, they bore into his skull and restore it. They take off his legs and arms, and refurnish him from the mechanical junk-shop, and he is as good as new. They give him a new nose if he needs it; new entrails; new bones; new teeth; glass eyes; silver tubes to swallow through; in a word, they take him to pieces and make him over again, and he can stand twice as much wear and tear as he could before. They do these things by the help of antiseptics and anaesthesia, and there is no gangrene and no pain. Thus war has become nearly valueless; out of a hundred wounded that would formerly have died, ninety-nine are back in the ranks again in a month.

"What, then, is the grand result of all this microbing and sanitation and surgery? This—which is appalling: the death-rate has been reduced to *twenty-two in the million.* And foolish people rejoice at it and boast about it! It is a serious matter. It promises to double the globe's population every twelve months. In time there will not be room in the world for people to stand, let alone sit down.

"Remedy? I know of none. The span of life is too long, the death-rate is too trifling. The span should be 35 years—a mere moment of time—the death-rate should be 20 or 30 in the *thousand,* not million. And even then the population would double in 35 years, and by and by even this would be a burden again and make the support of life difficult."

⟨It was some centuries ago that he had said those things. Yesterday he said—

"You will grant that in the main I was right. War⟩ has saved us. Not that the killed and wounded amount to anything as a relief, for they do not; but the poverty and desolation caused by war sweep myriads away and make space for immigrants. ⟨**Blessed war! benevolent war is the race's best friend!**⟩ It keeps us down to 60,000,000,000 and saves the hard-grubbing world alive. It is all that the globe can support." * * *

Received the Mad Prophet to-day.

He is a good man, ⟨**the Mad Prophet,**⟩ and I think his intellect is better than its reputation. He got his nickname long ago, and did not deserve it; for he merely builds prognostications, not prophecies. He pretends to nothing more. Builds them out of history and statistics, using the facts of the past to forecast the probabilities of the future. It is merely applied science. An astronomer foretells an eclipse, yet is not obnoxious to the charge of pretending to be a prophet. Noah is a prophet; and certainly no one has more reverence for him and for his sacred office than has this modest dealer in probabilities and progostications.

I have known the Mad Prophet—or the Mad Philosopher, for he has both names—ever since he was a student in college, in the beginning of the third century. He was nineteen or twenty, then. I have always had a kindly feeling for him; partly, of course, because he was a relative, (though distant), but mainly, I am sure, because of the good qualities of his head and heart. He married when he was 24, and when neither he nor the girl was properly situated to marry, for they were poor and belonged to families which had the same defect. Both families were respectable enough, and in a far-away fashion were allied to the nobility; but as Adam always said, "Respectability butters no parsnips," and it was not just the right capital to marry on. I advised them to wait a while, and of course they did it, since advice from ⟨**me**⟩ was—and is—law, by courtesy and custom of the race; but they were an impatient little pair and dreadfully in love with each other, and they only waited long enough to cover the bare necessities of etiquette. My influence got the lad a small mathematics-professorship in his university and kept him in possession of it, and he worked hard and saved faithfully. Poor things, they endured the suspension of life, as they called it, as long as they could; they waited sixty years, then they got married. She was a lovely little rat, and sweetly captivating: slender, lissom, brown-eyed, dimpled, complexioned like a peach-blossom, frisky, frolicsome, graceful—just a picture, she was, just a poem. She was of foreign extraction; her little drop of nobility had trickled down to her, in the lapse of time, from a great lord whose habitat was ⟨**on the other side of the globe,**⟩ the Duke of Washoe. He was descended from me through—I forget the name now—but the source was ⟨**Edwina's**⟩ branch, I mean the one proceeding from ⟨**Edwina's**⟩ second marriage. ⟨**No, I remember now, it was Gladys's.**⟩ He was second cousin to—but I have forgotten that name, too. The little bride's name was Red Cloud, and was as foreign as her extraction. It was a kind of inheritance.

The couple remained poor, and are poor yet, but as happy as many that are richer. They have always had enough for their needs, for my influence has kept him in his post, and has also augmented his salary a little, more than once. Their tranquil life has suffered one blight, one heavy sorrow, which fell upon them toward the end of the first century of their union, and whose shadow lies upon their hearts yet. They lost sixteen children in a railway accident.

* * * *

Before he came, ⟨**yesterday, Reginald**⟩ had been examining the mobile which is propelled by the wonderful new force, liquified thought. He was profoundly impressed. He said he could see no reason why this force should not displace steam and electricity, since it is much more powerful than those agents, occupies almost no space, and costs next to nothing. That is, the cost to the Trust that owns the patent is next to nothing. It is the same Trust that owns the globe's railways and ships—the globe's transportation, in a word.

"Five years ago," said ⟨**Reginald,**⟩ "this new force was laughed at by the ignorant, and discounted by the wise—a thing which always happens when there is a new invention. It happened with the Liograph, it happened with the Hellograph, it happened with the Mumble'n'screechograph, and it will go on happening with new inventions to the end of time. Why cannot people learn to wait for developments before they commit themselves? Surely experience has given them warnings enough. Almost as a rule the apparently insane invention turns out well by and by, through the discovery and application to it of improvements of one kind and another. Five years ago liquified thought had no value but as an Imperial-Academy show on Ladies' Night. The cost of production was prohibitory, as far as business and commerce were concerned, for at that stage of development the only raw material which would answer had to be taken from statesmen, judges, scientists, poets, philosophers, editors, sculptors, painters, generals, admirals, inventors, engineers, and such like, but now—as [ ] says—you can get it from politicians and idiots; adding, in his unpleasant way, 'But that is tautology; Politician and idiot are synonymous terms.'

"I am of the opinion that the development of this mysterious new force has not yet proceeded beyond the infancy stage. I think we know but little about it now, compared with what we shall know a few decades hence. Why, it may turn out to be the renowned and lamented Lost Force of old tradition! And it isn't mere tradition, there is history for it. You know the tradition yourself, gracious Excellency—like the rest of the world—but you do not know the history. It has just been deciphered from the clay archives of an exhumed city of the Double Continent; and when it is published the nations will perceive that when the amazing man called 'the Prodigy,' who rose out of obscurity in the middle of the fifth century and in a few years conquered the world and brought all its kingdoms under his imperial sceptre, where they still abide under the sceptre of his son to-day, had formidable help in his stupendous work from a source outside of his colossal genius for war, statesmanship and administration, unrivaled and unapproachable as these confessedly were. That source was the agent known to tradition, romance and poetry as the Lost Force. It is true that that humble young shoemaker did sweep the Double Continent from end to end with fire and sword without that help, and establish his autocratic sway over all its monarchies by merely the faculties that were born in him, and that he handled a billion men in the field under a million generals trained by himself and subject to his sole will unhampered by meddling ministries and legislatures, and left mountains of dead and wounded upon his battle fields, but he subdued the rest of the globe without spilling blood, except in a single instance.

"That mystery is explained, now, by the clay records. It came to his knowledge that one Napeer, an obscure person but learned in science, had stated in his will that he had discovered a means whereby he could sweep a whole army out of existence in an instant, but that he would not reveal his secret, since war was already terrible enough and he would not be party to the augmentation of its destructiveness.

"The shoemaker-emperor said, 'The man was foolish—his invention would abolish war altogether,' and commanded that all papers left behind by him should be brought to him. He found the formula, mastered its details, then destroyed it. He privately manufactured that tremendous agent, and went out alone against the sovereigns of the eastern world, with it in his pocket. Only one army ever came against him. It formed itself in battle array in a great plain, and at a distance of twelve miles he blew it into the air, leaving no vestige of it behind but a few rags and buttons.

"He claimed the sovereignty of the globe, and it was accorded him without an objecting voice. As you are aware, his reign of thirty years was a reign of peace; then, by accident, he blew himself up with his machine, along with one of his vice-regal capitals, and his formidable secret died with him. Then the dreadful wars began again, and for the world's sins they still continue. But the universal empire which he established was founded in wisdom and strength, and to-day his son sits as securely upon its throne as he did when he mounted it so many centuries ago."

It was quite interesting. He was just beginning to speak about his "Law of Periodical Repetition"—or perhaps it was about his "Law of the Permanency of the Intellectual Average"—but was interrupted. He was to be received by her Grandeur, and was now called to that privilege by an officer of the Household.

* * * *

⟨I said—

"It created the wonderful civilization of our time."

He said he had an engagement.

I only said it to furnish him another text. I know that he was not an enthusiast about our civilization; still that theme could be a protection for me for a little while at least, by postponing Selkirk's Law of Periodical Repetition, or the Permanency of the Intellectual Average, or some other pet of his. Postponement was the best that could be hoped for; his own Law of Periodical Repetition was security for that. He sighed & said—

"Wonderful civilization? I will not object to the adjective—it rightly describes it—but⟩ I do object to the large and complacent admiration which it implies. By all accounts—yours in chief, Excellency—the pure and sweet and ignorant and unsordid civilization of Eden was worth a thousand millions of it. What *is* a civilization, rightly considered? Morally, it is the evil passions repressed, the level of conduct raised; spiritually, idols cast down, God enthroned; materially, bread and fair treatment for the greatest number. That is the common formula, the common definition; everybody accepts it and is satisfied with it.

"Our civilization is wonderful, in certain spectacular and meretricious ways; wonderful in scientific marvels and inventive miracles; wonderful in material inflation, which it calls advancement, progress, and other pet names; wonderful in its spying-out of the deep secrets of Nature—and its vanquishment of her stubborn laws; wonderful in its extraordinary financial and commercial achievements; wonderful in its hunger for money, and in its indifference as to how it is acquired; wonderful in the hitherto undreamed-of magnitude of its private fortunes and the prodigal fashion in which they are given away to institutions devoted to the public culture; wonderful in its exhibitions of poverty; wonderful in the surprises which it gets out of that great new birth, ORGANIZATION, the latest and most potent creation and miracle-worker of the commercialized intellect, as applied in transportation-systems, in manufactures, in systems of communication, in news-gathering, book-publishing, journalism; in protecting labor; in oppressing labor; in herding the national parties and keeping the sheep docile and usable; in closing the public service against brains and character; in electing purchasable legislatures, blatherskite Congresses, and city governments which rob the town and sell municipal protection to gamblers, thieves, prostitutes and professional seducers for cash. It is a civilization which has destroyed the simplicity and repose of life; replaced its poetry, its soft romance-dreams and visions with the money-fever, sordid ideals, vulgar ambitions, and the sleep which does not refresh; it has invented a thousand useless luxuries, and turned them into necessities, it has created a thousand vicious appetites and satisfies none of them; it has dethroned God and set up a shekel in His place.

"Religion has removed from the heart to the mouth. You have the word of Noah for it. Time was, when two sects, divided but by a simple hair of doctrine, would fight for that hair, would kill, torture, persecute for it, suffer for it, starve for it, die for it. *That* religion was in the heart; it was vital, it was a living thing, it was the very man himself. Who fights for his religion now, but with the mouth? Your civilization has brought the flood. Noah has said it, and he is preparing."

⟨"Not preparing!"

"Yes, preparing."

"I thought—I thought—well, prophecies—why, you know that as a rule prophecies deal with a distant and indefinite future."

"This one deals with the present. The keel of the Ark is laid."

"Are you sure? Do you know?"

"It was laid three days ago."

It was a great shock. I was not expecting it.

"When will it be completed?"

"It must be ready eleven months and four days hence; for then the rains will begin, and last forty days."

"It is awful. I was not suspecting that it was so near. It is terrible to think of—the billions that will be drowned. Will the Ark be very large?"

"Yes—prodigious."

"I have seldom been on the water, and have always been afraid of it. But an Ark that is large—and strong— Must one enter it before the rains begin? That is, *long* before?"

"No, I believe not. The last day will answer, I think."

It was a comfort to me to hear him say that.

For a while my mind was thronged and oppressed with pathetic images of that coming calamity—appealing faces, imploring faces, despairing faces—multitudes upon multitudes, the rocks and crags and mountain ranges dense with them, and all bone of my bone, flesh of my flesh; some, little and helpless; some, comrades for centuries, friends of my youth, mates in unforgetable Eden— I could not bear it!

"Speak!" I said.

"What shall I speak of, Excellency?"

"Oh, anything, anything! Tell me what the desolate world will look like when we see it again; and tell me, oh, tell me that there will be no more floods."

"Ah, madam, I would I could, but I cannot. By the Law of Periodical Repetitions—"

"Oh, go on—why do you stop?"

"I thought you were in pain."

"Never mind it; it was nothing; it has passed. I brought it upon myself."

"The pain?"

"The *cause* of it. Pray go on."

"Well, then, as I was about to say, by that Law,〉 nothing whatever can happen a single time only: everything happens again, and yet again, and still again—monotonously. Nature has no originality—I mean, no large ability in the matter of inventing new things, new ideas, new stage-effects. She has a superb and amazing and infinitely varied equipment of old ones, but she never adds to them. She repeats—repeats—repeats—repeats. Examine your memory and your experience, you will find it is true. When she puts together a man, and is satisfied with him, she is loyal to him, she stands by him through thick and thin forevermore, she repeats him by billions and billions of examples; and physically and mentally the *average* remains exactly the same, it doesn't vary a hair between the first batch, the middle batch and the last batch. If you ask—"

"But really—do you think all men are alike?" I reply—

"I said the *average* does not vary."

"But you will have to admit that some individuals do far overtop the average—intellectually, at least."

"Yes, I answer, and Nature repeats *those*. There is nothing that she doesn't repeat. If I may use a figure, she has established the general intellectual level of the race at say, six feet. Take any billion men and stand them in a mass, and their head-tops will make a floor—a floor as level as a table. That floor represents the intellectual altitude of the masses—and it never changes. Here and there, miles apart, a head will project above it a matter of one intellectual inch, so to speak—men of mark in science, law, war, commerce, etc; in a spread of five thousand miles you will find three heads that project still an inch higher—men of national fame—and *one* that is higher than *those* by two inches, maybe three—a man of (temporarily) world-wide renown; and finally, somewhere around the circumference of the globe, you will find, once in five centuries of waiting, one majestic head which overtops the highest of all the others—an author, a teacher, an artist, a martyr, a conqueror, whose fame towers to the stars, and whose name will never perish, never fade, while time shall last; some colossus supreme above all the human herd, some unmated and unmateable prodigy like him who, by magic of the forces born in him, turned his shoe-hammer into the sceptre of universal dominion. Now in that view you have the ordinary man of all nations; you have the here-and-there man that is larger-brained and becomes distinguished; ⟨**and in the isolated highest head you have the poet or the general or the orator or the statesman who appears in the earth once in an age and is known forever after as 'the Prodigy' or by some equivalent great word. Allow me to take down a volume of your Diary—volume I. Here it is. *First* edition! How quaint—and what funny crude wood-cuts; your autograph in it, too, in faded ink. If that were put up at auction—oh, Peerpontibusmorganibus but it would make a stir in the world! I wish to read a passage which has been recited in the public schools some centuries, and which— Here it is:**

> **Several days ago little Abel found a clover with four leaves. Naturally it caused great excitement. Adam could hardly believe his eyes, yet there it was, that impossible thing. There it was—and more-**

over, possible. Adam said there might be others; it wasn't likely, but there might be. So the first thing in the morning, we started, the eager children scampering on ahead, Cain and Abel in the lead, little Gladys and Edwina toddling after—

And so forth and so-on.〉

APPENDIX 2

Planning Notes for "Autobiography of Eve"†

a. [This first set of planning notes is written on a cardboard—probably a tablet-back from one of the Par Value writing tablets that Mark Twain was currently using. The entries here consist of one reference to the "Mad prophet," suggestions for development of family activities, which were never expanded, and notes for a discussion that Mark Twain did develop in "Passage from Satan's Diary." This document in the Mark Twain Papers is here first published.]

Mad prophet. ^1st Century poor old pachyderm.^
July, Year 3, Cain born
April " 4 Abel "
Year 5, Gladys; ^yr 6,^ Edwina born^.^
⟨twins.⟩
Would that Wash^n & his little hatchet had come ere this.
This is the first time I have ever had a nasty thought.
FIRST BLUSH. Adam sees it. They must hide from children.
If this is to be as the gods, let me be as the beasts.

[Written sideways in left margin next to the above items: "A.M. 32."]

They now have 32 children (one pr twins). The older brothers and sisters have ⟨considerable⟩ families started.

Mere nursery tots as yet—Cain's eldest is 5 or 6/ — Gladys is his wife & sister. First Daughter & Widow—

(Put in domestic & other scenes to make these people real.

Serpents standing on end.

Satan: He knows good & evil but has no way to explain them to people who, like the animals, still lack a sense, the Moral Sense. "Suppose Ad tells you to do so & so & you don't do it—how do you feel about it?"—& would you do it?" "Why shouldn't I?" Certainly, why shouldn't she? (Satan, aside: I was once without the M S myself—one is like a turnip for naievety.

What is death? S. ⟨pretends to⟩ knows, but can't make an inexperienced person understand. "When you are asleep, that is death substantially—yet not the same." "Why?" "Death is long—long—forever." "Then it is very pleasant; sleep is very pleasant." "But this is a long, infinitely long sleep." ^A. The longer the better.^ ^E.^"Oh, it must be lovely!

The young loves of Cain & Gl; & Abel & Edw.*

b. [This group of notes, with suggestions for developing the story beyond the extant portion, is written on the cover of a Par Value writing tablet (in Mark Twain Papers). At some point Mark Twain scribbled over the notes, and apparently used this cover as a title page for his manuscript of "The Czar's Soliloquy," for that title is written in large script near the bottom of the cover. These notes were first published (in error) as group C-1 of the working notes for "The Secret History of Eddypus, The World-Empire" (*FM*, 471–72). They read:]

Clover. Be another flood & others. Average of life 1000 yr. Geology shows 1,000,000 years—fossils to tell its age by. Webster, Snakspeer, Appolyon. Prodigy, Pitt

General average of pulpit &c raised, but no supremacies any more—no great book or statesman.

Religion become perfunctory—X_n Science & Health—hence a flood. X_n S. will come again & in ⟨2⟩300 yrs be supreme—then another flood.

Gospel of Selfishness.

Adam died 930.

Discov. of America, yr 314

Eve dies ⟨1032?⟩ 972

Decay of civiliz^n begins then: spread of X^n Sci. Religious wars produced.

By 1200 civ. is dead, & X^n S with it. Savagery the result of X^n S—flood results.

No trade for life ins. except insuring the Ins. Companies.

Ruined monument to Adam. A savage discourses upon it.

SUSY [two-thirds of way
down the page]

Condemned [near bottom of page]

The Czar's Soliloquy
[written in large letters over "Condemned"]

[in margin]
Popoatahual⟨l⟩ pacatapetal I
II
pronounced pie-crust
⟨necess [unrecovered words]⟩

APPENDIX 3

"Extracts from Adam's Diary" from the Original Niagara Book *Version*

["Extracts from Adam's Diary" as first printed in *The Niagara Book. A Complete Souvenir of Niagara Falls Containing Sketches . . . by W. D. Howells, Mark Twain . . . and Others.* Buffalo: Underhill & Nichols, 1893, pp. 93–109.]

The Earliest Authentic Mention of Niagara Falls

Extracts from Adam's Diary

Translated from the Original MS.

By Mark Twain

MONDAY.—This new creature with the long hair is a good deal in the way. It is always hanging around and following me about. I don't like this; I am not used to company. I wish it would stay with the other animals. . . . . Cloudy today, wind in the east; think we shall have rain. . . . . *We?* Where did I get that word? . . . . I remember now,—the new creature uses it.

TUESDAY.—Been examining the great waterfall. It is the finest thing on the estate, I think. The new creature calls it Niagara Falls—why, I am sure I do not know. Says it *looks* like Niagara Falls. That is not a reason, it is mere waywardness and imbecility. I get no chance to name anything myself. The new creature names everything that comes along, before I can get in a protest. And always that same pretext is offered—it *looks* like the thing. There is the dodo, for instance. Says the moment one looks at it one sees at a glance that it "looks like a dodo." It will have to keep that name, no doubt. It wearies me to fret about it, but it does no good, anyway. Dodo! It looks no more like a dodo than I do.

WEDNESDAY.—Built me a shelter against the rain, but could not have it to myself in peace. The new creature intruded. When I tried to put it out it shed water out of the holes it looks with, and wiped it away with the back of its paws, and made a noise such as some of the other animals make when they are in distress. I wish it would not talk, it is always talking. That sounds like a cheap fling at the poor creature, a slur; but I do not mean it so. I have never heard the human voice before, and any new and strange sound intruding itself here upon the solemn hush of these dreaming solitudes offends my ear and seems a false note. And this new sound is so close to me; it is right at my shoulder, right at my ear, first on one side then on the other, and I am used only to sounds that are more or less distant from me.

FRIDAY.—The naming goes recklessly on, in spite of anything I can do. I had a very good name for the estate, and it was musical and pretty—GARDEN-OF-EDEN. Privately, I continue to call it that, but not any longer publicly. The new creature says it is all woods and rocks and scenery, and therefore has no resemblance to a garden. Says it *looks* like a park, and does not look like anything *but* a park. Consequently, without consulting me it has been new named—NIAGARA FALLS PARK. This is sufficiently high-handed, it seems to me. And already there is a sign up:

KEEP OFF
THE GRASS

My life is not as happy as it was.

SATURDAY.—The new creature eats too much fruit. We are going to run short, most likely. "We" again—that is *its* word; mine, too, now, from hearing it so much. Good deal of fog this morning. I do not go out in the fog, myself. The new creature does. It goes out in all weathers, and stumps right in with its muddy feet. And talks. It used to be so pleasant and quiet here.

SUNDAY.—Pulled through. This day is getting to be more and more trying. It was selected and set apart last November as a day of rest. I already had six of them per week before. This is another of those unaccountable things. There seems to be too much legislation; too much fussing, and fixing, and tidying up, and not enough of the better-let-well-enough-alone policy. [*Mem.*—Must keep that sort of opinions to myself.] This morning found the new creature trying to clod apples out of that forbidden tree.

MONDAY.—The new creature says its name is Eve. That is all right, I have no objections. Says it is to call it by when I want it to come. I said it was superfluous, then. The word evidently raised me in its respect; and indeed it is a large, good word and will bear repetition. It says it is not an It, it is a She. This is probably doubtful, yet it is all one to me; what she is were nothing to me if she would but go by herself and not talk.

TUESDAY.—She has littered the whole estate with execrable names and offensive signs:

☛ THIS WAY TO THE WHIRLPOOL.

☛ THIS WAY TO GOAT ISLAND.

☛ CAVE OF THE WINDS THIS WAY.

She says this park would make a tidy summer resort, if there were any custom for it. Summer resort—another invention of hers—just words, without any meaning. What is a summer resort? But it is best not to ask her, she has such a rage for explaining.

FRIDAY.—She has taken to begging and imploring me to stop going over the Falls. What harm does it do? Says it makes her shudder. I wonder why; I have always done it—always liked the plunge, and the excitement and the coolness. I supposed it was what the Falls were for. They have no other use that I can see, and they must have been made for something. She says they were only made for scenery—like the rhinoceros and the mastodon.

I went over the Falls in a barrel—not satisfactory to her. Went over in a tub—still not satisfactory. Swam the Whirlpool and the Rapids in a fig-leaf suit. It got much damaged. Hence, tedious complaints about my extravagance. I am too much hampered here. What I need is change of scene.

SATURDAY.—I escaped last Tuesday night, and traveled two days, and built me another shelter, in a secluded place, and obliterated my tracks as well as I could, but she hunted me out by means of a beast which she has tamed and calls a wolf, and came making that pitiful noise again, and shedding that water out of the places she looks with. I was obliged to return with her, but will presently emigrate again, when occasion offers. She engages herself in many foolish things: among others, trying to study out why the animals called lions and tigers live on grass and flowers, when, as she says, the sort of teeth they wear would indicate that they were intended to eat each other. This is foolish, because to do that would be to kill each other, and that would introduce what, as I understand it, is called "death"; and death, as I have been told, has not yet entered the Park. Which is a pity, on some accounts.

SUNDAY.—Pulled through.

MONDAY.—I believe I see what the week is for: it is to give time to rest up from the weariness of Sunday. It seems a good idea, in a region where good ideas are rather conspicuously scarce. Will try it. [*Mem.*—Must keep this sort of remarks private.] . . . . She has been climbing that tree again. Clodded her out of it. She said nobody was looking. Seems to consider that a sufficient justification for chancing any dangerous thing. Told her that. The word justification moved her admiration—and envy, too, I thought. It is a good word.

THURSDAY.—She told me she was made out of a rib taken from my body. This is at least doubtful, if not more than that. I have not missed any rib. . . . She is in much trouble about the buzzard; says grass does not agree with it; is afraid she can't raise it; thinks it was intended to live on decayed flesh. The buzzard must get along the best it can with what is provided. We cannot overturn the whole scheme to accommodate the buzzard.

SATURDAY.—She fell in the pond yesterday, when she was looking at herself in it, which she is always doing. She nearly strangled, and said it was most uncomfortable. This made her sorry for the creatures which live in there, which she calls fish, for she continues to fasten names on to things that don't need them and don't come when they are called by them, which is a matter of no consequence to her, she is such a fool anyway; so she got a lot of them out and brought them in and put them in my bed to keep warm, but I have noticed them now and then all day and I don't see that they are any happier there than they were before. When night comes I shall throw them outdoors; I will not sleep with them, for I find them clammy and unpleasant to lie among when a person hasn't anything on.

SUNDAY.—Pulled through.

TUESDAY.—She has taken up with a snake, now. The other animals are glad, for she was always experimenting with them and bothering them; and I am glad, because the snake talks, and this enables me to get a rest.

FRIDAY.—She says the snake advises her to try the fruit of that tree, and says the result will be a great and fine and noble education. I told her there would be another result, too—it would introduce death into the world. That was a mistake—it had been better to keep the remark to myself: it only gave her an idea—she could save the sick buzzard, and furnish fresh meat to the despondent lions and tigers. I advised her to keep away from the tree. She said she wouldn't. I foresee trouble. Will emigrate.

WEDNESDAY.—I have had a variegated time. I escaped that night, and rode a horse all night as fast as he could go, hoping to get clear out of the Garden and hide in some other country before the trouble should begin; but it was not to be. About an hour after sun-up, as I was riding through a flowery plain where thousands of animals were grazing, slumbering, or playing with each other, according to their common wont, all of a sudden they broke into a tempest of frightful noises and in one moment the plain was a frantic commotion and every beast was destroying its neighbor. I knew what it meant—Eve had eaten that fruit, and death was come into the world. . . . . The tigers ate my horse, paying no attention when I ordered them to desist, and they would even have eaten me if I had stayed—which I didn't, but went away in much haste. . . . . I found this place, outside the Garden, and was fairly comfortable for a few days, but she has found me out. Found me out, and has named the place Tonawanda—says it *looks* like that. In fact I was not sorry she came, for there are but meagre pickings here, and she brought some of those apples. I was obliged to eat them, I was so hungry. It was against my principles, but I find that principles have no real force except when one is well fed. . . . She came curtained in boughs and bunches of leaves, and when I asked her what she meant by such nonsense, and snatched them away and threw them down, she tittered and blushed. I had never seen a person titter and blush before, and to me it seemed unbecoming and idiotic. She said I would soon know how it was myself. This was correct. Hungry as I was, I laid down the apple half eaten—certainly the best one I ever saw, considering the lateness of the season—and arrayed myself in the discarded boughs and branches, and then spoke to her with some severity and ordered her to go and get some more and not make such a spectacle of herself. She did it, and after this we crept down to where the wild-beast battle had been, and collected some skins, and I made her patch together a couple of suits proper for public occasions. They are uncomfortable, it is true, but stylish, and that is the main point about clothes. . . . I find she is a good deal of a companion. I see I should be lonesome and depressed without her, now that I have lost my property. Another thing, she says it is ordered that we work for our living hereafter. She will be useful. I will superintend.

TEN DAYS LATER.—She accuses *me* of being the cause of our disaster! She says, with apparent sincerity and truth, that the Serpent assured her that the forbidden fruit was not apples, it was chestnuts. I said I was innocent, then, for I had not eaten any chestnuts. She said the Serpent informed her that "chestnut" was a figurative term meaning an aged and mouldy joke. I turned pale at that, for I have made many jokes to pass the weary time, and some of them could have been of that sort, though I had honestly supposed they were new when I made them. She asked me if I had made one just at the time of the catastrophe. I was obliged to admit that I had made one to myself, though not aloud. It was this. I was thinking about the Falls, and I said to myself, "How wonderful it is to see that vast body of water tumble down there!" Then in an instant a bright thought flashed into my head, and I let it fly, saying, "It would be a deal more wonderful to see it tumble *up* there!"—and I was just about to kill myself with laughing at it when all nature broke loose in war and death and I had to flee for my life. "There," she said, with triumph, "that is just it; the Serpent mentioned that very jest, and called it the First Chestnut, and said it was coeval with the creation." Alas, I am indeed to blame. Would that I were not witty; oh, would that I never had that radiant thought!

Next Year.—We have named it Cain. She caught it while I was up country, trapping on the North Shore of the Erie; caught in the timber a couple of miles from our dug-out—or it might have been four, she isn't certain which. It resembles us in some ways, and may be a relation. That is what she thinks, but this is an error, in my judgment. The difference in size warrants the conclusion that it is a different and new kind of animal—a fish, perhaps, though when I put it in the water to see, it sank, and she plunged in and snatched it out before there was opportunity for the experiment to determine the matter. I still think it is a fish, but she is indifferent about what it is, and will not let me have it to try. I do not understand this. The coming of the creature seems to have changed her whole nature, and made her unreasonable about experiments. She thinks more of it than she does of any of the other animals, but is not able to explain why. Her mind is disordered—everything shows it. Sometimes she carries the fish in her arms half the night when it complains and wants to get to the water. At such times the water comes out of the places in her face that she looks out of, and she pats the fish on the back and makes soft sounds with her mouth to soothe it, and betrays sorrow and solicitude in a hundred ways. I have never seen her do like this with any other fish, and it troubles me greatly. She used to carry the young tigers around so, and play with them, before we lost our property, but it was only play; she never took on about them like this when their dinner disagreed with them.

Sunday.—She don't work, Sundays, but lies around all tired out, and likes to have the fish wallow over her; and she makes fool noises to amuse it, and pretends to chew its paws, and that makes it laugh. I have not seen a fish before that could laugh. This makes me doubt. . . . . I have come to like Sunday myself. Superintending all the week tires a body so. There ought to be more Sundays. In the old days they were tough, but now they come handy.

Wednesday.—It isn't a fish. I cannot quite make out what it is. It makes curious devilish noises when not satisfied, and says "goo-goo" when it is. It is not one of us, for it doesn't walk; it is not a bird, for it doesn't fly; it is not a frog, for it doesn't hop; it is not a snake, for it doesn't crawl; I feel sure it is not a fish, though I cannot get a chance to find out whether it can swim or not. It merely lies around, and mostly on its back, with its feet up. I have not seen any other animal do that before. I said I believed it was an enigma; but she only admired the word without understanding it. In my judgment it is either an enigma or some kind of a bug. If it dies I will take it apart and see what its arrangements are. I never had a thing perplex me so.

Three Months Later.—The perplexity merely augments instead of diminishing. I sleep but little. It has ceased from lying around, and goes about on its four legs, now. Yet it differs from the other four-legged animals, in that its front legs are unusually short, consequently this causes the main part of its person to stick up uncomfortably high in the air, and this is not attractive. It is built much as we are, but its method of traveling shows that it is not of our breed. The short front legs and long hind ones indicate that it is of the kangaroo family, but it is a marked variation of the species, since the true kangaroo hops, whereas this one never does. Still it is a curious and interesting variety, and has not been catalogued before. As I discovered it, I have felt justified in securing the credit of the discovery by attaching my name to it, and hence have called it *Kangaroorum Adamiensis*. . . . . It must have been a young one when it came, for it has grown exceedingly since. It must be five times as big, now, as it was then, and when discontented is able to make from twenty-two to thirty-eight times the noise it made at first. Coercion does not modify this, but has the contrary effect. For this reason I discontinued the system. She reconciles it by persuasion, and by giving it things which she had told it she wouldn't give it, before. As observed previously, I was not at home when it first came, and she told me she found it in the woods. It seems odd that it should be the only one, yet it must be so, for I have worn myself out these many weeks trying to find another one to add to my collection, and for this one to play with; for surely then it would be quieter and we could tame it more easily. But I find none, nor any vestige of any; and strangest of all, no tracks. It has to live on the ground, it cannot help itself; therefore, how does it get about without leaving a track? I have set a dozen traps, but they do no good; I catch all small animals except that one; animals that merely go into the trap out of curiosity, I think, to see what the milk is there for. They never drink it.

Three Months Later.—The Kangaroo still continues to grow, which is very strange and perplexing. I never knew one to be so long getting its growth. It has fur on its head, now; not like kangaroo fur, but exactly like our hair except that it is much finer and softer, and instead of being black, is red. I am like to lose my mind over the capricious and harassing developments of this unclassifiable zoological freak. If I could catch another one—but that is hopeless; it is a new variety, and the only sample; this is plain. But I caught a true kangaroo and brought it in, thinking that this one, being lonesome, would rather have that for company than have no kin at all, or any animal it could feel a nearness to or get sympathy from in its forlorn condition here among strangers who do not know its ways or habits, or what to do to make it feel that it is among friends; but it was a mistake—it went into such fits at the sight of the kangaroo that I was convinced it had never seen one before. I pity the poor noisy little animal, but there is nothing I can do to make it happy. If I could tame it—but that is out of the question; the more I try the worse I seem to make it. It grieves me to the heart to see it in its little storms of sorrow and passion. I wanted to let it go, but she wouldn't hear of it. That seemed cruel, and not like her; and yet she may be right. It might be lonelier than ever; for since I cannot find another one, how could *it?*

FIVE MONTHS LATER.—It is not a kangaroo. No, for it supports itself by holding to her finger, and thus goes a few steps on its hind legs, and then falls down. It is probably some kind of a bear; and yet it has no tail—as yet—and no fur, except on its head. It still keeps on growing—that is a curious circumstance, for bears get their growth earlier than this. Bears are dangerous—since our catastrophe—and I shall not be satisfied to have this one prowling about the place much longer without a muzzle on. I have offered to get her a kangaroo if she would let this one go, but it did no good—she is determined to run us into all sorts of foolish risks, I think. She was not like this before she lost her mind.

A FORTNIGHT LATER.—I examined its mouth. There is no danger yet; it has only one tooth. It has no tail yet. It makes more noise, now, than it ever did before—and mainly at night. I have moved out. But I shall go over, mornings, to breakfast, and to see if it has more teeth. If it gets a mouthful of teeth it will be time for it to go, tail or no tail, for a bear does not need a tail in order to be dangerous.

FOUR MONTHS LATER.—I have been off hunting and fishing a month up in the region that she calls Buffalo; I don't know why, unless it is because there are not any buffalos there. Meantime the bear has learned to paddle around all by itself on its hind legs, and says "poppa" and "momma." It is certainly a new species. This resemblance to words may be purely accidental, of course, and may have no purpose or meaning; but even in that case it is still extraordinary, and is a thing which no other bear can do. This imitation of speech, taken together with general absence of fur and entire absence of tail, sufficiently indicates that this is a new kind of bear. The further study of it will be exceedingly interesting. Meantime I will go off on a far expedition among the forests of the north and make an exhaustive search. There must certainly be another one somewhere, and this one will be less dangerous when it has company of its own species. I will go straightway; but I will muzzle this one first.

THREE MONTHS LATER.—It has been a weary, weary hunt, yet I have had no success. In the meantime, without stirring from the home-estate, she has caught another one! I never saw such luck. I might have hunted these woods a hundred years, I never would have run across that thing.

NEXT DAY.—I have been comparing the new one with the old one, and it is perfectly plain that they are the same breed. I was going to stuff one of them for my collection, but she is prejudiced against it for some reason or other; so I have relinquished the idea, though I think it is a mistake. It would be an irreparable loss to science if they should get away. The old one is tamer than it was, and can laugh and talk like the parrot, having learned this, no doubt, from being with the parrot so much, and having the imitative faculty in a highly developed degree. I shall be astonished if it turns out to be a new kind of parrot; and yet I ought not to be astonished, for it has already been everything else it could think of, since those first days when it was a fish. The new one is as ugly now as the old one was at first; has the same sulphur-and-raw-meat complexion and the same singular head without any fur on it. She calls it Abel.

TEN YEARS LATER.—They are boys; we found it out long ago. It was their coming in that small, immature shape that fooled us; we were not used to it. There are some girls now. Abel is a good boy, but if Cain had stayed a bear it would have improved him. After all these years, I see that I was mistaken about Eve in the beginning; it is better to live outside the Garden with her than inside it without her. At first I thought she talked too much; but now, I should be sorry to have that voice fall silent and pass out of my life. Blessed be the chestnut that brought us near together and taught me to know the goodness of her heart and the sweetness of her spirit!

APPENDIX 4

Planning Notes for Methuselah's Diary †

[These notes are here published in full for the first time from manuscripts in the Mark Twain Papers. They have been grouped according to physical characteristics, comparison with the manuscript, matters treated in each set, internal cohesion, and topical references. A number has been given to each manuscript leaf within a sequence.]

Group 1

[This group consists of pages numbered 1–9, all written in dark brown ink on Towgood's Superfine stationery, the same stationery used in the first segment of "Methuselah's Diary," 31–41.]

1-A [page 1]

Mastodon—pets.

Travels to Enoch & other strange cities, noting manners, customs, literature, laws & religion.

The god Baal—followers of many sects, with trivial differences, like Christians.

Get some customs from Mosaic law & alter them.

Traditions of prophecies of flood.

1-B [page 2]

Mails.
Menagerie
Circus.
Fire Eaters.
Gymnasts.
Fire-works.

Wandering Jabals come to town & wondered at.
They scalp & paint faces in war.

Announcing Royal proclamations & new laws from rostra in the market.

1-C [page 3]

Six-legged calves & fat women & skeleton men.

Prices of admish.

Baalish missionaries—Mis^{h} Society for propagating religion in foreign parts. Each convert costs lives & piles of money.

Ginx Baby charities.

Demagogue politicians & elective judgeships—suffrage.

1-D [page 4]

Women's rights.
Groceries, concubines & other household furniture for sale.
The Slave mart.
Drunk man.
Magicians, with old slight-of-hand tricks.
Dinner customs.
Executions.
Child of 22—toys for him.
Aged dog.

1-E [page 5]

The Princess of the house of —— proposed for Meth. Too old and ill-tempered.

Mr. & Mrs. Turner met on travels.

Zillah is mean birth—supposed to be.

Meets Cain.

Adam coming—grand preparations.

Eve ditto.

1-F [page 6]

Adam's visit—preparations—Exodus XIX.
Graven images permissable of old—Ex. 20. (only to Baal
Also swearing.
Sabbath Breaking

———

Baal's Sabbath Tuesday, ⟨third⟩ second day of week.
Jewish, 7th day.

———

Plain stones for altars to God, but set in grand temples.
Some dissent & have only the stones. Stone on level ground.—Ex. 20.
Hebrew slaves were only for 7 years.—Ex 21.

1-G [page 7]

Slavery in full—Ex. 21.
Buying the man made his free wife a slave for 7 years.
⟨Refuge⟩

Amurath Assizes.

Murder

—

Murder—penalty death.

2. But has priv. of refuge.
3. No refuge for assassins.
4. " " " parricides.
5. Nor for men-stealers.
6. " " cursers of parents.

If wound a man, must pay lost time & doctor bills.

———

To kill a servant—mere punishment, if death be quick. None if a day or two elapse. For he is his money.

1-H [page 8]

⟨Kill⟩ Hurting a woman with child. Punishment. And death. Eye for eye. foot for foot.
The ox—finable in shekels.

Ex. 22.

Theft, damage, trespass,—
Borrowing, fornication,
Idolatry (inoperative)
Strangers, widows &c.

See laws in Josephus.

Destroying altars & groves, Ex. 34.

Can't intermarry—ibid.

Introduce a recreant priest—who breaks the above rules.

1-I [page 9]

No fire on Sunday—Ex. 35.

Group 2

[Written probably close to same time as above in same ink, on two sides of a sheet, original seven-inch length torn to five inches. On recto Mark Twain drafted a telegram to Elisha Bliss and then at some time turned the paper around and began figuring birth and death dates of various biblical characters (upside down in relation to the telegram). On the verso of the sheet, he continued the figuring. The dates here and in group 4 below, he undoubtedly derived from Genesis 5.]

2-A

American Telegram
E. Bliss,
Hartford, Conn.
Stop that Pamphlet.
Clemens.

622	622	687
365	65	969
987	687	1656
57	187	
30	874	
	182	
	1056	

2-A verso

910	905	912	687
395	235	130	969
1305	1140	1042	1656

325	395	962	777
910	895	460	874
1235	1290	1422	1651

365
622
987

Meth died 1656

950
1056
2006

Edinburgh

Edinburgh
Edinburgh
Edinburgh

[The "Edinburghs" become increasingly longer as the column descends.]

Group 3

[Groups 3-A and 3-B are written in pencil on the first and last pages of a four-page folded letter paper, like Towgood's Superfine, but slightly different, as are 3-C and 3-D (this is the same paper as pp. 1–30 of the ms.). A brown-ink blot at the top left-hand corner of the first page of each of these items is like the inkblots on the pages of group 1. Hence these sheets were probably used fairly close to the same time.

Groups 3-A and 3-B seem to develop the suggestion on 1-A to "Get some customs from Mosaic law & alter them." 3-E is written in brown ink on page 1 of the same sort of folded letter paper, and is the only note on the four pages, but this folded paper is Towgood's Superfine.]

3-A

Sackcloth—Gen. 37.
See Ruth.
She veiled her face like a harlot—Gen. 38
Burn harlot—Gen. 38.
Slave caravan.—Gen. 39.
Interpreting dreams by ^"wise men"^—Gen. 40.
My cup-bearer, ^&^ chief baker & overseer.
 Dream won't come true unless dreamt twice—Gen. ^41^ ⟨42⟩
 Unclean beasts &c—Levit. 11.
 Purifying after childbirth—12
 Leprosy—Lev. 13, v. 45.
 Cleansing a house, Lev. 14.

Levit—if you stub yr toe, you must run to the priest—so says old carping Uzziel—who is neither for God nor Baal. Priest hears women & all confess their closest secrets.

3-B

Scapegoat—Lev. 16.
Eating blood—17.
Gleaning, Lev. 19 & Ruth.
Mingled linen, 19, v. 19

3-C

Blessed be God have succeeding thereof; above 100 cats
A maid's [?] oath.
Same language everywhere, but many dialects—

My 1200 bros. & sisters mustered, inspected, counted, tallied invoiced, ac/of stock twice a year.—this is when M. is old—or he can see it done with Seth's or Enos's—especially if there were concubines. Quote & begat sons & daughters.'

In his age, on one of thes occasions is introduced to brothers & sisters never met before. Invites 40 or 50 to dine. Sees resemblance—have much family talk about What ever became of Jim?—Married so & so & moved out into so & so 200 ys ago &c

3-D

Remains 20 years. in Enoch (short stay—is hurried) ⟨marries;⟩ returns there 500 yrs later—everybody married or dead or moved away—inquires for all—reads mouldering monuments to them—asks after this & that one—is all very sad—so many changes—finally finds one withered wretch who was a humble youth & befriended him in the old time—shows him graves, ruined houses, & tells everything.

Changes in town's appearance & customs. Men kissing going out of fashion—been out twice before in his time.

Raising seed to a brother Gen—38.

3-E

Sleeping upon the House-tops coming into vogue. 797.

Group 4

4-A

[Written in pencil. Seems to be a chart resulting from the computations of group 2.]

Year Born		How old when son born	Year Died
1.	Adam	130	930
130.	Seth	105	1092
235	Enos	90	1140
325	Cainan	70	1235
395	Mahalaleel	65	1290
460	Jared	162	1422
622	Enoch	65	987
	died—not translated		
687	Methuselah	187	1656
874	Lamech	182	1651
1056	Noah	500	2006
1556	Shem, Ham, & Jap		

1656 The flood came, began to rain the 17th of the 2d month of Noah's 600th year. The waters remained upon the earth 155 days: "The rains were [then) restrained." So it rained *more* than 40 days.

The 17th of the 7th month the Ark grounded on Ararat.

The 1st of the

4-B

[This beginning of an additional list, in pencil, possibly belongs to this group.]

Adam, Cain, Abel, Seth.

⟨Adam 130⟩

⟨Adam 130 when Seth born⟩	Year
Seth born - - - -	130
	1042

4-C

[Written in dark brown ink on Towgood's Superfine stationery, and seems related to this group.]

Adam, Enoch's grandfather.

City of Enoch, built by Cain, Enoch's father.

Enoch was Lamech's great-great-grandfather.

⟨Cain⟩ Adam was his gre-gr. g. gr-.

Lamech's sons were Jabal

1. (lived in tents & had cattle)—not considered altogether respectable. —
2. & Jubal-the musician (harp & organ.)
3. & Tubal-cain iron & brass machinist.

Adam was these boys' great-great-great-great-great grandfather.

And then Adam had another son, Seth, when 130 yrs old. Seth's son was Enos—Ad. was then 235, & a revival began—

Savages before. "Then began men to call upon the name of the Lord." [Last sentence added in pencil.]

Group 5

[These notes are written in pencil on Crystal Lake Mills stationery, which Mark Twain used for the second segment of "Methuselah's Diary." Hence these notes date from the fall of 1877. They are in part a summary of what he had already written.]

5-A

The Sage Uz, ^the learned idolater^ from the far North-eastern land of Nod, in the old city Enoch—gone home. Their religion is cramped by law.

Zillah, his gr-gr-grand-daugh remains, visiting her kinsman Habakkuk. ⟨supposed⟩ to be of mere civilian degree & of no estate.

Amurath, Meth's capital city—covering 5 hills & valleys, a vast population—city all stone.

Luz, the new actor of Adam in The Expulsion from Eden.

Jebel, that never-failing ½ brother of my ^gr.^ grt-gr-grandfather Enos, the smirking critic, about 500 yr old Talks about

Uzziel, the great tragedian of 4 or 500 yr ago.

Zuar, a Hebrew slave, purchased from Z's father—could only hold a Hebrew slave 6 years. Has wife & children born in slavery.

[Written along left margin] You dissipate so you will be an old man at 600.

5-B

Meth sets them all free. Zuar & his wife Malah appointed master of the pages & "serve in the apartments of the women" (harem).

Princess Sarah, grand-daugh of my kinsman Eliah, a rich great & ancient house. She is turned 61 (<u>page</u> 26)—folks want him to marry her. "Not for Joe." ["<u>page</u> 26" refers to page 26 of the *first* segment of Methusaleh's diary.]

Jabelites, savages, dwellers in tents. Give them Sitting-Bull names.

Meth's first child.—foolish fondnesses.

Mastodon fight in arena in presence of 400,000. Good house. [This last item is written in purple ink, much finer writing.]

Group 6

[This group consists of five individual sheets of Crystal Lake Mills paper, written in pencil. We have simply guessed about the order.]

6-A

Cain
Enoch (<u>not</u> the translated.)
Irad
Mehujael
Methusael
Lamech (<u>not</u> the regular line)

Lamech's wives, Adah & Zillah
Adah's sons—Jabel, (tents) & Jubal, (music)
Zillah's son Tubal-cain—(brass & iron)—his sister Naamah.

6-B

Adam
Cain, Abel, Seth
Enoch   Enos
Irad
Mehujael
Methusa⟨leh⟩^el^
Lamech (Adah & Zillah his wives)
brothers (Jabal (Tubal-cain
            (Jubal (Naamah, ⟨his⟩ T.-c's
                        sister.

Lamech was a murderer of ^a youth of 70 or 80^& ⟨impressed with the idea that he must suffer 70-& 7-fold⟩ charmed with the idea that any man that shall avenge this murder will have to suffer 70- & 7-fold if Cain's must suffer 7-fold. Why? ⟨Because⟩ Did he misconstrue God & imagine that murderers were His special pets?

Don't confound the murderer Lamech with Adam's holy descendant.

6-C

Land of Nod, East of Eden
Meth is living ⟨west⟩
        South "   "
(None allowed to visit the mysterious Eden—terrible legends concerning it.

Talk about Cain the first murderer.

Eve outlives Adam.

6-D

Poor foreign devils lost & starving in the desert.

Republican govt of Meth can't relieve or rescue them.

⟨Chief Minister⟩ ^Somebody^observes that if you can pretend that they are robbers or other criminals govt will hunt them up with alacrity——which is done.

Disgust of govt to find they are honest & harmless.

6-E

The giants & the sons of God can be referred to shortly after Noah's birth (1056) when Meth about 350 yr old.

6-F

Meth gets onto scientific religion, his faith weakens, he finally becomes a regular free-thinker—bothers over the foolish prophecies about a flood; & ends, through his love for Zillah, in becoming an idolater (it is only hinted) since he did not sail in the ark. Baalite.

APPENDIX 5

Passages from "Stormfield" Preserved in the Manuscript but Deleted from Typescript or Proof

a. Original Mrs. Rushmore and Daughter Episode

[At some period before sending "Stormfield" to *Harper's* Mark Twain removed this episode (originally on pages 11.9–19.18 of the second section of the manuscript) by deleting pages 1,138–41 (originally 33–36) and crossing out the first nine lines of page 1,142 (37) of his typescript. Possibly he decided the episode was too sentimental, but more likely he sought to avoid complications arising from his use of the name Rushmore. In July 1907, not long before the story went to Harper's, he had been treated for bronchitis by a Dr. Edward C. Rushmore, who also advised against having an operation—possibly for the hernia Clemens had suffered in 1893—since at his time of life such an operation would be too dangerous (*MTHHR*, 630–31, 634). And he may well have thought that Dr. Rushmore might take offense at having his name appropriated.

In another direction Mrs. Rushmore's reactions to the death of her first-born (a sixteen-month-old baby daughter) doubtless reflected the Clemenses' grief when their own first-born died of diphtheria on 2 June 1872. Olivia, like Mrs. Rushmore, was "about twenty-five" (actually 26) at the time, and their son Langdon was just short of nineteen months old.

The deleted passage would have followed the sentence on 161.34–35 of the present text of "Stormfield": "You are making heaven pretty comfortable in one way, but you are playing mischief with it in another."

The original manuscript text, (first published in *MTQH*, 123–26), reads as follows:]

"As how?"

"Well, for instance. You make the baby *grow up*—you make the young girl and the young man progress along into age, and *take on the look of it and the signs of it!* My land, it chills me all through to think of it! Imagine a sweet young mother seeing her little baby die, twenty years ago, and keeping her heart from breaking by saying a million times, through her tears. 'I shall see my darling again in heaven'—and imagine that mother soaring into this place now, crazy to get that child in her arms again—and suppose—"

"Sh!—hold still," says Sandy. "I've seen it a hundred times. I had an instance last week. Mildred Rushmore—neighbor of ours, below—lost a baby sixteen months old, a couple of years before I died, It was her first—she was about twenty-five years old—and it seemed as if she would go stark mad with the grief of it. It would have broken anybody's heart to see the poor thing, and hear her wail and cry. All the comfort she could get was out of those very words, 'I shall see my child in heaven—I shall see her in heaven, and there we'll meet to part no more forever'—and then she would break down and wail and cry again.

"Well Mildred died, in her own good time, and last week she arrived here; I was passing by that house yonder when I heard the whir of wings, and down she lit by me, and fell flat. I lifted her up and brushed her off. She had recognized me, but I couldn't make her out till she told me who she was, for she is over fifty, now, and pretty gray, whereas she was plump and young when I died.

"She was all aglow, her eyes were dancing. 'My child!' she says, 'take me to my child! O, take me to my baby, take me to my darling!'

"Just at that minute, out of that house steps a woman of about thirty, with five children following behind her.

" 'This is your baby,' says I—'your daughter, I mean—she is Mrs. McLaughlin, now, and these are her children.'

"The poor old thing stopped stock still, her eyes stared glassy as a corpse's, and her wings drooped till they trailed the ground; never did I see anybody so stricken. She moaned out—

" 'This my sweet lost baby!—O, there is some dreadful mistake, some cruel mistake! Take me back to the grave—O, please, I cannot bear to live.'

"The other lady looked wonderingly and pityingly at her, as one would look at a harmless strange madman, and was about to move on.

" 'Wait a minute,' says I, 'wait a minute, Mrs. McLaughlin, let me introduce you; this is your mother—the late Mrs. Rushmore.'

" '*My* mother?' she said, opening her kind eyes wide, but sort of half-shrinking back, as if she judged it was a mistake or a joke.

"Mrs Rushmore burst out crying, and fell limp in my arms, saying over and over again—

" 'O, why did I die? I wish I had never died! Go away woman, I cannot bear you! Give me my child, O, give me my child!'

"It was very embarrassing to us all. Mrs. McLaughlin said, in a hurt voice—

" 'Do not speak so to me, madam, I have never done you any harm. I do not know you, I have not heard of you before. Trouble has disordered your mind; but if you will come in my house I will do all I can to comfort you. And do not grieve, nor be afraid, poor lady, for here in heaven you cannot be unhappy long.'

"But Mrs. Rushmore waved her away and would not look at her, but went on wailing and begging to be taken to her child. So presently Mrs. McLaughlin went away with her children, on some business, whatever it was, and I took Mrs. Rushmore to my house."

"Is that all? What happened afterwards?"

"O well, what always happens. The two women got acquainted, and visited a little for a day or so and called each other mother and daughter, and all that, but nothing came of it. They were strangers, and hadn't anything in common. Mrs. McLaughlin had been head over heels in astronomy for years, and didn't care to talk about anything else, whereas her poor old mother didn't know one star from t'other, and didn't want to. So of course they drifted apart inside of four days. They haven't any sympathies that they can hitch to—inside of a month they'll stop this fol-de-rol and just be acquaintances, nothing more."

"Well, but goodness! what will this poor old woman do, all alone in heaven? She can't be happy here, of course, after such a disappointment?"

"O, but can't she, though? She is already happy. She has raked up twenty or thirty friends and relations who died within two or three years before she did, and it would have done your heart good to see these old cronies meet again. She has raked up her husband, too—he died about five years ahead. Happy? there ain't anybody in these realms that is happier than Mrs. Rushmore. She has got acquainted with a lot of simple-minded, harmless, ignorant Jersey people,—regular gossips—and they get together every day and pull other people's reputations to pieces, and slander the elect in general, wholesale and retail, and have a noble good time. Much she will be bothering about her lost child a month from now!"

"No, but do they really deal in that kind of gossip in heaven?" . . .

[In printing that passage in *Mark Twain's Quarrel with Heaven*, appendix B, Browne also included the fifteen lines that Mark Twain omitted from the ending of part I (*Harper's Monthly*, December 1907, 49) when he revised the passage for the book publication in order to include a condensed version of the Rushmore incident. In the manuscript (second section, 19.18–20.14) those lines read as follows:]

"How you talk! Would heaven be heaven if you couldn't slander folks?"

"Come to think, I don't believe it would—for some people—but I hadn't thought of it before."

"For 'some people?'—There you hit it. The trouble on earth is, that they leave out the *some-people* class—they try to fix up a heaven for only one kind of people. It won't work. There's all kinds here—and God cares for all kinds. He makes all happy; if he can't do it in one way, he does it in another. He doesn't leave anybody out in the cold."

[End of chapter. Also end of *Harper's* part I.]

b. Stormfield's Trouble with Wings†

[In "Mental Telegraphy?" (q.v.), the piece he wrote in November 1907, Mark Twain mentioned that "three weeks ago" in reading and revising the *Harper's Monthly* proofs for "Captain Stormfield's Visit to Heaven," he had "struck out one or two of the Captain's adventures." This substantial passage (second section of MS, 25.9–36.end, and TS, 1144.21–1150.6 [originally pp. 39–45]) was the only one that could really qualify as one of Stormfield's "adventures." In this case Twain must have decided that the episode had gone on too long, and so removed all but a few paragraphs to document the captain's aerial misadventures.

This passage originally followed the second paragraph of the present chapter 5 of "Stormfield," which ends: "You could lay to, with your head to the wind—that is the best you could do, and right hard work you'd find it, too. If you tried any other game, you would founder sure."

The passage deleted in proof, and here first published, reads:]

I argued this all out to myself, but I went on practising, to make certain. With my first few experiments, I naturally stuck to the flop, of course—any beginner would. But says I to myself, an angel of my weight (230) can never flop such a pair of wings as these but a little while without tiring himself out—no, it stands to reason that he must soar, he must float, like a buzzard, or an eagle. So I got up on the rock again, and got a good start, and tried for a long go. When I had gone a mile, I was fagged out, and sweating like the dewy meadows; then I spread out my wings and held them still. It was very nice and smooth, though I came downwards faster than was convenient; so I had to give a flop or two—and pretty often—to keep up. But as I began to get the hang of soaring, I commenced to throw in some embellishments, and that wasn't a lucky idea. I tilted up my port side and soared off on a half circle; then I tilted up my weather side—and right there is where the mistake occurred; the wind got in under that wing and whirled me upside down; and the next minute I smashed down into a brier bush and tore my robe and lost as much as a hatful of feathers. Says I, "Earth has got some advantages that this region don't possess; if I was down there, now, I could swear this thing out and get it off of my mind, but here a body has got to hold in and let it fester."

I had timed myself from the rock. I timed myself again, now, and walked back. I took one or two more flights and walks, and timed myself. I made a little calculation, and I could see that as a general thing there wasn't any mighty advantage in flying, over walking. With the wind fair, I could fly fifteen miles in an hour—and be dead tired and beat-out when I got through, with the flopping. Sailing close to the wind, I couldn't fly much faster than I could walk, and would get beat out twice as quick. The wings would be good in muddy weather—that was about all there was to it.

Another thing. When I walked, I could go to my target, every time, of course; but with the wings it was different; if there was any wind at all, a body was bound to drift to looard, do what he might—at least a new hand was, anyway. I always fetched up away to one side of where I started to go to. There didn't seem to be any way to steer.

I went and sat down, and thought over it. Now, says I, what does a bird do? Well, the birds that are the most like a man are the crane kind; they stick their long legs straight out behind, and I reckon they steer with them. I tried it, but it wouldn't work. My legs were long enough, but they were too heavy; they wouldn't stick out, but wanted to hang down. I tried striking out with them, like a frog, but they kept catching in my robe—it was like trying to swim with a night shirt on. So I tied my robe up around my neck and tried it again. But it was no use; my legs were too heavy, and besides I felt embarrassed, there being considerable company around.

I thought over the birds again, and judged that what I wanted was a tail. I belted my gown tight and fastened a sheaf of feathers on behind. It was a failure. They were not part of me, and I couldn't work them; they only just stuck out behind in a foolish bunch, like a feather-duster, and didn't do any good. And then some boys came along and one of them said—

"Oh, here's fun! Here's an angel with a tail. Let's clod him."

They did clod me, too, and I had to fly into some woods a mile off to get away from them. I experimented every way I could think of, but I couldn't see that for ordinary purposes wings were any advantage, and besides it was most awful fatiguing to flop them. I could see, after cogitating over it, that I wasn't rightly built for wings. I hadn't any muscles about my shoulders suited for working such things as wings—no muscles situated to take hold of them rightly.

But I hated to give them up, for I had always wanted to be a regulation angel. Still they were such a trouble to me that I stopped using them except when I was going to cut around in public. Another thing; I found I had to have considerable rigging, when I went any distance, and this was another bother. Of course I found that out by experience; I got caught in a gale one day, and was blown a hundred miles out of my course; I found I couldn't lay to, you see; well, I had no instruments, I got lost, and had a time of it finding my way home again.

Next time I started on such a trip, I took along a little three-hooked grapnel and thirty fathom of line, which I coiled around my neck. I had a sextant and a compass in a carpet sack hanging to my belt. Well, it came on to blow like sixty, and I lay to, over a mighty wide lake. I let go my anchor—the rope was fast around my neck—but it struck deep water and snatched me down head first to within fifty foot of the water before it found bottom. Well, I lay to, there, a couple of hours, flopping away, with my head to the wind. Then the gale went down and it was time, too, for I hadn't strength left to flop much longer. I got up my anchor, and got away on a fair wind, but by and by it came on to blow worse than ever. I didn't want to try laying to, any more, so I set my helm amidships, so to speak, and thought I would run before the wind and see what would come of it. The thing that come of it, was, that I fetched up in an unknown land, by and by, and had to lay idle there a couple of days, because the weather was thick and I couldn't get an observation. However, things cleared a little the third day, and I out with my sextant and got an observation. I was in latitude 17,244,514° 40′ 43″ N, and longitude 9,454,610° 32′ 15″ west of the New Jerusalem. How the mischief I could have made all that latitude I couldn't make out; but such was the case, and there was nothing for it but to set my course and scud for home.

By the time I got there I had about made up my mind that if there was a saint around that wanted to trade a paper of tacks for a second-hand pair of wings a little the worse for wear and weather, I could tell him where he could get a chance.

Well, I was home again, and that was a comfort, anyway. I rolled up my wings in an old last week's *Zion's Herald*, and tucked them away in the pantry, and says I, "You lay there and take a rest till the mud's too deep for stilts; for if I ever meddle with you in the meantime it will be because there's an official pow-wow of some sort where the elect will have to go in their regimentals." †

APPENDIX 6

Discussion of the Fall from "Schoolhouse Hill"

[One of the three surviving tales about a mysterious stranger's visit to earth that Mark Twain worked on from 1897 until 1908 (later known as the "Mysterious Stranger" manuscripts), the "Schoolhouse Hill" fragment (1898), has direct links to the Captain Stormfield materials, to "Passage from Satan's Diary" and "Passage from Eve's Diary" in "Diaries Antedating the Flood," and to "Letters from the Earth."

In chapter 5 of "Schoolhouse Hill" an important dialogue occurs between Oliver Hotchkiss and the youth who calls himself Quarante-Quatre (Forty-four) and has just revealed that he is the son of Satan. During their discussion Quarante-quatre explains that it was his father's involvement with Adam and Eve in Eden that caused both the Fall and Satan's banishment from Heaven. Mark Twain later developed a similar discussion in "Passage from Satan's Diary," in which Satan himself describes the origin of evil and the discovery of death. In "Passage from Eve's Diary" Eve addresses serious events rather than idyllic memories when she recounts the loss of Eden and the death of Abel.

In addition, Mark Twain here introduced his concept of the differences between human and heavenly time, which he also touched upon in the "Stormfield" manuscripts and, more fully, in "Letters from the Earth."]

From "Schoolhouse Hill"

Chapter 5

Hotchkiss sank into his chair weak and limp, and began to pour out broken words and disjointed sentences whose meanings were not always clear but whose general idea was comprehensible. To this effect: from custom bred of his upbringing and his associations he had often talked about Satan with a freedom which was regrettable, but it was really only talk, mere idle talk, he didn't mean anything by it; in fact there were many points about Satan's character which he greatly admired, and although he hadn't said so, publicly, it was an oversight and not intentional—but from this out he meant to open his mouth boldly, let people say what they might and think what they chose—

The boy interrupted him, gently and quietly—

"*I* don't admire him."

Hotchkiss was hard aground, now; his mouth was open, and remained so, but no words came; he couldn't think of anything judicious to say. Presently he ventured to throw out a feeler—cautiously, tentatively, feelingly, persuasively:

"You see—well, you know—it would only be natural, if I was a devil—a good, kind, honorable devil, I mean—and my father was a good, kind, honorable devil against whom narrow and perhaps wrongful or at least exaggerated prejudices—"

"But I am not a devil," said the boy, tranquilly.

Hotchkiss was badly confused, but profoundly relieved.

"I—er—I—well, you know, I suspected as much, I—I—indeed I hadn't a doubt of it; and—although it—on the whole—oh, good land, I can't understand it, of course, but I give you my word of honor I like you all the better for it, I do indeed! I feel good, now—good, and comfortable, and in fact happy. Join me—take something! I wish to drink your health; and—and your family's."

"With pleasure. Now eat—refresh yourself. I will smoke, if you don't mind. I like it."

"Certainly; but eat, too; aren't you hungry?"

"No, I do not get hungry."

"Is that actually so?"

"Yes."

"Ever? Never?"

"No."

"Ah, it is a pity. You miss a great deal. Now tell me about yourself, won't you?"

"I shall be glad to do it, for I have a purpose in coming to the earth, and if you should find the matter interesting, you can be useful to me."

Then the talking and eating began, simultaneously.

"I was born before Adam's fall—"

"Wh-at!"

"It seems to surprise you. Why?"

"Because it caught me unprepared. And because it is six thousand years ago, and you look to be only about fifteen years old."

"True—that is my age, within a fraction."

"Only fifteen, and yet—"

"Counting by *our* system of measurement, I mean—not yours."

"How is that?"

"A day, with us, is as a thousand years with you."

Hotchkiss was awed. A seriousness which was near to solemnity settled upon his face. After a meditative pause he said—

"Surely it cannot be that you really and not figuratively mean—"

"Yes—really, not figuratively. A minute of our time is $41\frac{2}{3}$ years of yours. By our system of measurement I am fifteen years old; but by yours I am five million, lacking twenty thousand years."

Hotchkiss was stunned. He shook his head in a hopeless way, and said, resignedly—

"Go on—I can't realize it—it is astronomy to me."

"Of course you cannot realize these things, but do not be troubled; measurements of time and eternity are mere conveniences, they are not of much importance. It is about a week ago that Adam fell—"

"A week?—Ah, yes, *your* week. It is awful—that compression of time! Go on."

"I was in heaven; I had always lived in heaven, of course; until a week ago, my father had always lived there. But I saw this little world created. I was interested; we were all interested. There is much more interest attaching to the creation of a planet than attaches to the creation of a sun, on account of the life that is going to inhabit it. I have seen many suns created—many indeed, that you are not yet acquainted with, they being so remotely situated in the deeps of space that their light will not reach here for a long time yet; but the planets—I cared the most for them; we all did; I have seen millions of them made, and the Tree planted in the Garden, and the man and the woman placed in its shade, with the animals about them. I saw your Adam and Eve only once; they were happy, then, and innocent. This could have continued forever, but for my father's conduct. I read it all in the Bible in Mr. Ferguson's school. As it turned out, Adam's happiness lasted less than a day—"

"Less than one day?"

"By our reckoning, I mean; by yours he lived nine hundred and twenty years—the bulk of it unhappily."

"I see; yes, it is true."

"It was my father's fault. Then hell was created, in order that Adam's race might have a place to go, after death—"

"They could go to heaven, too."

"That was later. Two days ago. Through the sacrifice made for them by the son of God, the Savior."

"Is hell so new?"

"It was not needed before. No Adam in any of the millions of other planets had ever disobeyed and eaten of the forbidden fruit."

"It is strange."

"No—for the others were not tempted."

"How was that?"

"There was no tempter until my father ate of the fruit himself and became one. Then he tempted other angels and they ate of it also; then Adam and the woman."

"How did your father come to eat of it this time?"

"I did not know at the time."

"Why didn't you?"

"Because I was away when it happened; I was away some days, and did not hear of it at all and of the disaster to my father until I got back; then I went to my father's place to speak with him of it; but his trouble was so new, and so severe, and so amazing to him that he could do nothing but grieve and lament—he could not bear to talk about the details; I merely gathered that when he made the venture it was because his idea of the nature of the fruit was a most erroneous one."

"Erroneous?"

"Quite erroneous."

"You do not know in what way it was erroneous?"

"Yes, I think I know now. He probably—in fact unquestionably—supposed that the nature of the fruit was to reveal to human beings the knowledge of good and evil—that, and nothing more; but not to Satan the great angel; he had that knowledge before. We always had it—always. Now why he was moved to taste it himself is not clear; I shall never know until he tells me. But his error was—"

"Yes, what was his error?"

"His error was in supposing that a knowledge of the difference between good and evil was *all* that the fruit could confer."

"Did it confer more than that?"

"Consider the passage which says *man is prone to evil as the sparks to fly upward.* Is that true? Is that really the nature of man?—I mean your man—the man of this planet?"

"Indeed it is—nothing could be truer."

"It is not true of the men of any other planet. It explains the mystery. My father's error stands revealed in all its nakedness. The fruit's office was not confined to conferring the mere knowledge of good and evil, it conferred also the passionate and eager and hungry *disposition to* DO *evil.* Prone as sparks to fly upward; in other words, prone as water to run down hill—a powerful figure, and means that man's disposition is wholly evil, uncompromisingly evil, inveterately evil, and that he is as undisposed to do good as water is undisposed to run *up* hill. Ah, my father's error brought a colossal disaster upon the men of this planet. It *poisoned* the men of this planet—poisoned them in mind and body. I see it, plainly."

"It brought death, too."

"Yes—whatever that may be. I do not quite understand it. It seems to be a sleep. You do not seem to mind sleep. By my reading I gather that you are not conscious of either death *or* sleep; that nevertheless you fear the one and do not fear the other. It is very stupid. Illogical."

Hotchkiss put down his knife and fork and explained the difference between sleep and death; and how a person was not sorry when asleep, but sorry when dead, because—because—

He found it was not so easy to explain why as he had supposed it was going to be; he floundered a while, then broke down. But presently he tried again, and said that death *was* only a sleep, but that the objection to it was that it was so *long;* then he remembered that time stands still when one sleeps, and so the difference between a night and a thousand years is really no difference at all so far as the sleeper is personally affected.

However, the boy was thinking, profoundly, and heard none of it; so nothing was lost. By and by the boy said, earnestly—

"The fundamental change wrought in man's nature by my father's conduct must remain—it is permanent; but a part of its burden of evil consequences can be lifted from your race, and I will undertake it. Will you help?"

He was applying in the right quarter. Lifting burdens from a whole race was a fine and large enterprize, and suited Oliver Hotchkiss's size and gifts better than any contract he had ever taken hold of yet. He gave in his adhesion with promptness and enthusiasm, and wanted the scheme charted out at once. Privately he was immeasurably proud to be connected in business with an actual angel and son of a devil, but did what he could to keep his exultation from showing. The boy said—

"I cannot map out a definite plan yet; I must first study this race. Its poisoned condition and prominent disposition to do evil differentiate it radically from any men whom I have known before, therefore it is a new race to me and must be exhaustively studied before I shall know where and how to begin. Indefinitely speaking, our plan will be confined to ameliorating the condition of the race in some ways in *this* life; we are not called upon to concern ourselves with its future fate; that is in abler hands than ours."

"I hope you will begin your studies right away."

"I shall. Go to bed, and take your rest. During the rest of the night and to-morrow I will travel about the globe and personally examine some of the nationalities, and learn languages and read the world's books in the several tongues, and to-morrow night we will talk together here. Meantime the storm has made you a prisoner. Will you have one of my servants to wait on you?"

A genuine little devil all for his own! It was a lovely idea, and swelled Hotchkiss's vanity to the bursting point. He was lavish with his thanks.

"But he won't understand what I say to him."

"He will learn in five minutes. Would you like any particular one?"

"If I could have the cunning little rascal that sat down in the fire after he got cooled off—"

There was a flash of scarlet and the little fiend was present and smiling; and he had with him some books from the school; among them the French-English dictionary and the phonographic shorthand system.

"There. Use him night and day. He knows what he is here for. If he needs help he will provide it. He requires no lights; take them, and go to bed; leave him to study his books. In five minutes he will be able to talk broken English in case you want him. He will read twelve or fifteen of your books in an hour and learn shorthand besides; then he will be a capable secretary. He will be visible or invisible according to your orders. Give him a name—he has one already, and so have I, but you would not be able to pronounce either of them. Good-bye."

He vanished.

Hotchkiss stood smiling all sorts of pleasant smiles of intricate and variegated pattern at his little devil, with the idea of making him understand how welcome he was; and he said to himself, "It's a bitter climate for him, poor little rascal, the fire will go down and he will freeze; I wish I knew how to tell him to run home and warm himself whenever he wants to."

He brought blankets and made signs to him that these were for him to wrap up in; then he began to pile wood on the fire, but the red stranger took that work promptly off his hands, and did the work like an expert—which he was. Then he sat down on the fire and began to study his book, and his new master took the candle and went away to bed, meditating a name for him. "He is a dear little devil," he said, "and must have a nice one." So he named him Edward Nicholson Hotchkiss—after a brother that was dead.

APPENDIX 7

God of the Bible vs. God of the Present Day (1870s)

[Written in the early 1870s, probably close to the time of the January 1870 letter to Olivia quoted in the introduction to this volume, this piece reflects a concept of the Creator that Mark Twain would hold well into the 1890s. Like the letter it also introduces the theme that would continue to fascinate him for the rest of his life, namely, the almost unimaginable magnitude of the universe as revealed by science.

Mark Twain's first real departure from the Presbyterian fundamentalism of his youth, with its emphasis on God's punishment for one's sins, came during his years on the river. There he first read Thomas Paine's *The Age of Reason*, as he later said, "with fear and hesitation, but marveling at its fearlessness and wonderful power" (*MTB* 3:1445). Obviously impressed by Paine's Deism, with its vision of an immense universe governed by immutable natural law, he was also struck by the author's discussions of the inconsistencies and limitations of the biblical concepts of God and nature. And the ideas of *The Age of Reason* became one of the major influences on his thought (for the best discussion of that influence, see Sherwood Cummings, *Mark Twain and Science*, [1988]).

In presenting his contrast between the biblical God and the "real" God, Mark Twain drew strongly upon the *Age of Reason*, especially chapters 13–15. In the first of these, for instance, Paine describes how, after mastering the "use of the globes and of the orrery" (an orrery is a mechanical model of the solar system, so named after one was made for Charles Boyle, fourth earl of Orrery) and conceiving some idea of the "infinity of space," he began to compare the evidence of those studies with accepted beliefs, and goes on to contrast what he saw as the foolish concept of a geocentric universe with the immensity of the solar system as revealed by "natural philosophy," that is, science. Later he remarks that far from being the center of the universe, the earth "is infinitely less in proportion than the size of a grain of sand is to the size of the world."

Mark Twain's discussion is very similar, declaring that the universe discovered by "modern men" consists of "countless worlds of so stupendous dimensions that in comparison ours is grotesquely insignificant; they swing in spaces so vast that in comparison the spaces of the Biblical universe are but as those of an orrery." Elsewhere he comes even closer to Paine's imagery, declaring that "one might represent the Biblical God by a grain of sand on the shore and then draw the proportions of the modern Deity upon the boundless expanse of the waters."

Many other similarities could be cited, but this is not to say that Paine was the only influence. Once his interest in astronomy was aroused, Mark Twain read a good deal in the periodicals of the time. The letter to Livy, referred to above, reflected two articles in the *Eclectic Magazine* for January 1870: "The Early History of Man," which also dealt with the conflict between biblical history and the discoveries of science, and "Solar Wonders," which described the magnitude of the sun and its solar flares. And his continuing fascination led him to purchase from time to time a number of popular works on astronomy, including those of two of the most famous nineteenth-century astronomers, Norman Lockyer and Simon Newcomb.

For Mark Twain's final views on God and the Bible see the Autobiographical Dictations of June 1906, which follow, and "Letters from the Earth."

We have borrowed the title of this selection from the listing of the manuscript in the Mark Twain Papers.]

God of the Bible vs. God of the Present Day†

The difference, in importance, between the God of the Bible and the God of the present day, cannot be described, it can only be vaguely and inadequately figured to the mind. It is as the difference between an ant and the Emperor of Russia. One cannot diagram the two proportions on a piece of paper, or any surface, indeed, unless it be one like that of the Atlantic ocean—in which case, one might represent the Biblical God by a grain of sand on the shore and then draw the proportions of the modern Deity upon the boundless expanse of the waters. It suggests those vast astronomical dimensions which cannot be mapped, because no map can afford the requisite space. If you make figures to represent the earth and moon, and allow a space of one inch between them to represent the 400,000 miles of distance which lie between the two bodies, the map will have to be eleven miles long in order to bring in the nearest fixed star. So one cannot put the modern heavens on a map, nor the modern God; but the Bible God and the Bible heavens can be set down on a slate and yet not be discommoded.

The Biblical universe consisted of but one important feature, a miniature world 8,000 miles in diameter; the minor features were a roof a rocket-flight overhead, containing a toy sun and moon, and speckled with some dimensionless sparks, placed there with the avowedly sole object of confining their homage to that little world and humbly serving it. The difference between that universe and the modern one revealed by science, is as the difference between dust-flecked ray in a barn and the sublime arch of the Milky Way in the skies. Its God was strictly proportioned to its dimensions. His sole solicitude was about a handful of truculent nomads. He worried and fretted over them in a peculiarly and distractingly human way. One day he coaxed and petted them beyond their due, the next he harried and lashed them beyond their deserts. He sulked, he cursed, he raged, he grieved, according to his mood and the circumstances, but all to no purpose; his efforts were all vain, he could not govern them. When the fury was on him he was blind to all reason—he not only slaughtered the offender but even his harmless little children and dumb cattle. So he got his little company of chosen ones to behave themselves after a fashion, he was indifferent about the world's worthier myriads.

He was an unfair God; he was a God of unsound judgment; he was a God of failures and miscalculations; he was given to odd ideas and fantastic devices.

He was unfair in Adam's case. He commanded Adam not to eat of the tree of the knowledge of good and evil; To disobey could not be a sin, because Adam could not comprehend a sin *until* the eating the fruit should reveal to him the difference between right and wrong. So he was unfair in punishing Adam for doing wrong when he could not know it was wrong.

It is plain that God thought man would be a successful invention. The result proved that his judgment in this matter was unsound. After some ages of experiment, he saw that Man was a failure; he "repented him" that he had made him—so he swept him away. But he retained a remnant, and tried him again. This was another error of judgment, as far as the chosen people were concerned, for the second crop were no better than the first.

He made all the animals in the world in a single day; he could have swept them all away in the flood and re-created them in one day when they were again needed. Therefore it was an odd idea to save specimens of them for eleven months in the ark, whilst aware that eight persons could *not* feed or water them by any human possibility. If they were to be preserved by miracle, the ark was not necessary—to let them swim would have answered the purpose and been more indubitably miraculous.

The ark was a peculiarly fantastic device. A man of reputation who should contrive so inadequate a thing for such a purpose would cease to be admired. There was no way to propel it, no way to steer it, no way to get the leakage-water out of it; if there was room for all the necessary animals, there was certainly not room for provender enough for them during so long a voyage.

There is one very impressive thing about the Deity of the Bible, and that is his lack of information. He did not know there was an America; he did not know the globe was round, he supposed it was flat; he did not know it moved, he imagined it stood still; he did not know the sun stood still, he supposed it moved; he did not know the globe was a mere berry, he thought it was the mightiest mass in the universe. In knowledge—in a word—he was not strong.

He made Man. He made man in such a way that multitudes of facts can be so demonstrated to him that he can *not* doubt their absoluteness; but when he wrote a book whose purpose was to convince all men of the truth of certain things, this book was capable of convincing only about one-tenth of them. He can visit every nostril in every corner and byway of the broad earth with his life-giving air, and every secret spot with his sun's beneficent light, but his "truth" he cannot spread—entire nations have not even heard of it; the many among such peoples as have heard of it only achieve a saddening and oppressive uncertainty by reading it. Plainly, his powers are limited, he is not Almighty; some things he can do, others are to him impossible.

Yes, the God of the Bible is justly meted to the scale of the Bible's universe. He found his most consonant employment in superintending the minute domestic affairs of a small coterie of vicious and turbulent fantastics, and his chief joy in inhaling the odors of burnt meat ascending from this toy globe; unconscious, the while, of the processions of majestic worlds which were marching through the awful wastes of space about him, ignorant as a babe of the stupendous nature of the *real* universe. He made the stars—such as those prodigious spheres, Jupiter, Saturn, etc.—to "give light" to this remote and wandering bubble of ours.

Some of the star-light created especially for us was made 50,000 years before it was needed—it takes it that long to reach us. This was another miscalculation. A great and needless waste of material.

The universe discovered by modern men comports with the dignity of the modern God, the God whom we trust, believe in, and humbly adore. It consists of countless worlds of so stupendous dimensions that in comparison ours is grotesquely insignificant; they swing in spaces so vast that in comparison the spaces of the Biblical universe are but as those of an orrery. The nearest star of the Biblical universe could not have been more than a bird's flight removed. The nearest fixed star in the modern heavens is twenty trillions of miles away. To merely *count* these miles—counting with good rapidity (150 per minute ten hours a day, three hundred and sixty-five days in the year,) would occupy a man close upon *four hundred thousand years*.

The God of the Bible did not know that the mountains and the everlasting rocks are built of the bones of his dead creatures—he supposed he built them himself, in a single day, out of nothing. He did not know that every drop of water and every grain of matter is populous with living forms. The very microscope has created a world compared with which the entire universe of the Bible is meagre, unmarvelous, and inconsequent. A man could contrive the Bible's universe—and manifestly did; but only God could imagine the real universe. The one had neither variety nor grandeur in it—the other bewilders with its variety and appals with its sublimity.

To trust the God of the Bible is to trust an irascible, vindictive, fierce, and ever fickle and changeful master; to trust the true God is to trust a Being who has uttered no promises, but whose beneficent, exact, and changeless ordering of the machinery of his colossal universe is proof that he is at least steadfast to his purposes; whose unwritten laws, so far as they affect man, being equal and impartial show that he is just and fair; these things, taken together, suggest that if he shall ordain us to live hereafter, he will still be steadfast, just and fair toward us. We shall not need to require anything more.†

APPENDIX 8

Selected Passages on God and the Bible from Autobiographical Dictations of June 1906

[In May 1906 Mark Twain again took up summer residence near Dublin, New Hampshire, where he continued dictating his autobiography, parts of which he had begun in Florence in January 1904 and had resumed in New York in January 1906. With him during that summer of 1906 were his daughter Jean, a stenographer and typist named Josephine Hobby, and Albert Bigelow Paine, who had requested and received permission to write the author's biography.

The sections of the so-called "Autobiography" written in June 1906 were less autobiographical in nature than they were contemplative reflections on subjects, especially religious ones, that were occupying his thoughts (and writing) during this period.

Mark Twain clearly recognized how controversial his thoughts would be, should they find their way into print. On 17 June 1906 he wrote to his friend William Dean Howells: "To-morrow I mean to dictate a chapter which will get my heirs & assigns burnt alive if they venture to print it this side of 2006 A.D.—which I judge they won't. There'll be lots of such chapters if I live 3 or 4 years longer. The edition of A.D. 2006 will make a stir when it comes out. I shall be hovering around taking notice, along with other dead pals. You are invited" (*MTHL*, 2:811). On 26 June he again wrote to Howells: "I have been dictating some fearful things, for 4 successive mornings—for no eye but yours to see until I have been dead a century—if then. But I got them out of my system, where they had been festering for years—& that was the main thing. I feel better, now" (*MTHL*, 2:815).

We include these selections from the June 1906 dictations because they provide direct links to others of Mark Twain's writings, both published and unpublished, and particularly to "Diaries Antedating the Flood," "Adam's Soliloquy," "Letters from the Earth," and "God of the Bible vs. God of the Present Day" in this volume. And together with the latter piece, written in the early 1870s near the beginning of his literary career, they furnish a useful framework for understanding the continuity of the author's religious thought into the final decade of his life.

In the dictation for 20 June, though we have retained the initial label for the selection, we have omitted the five-and-a-half-page attack on the concept of the virgin birth (mistakenly referred to as the immaculate conception) because that discussion is not closely related to the writings in this volume.]

Tuesday, June 19, 1906

About the character of God,
as represented in the New and Old Testaments.

Our Bible reveals to us the character of our God with minute and remorseless exactness. The portrait is substantially that of a man—if one can imagine a man charged and overcharged with evil impulses far beyond the human limit; a personage whom no one, perhaps, would desire to associate with, now that Nero and Caligula are dead. In the Old Testament His acts expose His vindictive, unjust, ungenerous, pitiless and vengeful nature constantly. He is always punishing—punishing trifling misdeeds with thousandfold severity; punishing innocent children for the misdeeds of their parents; punishing unoffending populations for the misdeeds of their rulers; even descending to wreak bloody vengeance upon harmless calves and lambs and sheep and bullocks, as punishment for inconsequential trespasses committed by their proprietors. It is perhaps the most damnatory biography that exists in print anywhere. It makes Nero an angel of light and leading, by contrast.

It begins with an inexcusable treachery, and that is the keynote of the entire biography. That beginning must have been invented in a pirate's nursery, it is so malign and so childish. To Adam is forbidden the fruit of a certain tree—and he is gravely informed that if he disobeys he shall die. How could that be expected to impress Adam? Adam was merely a man in stature; in knowledge and experience he was in no way the superior of a baby of two years of age; he could have no idea of what the word death meant. He had never seen a dead thing; he had never heard of a dead thing before. The word meant nothing to him. If the Adam child had been warned that if he ate of the apples he would be transformed into a meridian of longitude, that threat would have been the equivalent of the other, since neither of them could mean anything to him.

The watery intellect that invented the memorable threat could be depended on to supplement it with other banalities and low grade notions of justice and fairness, and that is what happened. It was decreed that all of Adam's descendants, to the latest day, should be punished for the baby's trespass against a law of his nursery fulminated against him before he was out of his diapers. For thousands and thousands of years, his posterity, individual by individual, has been unceasingly hunted and harried with afflictions in punishment of the juvenile misdemeanor which is grandiloquently called Adam's sin. And during all that vast lapse of time, there has been no lack of rabbins and popes and bishops and priests and parsons and lay slaves eager to applaud this infamy, maintain the unassailable justice and righteousness of it, and praise its Author in terms of flattery so gross and extravagant that none but a God could listen to it and not hide His face in disgust and embarrassment. Hardened to flattery as our Oriental potentates are, through long experience, not even they would be able to endure the rank quality of it which our God endures with complacency and satisfaction from our pulpits every Sunday.

We brazenly call our God the source of mercy, while we are aware, all the time, that there is not an authentic instance in history of His ever having exercised that virtue. We call Him the source of morals, while we know by His history and by His daily conduct, as perceived with our own senses, that He is totally destitute of anything resembling morals. We call Him Father, and not in derision, although we would detest and denounce any earthly father who should inflict upon his child a thousandth part of the pains and miseries and cruelties which our God deals out to His children every day, and has dealt out to them daily during all the centuries since the crime of creating Adam was committed.

We deal in a curious laughable confusion of notions concerning God. We divide Him in two, bring half of Him down to an obscure and infinitesimal corner of the world to confer salvation upon a little colony of Jews—and only Jews, no one else—and leave the other half of Him throned in Heaven and looking down and eagerly and anxiously watching for results. We reverently study the history of the earthly half, and deduce from it the conviction that the earthly half has reformed, is equipped with morals and virtues, and in no way resembles the abandoned, malignant half that abides upon the throne. We conceive that the earthly half is just, merciful, charitable, benevolent, forgiving, and full of sympathy for the sufferings of mankind and anxious to remove them. Apparently we deduce this character not by examining facts, but by diligently declining to search them, measure them, and weigh them. The earthly half requires us to be merciful, and sets us an example by inventing a lake of fire and brimstone in which all of us who fail to recognize and worship Him as God are to be burned through all eternity. And not only *we*, who are offered these terms, are to be thus burned if we neglect them, but also the earlier billions of human beings are to suffer this awful fate, although they all lived and died without ever having heard of Him or the terms at all. This exhibition of mercifulness may be called gorgeous. We have nothing approaching it among human savages, nor among the wild beasts of the jungle. We are required to forgive our brother seventy times seven times, and be satisfied and content if on our death-bed, after a pious life, our soul escape from our body before the hurrying priest can get to us and furnish it a pass with his mumblings and candles and incantations. This example of the forgiving spirit may also be pronounced gorgeous.

We are told that the two halves of our God are only seemingly disconnected by their separation; that in very fact the two halves remain one, and equally powerful, notwithstanding the separation. This being the case, the earthly half—who mourns over the sufferings of mankind and would like to remove them, and is quite competent to remove them at any moment He may choose—satisfies Himself with restoring sight to a blind person, here and there, instead of restoring it to all the blind; cures a cripple, here and there, instead of curing all the cripples; furnishing to five thousand famishing persons a meal, and lets the rest of the millions that are hungry remain hungry—and all the time He admonishes inefficient man to cure these ills which God Himself inflicted upon him, and which He could extinguish with a word if He chose to do it, and thus do a plain duty which He had neglected from the beginning and always will neglect while time shall last. He raised several dead persons to life. He manifestly regarded this as a kindness. If it was a kindness it was not just to confine it to half-a-dozen persons. He should have raised the rest of the dead. I would not do it myself, for I think the dead are the only human beings who are really well off—but I merely mention it, in passing, as one of those curious incongruities with which our Bible history is heavily overcharged.

Whereas the God of the Old Testament is a fearful and repulsive character, He is at least consistent. He is frank and outspoken. He makes no pretense to the possession of a moral or a virtue of any kind—except with His mouth. No such thing is anywhere discoverable in His conduct. I think He comes infinitely nearer to being respectworthy than does His reformed self, as guilelessly exposed in the New Testament. Nothing in all history—not even

His massed history combined—remotely approaches in atrocity the invention of Hell.

His heavenly self, His Old Testament self, is sweetness and gentleness and respectability, compared with His reformed earthly self. In Heaven he claims not a single merit, and hasn't one—outside of those claimed by his mouth—whereas in the earth He claims every merit in the entire catalogue of merits, yet practised them only now and then, penuriously, and finished by conferring Hell upon us, which abolished all His fictitious merits in a body.

Wednesday, June 20, 1906

The defects about Bibles—
Remarks about the Immaculate Conception.

There are one or two curious defects about Bibles. An almost pathetic poverty of invention characterizes them all. That is one striking defect. Another is that each pretends to originality, without possessing any. Each borrows from the others, and gives no credit, which is a distinctly immoral act. Each, in turn, confiscates decayed old stage-properties from the others, and with a naïve confidence puts them forth as fresh new inspirations from on high. We borrow the Golden Rule from Confucius, after it has seen service for centuries, and copyright it without a blush. When we want a Deluge we go away back to hoary Babylon and borrow it, and are as proud of it and as satisfied with it as if it had been worth the trouble. We still revere it and admire it, to-day, and claim that it came to us direct from the mouth of the Deity; whereas we know that Noah's flood never happened, and couldn't have happened. The flood is a favorite with Bible makers. If there is a Bible—or even a tribe of savages—that lacks a General Deluge it is only because the religious scheme that lacks it hadn't any handy source to borrow it from. . . .

Saturday, June 23, 1906

Concerning the character of the real God.

Let us now consider the real God, the genuine God, the great God, the sublime and supreme God, the authentic Creator of the *real* universe, whose remotenesses are visited by comets only—comets unto which incredibly distant Neptune is merely an outpost, a Sandy Hook to homeward bound spectres of the deeps of space that have not glimpsed it before for generations—a universe not made with hands and suited to an astronomical nursery, but spread abroad through the illimitable reaches of space by the fiat of the real God just mentioned; that God of unthinkable grandeur and majesty, by comparison with whom all the other gods whose myriads infest the feeble imaginations of men are as a swarm of gnats scattered and lost in the infinitudes of the empty sky.

When we think of such a God as this, we cannot associate with Him anything trivial, anything lacking dignity, anything lacking grandeur. We cannot conceive of His passing by Sirius to choose our potato for a footstool. We cannot conceive of His interesting Himself in the affairs of the microscopic human race and enjoying its Sunday flatteries, and experiencing pangs of jealousy when the flatteries grow lax or fail, any more than we can conceive of the Emperor of China being interested in a bottle of microbes and pathetically anxious to stand well with them and harvest their impertinent compliments. If we could conceive of the Emperor of China taking an intemperate interest in his bottle of microbes, we should have to draw the line there; we could not, by any stretch of imagination, conceive of his selecting from these innumerable millions a quarter of a thimbleful of Jew microbes—the least attractive of the whole swarm—and making pets of them and nominating them as his chosen germs, and carrying his infatuation for them so far as to resolve to keep and coddle them alone, and damn all the rest.

When we examine the myriad wonders and glories and charms and perfections of this infinite universe (as we know the universe now), and perceive that there is not a detail of it—from the blade of grass to the giant trees of California, nor from the obscure mountain rivulet to the measureless ocean; nor from the ebb and flow of the tides to the stately motions of the planets—that is not the slave of a system of exact and inflexible law, we seem to know—not suppose nor conjecture, but *know*—that the God that brought this stupendous fabric into being with a flash of thought and framed its laws with another flash of thought, is endowed with limitless power. We seem to know that whatever thing He wishes to do, He can do that thing without anybody's assistance. We also seem to know that when He flashed the universe into being He foresaw everything that would happen in it from that moment until the end of time.

Do we also know that He is a moral being, according to our standard of morals? No. If we know anything at all about it, we know that He is destitute of morals—at least of the human pattern. Do we know that He is just, charitable, kindly, gentle, merciful, compassionate? No. There is no evidence that He is any of these things—whereas each and every day, as it passes, furnishes us a thousand volumes of evidence, and indeed proof, that he possesses none of these qualities.

When we pray, when we beg, when we implore, does He listen? Does He answer? There is not a single authentic instance of it in human history. Does He silently refuse to listen—refuse to answer? There is nothing resembling proof that He has ever done anything else. From the beginning of time, priests, who have imagined themselves to be His appointed and salaried servants, have gathered together their full numerical strength and simultaneously prayed for rain, and never once got it, when it was not due according to the eternal laws of Nature. Whenever they got it, if they had had a competent Weather Bureau they could have saved themselves the trouble of praying for that rain, because the Bureau could have told them it was coming, anyhow, within twenty-four hours, whether they prayed or saved their sacred wind.

From the beginning of time, whenever a king has lain dangerously ill, the priesthood and some part of the nation have prayed in unison that the king be spared to his grieving and anxious people (in case they were grieving and anxious, which was not usually the rule) and in no instance was their prayer ever answered. When Mr. Garfield lay near to death, the physicians and surgeons knew that nothing could save him, yet at an appointed signal all the pulpits in the United States broke forth with one simultaneous and supplicating appeal for the President's restoration to health. They did this with the same old innocent confidence with which the primeval savage had prayed to his imaginary devils to spare his perishing chief—for that day will never come when facts and experience can teach a pulpit anything useful. Of course the President died, just the same.

Great Britain has a population of forty-one millions. She has eighty thousand pulpits. The Boer population was a hundred and fifty thousand, with a battery of two hundred and ten pulpits. In the beginning of the Boer war, at a signal from the Primate of all England, the eighty thousand English pulpits thundered forth a titanic simultaneous supplication to their God to give the embattled English in South Africa the victory. The little Boer battery of two hundred and ten guns replied with a simultaneous supplication to the same God to give the Boers the victory. If the eighty thousand English clergy had left their prayers unshed and gone to the field, they would have got it, whereas the victory went the other way, and the English forces suffered defeat after defeat at the hands of the Boers. The English pulpit kept discreetly quiet about the result of its effort, but the indiscreet Boer pulpit proclaimed with a loud and exultant voice that it was *its* prayers that had conferred the victory upon the Boers.

The British Government had more confidence in soldiers than in prayer

—therefore instead of doubling and trebling the numerical strength of the clergy, it doubled and trebled the strength of its forces in the field. Then the thing happened that always happens—the English whipped the fight, a rather plain indication that the Lord had not listened to either side, and was as indifferent as to who should win as He had always been, from the day that He was evolved, down to the present time—there being no instance on record where He has shown any interest at all in any human squabble, nor whether the good cause won out or lost.

Has this experience taught the pulpit anything? It has not. When the Boer prayers achieved victory—as the Boers believed—the Boers were confirmed once more in their trust in the power of prayer. When a crushing finality of defeat overwhelmed them, later, in the face of their confident supplications, their attitude was not altered, nor their confidence in the righteousness and intelligence of God impaired.

Often we see a mother who has been despoiled, little by little, of everything she held dear in life but a sole remaining dying child; we have seen her, I say, kneeling by its bed and pouring out from a breaking heart beseechings to God for mercy that would get glad and instant answer from any man who had the power to save that child—yet no such prayer has ever moved a God to pity. Has that mother been convinced? Sometimes—but only for a little while. She was merely a human being, and like the rest—ready to pray again in the next emergency; ready to believe again that she would be heard.

We know that the real God, the Supreme God, the actual Maker of the universe, made everything that is in it. We know that He made all the creatures, from the microbe and the brontosaur down to man and the monkey, and that he knew what would happen to each and every one of them, from the beginning of time to the end of it. In the case of each creature, big or little, He made it an unchanging law that that creature should suffer wanton and unnecessary pains and miseries every day of its life—that by that law these pains and miseries could not be avoided by any diplomacy exercisable by the creature; that its way, from birth to death, should be beset by traps, pitfalls, and gins, ingeniously planned and ingeniously concealed; and that by another law every transgression of a law of Nature, either ignorantly or wittingly committed, should in every instance be visited by a punishment ten-thousandfold out of proportion to the transgression. We stand astonished at the all-comprehensive malice which could patiently descend to the contriving of elaborate tortures for the meanest and pitifulest of the countless kinds of creatures that were to inhabit the earth. The spider was so contrived that she would not eat grass, but must catch flies, and such things, and inflict a slow and horrible death upon them, unaware that her turn would come next. The wasp was so contrived that he also would decline grass and stab the spider, not conferring upon her a swift and merciful death, but merely half paralyzing her, then ramming her down into the wasp den, there to live and suffer for days, while the wasp babies should chew her legs off at their leisure. In turn, there was a murderer provided for the wasp, and another murderer for the wasp's murderer, and so on throughout the whole scheme of living creatures in the earth. There isn't one of them that was not designed and appointed to inflict misery and murder on some fellow creature and suffer the same, in turn, from some other murderous fellow creature. In flying into the web the fly is merely guilty of an indiscretion—not a breach of any law—yet the fly's punishment is ten-thousandfold out of proportion to that little indiscretion.

The ten-thousandfold law of punishment is rigorously enforced against every creature, man included. The debt, whether made innocently or guiltily, is promptly collected by Nature—and in this world, without waiting for the ten-billionfold additional penalty appointed—in the case of man—for collection in the next.

This system of atrocious punishments for somethings and nothings begins upon the helpless baby on its first day in the world, and never ceases until its last one. Is there a father who would persecute his baby with unearned colics and the unearned miseries of teething, and follow these with mumps, measles, scarlet-fever, and the hundred other persecutions appointed for the unoffending creature? And then follow these, from youth to the grave, with a multitude of ten-thousandfold punishments for laws broken either by intention or indiscretion? With a fine sarcasm, we ennoble God with the title of Father—yet we know quite well that we should hang His style of father wherever we might catch him.

The pulpit's explanation of, and apology for, these crimes, is pathetically destitute of ingenuity. It says that they are committed for the benefit of the sufferer. They are to discipline him, purify him, elevate him, train him for the society of the Deity and the angels—send him up sanctified with cancers, tumors, smallpox, and the rest of the educational plant; whereas the pulpit knows that it is stultifying itself, if it knows anything at all. It knows that if this kind of discipline is wise and salutary, we are insane not to adopt it ourselves and apply it to our children.

Does the pulpit really believe that we can improve a purifying and elevating breed of culture invented by the Almighty? It seems to me that if the pulpit honestly believed what it is preaching, in this regard, it would recommend every father to imitate the Almighty's methods.

When the pulpit has succeeded in persuading its congregation that this system has been really wisely and mercifully contrived by the Almighty to discipline and purify and elevate His children whom He so loves, the pulpit judiciously closes its mouth. It doesn't venture further, and explain why these same crimes and cruelties are inflicted upon the higher animals—the alligators, the tigers, and the rest. It even proclaims that the beasts perish—meaning that their sorrowful life begins and ends here; that they go no further; that there is no Heaven for them; that neither God nor the angels, nor the redeemed, desire their society on the other side. It puts the pulpit in a comical situation, because in spite of all its ingenuities of explanation and apology it convicts its God of being a wanton and pitiless tyrant in the case of the unoffending beasts. At any rate, and beyond cavil or argument, by its silence it condemns Him irrevocably as a malignant master, after having persuaded the congregation that He is constructed entirely out of compassion, righteousness, and all-pervading love. The pulpit doesn't know how to reconcile these grotesque contradictions, and it doesn't try.

In His destitution of one and all of the qualities which could grace a God and invite respect for Him, and reverence, and worship, the real God, the genuine God, the Maker of the mighty universe, is just like all the other gods on the list. He proves, every day, that He takes no interest in man, nor in the other animals, further than to torture them, slay them, and get out of this pastime such entertainment as it may afford—and do what He can not to get weary of the eternal and changeless monotony of it.

Monday, June 25, 1906

Only hearsay evidence that there is to be a Heaven hereafter. Christ does not prove that He is God. Takes up the human race. Man is a machine, and not responsible for his actions.

It is to these celestial bandits that the naïve and confiding and illogical human rabbit looks for a Heaven of eternal bliss, which is to be his reward for patiently enduring the want and sufferings inflicted upon him here below—unearned sufferings covering terms of two or three years, in some cases; five or ten years in others; thirty, forty, or fifty in others; sixty, seventy, eighty, in others. As usual, where the Deity is Judge, the rewards are vastly out of proportion to the sufferings—and there is no system about the matter anyhow. You do not get any more Heaven for suffering eighty years than you get if you die of the measles, at three.

There is no evidence that there is to be a Heaven hereafter. If we should find, somewhere, an ancient book in which a dozen unknown men professed to tell all about a blooming and beautiful tropical Paradise secreted in an inaccessible valley in the center of the eternal icebergs which constitute the Antarctic continent—not claiming that they had seen it themselves, but had acquired an intimate knowledge of it through a revelation from God—no Geographical Society in the earth would take any stock in that book; yet that book would be quite as authentic, quite as trustworthy, quite as valuable, evidence as is the Bible. The Bible is just like it. Its Heaven exists solely upon hearsay evidence—evidence furnished by unknown persons; persons who did not prove that they had ever been there.

If Christ had really been God, He could have proved it, since nothing is impossible with God. He could have proved it to every individual of His own time and of our time, and of all future time. When God wants to prove that the sun and the moon may be depended upon to do their work every day and every night, he has no difficulty about it. When He wants to prove that man may depend upon finding the constellations in their places every night—although they vanish and seem lost to us every day—He has no difficulty about it. When He wants to prove that the seasons may be depended upon to come and go according to a fixed law, year after year, He has no difficulty about it. Apparently He has desired to prove to us beyond cavil or doubt many millions of things, and He has no difficulty about proving them all. It is only when He apparently wants to prove a future life to us that His invention fails, and He comes up against a problem which is beyond the reach of His alleged omnipotence. With a message to deliver to men which is of infinitely more importance than all those other messages put together, which He has delivered without difficulty, He can think of no better medium than the poorest of all contrivances—a book. A book written in two languages—to convey a message to a thousand nations—which, in the course of the dragging centuries and eons, must change and change and become finally wholly unintelligible. And even if they remained fixed, like a dead language, it would never be possible to translate the message with perfect clearness into any one of the thousand tongues, at any time.

According to the hearsay evidence, the character of every conspicuous god is made up of love, justice, compassion, forgiveness, sorrow for all suffering and desire to extinguish it. Opposed to this beautiful character—built wholly upon valueless hearsay evidence—it is the absolutely authentic evidence furnished us every day in the year, and verifiable by our eyes and our other senses, that the real character of these gods is destitute of love, mercy, compassion, justice, and other gentle and excellent qualities, and is made up of all imaginable cruelties, persecutions, and injustices. The hearsay character rests upon evidence only—exceedingly doubtful evidence. The real character rests upon proof—proof unassailable.

Is it logical to expect of gods whose unceasing and unchanging pastime is the malignant persecution of innocent men and animals, that they are going to provide an eternity of bliss, presently, for these very same creatures? If King Leopold II, the Butcher, should proclaim that out of each hundred innocent and unoffending Congo negroes he is going to save one from humiliation, starvation, and assassination, and fetch that one home to Belgium to live with him in his palace and feed at his table, how many people would believe it? Everybody would say "A person's character is a permanent thing. This act would not be in accordance with that butcher's character. Leopold's character is established beyond possibility of change, and it could never occur to him to do this kindly thing."

Leopold's character *is* established. The character of the conspicuous gods is also established. It is distinctly illogical to suppose that either Leopold of Belgium or the Heavenly Leopolds are ever going to think of inviting any fraction of their victims to the royal table and the comforts and conveniences of the regal palace.

According to hearsay evidence, the conspicuous gods make a pet of one victim in a hundred—select him arbitrarily, without regard to whether he's any better than the other ninety-nine or not—but damn the ninety-nine through all eternity, without examining into their case. But for one slight defect this would be logical, and would properly reflect the known character of the gods—that defect is the gratuitous and unplausible suggestion that one in a hundred is permitted to pull through. It is not likely that there will be a Heaven hereafter. It is exceedingly likely that there will be a Hell—and it is nearly dead certain that nobody is going to escape it.

As to the human race. There are many pretty and winning things about the human race. It is perhaps the poorest of all the inventions of all the gods, but it has never suspected it once. There is nothing prettier than its naïve and complacent appreciation of itself. It comes out frankly and proclaims, without bashfulness, or any sign of a blush, that it is the noblest work of God. It has had a billion opportunities to know better, but all signs fail with this ass. I could say harsh things about it, but I cannot bring myself to do it—it is like hitting a child.

Man is not to blame for what he is. He didn't make himself. He has no control over himself. All the control is vested in his temperament—which he did not create—and in the circumstances which hedge him round, from the cradle to the grave, and which he did not devise and cannot change by any act of his will, for the reason that he has no will. He is as purely a piece of automatic mechanism as is a watch, and can no more dictate or influence his actions than can the watch. He is a subject for pity, not blame—and not contempt. He is flung head over heels into this world without ever a chance to decline, and straightway he conceives and accepts the notion that he is in some mysterious way under obligations to the unknown Power that inflicted this outrage upon him—and thenceforth he considers himself responsible to that Power for every act of his life, and punishable for such of his acts as do not meet with the approval of that Power—yet that same man would argue quite differently if a human tyrant should capture him and put chains upon him and make him a slave. He would say that the tyrant had no right to do that; that the tyrant had no right to put commands upon him of any kind, and require obedience; that the tyrant had no right to compel him to commit murder and then put the responsibility for the murder upon him. Man constantly makes a most strange distinction between man and his Maker, in the matter of morals. He requires of his fellow man obedience to a very creditable code of morals, but he observes without shame or disapproval his God's utter destitution of morals.

God ingeniously contrived man in such a way that he could not escape obedience to the laws of his passions, his appetites, and his various unpleasant and undesirable qualities. God has so contrived him that all his goings out and comings in are beset by traps which he cannot possibly avoid, and which compel him to commit what are called sins—and then God punishes him for doing these very things which from the beginning of time He has always intended that he should do. Man is a machine, and God made it—without invitation from any one. Whoever makes a machine, here below, is responsible for that machine's performance. No one would think of such a thing as trying to put the responsibility upon the machine itself. We all know perfectly well—though we all conceal it, just as I am doing, until I shall be dead, and out of reach of public opinion—we all know, I say, that God, and God alone, is responsible for every act and word of a human being's life between cradle and grave. We know it perfectly well. In our secret heart we haven't the slightest doubt of it. In our secret hearts we have no hesitation in proclaiming as an unthinking fool anybody who thinks he believes that he is by any possibility capable of committing a sin against God—or who thinks he thinks he is under obligations to God and owes Him thanks, reverence, and worship.

NOTES

The notes that follow are identified by a phrase from the text keyed to page and line number of the present volume, for example, 12.3 means page 12, line 3. Titles of selections are not included in line counts. Titles within selections *are* included.

Extracts from Adam's Diary

Copy-text for this piece is the book version of *Extracts from Adam's Diary* (New York: Harper and Brothers, 1904), as revised by Mark Twain in 1905. The volume that contains Mark Twain's revisions is now in the Clifton Waller Barrett Library, Special Collections, University of Virginia. Mark Twain intended this revision to be published together with "Eve's Diary" in a separate book, but his wishes were never realized. Mark Twain's original manuscript and a typescript are in the Berg Collection, New York Public Library.

8.13–14 new creature names everything] Here Mark Twain obviously alters the biblical account, in which Adam is the namer (Genesis 2:19–21). In 1906, after the publication of "Eve's Diary," the London *Westminster Gazette* would take him to task for this same "error" by pointing out that in Genesis the "naming" had of course occurred before the creation of Eve, so that Eve's taking over the job was illogical. Noting that he had received the *Gazette* clipping in that morning's mail, Mark Twain quoted the entire item in his autobiographical dictation of 10 August and then commented on how such critical nit-picking depressed him: "It always saddens the professional lightning-bug when he flares up under the mole's nose and finds that the mole doesn't know that anything has happened. The *Westminster* man is unaware of the privileges of our profession. He thinks we must stick to the facts . . . whereas by the privileges of our order we are independent of facts; we care nothing for them in a really religious way. . . . When we are hot with the fires of production we would even distort the facts of the multiplication-table, let alone the facts of Genesis. . . . If I had felt it best to turn the whole fable of creation inside out, I would have done it without compunction" † (Autobiographical Dictation, 8/10/06, TS, 1027–29, MTP).

10.8–9 tigers live on grass and flowers] Here Mark Twain makes somewhat more specific the biblical account (Genesis 1:30) where God gives to all the beasts and other living creatures "every green herb for meat." In "Eve's Diary" and the "Autobiography of Eve," he would make the vegetarian diet even more specific—strawberries in the former, strawberries, cabbages, and onions in the latter. Alison Ensor has pointed out that Mark Twain may have been partly inspired by Bible commentaries of the day, and cites Dan Beard's reminiscence of Mark Twain's reaction to one commentary that noted that the meat-eating animals on the ark became vegetarians during the voyage. According to Beard, Twain was intrigued with the thought of a Barbary lion shouting, "Noah! Noah! Bring me a bale of hay" (Ensor, 115, n. 48).

10.9–10 teeth . . . intended to eat each other] This discovery that the beasts' teeth were those of carnivores and Adam's comment that if that were so the beasts would have to kill each other and hence bring something called "death" into the world of course foreshadow the Fall, but here, unlike the situation in both "Eve's Diary" (in which the matter of teeth is not discussed) and the "Autobiography of Eve," Adam seems to have some knowledge of what death is.

11.27 frantic commotion . . . every beast was destroying its neighbor] In this brief description Adam's account is reminiscent of that in Milton's *Paradise Lost*, a work that Mark Twain knew well. Book 10, ll. 710–12, reads: "Beast now with beast 'gan war, and fowl with fowl,/ And fish with fish; to graze the herb all leaving,/ Devoured each other; . . ."

13.29–30 *Kangaroorum Adamiensis*] Here Mark Twain plays with scientific classification: the assigning of organisms to groups according to structure, origin, etc., a system generally credited to Linnaeus (1707–78).

14.15 instead of being black is red] In the very early Hannibal *Journal* piece "Oh, She Has a Red Head!" young Sam Clemens had argued that since Adam's name signified "red earth," Adam must have been red-headed (*ET&S1*, 102–5). Hence, by giving Cain red hair, Mark Twain (perhaps unconsciously) shows Cain taking after his father.

Eve's Diary

Since the location of the manuscript of "Eve's Diary," if extant, is unknown, the copy-text is the first published version in *Harper's Monthly* for December 1905, except for the italicized "*Extract from Adam's Diary*" (17.1–19.19) that Mark Twain added to the 1906 book version. For that passage, the manuscript in the Mark Twain Papers is copy-text. In a few cases the Harper text has been emended to incorporate variants occurring in the 1906 Harper book version that are attributable to Mark Twain.

20.15–16 eternal vigilance is the price of supremacy] Twain here has Eve echo Wendell Phillips's famous statement from a speech on "Public Opinion" delivered before the Massachusetts Antislavery Society on 28 January 1852, where he proclaimed that "Eternal vigilance is the price of liberty." Phillips, in turn, perhaps adapted the phrase from the 1790 "Speech Upon the Right of Election" of John Philpot Curran (1750–1817), in which Curran said, "The condition upon which God hath given liberty to man is eternal vigilance."

21.34 because they live on strawberries] See Genesis 1:30 for the implication that the beasts were at first vegetarians, and see also the related note to "Extracts from Adam's Diary."

22.3 *The scratched Experiment shuns the thorn*] Twain here seems to be adapting (loosely) the saying used by John Lyly in *Euphues, The Anatomy of Wit* (1579) and Ben Jonson in *The Devil is an Ass* (1616), that is, "The burnt child dreads the fire."

23.19 taken . . . the naming of things off his hands] Here, as in "Adam's Diary," Eve rather than Adam does the naming. See Genesis 2:19–21 for Adam's responsibility to name all creatures and also the related note to "Adam's Diary."

Autobiography of Eve and Diaries Antedating the Flood

Copy-texts for these pieces are the several related manuscripts in the Mark Twain Papers. Some of these passages were first published in *Letters from the Earth*, edited by Bernard DeVoto (New York: Harper, 1962).

Autobiography of Eve

42.13–14 reflection of my slender white body . . . yellow hair hang down] Here Twain seems to draw upon *Paradise Lost*, where Milton describes Eve's "unadorned golden tresses," which hang like "a veil down to the slender waist" (Book 4, 304–5) and later has her admire her reflection in the "clear/ Smooth lake that . . . seemed another sky" (458–59). Twain's description, however, emphasizes Eve's loneliness and contains only a small implication of the vanity or narcissism found in Milton, and carries no suggestion of Eve's submission or subjugation to Adam.

43.19 lost mate] The story of Eve's search for Adam possibly reflects some of Twain's memories of his courtship of Olivia, but many of its details seem related to his earlier love for and parting from Laura Wright, a sweetheart of his river years (see Baetzhold 1972, 426–28).

43.32 size of a hound. Five-toed] Probably eohippus, a small prehistoric horse which had four toes and a rudimentary thumb on its forefeet.

45.14–15 "Cheese it;"] Slang for "stop it" or "go away."

47.4 and oppresses my spirit] Between this paragraph and the following one, Twain wrote and circled "End of small type." It could be here that he decided to have Eve tell her story from a later perspective, because the next paragraph (ms., p. 19) begins: "I still remember that time as if it were yesterday." On the other hand, he could have decided on the change later on and substituted p. 19 for an earlier manuscript page, because p. 19 is an absolute fair copy, i.e., no strikeouts, revisions, etc.

At the time he added "End of small type," he also appears to have gone back to p. 1 and added in the upper right-hand corner "Autobiography of Eve." and under it "I." and under that "I will begin with a few extracts from my diary." This sets up the machinery for the several shifts from present (1012 AC—[After Creation], later 920) to the earliest days of Adam and Eve.

At the bottom of p. 18 Twain also wrote notes to himself in pencil: "Overproduction of animals will pack the world / Family troub. Adam a Presbyterian. Satan Xn Scientist / with 'little book' / Eve unclassified. Teething Inven Mul table to 6 times 7 / I shook my fist at the sky / Flood. Would worship no being who required me to desert my children."†

Most of these were not used, except for the multiplication table, but obviously by here he had decided to deal with the Flood.

47.5 I still remember . . .] Echoes Psalms 90:4—"For a thousand years in thy sight are but as yesterday when it is past, and as a watch in the night."

47.29 two long plaits down my back] Recalls Mark Twain's earlier description in *Tom Sawyer* of Becky Thatcher, a blue-eyed blond who is also described as having her hair "plaited into two long tails," and wearing a "white summer frock" (chapter 3).

47.33 four shining rivers] Genesis 2:10—"And a river went out of Eden to water the garden; and from thence it was parted and became into four heads."

49.8 Irish elks] Extinct species of huge elk or deer, over six feet tall with antlers that spread from twelve to fifteen feet; so named because of fossils found under the peat bogs of Ireland.

49.16 widowed] Twain at first intended that Adam should have died by the time Eve tells her story. That he later changed his mind is evident in the section entitled "Diaries Antedating the Flood" where he presents a "Passage from Eve's Diary. Year of the World, 920." The change of dates from 1012 to 920 now placed the time ten years *before* Adam's death. Cf. Genesis 5:5—"And all the days that Adam lived were nine hundred and thirty years; and he died."

49.22 a child that I have lost] This mention of a lost child echoes details from a poem entitled "Broken Idols," which Twain wrote in the Swiss village of Weggis on 18 August 1897 and revised in August 1902 as "In Dim and Fitful Visions: In Memoriam Olivia Susan Clemens." Both versions commemorate the death of his daughter Susy, 18 August 1896. In a related statement, which Tuckey has entitled "In My Bitterness" (and Twain called "blaspheming"), he attacked the God who "gives you a wife and children whom you adore, only that through the spectacle of the wanton shames and miseries which He will inflict upon them He may tear the palpitating heart out of your breast and slap you in the face with it" (*FM*, 131).

50.15 Curly brown hair, tumbling negligently about his shoulders] As with Eve's hair, Twain possibly drew on Milton's description of Adam in *Paradise Lost*, whose "hyacinthine locks/ Round from his parted forelock manly hung/ Clustering, but not beneath his shoulders broad" (Book 4, 301–3).

50.39 I made a lost of fossils] In a related manuscript, "The Secret History of Eddypus, the World-Empire," on which he was working in 1901–2, Twain highlighted the making of fossils, borrowing extensively from Andrew D. White's *A History of the Warfare of Science with Theology in Christendom*, 2 vols. (New York: D. Appleton and Company, 1901), the incident in which college boys "planted" small manufactured clay animal figures that were accepted by their mentor (Martin Luther in the Mark Twain version) as the original models used for the Creation (*FM*, 24–26). See also Twain's treatment of fossil hoaxes in "Some Learned Fables for Good Old Boys and Girls" in *Sketches New and Old* (1875).

51.2 Quaternary] The geologic period following the Tertiary (or Age of Mammals) in the Cenozoic period. Also known as the Age of Man. On 13 April 1902 Twain made notes for a love story set in the "Quarternary [*sic*] Epoch," two million years ago. He immediately thought of the solution to one problem: "For the early scenery & animals, see John Fiske's Discovery of America, vol. I" (Gribben, 1:233). It is possible that some of the early descriptions here are inspired by and perhaps even based on Fiske.

51.3 Primary] The earliest geologic epoch, up through the Paleozoic era. Twain attempts to reconcile science and religion by having the First Family create the fossils we attribute to evolutionary science. Cf. 62.8–10—"Cain . . . is really an expert at making fossils, and will soon be taking the most of that work off our hands, I think. And he has invented one fossil, all by himself." (See also Cummings, 32, about mixing geology and theology.)

51.4–5 blind staggers] A form of dizziness accompanied by staggers, as if one is ready to fall; also, extreme drunkenness. Originally referred to a disease of horses.

51.6 hydrocephalous plantigrade] Apparently Twain's coinage for an animal that walks on the sole of the foot ("plantigrade") and has an enlarged head such as that which is symptomatic of hydrocephalus, a disease of the brain caused by an accumulation of fluid in the cranial cavity. See Twain's planning notes for "Refuge of the Derelicts" A-11, 2. for a mention of giving up on naming the "dinotherium, the pterodactyl, the ornithorhyncus & all that family of ^protoplasmic^plantigrade⟨s⟩ invertebrates" (*FM*, 461).

53.24 "Yes, I saw you."] Immediately following this, Twain wrote "Over" at the bottom of ms., p. 41, where he developed on the verso of that page extensive planning notes† most of which are treated over the next twenty manuscript pages, and two of which deal with matters treated in the later "Passage from Eve's Diary":

II 10 Before Eve's birth—forenoon, Jan. 1. [This line squeezed in above original first line—not ultimately developed.]

Ad is to "dress the Garden & keep it"—but he doesn't fatigue himself.

9. Tree of life & knowledge

16. The prohibition

17. Shalt die.

19. Naming the things.—Before Eve's birth

"But for Adam (the others had mates)

Build house

[To far right side of items 9 and 16 is written: Fish prefers / water. / Land things / don't. To right side, and close to items 16 and 17: Make flint arrow / Picture mastodon / on living animal's tusk.]

III

In the Garden Cat. / and kits

Eve. "What is die?" Linseed oil—Spontaneous combustion on cotton waste

28. "Be fruitful." It is in the Garden

"Some of these creatures are carnivorous"

"as the gods"—are there several? What is a god?

What is death?

Ad kept Diary, but not reliable. And couldn't spell.

"She speaks of the tree. Talks with Satan. Being forbidden, / she wants the fruit."

⟨"Will⟩ Satan: "What is right & wrong. Eve. I don't know,/ —Sat. Then it isn't wrong to take the fruit.

The milk of the cow.

Water runs down-stream—blood up

The tadpole

No dictionary

Burnt child

Fire made

55.5 Adam's law of Fluidic Precipitation.] The nature of a fluid to fall, flow, or rush downward with violence and rapidity. By using a comically pretentious coinage, Twain is parodying scientific "laws" such as Newton's Laws of Motion. See also the "Law of Intellectual Averages" and the "Law of Periodical Repetition" developed in "Passage from a Lecture" in "Diaries Antedating the Flood."

56.25 William McKinley . . . the original first lion] McKinley (1843–1901) was 25th president, 1897–1901. Assassinated in Buffalo at the Pan-American Exhibition of 1901, he was succeeded by Theodore Roosevelt. Twain's reference to McKinley helps establish the date of composition of this manuscript at 1901 (the year of McKinley's death) or possibly 1902. Giving his name to the lion—often a symbol of imperialism, especially in the case of the British lion—indirectly reflects Twain's own opposition during the early 1900s to imperialism in general and the policies of McKinley in particular, in such works as "To the Person Sitting in Darkness" and "A Defence of General Funston" (*North American Review*, February 1901, May 1902). See "Passages from 'Glances at History' (suppressed.)" for a sustained indictment of American imperialism.

56.33 carnivorous, a flesh-eater!] Eve's discovery in this version seems more shocking than in either "Adam's Diary" (1893) or in the later "Eve's Diary" (1905), for whereas Adam's responses to her discovery are similar, especially in "Adam's Diary," here the horror of her find is presented first from her viewpoint, with Adam's "explanation" following. Since this episode occurs before the Fall, Adam and Eve, of course, do not yet have knowledge of death in the world. But the teeth of the lion are, in a sense, a harbinger of things to come.

57.12 larboard] nautical term for the left side of a ship, looking from stern to bow. "Port" is now more commonly used to avoid confusion with its opposite, "starboard."

57.14 halidome] Archaic term for "holiness." Commonly used up to the 16th century in oaths and abjurations. Hence the assertion "by my halidome." Note Twain's burlesque of medieval courtly speech in the following lines.

57.19 Statistics cannot lie] Recalls Twain's often quoted remark: "Figures often beguile me, particularly when I have the arranging of them myself; in which case the remark attributed to Disraeli would often apply with justice and force: 'There are three kinds of lies: lies, damned lies and statistics' " (*AMT*, 149).

57.19 graminivorous] Eating or feeding on grass.

57.32–33 we must not eat . . . surely die] Echoes directions given to Adam and Eve in Genesis 3:2–3. Twain again would stress the childlike innocence of Adam and Eve and the unfairness of the punishment following the Fall in "Refuge of the Derelicts," written in 1905–1906 (*FM*, 208–10); he also treats the broader theme of God's justice in "Autobiographical Dictations" and "Letters from the Earth."

58.7–8 I have never seen . . . conception of it?] Adam's question here and the discussion that follows reflect the empirical theory that knowledge comes only from observation: that the senses, especially sight, are the principal avenues of knowledge.

58.24–25 "How stupid . . . bother about it."] Compare the same account in Genesis 3:2–6, where the serpent makes the counter-arguments rather than the "logic" employed here by Adam and Eve.

58.26–33 reaching for the apple . . . he is a pterodactyl] Note that in Twain's version the Fall is postponed *because* of intellectual curiosity rather than brought about because of it. Also, Adam and Eve's chasing the pterodactyl in the western side of the valley further removes them from the east of Eden, where they will eventually be expelled (Genesis 3:24).

58.39 survival of the fittest] Term coined by Herbert Spencer in 1864 and adopted by Charles Darwin as more accurate and precise than the loosely synonymous phrase "natural selection" originally used by Darwin to explain the natural process that results in the survival of individuals or groups best adjusted to the conditions under which they live.

59.5 He spells cat with a *k* . . . same root] Compare Twain's fondness for playing with words beginning with "cat" in "A Cat-Tale" (*LE*, 123–34).

59.35–36 considerable lake three hundred miles up the valley] Possibly refers to the location of the Tethys Sea, a huge Mesozoic ocean, considered the probable center of whale evolution. The Tethys Sea, which encompassed the modern Mediterranean, Black, and Caspian seas, was approximately three hundred miles north of the supposed location of Eden.

59.38 little Cain was born] Twain here places Cain's birth before the Fall. Genesis 3 details the story of the Fall and the expulsion from Eden; Cain's birth occurs in Genesis 4:1—"And Adam knew Eve his wife; and she conceived, and bare Cain, and said, I have gotten a man from the Lord."

59.40 "It is the unexpected that happens."] Variant of an English proverb of the 19th century, "It is the unexpected that always happens."

60.4 *lusus naturae*] Literally "a sport of nature"; a deformed person or thing, a freak.

60.29 *Year* 10] The "year 10" was added, with a caret, sometime after the original composition. Actually, Twain probably did not leave sufficient time for *nine* children to be born. If Gladys and Edwina (Twain's inventions) were born in the years 5 and 6, Adam and Eve would have had to produce five more children in the next four years.

60.35 We have nine children, now] This sentence begins a new section that replaces the text that Twain originally wrote. For that text (original ms. pages 68–72) see Appendix 1.

61.4 orthography is just a calamity] Mark Twain himself several times complained about his wife's faulty spelling and at one point commented on the numerous misspellings found in his daughter Susy's biography of him (*MTA*, 2:66).

61.18 deadly nightshade] The belladonna, a poisonous plant, the leaves and roots of which can be made into medicine. Eaten in their natural state, its berries are deadly. Note how the children eat the berries and remain unharmed, indicating that death has not yet entered the world. Contrast this with Eve's earlier shocking discovery that the lion was meant to be carnivorous.

62.7 kitchen-middens] Term for the refuse heaps of shells and bones marking the site of a prehistoric settlement, and where stone implements and other relics of early human occupation are often found. As with the earlier mention of Eve making fossils, Twain alludes indirectly to some creationist arguments that fossils were premade, again probably borrowing from White's *History of the Warfare of Science with Theology in Christendom* (1901).

62.10 by himself.] Here the manuscript page breaks off abruptly in midsentence. We have emended the copy-text which reads "by himself—the" to "by himself." Below the broken-off phrase, at the very bottom of the page, Twain added a note: "planning & arranging prehistoric deposits." †

Diaries Antedating the Flood

63 *title* Passage from Satan's Diary] Although this new section was probably written at a later time than the preceding sections, the precise date has not been determined. In 1923 Paine

published this piece and the following "Passage from Eve's Diary" in *Europe and Elsewhere* as "That Day in Eden" and "Eve Speaks." Mark Twain here develops two of the notes on ms. p. 41 verso of the "Autobiography of Eve," the entire text of which is reprinted in the note to 53.24, as well as some additional planning notes of approximately 250 words that Twain wrote on cardboard (see appendix 2).

At some point he probably realized that he hadn't really treated the Fall, and so developed these passages. It seems probable also that this was the point at which he decided to provide a sort of documentary account, for at the top right of the first page he wrote the title "Passages from ⟨the⟩ Diaries / Antedating the Flood." This change, of course, shifted the narration away from Eve's point of view alone and set up the possibility of the other diaries: Lady of the Blood, Mad Philosopher, etc. (See Baetzhold, McCullough, and Malcolm, 23–38 for a full discussion of the development of this manuscript.)

63.1 Tree of Knowledge] Genesis 2:9—"And out of the ground made the Lord God to grow every tree that is pleasant to the sight, and good for food; the tree of life also in the midst of the garden, and the tree of knowledge of good and evil."

63.5 innocently unconscious of their nakedness] Genesis 2:25–"And they were both naked, the man and his wife, and were not ashamed."

66.14 The Moral Sense] The innate ability to know right from wrong. Here and in many of his other late writings—perhaps most vividly in "The Chronicles of Young Satan" (*Mysterious Stranger Manuscripts*, 35–174) Mark Twain presents the Moral Sense as the chief cause of human undoing. Creatures without that knowledge—Adam and Eve before the Fall—are innocent and cannot do wrong because they can have no conception of what wrong is. Twain's attitudes are also reflected in incidental comments like that from *Pudd'nhead Wilson's New Calendar:* "There is a Moral Sense, and there is an Immoral Sense. History shows us that the Moral Sense enables us to perceive morality and how to avoid it, and that the Immoral Sense enables us to perceive immorality and how to enjoy it" (epigraph to chapter 16, *Following the Equator*, 1897).

66.33 Eve reached for the apple!] Genesis 3:6—"And when the woman saw that the tree was good for food, and that it was pleasant to the eyes, and a tree to be desired to make one wise, she took of the fruit thereof, and did eat, and gave also unto her husband with her; and he did eat."

67.19–20 Then he gathered boughs for both and clothed their nakedness] Genesis 3:7—"And the eyes of them both were opened, and they knew that they were naked; and they sewed fig leaves together, and made themselves aprons."

67.24–25 They drove us . . . fierce cherubim] Genesis 3:23–24—"Therefore the Lord God sent him forth from the garden of Eden, to till the ground from whence he was taken. So he drove out the man; and he placed at the east of the garden of Eden Cherubims, and a flaming sword which turned every way, to keep the way of the tree of life."

68.17–18 we know the scorn . . . unclothed to the day.] Genesis 3:9–12—"And the Lord God called unto Adam, and said unto him, Where art thou? And he said, I heard thy voice in the garden, and I was afraid because I was naked; and I hid myself. And he said, Who told thee that thou wast naked? Hast thou eaten of the tree, whereof I commanded thee that thou shouldest not eat? And the man said, The woman whom thou gavest to be with me, she gave me of the tree, and I did eat."

68.29 That is our second-born—our Abel] From Genesis 4:2.

69.2–4 We found him . . . struck him down] Genesis 4:8—"And Cain talked with Abel his brother: and it came to pass, when they were in the field, that Cain rose up against Abel his brother, and slew him."

70.2–3 The family think ill of Death—they will change their mind] Cf. *Pudd'nhead Wilson's Calendar:* "Whoever has lived long enough to find out what life is, knows how deep a debt of gratitude we owe to Adam, the first great benefactor of our race. He brought death into the world" (epigraph to chapter 3, *Pudd'nhead Wilson*, 1894).

71.38 Honor to whom honor is due] Echoes Romans 13:7—"Render therefore to all their dues: Tribute to whom tribute is due; custom to whom custom; fear to whom fear; honour to whom honour."

72.26 "Respectability butters no parsnips"] First recorded as "fair words butter no parsnips" (i.e., "words don't feed the family") in John Clark's *Paroemiologia* (1639). Frequently quoted over the years and variously revised as "Mere praise butters no parsnips," etc.

73.6 Duke of Washoe] Washoe City, a lumber-milling community in western Nevada, was for a time the seat of Washoe county. When Twain was working for the *Territorial Enterprise* in nearby Virginia City, Nevada, Washoe was often used to refer to the whole region.

73.10 Red Cloud] Though Red Cloud here is female, Mark Twain doubtless borrowed her name from the famous chief of the Oglala Sioux who led many battles (known as "Red Cloud's War") against U.S. forces in the middle 1860s.

73.16 They lost sixteen children in a railway accident] As Paine points out, Mark Twain was very much concerned with the improvement of railway service, so as to reduce the numerous injuries and deaths, once estimating that the casualties from such accidents were more than those of all wars combined (*MTB*, 3:1,228–29). When a friend, St. Clair McKelway, narrowly escaped injury in a railroad accident, Twain wrote him on 30 April 1905: "The Government's Official report, showing that our railways killed twelve hundred persons last year and injured sixty thousand convinces me that under present conditions one Providence is not enough to properly and efficiently take care of our railroad business. But it is characteristically American—always trying to get along short-handed and save wages" (*MTL*, 2:771).

73.19 wonderful new force, liquified thought] Though the specific "invention" that Twain has in mind here is unclear, his enthusiasm for inventions, both his own and others, in some of which he invested, was immense. His own inventions ranged from a self-pasting scrapbook to a perpetual calendar, a board game for teaching history, and a bed clamp to prevent children from kicking off their sheets and blankets. To mention only a few of his other interests in inventions, he also owned a four-fifths interest in "Kaolatype" (a process for making printed plates). He was one of the first in the world to install a telephone in his private residence (though he said that he unfortunately passed up a golden opportunity to invest in the new invention in 1877), was the first famous author to use the typewriter and to double-space manuscripts, and lost a small fortune backing the typesetting machine invented by James W. Paige. In both "Mental Telegraphy" (1891) and "Mental Telegraphy Again" (1895), Twain discussed his lifelong interest in mental phenomena, instantaneous communication, telepathy, and other extrasensory phenomena. In "Mental Telegraphy" he posits an invention called the "phrenophone" which might communicate thoughts instantaneously, just as the telephone communicates the spoken word.

73.23 the Trust] Generally, an industrial monopoly such as Standard Oil (the first trust) or the United Steel Corporation, which attempts to control a certain market. As the formation of trusts began to accelerate between 1898 and 1904, government began to move against them with the Sherman Anti-Trust Law. Theodore Roosevelt had become president, and a fever of reform to bust the trusts began to sweep the nation.

73.27 Liograph] This is probably a play on words referring to the polygraph (or "lie detector"), an instrument for recording simultaneous variations in the subject's temperature, pulse, etc.

73.27 Hellograph] Another play on words, probably referring to the telephone. In the manuscript Twain first wrote "Talkograph," then replaced it with "Hellograph." He may also be punning on the heliograph, a print made from a chemical reaction as a result of exposure to light, or an apparatus for telegraphing by means of the sun's rays flashed from a mirror, or a device for measuring the sun—all new inventions in the 19th century.

73.28 Mumble'n'screechograph] Yet another coinage by Twain, possibly referring to the phonograph or dictaphone, also a relatively recent invention.

73.38–74.1 as [ ] says] In the ms. following "but now—," Twain inserted with a caret "—as says—". DeVoto, in *LE*, inserts the name Methuselah in the space, but there is no reason to believe that Twain intended these to be Methuselah's words, hence we leave the space blank, indicating the omission of a name by brackets.

74.6 Lost Force of old tradition] We have not discovered a source for this concept of the "Lost Force," which in some ways resembled atomic power, nor the following story of "the Prodigy" who conquered the world by its means. Mark Twain was deeply interested in the experiments of Marie Curie during the early 1900s, and especially in the potential forces connected with radium. In 1904, for instance, in "Sold to Satan" (*E&E*, 326–38), he described Satan's body as composed of radium, contained within a protective skin of polonium. If that skin were to be removed, Satan tells the narrator, "the world would vanish away in a flash of flame and a puff of smoke, and the remnants of the extinguished moon would sift down through space a mere snow-shower of gray ashes!" (333).

The story of the Prodigy (without the "Lost Force" concept) is further developed in "Passage from 'Outlines of History' (suppressed.)" Given the indirect allusions there to Incan and Mayan cultures, the "Double Continent" in the present passage probably refers to North and South America.

74.27 Napeer] Twain here was playing with famous names, as he did in "The Secret History of Eddypus, the World-Empire." He may have been referring to John Napier (1550–1617), a Scottish mathematician who discovered natural logarithms, but more likely the reference is to Sir Charles Napier (1782–1853), the British general who commanded an expedition of Victoria's army that destroyed the Amirs of Sind and led to the annexation of the province to the British empire. Napier wired the news of his victory in a single cryptic Latin word: *Peccavi*, a pun meaning "I have Sin(ne)d" (Kurian, 178).

74.37–75.6 Only one army . . . died with him.] A number of the details resemble the Yankee's destruction of the knights in *A Connecticut Yankee in King Arthur's Court* (chapter 43).

75 *section title* . . . her Grandeur the Acting Head of the Human Race] Here we have borrowed DeVoto's title for this passage (*LE*, 97) that he himself doubtless borrowed from the later "Passage from the Diary of the Mad Philosopher." She is "Acting Head" because Adam had delegated his position to her eighty years earlier and had been under the care of physicians for the past seventy-five.

75.23–27 Morally . . . satisfied with it.] This passage echoes the tenets of Utilitarianism, which is often characterized, though oversimplified, in the phrase "the greatest good for the greatest number." Its chief exponents were Jeremy Bentham and John Stuart Mill, whose *Utilitarianism* (1861) argued that "utility, or the greatest happiness for the greatest number, is the foundation of morals." Over the years Mark Twain grew increasingly attracted to this philosophy, primarily through the long summary in W. E. H. Lecky's *History of European Morals*, and ultimately formulated his own version thereof in *What is Man?* (1906). See Baetzhold 1970, *passim* for Lecky's influence on Twain's works; for additional references, see Gribben, 1:400–3.

75.33–76.4 extraordinary financial . . . public culture] In the upper right-hand corner of the ms., p. 90, which contains this passage, Twain originally wrote and later lined out, "Carnegie/ Rockefel[ler]/ Morgan."† Andrew Carnegie (1835–1919) was a philanthropic steel magnate and friend of Mark Twain, best known for the establishment of the Carnegie Libraries; John D. Rockefeller (1839–1925) was the owner of the Standard Oil Company; and J. Pierpont Morgan (1837–1913) was a famed American banker. See also Twain's pun on Morgan's name ("Peerpontibusmorganibus") in the original continuation of this manuscript (Appendix 1, 273.32), which also suggests Morgan's reputation for collecting manuscripts ultimately placed in the J. Pierpont Morgan Library in New York City.

76.12 blatherskite] One of Mark Twain's favorite words, meaning balderdash, nonsense, or a contemptible person, one who blathers and blusters.

76.29 Forty Immortals] Probably a play on the Académie Français, founded in 1634 for the surveillance of language and published works, the membership of which was set at forty in 1639. Those so honored came to be known as the "immortals," doubtless to invite comparison with the gods of the Greek and Roman pantheon. They were not always so revered, as one historian has noted: "The list of the Academicians who occupied the forty chairs in 1731, the year when Voltaire first considered entering the Citadel of the Immortals shows us a changed Academy, lacking much of the brilliance that had formerly been associated with its status as 'tribunal litteraire' " (Racevskis, 18).

76.31–32 Laws of Angina Pectoris] Again, as he does elsewhere, particularly in "The Secret History of Eddypus," Twain provides an outrageous name for his character. Angina Pectoris is the name of a heart disease from which Twain himself suffered in his last years, characterized by spasms of pain in the chest and feelings of suffocation, and often associated with a sense of apprehension or fear of death. Why Twain gave this name to his lecturer, who was really expounding the theories of Reginald Selkirk (also known as the Mad Prophet or Mad Philosopher) is not known. Perhaps Twain decided to remove this lecture from the rest of the manuscript, possibly for separate publication.

78.16 occultation of Venus] The disappearance or hiding of Venus as morning or evening star behind another heavenly body, such as the sun or moon.

78.38 Science of Health] A direct allusion to Christian Science, founded in 1866 by Mary Baker Eddy (1821–1910), which teaches that all ill may be cured by mental or spiritual means. After providing the movement with its textbook, *Science and Health, with a Key to the Scriptures* (1875), she established the Church of Christ, Scientist, in Boston (1879). Twain's hostility to Eddy's dictatorial rule and the practice of Christian Science here is but a sample of his many related writings on the subject, which include articles in the *Cosmopolitan* (October 1899) and the *North American Review* (January 1902; January, February, April 1903), a full-length book, *Christian Science*, published in 1907, and the unfinished "Secret History of Eddypus, The World Empire" (written in

1901–1902 and published in 1972 in *FM*, 315–82, 384–85). *Christian Science* is reprinted in *WIM*, along with related fragments (215–397, 504–20). For useful discussions of Mark Twain's views on Christian Science, see *FM*, 18–29, *WIM*, 20–28, and Gribben, 1:212–13.

80.10 Nanga Parbat] The dissolute and cynical Eden-born "Scion of the First Blood," grandson of Eve, who is maliciously bitter, especially on the subject of nepotism. Nanga Parbat's name, interestingly enough, is that of the highest mountain in the Himalayan chain in northern Pakistan. Before settling on Nanga Parbat, Twain played with "Israfel" and "Azrubbledubble" in the manuscript.

80.23 be they in the right or in the wrong] Paraphrase of the motto, "My country right or wrong." See also note to "Passage from Glances at History (suppressed.)" below (87.20).

80.29 Patriotism . . . 'the last refuge of a scoundrel.'] Nanga Parbat here credits Adam with a statement by Samuel Johnson (Boswell, *Life of Johnson* I, 547 [April 7, 1775]). His harsh tone here is also mirrored in many of Twain's other unpublished writings during these years and later. For example, in his copy of H. G. Wells's *The Future in America: A Search after Realities* (1906), Twain underscored a passage where Wells proclaimed: "Patriotism has become a mere national self-assertion, a sentimentality of flag cheering, with no constructive duties." At the top of the following pages, Twain wrote: "We have a bastard Patriotism, a sarcasm, a burlesque; but we have no such thing as a public conscience. Politically we are just a joke" (Gribben, 2:755). In his notebook he commented in 1905: "In any civic crisis of a great and dangerous sort the common herd is not anxious privately about the rights and wrongs of the matter, it is only anxious to be on the winning side. . . . There are two kinds of patriotism—monarchical patriotism and republican patriotism. In the one case the government and the king may rightfully furnish you their notions of patriotism; in the other, neither the government nor the entire nation is privileged to dictate to any individual what the form of his patriotism shall be. The Gospel of the Monarchical Patriotism is: 'The King can do no wrong.' We have adopted it with all its servility, with an unimportant change in the wording: 'Our country, right *or* wrong!' " (*MTN*, 394–95).

81.3–4 before clothes and the accident of birth] Twain here echoes Thomas Carlyle's "clothes philosophy," that he had encountered in both the Scotsman's *History of the French Revolution* (one of his favorite books) and *Sartor Resartus.* Twain often used the clothes metaphor, especially in *A Connecticut Yankee in King Arthur's Court* (1889), "Diplomatic Pay and Clothes" (*Forum*, March 1899), and "The Czar's Soliloquy" (*North American Review*, March 1905).

81.22 'They seldom die and never resign'] Adam here echoes a widely known comment by Thomas Jefferson, in his "Letter to Elias Shipman and Others of New Haven," 12 July 1801: "If a due participation of office is a matter of right, how are vacancies to be obtained? Those by death are few; by resignation, none." This is usually quoted: "Few die and none resign" (Bartlett, 12th ed. 1951, 274).

81.25 Bar Sinister] In heraldry, a horizontal stripe (bar) on the left (sinister) side of a shield or coat of arms, popularly but erroneously considered to be the heraldic symbol of illegitimacy. Also sometimes connected to a morganatic (or "left-handed") marriage, a valid union contracted by a member of a European royal or noble family with a person of inferior rank with the understanding that the inferior partner does not share the title, and children of the marriage, though legitimate, do not succeed to the title or entailed property of the parent of higher rank.

81.25 'no Irish need apply'] Popular in late 19th and early 20th century, when so many Irish fled to the United States because of the recurrent potato famine in Ireland. Originally used by business owners advertising for employees, it soon became a catchphrase meaning "Don't bother trying for that job—you won't get it."

81.29 "tell it to the marines."] Originally quoted as "Tell that to the marines—the sailors won't believe it," in Byron's *The Island* (1823), followed closely by Sir Walter Scott's *Redgauntlet* (1824). The comment expresses disbelief, because regular sailors looked down upon marines as inexperienced and gullible.

83.7 do some taffy] A colloquial expression from the late 1800s, now obsolete, meaning a crude or vulgar compliment or flattery.

83.11 doctor-sickness] The satire here expresses Twain's dislike and distrust of physicians, especially their practice of exaggerating illnesses and then claiming improvements. His comments on their practices very likely reflect his reactions to his own experience with physicians, especially during the summer and fall of 1902, when Olivia Clemens was under the constant care of doctors, whose reports could have inspired this passage. Twain then goes on to compare doctors to stock-market manipulators.

83.23 bulls] Stock-market term for persons who buy stocks or securities in the expectation that the market price will rise, so that they can sell at a profit.

83.26 it's a [word illegible] of a world!] The "[word illegible]" is Twain's own notation.

Documents Related to "Diaries Antedating the Flood"

Passage from "Glances at History" (suppressed.) and Passage from "Outlines of History" (suppressed.)

The copy-texts for these pieces are the manuscripts in the Mark Twain Papers. They were first published in *Mark Twain's Fables of Man*, edited by John S. Tuckey (Berkeley: U of California P, 1972), 389–96.

87.20 *Our Country, right or wrong!*] Popular adaptation of a portion of a toast originally given by the American naval officer Stephen Decatur (1779–1820): "Our country! In her intercourse with foreign nations may she always be in the right; but our country right or wrong." See also 80.23 in "Diaries Antedating the Flood" and corresponding note.

89.2–6 But it was impossible . . . their own persons] Refers to American imperialism in the Philippines.

89.11 trading their daughters] Twain earlier had fulminated on a number of occasions against the practice of American families marrying their daughters to titled Europeans, perhaps most notably expressed in a letter to newspaperman Sylvanus Baxter on 20 November 1889, when he referred to "the spectacle of these bastard Americans—these Hamersleys and Huntingtons and such—offering cash, encumbered by themselves, for rotten carcases and stolen titles" (*MTL*, 2:520).

89.18–19 It drove the money-changers from the temple] See Mark 11:15–16—"And they come to Jerusalem: and Jesus went into the temple, and began to cast out them that sold and bought in the temple, and overthrew the tables of the moneychangers, and the seats of them that sold doves; And would not suffer that any man should carry any vessel through the temple." Cf. Matthew 21:12–13; Luke 19:45–46; John 2:14–16.

89.21 soldier-pensions] Though these pieces were probably written in 1901 or 1902, Mark

Twain's anger at what he considered the abuse of soldier pensions would be even stronger in 1904 when Theodore Roosevelt further expanded the pension rolls. In March 1904 Roosevelt succumbed to pressure from the Grand Army of the Republic, who demanded more liberal pension payments, and issued the politically expedient Pension Order 78 (also called Executive Order 78). By this executive order, he established pensions for all veterans, disabled or not, between 62 and 70 years old. The cost was about $5,000,000 a year (Pringle, 242). Twain frequently expressed his outrage at this blatant attempt to secure votes. In "Purchasing Civic Virtue" (1907), for example, he stated: "Everybody laughs at the grotesque additions to the pension fund; everybody laughs at the grotesque-est of them all, the most shameless of them all, the most transparent of them all, the only frankly lawless one of them all—the immortal Executive Order 78" (*MTE*, 70). Elsewhere, in several letters to the Reverend J. H. Twichell, including one on 16 February 1905, he expresses similar sentiments, saying that "whenever (as a rule) I meet Roosevelt the statesman and politician, I find him destitute of morals and not respectworthy . . . whenever he smells a vote, not only willing but eager to buy it, give extravagant rates for it and pay the bill—not out of his own pocket or the party's [Republican], but out of the nation's, by cold pillage. As per Order 78 and the appropriation of the Indian trust funds" (*MTL*, 2:766–67).

90.13 Popoatahualpacatapetl] "The Prodigy" mentioned earlier who "rose in the far South" (89.15). Although, as indicated earlier, it is not known whether or not Twain had a specific person in mind as a model for his shoemaker-emperor legend, this name combines Popocatapetl, the famous volcano 45 miles southeast of Mexico City, and Atahualpa, the last Incan emperor (1532–33). Atahualpa's father, Huayana Capac, assembled a great army and started northward on a campaign of pacification and conquest, taking with him two of his natural sons, one of them Atahualpa, who later became the emperor captured and executed by Pizarro. Huayana Capac was able to subjugate unconquered tribes without great difficulty as he extended his empire. Just before his death, in 1523, the Incan empire was attacked by a foreign enemy, and the Inca had their first sight of a white man, who accompanied the invaders (Mason, 11, 130–33).

Twain may also be playing with additional aspects of Incan history here. The Incas were the reigning and aristocratic order in ancient Peru from the 13th to 16th centuries. The Inca sovereigns always married their own sisters, and the throne was inherited, in general, by the oldest son proceeding from this marriage. Children by their other wives could not, by custom or law, receive the crown, though the rule was broken when Atahualpa inherited a part of the empire in 1523 (see Gribben, 2:559, for Twain's reading on this subject).

Two Additional Pre-Deluge Diarists

Copy-texts for these passages are the manuscripts in the Mark Twain Papers. Except for "Shem's Diary, Later Passage" these fragments were first published in *Letters from the Earth*, ed. Bernard DeVoto (New York: Harper, 1962).

Passages from Methuselah's Diary

97.5–6 my father Enoch . . . great-great-grandfather Canaan] See Genesis 5 for Methuselah's genealogy. A number of Mark Twain's planning notes also deal with the line of descent and the respective ages of his forebears. See appendix 4.

Mark Twain's first start on the diary (five ms. pages, with page 3 missing) presented Methuselah as a *child* of 67. The diary then read "—This day I am sixty years old & have divers toys, and things wherewith to play, & have abundant joy in them, I being born in the year from the beginning of the world, 687. Though I be but small & weak, yet can I read passing well, & likewise write, albeit the letters be of an ill fashion & do trouble my father sore to make them out, who saith he cannot, but that I shall abide in my studies & be of good cheer until years and judgment shall enlarge my art."† Twain doubtless then decided that making Methuselah almost infantile was too ridiculous, and broke off halfway down page two. Whether he then began again on the missing page 3 cannot be ascertained, but page 4 picks up with the genealogy, as in the final version, but after "my great-great-grandfather Cainan," he went on, following a semi-colon with: "my great-great-great grandfather Enos; my great-great-great-great-great-grandfather Seth; & ⟨my⟩ the High & Mighty ⟨the King⟩ Prince of Princes, King of Kings, The Father of Men, His Grace the most Noble & Supreme my great-great-great-great-grandfather ADAM, unto whom let prosperity & peace continue to the End! Amen."† Following that passage, he then wrote (and crossed out: "Meth by no means," and below it: "Have Meth speak of somebody who killed himself by a ⟨long⟩ life of smoking, at 698 years—& served him right."†

97.16 the sage Uz] In the Bible Uz was the son of Aram, and grandson of Shem (Genesis 10:23). Later in the Bible it was also the name of the homeland of Job (Job 1:1).

97.16 land of Nod . . . city called Enoch] After slaying Abel, Cain fled to the land of Nod, somewhere "on the east of Eden," and built a city there, naming it for his son Enoch (Genesis 4:16–17).

97.18–19 children of Jabal] Jabal was the son of Lamech and Adah (and grandson of Methuselah), and became "the father of such as dwell in tents" (Genesis 4:20), hence Mark Twain's parallels with American Indians.

97.20 Zillah] Here Mark Twain borrowed the name of Lamech's other wife, mother of Tubal-cain (Genesis 4:19, 22).

97.20 Habbakuk] A prophet of Judah in the seventh century B.C. prior to the fall of Jerusalem, author of the 35th book of the Old Testament.

97.23 Aumrath] Mark Twain apparently invented this name of Methuselah's city. Among the notes he wrote prior to taking up the second section of the diary he listed "Amurath [*sic*], Meth's capital city—covering 5 hills & valleys, a vast population—city all stone."†

98.10 marketh the doer for a fool.] This slap at tourist graffiti echoes Mark Twain's reactions to similar desecrations during his trip to the Mediterranean a few years earlier, as recorded in *The Innocents Abroad* (1869).

98.28 new actor Luz] In the Bible Luz was the city where Jacob had his dream, and set up as a pillar the stone he had used for his pillow. Jacob named the place Bethel (Genesis 28:18–19; Luz also mentioned in Genesis 35:6, 48.3, and Judges 1:23).

98.33 Jebel] Mark Twain invented the name of this overly critical "theatrical reviewer," allegedly the half-brother of Enos, son of Seth (third son of Adam).

99.5 Uzziel] Here Mark Twain probably borrowed this name from Uzziel the son of Kohath of the tribe of Levi (Exodus 6:18, and also mentioned in Numbers, Leviticus, and I Chronicles), or possibly from the goldsmith Uzziel, who helped rebuild Jerusalem's wall (Nehemiah 3:8).

99.15 Zuar] Here Mark Twain borrowed the name of the father of Nethaneel, prince of the tribe of Issachar, who was chosen to help Moses number the people of Israel (Numbers 1:8, 2:5;

7:18–23; 10:15). In this episode, though he drew on the rules concerning slavery that he found in Exodus (see planning notes, appendix 4), Mark Twain introduces the poignancy of the potential separation of a slave family, a theme he had portrayed strongly in "A True Story" (*Atlantic Monthly*, November 1874).

100.12–13 Sarah, grand-daughter of my kinsman Eliah] In the Bible the most famous Sarah was the wife of Abraham, who bore Isaac when she was 90 and her husband 100 (Genesis 17:17, 21:5). For Eliah, Mark Twain perhaps borrowed the name of a head man of the tribe of Benjamin, one of the sons of Jeroham (I Chronicles 8:27) or, more probably, that of one of the Sons of Elam in the time of Ezra (Ezra 10:26). At the end of a long list of names, the last verse (44) of the same chapter notes: "All these had taken strange wives: and some of them had wives by whom they had children." That statement might well have intrigued Mark Twain. Though "strange" here doubtless means "foreign" wives, he would especially have appreciated "strange."

100.32 Mahlah] For the wife of Zuar Mark Twain borrowed the name of one of the daughters of Zelophehad, who pleaded with Moses to let their father's inheritance pass to them, because he had no sons. They ultimately were allowed the inheritance so long as they married members of "the family of the tribe of their father" (Numbers 26:33, 27:1–11, 36:6–7).

101.13 Jabalites] See note to Jabal, above, and to Sitting Bull, Custer, and Howard below.

102.4 brief republican form of government] This phrase seems to reflect the implications of another note written on a separate sheet, very likely close to the same planning session. It could not, however, have been written earlier than late September 1877 because of the event described. The note read:

> Poor foreign devils lost & starving in the desert. Republican govt. of Meth can't relieve or rescue them.
>
> ⟨Chief Minister⟩ ^Somebody^ observes that if you can pretend that they are robbers or other criminals govt. will hunt them up with alacrity———— which is done.
>
> Disgust of govt to find they are honest & harmless"† (see appendix 4).

That plan resulted from a personal experience that had left a deep impression. On the return trip from Bermuda in May 1877, Clemens's ship had encountered a schooner, the *Jonas Smith*, whose crew of "innocent, marvelling chuckleheaded Bermudians," allegedly on a pleasure cruise to New York, had begged food and water. Describing the meeting at the time, the humorist closed his notebook entry with "Evidence of the foolhardiness of man. Shall we ever hear of these negroes again?" (*N&J2*, 33). His question was answered on 19 September when the newspapers reported that the *Jonas Smith* had been drifting for the past four and a half months and was now 250 miles farther away from its New York destination than it had been in May. Annoyed at the stupidity of the sailors, but convinced that they needed assistance, Clemens not only wrote a long letter to the Hartford *Courant* (reprinted in the New York *Times*, 20 September 1877, p. 20, col. 3), but also telegraphed President Rutherford B. Hayes, requesting a full investigation. Hayes referred him to Treasury Secretary John Sherman, who replied on the 22nd that because the commander of the revenue cutter *Colfax* had found no need for assistance when he had boarded the *Jonas Smith* on 16 September, it was unnecessary to send the *Colfax* out again.

That answer could hardly have pleased Clemens, who knew of the earlier incident. After describing his own experience with the *Jonas Smith* to his friend Howells on the 19th, he mentioned that "the other day," the *Colfax* had gone "a little way in search of them . . . & then struck a fog & gave it up." Thoroughly incensed, he added an afterthought to his letter, declaring that the cutter had gone to the *Jonas Smith* "thinking there was mutiny or other crime aboard." But, he continued, "It occurs to me now that since there is only suffering & misery & nobody to punish, it ceases to be a matter in which (a republican form of) government will feel authorized to interfere in further. Dam a republican form of government" (*MTHL*, 1:203–4).

102.5 Custer and Howard and the Peace Commission] See the *New York Times Index*, 1877, for more than 38 news stories dealing with the wars against the Sioux and the Nez Percés.

102.6 Modoc Lava Beds] During the Modoc War of 1872–73 Chief Kintpuash (known to the whites as Captain Jack) and a small band of braves held off large units of regular army and volunteers in the rugged lava beds of northern California. When a peace commission finally met with the chief and his party on 11 April 1873, the Indians, though surrounded by nearly 1,000 troops, killed Gen. E. R. S. Canby and the Reverend Eleazar Thomas, and wounded the other two commission members. Retreating again to the lava beds, the Modocs held out until the army finally rounded them up in late June. That October, Captain Jack and several companions were executed and the other members of the tribe were transported to a reservation in the Oklahoma Territory. As one modern historian has put it: "The monetary cost of subduing this handful of Indians (only fifty-three warriors) was over half a million dollars; the human cost was the life of at least eighty-three. The Modocs themselves lost only seventeen warriors killed in battle or executed. It was all a tragic waste, since if the Modocs had been allowed to live on their own land, a strip of worthless territory in the lava beds, the whole conflict would have been avoided," Roske, 380–83.

Obviously the spectacle of hundreds of soldiers trying to capture so small a band of Indians struck Mark Twain's sense of the ridiculous, and the wastefulness of the action surely would have aroused his ire. He had expressed that concern semihumorously, but with a sting, in his Fourth of July speech in 1873 to Americans living in London. Ironically describing the "progress" enjoyed by the United States—"a land which has developed a Washington, a Franklin, a William M. Tweed, a Motley, a Jay Gould, a Samuel C. Pomeroy, a recent Congress which has never had its equal—(in some respects)," he concluded his series with "a United States Army which conquered sixty Indians in eight months by tiring them out—which is much better than uncivilized slaughter, God knows" (*MTS*, 75).

Following the note on ms. page 41 Mark Twain wrote and later lined out "From 34 to 41 must come in" and under it, "The Jabalites are descended from Cain."† Then he began a new segment with page 42. Later he lined out that page number and substituted 34. Hence he originally intended to bring in the Jabalites at a later time but evidently took a different tack and abandoned the manuscript before returning to his "Indian" theme. We have left the passage as he originally wrote it, because it does not easily fit in later.

102.10 game, played with a ball] The passage parodying the playing of baseball and the "strange" language of the game also helps place the time of composition, at least of this segment, in late 1877. The "two years gone by" surely reflects the publicity that greeted the formation of baseball's National League in February 1876. Clemens's attention would have been drawn to that event not only because Hartford's team was one of the original members, but also because the Hartford club's president, M. G. Bulkeley, was named first president of the new league. Besides Hartford the league included Philadelphia, Brooklyn, New Haven, Boston, Chicago, St. Louis, Louisville, and Cincinnati (New York *Times*, 7 February 1876, p. 2., col. 2). Sometime during these years, very possibly during the 1877 season, Mark Twain had jotted down two pages of notes about a particular game between the Boston Red Stockings and the Hartford Blue Stockings. One item,

"Carey got a baser" †—probably a remark by one of the children—clearly places the game in the late 1870s, for Thomas Carey, the Hartford shortstop, was one of the team's most valuable players during these years and in the fall of 1877 was named captain for the 1878 season (New York *Times*, 2 November 1877, p. 5, col. 4). These notes also contain numerous references to the sort of "calls" by the umpires that Methuselah described. A much later comment attached to these pages by the author's secretary Isabel Lyon reads: "Along in 1905 Mr. Clemens handed this baseball scoring to me saying, 'Someday we'll talk about that Hartford game for the Autobiography'" (MTP).

104.1 To the museum . . .] The following episode echoes a number of Mark Twain's reactions to museums, guides, and relics as reported in *The Innocents Abroad* (1869).

105.21 Perish the generation of Jubal!] Jubal was another son of Lamech and Adah, brother to Jabal (and grandson of Methuselah), and the "father of all such as handle the harp and organ" (Genesis 4:21).

105.35 "O, Kiss Haggag for His Mother."] For the name of the character in this parody of popular sentimental song titles Mark Twain perhaps plays with the name of Haggi, one of the sons of Gad (Genesis 46:16) or with that of Haggai, the prophet (37th book of the Old Testament). The change in the final syllable is suggestive.

Passages from Shem's Diary

107.16 nine hundred and sixty-eight years] This figure would place the time as the year before Methuselah's death at age 969.

107.17 if he were not a relative] Methuselah was Shem's great-grandfather, though Mark Twain in the later fragment of the diary (1908 or 1909) would have him related to Shem's wife.

107.24 young girl in his dreams] Here, as in the "Autobiography of Eve," Mark Twain seems to be recalling his own experience with recurrent dreams of a youthful sweetheart (see Baetzhold, "Found: Mark Twain's 'Lost Sweetheart'").

108.15 title] Present title is supplied. Mark Twain originally drafted a fairly elaborate title page for this fragment from late 1908 or early 1909, headed: "Life in the Ark. / from / Shem's Diary Translated from the original hieroglyphics / by Mark Twain"; and near the bottom of the page was "Copyright by Shem B.C. . . . / Copyright by Mark Twain A.D. . . ." †

108.35 isn't the oldest person] In the Bible Methuselah *was*, of course, the oldest person who had ever lived (died at 969). In the earlier passage Mark Twain had set Methuselah's age at 968, just a year before his death. Here he again suggests, as he did in the first entry in the original section of Shem's diary, that there were older "undistinguished" people in the world who would not have been deemed important enough for mention in the Bible.

109.7 cake-walk gait] the strutting manner characteristic of the "cake walk," a promenade featuring elaborate steps and posturing, with a cake as a prize for the person who performed the most complex routine.

109.10–11 related to him by marriage] Mark Twain here either forgot or, more likely, chose to ignore the fact that Methuselah was Shem's paternal great-grandfather.

109.26 Japheth] Noah's fourth son.

Adam's Expulsion

The 1877 manuscript (revised slightly by Mark Twain in 1881) is copy-text for "Adam's Expulsion." Formerly housed in the Doheny Collection, St. John's Seminary, Camarillo, California, that manuscript has since been sold at auction, and its current whereabouts is unknown. This present version has been emended in a few instances from a fair copy of the same manuscript dated "Hartford Oct. 28 1877,"† which is housed in the Walter Hampden Memorial Library, 16 Gramercy Park, New York.

113.22–114.1 men be made each after his kind] Compare Genesis 1:25–26 where God made fish and fowl "after their kind," but man "in our image."

114.1 put not off until the morrow] Lord Chesterfield's letter of 26 December 1749 cautioning his son, "Never put off till tomorrow what you can do today," is apparently responsible for the advice that procrastinators find so irritating (Mencken, 976).

114.4–5 whosoever is without guile . . . lie down with the lion and the lamb] Compare Psalms 32:2—"Blessed is the man . . . in whose spirit there is no guile" and Isaiah 11:6—"The wolf also shall dwell with the lamb, and the leopard shall lie down with the kid; and the calf and the young lion and the fatling together."

114.5 be not ashamed of his nakedness] Compare Genesis 2:25—"And they were both naked . . . and were not ashamed." See also Genesis 3:10–11 for Adam's change of attitude.

114.5–7 for they shall put a ring . . .] The next four details echo the story of the prodigal son (Luke 15:11–32), a passage that Twain alluded to very frequently over the years.

114.7–8 mote that is in his brother's eye] Compare Matthew 7:3–4; Luke 6:41–42.

114.8 rich man to go through the eye of a camel] Compare Matthew 19:24—"It is easier for a camel to go through the eye of a needle, than for a rich man to enter into the kingdom of God" (also in Mark 10:25, Luke 18:25).

114.9 break the Sabbath day and keep it holy] Compare Moses' sixth commandment to "Remember the sabbath day, to keep it holy" (Exodus 20:8).

114.16–17 one day he cometh up as a flower . . . cut down] Compare Job 14:1–2—"Man . . . is of few days and full of trouble. He cometh forth like a flower, and is cut down."

114.8 trampled under foot of men] Compare Matthew 7:6, directly following the "mote" reference, where the listeners are advised not to cast pearls before swine, "lest they trample them under their feet."

114.18 cast into outer darkness] Compare Matthew 8:12—"the children . . . shall be cast into outer darkness: there shall be weeping and gnashing of teeth" (see also Matthew 22:13; 25:30).

114.18–19 where the grasshopper is a burden] Compare Ecclesiastes' dire predictions in chapter 12, among which are that "the grasshopper shall be a burden and desire shall fail" (12:5).

114.19 thieves break through and steal] Compare Jesus' advice about not laying up treasures on earth (Matthew 6:19).

114.19–20 naught of raiment but camel's hair and ashes] Compare the description of John the Baptist, Matthew 3:4—who "had his raiment of camel's hair, and a leathern girdle about his loins." The reference to ashes also suggests "sackcloth and ashes," Hebrew symbol of mourning mentioned throughout the Bible (e.g., Matthew 11:21; Luke 10:13).

114.20 girdle about his loins.] See preceding note. At this point in the manuscript Mark

Twain crossed out "For the Preacher saith, Vanity of vanities, all is vanity, & none but the brave deserve the fair,"† a ludicrous juxtaposition of Ecclesiastes 1:2 and the familiar line that forms the refrain of the first section of Dryden's "Alexander's Feast."

115.9 Clothed in sack-cloth and fine linen] See note to "naught of raiment" above. Among the many biblical references to "fine linen," Twain seems to be echoing the "purple and fine linen" of Luke 16:19.

115.9 even as did the children the fatted calf] Here the author combines the "fatted calf" of the prodigal son story (see note to "put a ring" above) with the setting up of the golden calf by Aaron during the Exodus (Exodus 32:4). The original manuscript reads "as did the children of Israel the fatted calf." In making a fair copy of the text, Twain deleted "of Israel." It seems likely that in making his fair copy, Twain may have considered that Adam would have been speaking considerably before the Exodus and so decided to blur the anachronism. While it is possible that the omission of the phrase *could* have been a slip, we are inclined toward the former possibility.

115.11–12 floods came . . . founded upon a rock] A close paraphrase of lines from Jesus' parable in Matthew 7:25.

115.13–14 limbs clove to the roof of their mouths] This absurdity seems to echo Job's memory of his earlier eminence, when in his presence "the nobles held their peace, and their tongue cleaved to the roof of their mouth" (Job 29:10).

115.14–15 fled away to the mountains . . . "Hold the fort for I am coming"] Here the humorist juxtaposes Jesus' advice concerning his second coming and the end of the world—that the people of Judea should "flee to the mountains" (Luke 21:21)—with the message reportedly signaled by Gen. William T. Sherman (1820–91) to Gen. John M. Corse (1838–93) at Allatoona Pass, Georgia, on 5 October 1864: "Hold the fort! I am coming!" Philip Bliss (1838–76), a singing evangelist and author of "Let the Lower Lights be Burning" and "Jesus Loves Me," commemorated the battle and the message in the popular hymn, "Hold the Fort."

115.16 Read, mark, and inwardly digest this parable] Here Twain adapts the collect for the second Sunday in Advent from the *Book of Common Prayer*, which asks that God grant us the power to "read, mark, learn, and inwardly digest" the Scriptures in such a way that the "comfort of thy Holy Word" may help us hold fast "the blessed hope of everlasting life."

Adam's Soliloquy

The copy-text for this piece is the manuscript in the Mark Twain Papers. It was first published in *Europe and Elsewhere* (1923) by Alfred Bigelow Paine, who took certain liberties with the manuscript.

120.3 The mere *skeleton* 57 feet long and 16 feet high!] Even here there is a casual link with "King Leopold's Soliloquy," in which Leopold, referring to a dinosaur with the same dimensions as the one mentioned here, says: "This long time I have been 'the monster'; that was their favorite—the monster of crime. But now I have a new one. They have found a fossil Dinosaur fifty-seven feet long and sixteen feet high, and set it up in the museum in New York and labeled it 'Leopold II.' "

120.7 alongside of the biggest Normandy] Twain here refers to the breed of powerful draft horses more commonly known as Percherons. Originally Percheron-Norman, one of the first great stallions of that breed in the United States was actually named Normandy, and was reputed to have sired about sixty colts a year for eighteen years.

120.18 stocking the Ark] the stipulations referred to are developed in Genesis 6:9–22, 7:1–7.

120.20 the boys were to blame for this] Noah's three sons, Shem, Ham, and Japheth.

121.28 salt seawater got mixed with the fresh] The one extensive treatment of Noah that Twain saw published during his lifetime was a section titled "Noah's Ark" in his essay "About All Kinds of Ships" (in *The £1,000,000 Bank-Note, Etc.*, 1893). In it, Noah points out to an inspector of the Ark that water could be obtained from the outside by lowering buckets. The inspector argues that this could not be done because the salt oceans would have mixed with the fresh water to such an extent that all water would be too salty to drink. Obviously struck by the logical improbabilities of the biblical account of the Flood, Twain also makes the point about the unavailability of fresh water in "Letters from the Earth." And in the "Autobiography of a Damned Fool," written in 1877, he suggested that "the account of the deluge could not have been written from sacred inspiration, but must have been interlarded by some person of a light mind during the early ages of the world," before going on to detail the specific improbabilities (*S&B*, 138).

121.29 cholera-germ] This continues Twain's preoccupation with the introduction of and continued presence of diseases in the world. For related discussions, see similar treatments in "Letters from the Earth," "Diaries Antedating the Flood," and "Selected Passages on God and the Bible from Autobiographical Dictations of June 1906" in this volume. Twain was certainly aware of the many crises confronting nineteenth-century urbanites, none of which loomed more obvious or important than environmental pollution. Unpaved or poorly paved streets, inefficient collection of garbage, excrement from thousands of horses, sooty dust from manufacturing establishments, and, above all, inadequate sewerage systems threatened the safety of most urban Americans by midcentury. Successive cholera, typhoid, and diphtheria epidemics claimed the lives of thousands. The discovery during the 1880s that many diseases, especially the killer typhoid, were waterborne accelerated campaigns for pure water, for sewer construction, and for the filtration of both water and sewage (Schultz and McShane, 389–411).

121.35 As for what Ham thinks, it is not important. Ham is biased] Though clearly extrabiblical, Twain's comic treatment of Ham here draws upon popular myths surrounding his character. According to legend, because Noah and his family alone survived the Flood, their descendants populated the earth. Egypt was called "The Land of Ham" and he was considered to be the ancestor of the Hamitic peoples—the Egyptians and the inhabitants of the regions in Africa south of Egypt. Their dark skins were said to be the result of Ham's iniquity in viewing his father drunk and naked, while his brothers walked backward with averted eyes to "cover" Noah (Genesis 9:22–26). When Noah awoke, he knew of his son's transgression and cursed Ham's *son*, Canaan, saying that henceforth he would be a servant to his brothers—with the implication that all his descendants would also be servants, thus providing a biblical justification for enslavement of blacks.

122.16 three hundred thousand years ago come Tuesday;] As Allison Ensor points out, while Twain followed Archbishop James Ussher's calculation of scriptural chronology in the passage at Adam's tomb in *The Innocents Abroad* (chapter 53), making the creation of Adam occur 6,000 years ago, here Twain's figure of 300,000 years is fifty times the age of the earth as calculated by Ussher (Ensor, 112, n. 23; 114, n. 38).

123.29 I do speak English with a heavenly accent] Compare the comment which Mark Twain wrote in his daughter Clara's copy of *Pudd'nhead Wilson* (1894): "I have traveled more than any-one else, and I have noticed that even the angels speak English with an accent."

124.8 the Man Without a Country] Readers would remember the story with that title by Edward Everett Hale, first published in the *Atlantic Monthly* in 1863 and widely reprinted. Its main character, Philip Nolan, a participant in Aaron Burr's conspiracy, curses the United States at his trial, whereupon he is sentenced to spend the rest of his life aboard a naval vessel and is never again to hear news of the country he has claimed to despise.

124.31 gates of pearl . . . New Jerusalem] For the biblical description of the New Jerusalem, which includes the twelve gates of pearl, see Revelation 21:10–22.

Captain Stormfield's Visit to Heaven

Headnote

129.22–23 told his remarkable dream] Chicago *Republican* (23 August 1868, p. 2, col. 1), letter dated 17 August. This Chicago *Republican* article would seem to refute Ray B. Browne's conjec-ture that Wakeman did not really furnish the idea for "Stormfield," but that a widely known joke, "Old Abe's 'Slap' at Chicago," may have inspired the story (*MTQH*, 21–22, 24–27).

One other intriguing possibility, at least for one of the revisions of the story, lies in a letter to Howells on 23 November 1875, in which Clemens incidentally remarked on the prevalence of un-conscious plagiarism among authors, and noted that he had once charged his friend and neighbor Charles Dudley Warner with just such plagiarism. That thought in turn reminded him, he said,

> that I have been delighting my soul for two weeks over a bran new and ingenious way of be-ginning a novel—& behold, all at once it flashes upon me that *Charley Warner* originated the idea 3 years ago [i.e., in 1872] & told me about it! Aha! so much for self-righteousness! I am well repaid. Here are 108 pages of MS, new & clean, lying disgraced in the waste paper basket, & I am beginning the novel over again in an unstolen way (*MTHL*, 1:112).

Very possibly the story he was beginning anew was "Stormfield," and the tale told him was one that Warner had written in 1872 for *Backlog Studies* (1873) involving the dream of a young man who had recently given up smoking. In the dream the youth dies, spends some time hovering about observing the reactions of various friends, but then soars past the solar system to heaven and, on arrival, is questioned by St. Peter. In his answers, he admits to minor sins and is forgiven, until one last question, "Have you ever used tobacco?" With his affirmative answer, St. Peter im-mediately banishes him to hell, where he observes numerous torments, and finally awakes just as he is about to be thrown into a flaming furnace. Assuring the reader that everything he had de-scribed was true, he adds a moral: "*Haec fabula docet:* It is dangerous for a young man to leave off the use of tobacco" (Warner, 97).

Warner's story contains a number of details similar to those in "Stormfield," and perhaps even more to some in "Captain Simon Wheeler's Dream Visit to Heaven." Hence, memories of Warner's story, written in the fall of 1872, may well have caused the problem mentioned in the letter to Howells, especially since Mark Twain specifically related it to a story that Warner had told him in 1872.

Most of the "Backlog Studies" had originally appeared serially in *Scribner's Monthly*, but the one describing the dream was first published in the collected volume, copyright 1872, issued in 1873. Mark Twain owned a copy of this edition (Gribben, 2:745).

130.18 "got it."] *MTL*, I, 323.

130.28 size of Rhode Island] *MTE*, 247.

130.37 actual borrowing] See Robert A. Rees, "*Captain Stormfield's Visit to Heaven* and *The Gates Ajar*," *English Language Notes* (7 March, 1970): 197–202; and see Gibson 1976, 84–85; 215, n. 27.

131.3 "Some Rambling Notes . . .] *Atlantic Monthly*, October 1877–January 1878.

131.24 as much like . . . Wakeman] *MTHL*, 1: 207.

131.36–37 major work on the story] The dating of this period of composition (March 1878 until the fall of 1881) is based on the paper and ink of the manuscript itself and other correspondence with Howells.

132.3–18 awkward new arrival" . . . Have all sorts of heavens . . . *between* solar systems."] *N&J2*, 55, 56.

132.29–34 Ollendorff . . . unrestricted suffrage."] *N&J2*, 66, 68. Heinrich George Ollendorf (1803–65) was the author of a famous series of "teach-yourself" language lessons, the German version of which Mark Twain would later use as a basis for his play, "Meisterschaft," first published in the *Century* magazine for January 1888. He would develop the concept of heaven's political and social structure in the angel Sandy's explanation to Stormfield in present chapter 4. The antipathy toward an "unrestricted suffrage" here closely reflects Clemens's own political and social views of the 1870s (see Baetzhold 1970, chapter 2).

132.38 before next year."] *MTHL*, 1:233, 236.

133.4 Guillemin's *The Heavens*] Clemens's copy of Guillemin's *The Heavens: An Illustrated Handbook of Popular Astronomy* (ed. by J. Norman Lockyer, F.R.A.S., F.R.S.; rev. by Richard A. Proctor, B.A., F.R.A.S.; 7th edition [London: Richard Bentley & Son, 1878]), now in the Mark Twain Papers, is inscribed "S. L. Clemens / Munich, Dec. 1878." In the chapter on "The Moon," for instance, Twain proposed to "let Wakeman visit the moon & find groveling beings who go naked, eat lava, don't breathe or drink—are capable of sleeping through their night of a fortnight's length—or let them be intelligent *with* strong telescopes & well informed about us, whom they despise. Their religion & the age (very great) to which they live. W. has an interpreter—a former Moonite."† And next to a scored and underlined statement that "the Earth is unknown to the lunarian observer situated on the invisible hemisphere," he wrote: "Speak of *these* people, too," and above that: "They can't stand strong light."† (144, 145). On the last page of the chapter on Neptune: "Wakeman finds that these various worlds, except Jupiter are no denser than water, the people are very light, & able to walk on water. Jupiter offers foothold as good as thick mud."† (234).

133.17 two books ready"] quoted in *N&J2*, 217. The first, of course, was *A Tramp Abroad*, and the second almost certainly the "Wakeman book."

133.20–21 at once." . . . for a long time.] SLC to Howells, 30 January 1879, *MTHL*, 1:250. The only evidence of continued attention to the Wakeman/Stormfield story at this time and in the succeeding months was two notes, neither of which was ultimately developed, and several references to Wakeman himself (*N&J2*, 275, 311, 347).

133.30 off my back."] *MTHL*, 1:287.

133.32 middle of the following June] The segments indicated here are written in purple ink, which, as Walter Blair has determined (Blair, 201), Clemens did not use for at least four years after that mid June of 1880. Moreover, the paper of both segments is like that used in other manuscripts during this period.

133.37–38 rename his narrator . . . uncertain.] Mark Twain first used the name in his notebook sometime early in August 1880 in a long entry which began: "Early in heaven Stormfield is delighted with the social equalities," and went on to detail the captain's subsequent disillusionment at being embraced and wept upon by "all sorts of disagreeable people" (*N&J2*, 368–69). And when he made a new start at the beginning of present chapter 4 (manuscript chapter 5, MS2, 54), Twain had Sandy enlighten Stormfield about the far-less-than-democratic social structure of heaven.

134.13 purpose at present."] *MTHL*, 1:376.

134.21–22 episodes or incidents] *N&J3*, 31, 32, 56.

134.30 live long enough."] New York *World*, 12 January 1890, p. 14.

134.37 "dinner table yarn."†] (SLC to OLC, 11–17 February 1894, MTP.

135.5 & still in MS.)"] Notebook 39, TS, p. 55, MTP.

135.6 listed "Stormfield"] *N&J3*, 72, 617, Notebook 46 (1903–4), TS, p. 7.

135.7 must rewrite the tale] Notebook 41, TS, pp. 37, 46; 42, TS, p. 55, MTP.

135.9 retrieve it from the "manuscript trunk"] Evidently Whitmore did not find the right manuscript, for a few days later, when Whitmore responded, Clemens chided him for sending the wrong one: "What I want is 'A Visit to Heaven.' . . . It is certainly in the safe or in the pigeon-holes & is worth as much as the house"† (SLC to Whitmore 15, 18, 23 October 1902, Hartford Memorial, TS, MTP).

135.17–29 early months of 1906 . . . Reminiscences"] All of these new passages are written on paper which John Tuckey has determined was used only after mid 1905. Obviously the discussion of light-years was written before the autobiographical dictation of 29 August 1906, in which Twain said: "Toward the end of the book my heaven grew to such inconceivable dimensions on my hands that I ceased to apply poor little million-mile measurements to its mighty territories, and measured them by light-years only! and not only that, but a million of them linked together in a stretch." And here Mark Twain inserted the following footnote: "Light-year. This is without doubt the most stupendous and impressive phrase that exists in any language. It is restricted to astronomy. It describes the distance which light, moving at the rate of 186,000 miles per second, travels in our year of 52 weeks" (*MTE*, 247).

It seems likely that these passages were written shortly after Mark Twain obtained a copy of *Sidelights on Astronomy and Kindred Fields of Popular Science* (New York: Harper, 1906) by Simon Newcomb (1835–1909), one of the most distinguished of nineteenth-century astronomers. On the front pasted down endpaper of his own copy of this book, inscribed "SL. Clemens / 21 Fifth Avenue / New York. / 1906," Twain computed the distance in miles of a light-year, as well as the distance to Alpha Centauri, the nearest star (Gribben 2:500). A reference to "p. 45" on that sheet shows that Paine's reproduction of those computations, which he seems to imply were from 1909 (*MTB*, 3:1510) actually came from Newcomb's book, page 45 of which deals with the light-year and the distance of Alpha Centauri.

136.10–11 in his working notes] Group A-6. The "dream" is also referred to in two other notes, A-9, A-10, *FM*, 458, 460.

136.19 from the same ms."] Lyon Journal, TS, p. 165, MTP.

136.26 until I am dead."] *MTHL*, 2: 811.

136.33 closing two-thirds of it] TS, p. 1102, MTP; *RP*, xxii.

137.8 couldn't help it."] TS, p.1188 (renumbered 1106 after "Stormfield" text removed), first published in *MTQH*, 19. When Twain subsequently circled the three sentences for deletion, he inserted a paragraph sign before "There has never been a time in the past thirty-five years when my literary shipyard hadn't two or more half-finished ships on the ways," the sentence that begins the published portion of the dictation of 30 August in *MTE*, 196.

137.15 play in its financing.] In October 1908, after his daughter Clara had objected to his proposal to name the new house in Redding, Connecticut, "Innocence at Home," he had agreed with her that its new name should be "Stormfield." And to his younger daughter Jean he declared "Stormfield" to be the better name because its lofty position on the hilltop would expose it to the onslaught of all the storms that came, and also because the payment he had received from the magazine publication of the story had financed construction of one whole end of the building (SLC to Jean, 2 October 1908, TS, MTP).

137.17–20 "exact, truthful . . . tell the truth."] *MTMary*, 59–60.

137.22 & the magazines (sic)."] Lyon, Secretary Notebook No. 1, 1906, on page headed "Sept. 7," MTP.

137.24 "formulated a scheme"] Harvey to SLC, 9/11/06, MTP.

137.27 returned the "original copy"] Duneka to SLC, 2/26 1907, MTP.

137.32–33 male transvestite.] This story was one of Mark Twain's several attempts to fictionalize an actual happening in the Clemens household in 1877. At that time one of the Clemenses' maids was thought to have been harboring a suspected burglar. When she revealed that the man was actually her lover and fiancé, though now unwilling to marry her, Clemens (Jackson in the story, set in London) forced the unwilling paramour to go through with the wedding. The revelation that "she" was a male was a later addition. (*MTB* 2: 600–1; Emerson, 215; Hill, 190).

137.36–138.5 On 9 August . . . might later be deleted] *Lyon Journal*, TS, 268, MTP; Quick, 99).

138.8–9 wholly positive] Lyon Journal, TS, p. 279, MTP.

138.10–12 proofs arrived . . . cut out all but a few paragraphs] H. R. Rood to SLC, 30 September 1907, MTP. The deleted section was the portion originally included in MS2, 25.8–36.23, and TS, 1144 (39).20–1150 (45).6. See also "Mental Telegraphy?" later in this volume. For the omitted passage itself, see appendix 5b.

138.17 in book form] Lyon to Major Leigh, 10 April 1909; MTP and Duneka to SLC 2 July 1909; Hill, 238 and note to 238.14.

138.21–22 In the original . . . Mrs. Rushmore] See appendix 5a for the original manuscript version of the Rushmore episode.

Text

The copy-texts for Mark Twain's introductory note, the first two and the last two chapters, and the segment at the end of chapter 3 involving the mother's search for her daughter who had died in infancy are manuscripts in the Mark Twain Papers. For chapters 3 and 4 (except for the last mentioned segment which ends chapter 3), the two-part manuscript (paged 1–62, 1–114) in the American Academy and Institute of Arts and Letters, New York City, is copy-text.

Since both the American Academy manuscript and the typescript originally made for Mark Twain's autobiography differ in their delineation of chapters, we have chosen to follow the two-part division made by *Harper's Monthly*, and have designated these passages chapters 3 and 4.

Twain's introductory note and chapters 1 and 2 were first published in *Report From Paradise*, edited by Dixon Wecter (New York: Harper, 1952); chapters 5 and 6 in *Mark Twain's Quarrel with Heaven*, edited by Ray B. Browne (New Haven: College and University Press, 1970).

Note

139.1 knew Captain Stormfield well] The characteristics described here were based chiefly on Mark Twain's memories of Captain Edgar "Ned" Wakeman (1818–75). Twain repeats details concerning the captain's birth and current age that he had used earlier in describing "Hurricane Jones" in "Some Rambling Notes of an Idle Excursion" (*Atlantic Monthly*, November 1877). Wakeman was not born in his father's ship, however, but in Westport, Connecticut. He went to sea when he was fourteen. When Clemens met him he was forty-eight, not sixty-five; he died in 1875, aged fifty-seven (Browne, 327). And though Mark Twain's notebooks record many anecdotes involving Wakeman, reference to "the Devil's Race Track" is not among them. But the captain's vivid imagination and story-telling abilities, his tenderness and toughness, were apparently much as described, though in Stormfield's story Mark Twain does not recapture Wakeman's characteristic manner of expression as recorded in a number of notebook entries and in "Some Rambling Notes."

139.18 Devil's Race-Track] Presumably a circular region between the Cape of Good Hope and the South Pole 500 miles in diameter, the outer four-fifths of which is "lashed and tossed and torn by eternal storms." Mark Twain described the experience of being caught in the Devil's Race-Track more fully in "The Enchanted Sea-Wilderness," a fragment originally written in November or December 1896 for inclusion in *Following the Equator* (1897) (*WWD*, 76, 81–82).

Chapter 1

140.12 Chips the carpenter] On merchant and naval ships, various crew members were traditionally given nicknames appropriate to their duties; for example, the carpenter was "Chips," the doctor, "Bones," etc.

140.18 Eight bells] Aboard ship, the 24-hour day is divided into six four-hour periods—"watches"—with "bells" every half hour. Noon is eight bells, 12:30 is one, 1:00 is two, and so on until 4:00, which is eight bells, after which the cycle repeats every four hours. The later references to time indicate that "eight bells" here is midnight.

140.23 "Sheet home . . . "Reef tops'ls and sky-scrapers] A "sheet" refers both to a sail itself and to a rope or chain that regulates the angle at which a sail is set in relation to the wind. "Sheet home," then, means to extend a square sail by hauling upon the sheets (ropes) until the sail is as flat as possible, and therefore does not catch as much wind. To "reef" is to reduce the area of a sail by rolling or folding a portion of it and fastening it to the spar by means of "reef points" (small pieces of rope).

To clarify this and later references to sails, "Sky-scrapers" or skysails are the topmost and smallest of the six principal sails on each of the three masts (fore, main, and mizzen) of a full-rigged sailing ship. Then, in descending order come the "royals," the "topgallants," the "upper-topsails," the "lower-topsails," and the "sails."

141.32 Chatham street] Though there is no Chatham Street there, Mark Twain was probably thinking of the area around Chatham Square on the Lower East Side of New York City, the site of the garment district in the late nineteenth century. Moreover, the oldest Jewish cemetery in Manhattan lies just south of the square.

142.2 prejudice against Jews] Mark Twain's own opinions of Jews and the nature of and reasons for prejudice against them are most fully discussed in his article, "Concerning the Jews," first published in *Harper's Monthly* magazine for September 1899. The section of "Stormfield" featuring Solomon Goldstein was probably written sometime between mid 1905 and early June 1906. An excellent discussion of Twain's opinions may be found in Sholom Kahn's "Mark Twain's Philosemitism: 'Concerning the Jews,'" *Mark Twain Journal*, 23 no. 2 (Fall 1985): 18–25.

142.33 loss my little taughter] The loss of a child was especially poignant to Mark Twain because of the death of his eighteen-month-old son Langdon in 1872 and of his daughter Susy in 1896. See also the later episode (and accompanying note) near the end of chapter 3, which features a mother searching for her child who had died in infancy.

Chapter 2

144.14 weather bow] The side of the ship's bow, or prow, that is turned toward the direction from which the wind is blowing.

144.22 marlin-spike] A sharp-pointed iron tool used to separate the strands of a rope for splicing.

144.37 persuadest me to pe a Ghristian."] Here Solomon Goldstein echoes King Agrippa's comment in Acts 26:28 after hearing Paul's account of his own conversion and its aftermath.

Chapter 3

147.34–35 Encke's and Halley's comets] In 1819, Johann Franz Encke (1791–1865) proved that the apparently different comets of 1786, 1795, 1805, and 1818 were actually the same one, and that comet thereafter was named for him. Halley's comet was likewise named for its discoverer, English astronomer Edmund Halley (1656–1742). In 1704, in calculating the orbits of 24 comets beginning with that of 1337, Halley discovered that three of them—in 1531, 1607, and 1682—were almost identical and predicted that comet's return in 1758. His calculations were verified by the reappearance of the comet in 1759, 1835, and 1910. In his own copy of Amédée Guillemin's *The Heavens: An Illustrated Handbook of Popular Astronomy*, which he bought in Munich in December of 1878, the year it was published, Clemens drew a marginal line next to the first two of the paragraphs discussing Halley's comet (p. 243; copy in MTP).

Halley's comet was of particular interest to him, for not only was it in the sky in 1835, but it reached its perihelion (the point nearest the sun) on 16 November 1835, just two weeks before his birth on 30 November. And Paine reports that during a discussion of astronomy in July of 1909 Clemens remarked that he had "come in" with Halley's comet, which was "coming again next year," and that he hoped to "go out" with it (*MTB* 3:1511). His wish was granted when, in 1910, the comet made its spectacular reappearance. Even more remarkably, this time the perihelion occurred just one day before his death on 21 April.

148.8 three points off my starboard bow] In nautical terms "points" refer to the 32 divisions of horizontal direction as indicated on the card of a compass, or measured in reference to the direction a ship is heading. Each "point" indicates a distance of 11 degrees, 15 minutes. "Starboard" is the right side of the ship, when one faces the bow.

148.9 north-east-by-north-half-east] Since "north-east by north" is 11 degrees, 15 minutes north of due northeast, "by north half east" would be 5 degrees, 35 minutes north of due northeast.

148.35 "Pipe the stabboard watch] That is, starboard watch—the group of sailors responsible for the right side of the ship. The "pipe" is a whistle with which the boatswain (bosun, or bo's'n, an officer in charge of rigging, anchors, cables, etc.) signals various activities.

148.37–38 royals and sky-scrapers] See note to "Reef tops'ls and sky-scrapers," above.

149.2 stuns'ls] Studding sails. Light sails set at the side of a larger or principal sail in free winds to increase the ship's speed.

149.2–3 from stem to rudder-post] That is, from the bow or prow of a ship to the stern post, a timber that extended from the keel to the deck, and to which the rudder was attached.

149.17 bound to beat this one] Stormfield's race with the comet, and especially the comet captain's commands, strongly resembles the steamboat race featured in chapter 4 of *The Gilded Age* (1873), which in turn was doubtless inspired by the race and collision between the *Pennsylvania* and the *Vicksburg* on 26 November 1857 (Michael H. Marleau, "'The Crash of Timbers Continued—the Deck Swayed under Me': Samuel L. Clemens, Eyewitness to the Race and Collision between the *Pennsylvania* and the *Vicksburg*," *Mark Twain Journal* 28, no. 1 [Spring 1990]: 1–36). In "A Curious Pleasure Excursion" (New York *Herald*, July 6, 1874; *Sketches, New and Old* [1875]), presumably concerned with the dangers of such races, Mark Twain's prospectus for a cosmic tour by comet assures its potential passengers that, though they may be traveling at 40,000,000 miles a day, they will take all proper precautions, "and we shall rigidly prohibit racing with other comets."

150.5 eighteen hundred thousand billion quintillions of kazarks] A "kazark," which Stormfield learns equals "the bulk of *a hundred and sixty-nine worlds like ours*," is obviously a coined term. Since a quintillion is a unit followed by 18 zeros, Mark Twain's hyperbolic number here would be 1,800,000,000,000,000,000,000,000,000,000 kazarks.

150.14 after-davits] Cranes projecting over the side of the rear area of the ship for hoisting cargo, boats, and the like.

155.32 *o revoor*] *Au revoir*. French for "till we meet again."

156.1 Pi Ute Injun] The Piutes or, more properly, Paiutes, were a Shoshonian group, inhabiting several western states including California, Nevada,and Utah. Mark Twain mentions the "Pi-Utes," among other tribes, in a letter of 20 March 1862, ostensibly to his mother but designed for publication in his brother's newspaper, the Keokuk *Gate City* of 25 June 1862 (*Letters1*, 174–80). There he satirizes romanticizing of Indians by writers like James Fenimore Cooper, as he would later do in *Roughing It* (1872).

156.2 Tulare county] Tulare County is in California, largely in the Sierra Nevada mountains southeast of Fresno.

157.32 Sam Bartlett] Perhaps an invented name, but possibly borrowed from Samuel Colcord Bartlett (1817–98), distinguished Congregational clergyman, author, and president of Dartmouth College from 1877 to 1892, noted for his lectures on "The Bible and its Relations to Science and Religion."

159.8–9 different from her own wax-figger.] These words end manuscript page 62, the last page of the beginning section. A single unnumbered page follows, written on the long dimension of the sheet in pencil, and framed by a wavy line. Suggesting an illustration, it reads as follows:

Map of Section No. *4,785 696* of Heaven—showing position of our world—also, smallness of our world as compared with that division of Heaven. A map of *all* heaven, drawn to this scale would stretch in all directions farther than any star visible through the most powerful telescope is removed from us,—say 5600000000000 miles long and wide.

(A school map of our own system would be *12 miles* long, to include Neptune & Uranus; so Proctor says.)

The Wart—enlarged slightly beyond its just size, to make it be seen with the naked eye.

(quoted by Browne, *MTQH*, 36, n. 25. In the ms. the last sentence is near the bottom of the page.)

"Proctor" was undoubtedly Richard A. Proctor (1837–88), author of a number of popular books on astronomy in the 1870s and later. We have been unable to locate the exact reference.

159.14–15 Sandy McWilliams.] Mark Twain used the name McWilliams in three other stories written close to the same period in which he wrote present chapters 3 and 4: "Experiences of the McWilliamses and the Membranous Croup" (1875), "Mrs. McWilliams and the Lightning" (1880), and "The McWilliamses and the Burglar Alarm" (1882). He doubtless borrowed the name from a friend, John J. McWilliams, a bookkeeper in the Buffalo branch of Jervis Langdon's coal company. The use of his friend's name in the McWilliams stories, as well as in the present one, suggests considerable affection for McWilliams and his wife, who befriended Clemens during the early days in Buffalo, before his marriage to Olivia Langdon (*Mark Twain Society Bulletin*, 12, no.2 [July 1989]: 1, 3). The name Sandy could have been suggested by Clemens's memories of a slave boy who had worked for his family in Hannibal (*MTA*, 101–2, 127–28; *HH&T*, 50), or of an attorney friend in Nevada, Sandy Baldwin (Alexander W., 1840–69; *Letters1*, 275, 280, n.11, 318, 365.

162.6 hunting for her child!] Besides the much longer version of this episode which he had originally included in "Stormfield" (see appendix 5b), featuring a Mildred Rushmore as the mother, Twain also described "a young mother whose little child disappeared one day and was never heard of again, and so her heart was broken" in a segment of "No. 44, The Mysterious Stranger" written in 1908 (*MSM*, 402); and in 1910, in the last extended piece of writing he ever did (included in this volume as "Etiquette for the Afterlife: Advice to Paine") he adapted a notebook entry of January 1897 that described a mother looking down from heaven, seeing her lost child in hell.

Chapter 4

163.21 sail pretty close to the wind] That is, close to the direction from which the wind is blowing.

163.26 shorten sail—like reefing] That is, to reduce the area of sail by rolling or folding part of it and fastening it to or around the yard or spar.

163.27–28 lay to, with your head to the wind] In the case of a ship: to stop its motion, with the bow facing into the wind.

163.32 manna and quails] An appropriate heavenly menu. In Exodus 16:13–15 God provided manna and quails to feed the children of Israel in the wilderness.

165.9 wishing-carpet of the Arabian Nights] A means of transportation featured notably in "The History of Prince Ahmed," one of Scheherezade's tales in *The Thousand and One Nights*, sometimes called *Arabian Nights Entertainments*, a collection of Arabic and other eastern tales, handed down by word of mouth for hundreds of years. This was one of Clemens's favorite books (see Gribben, 1:26). As he often did with things he liked, Mark Twain burlesqued these tales in "1002d Arabian Night," which he wrote in the early summer of 1888 (first published in *S&B*, 88–133).

165.24 Moody and Sankey] Preacher Dwight Lyman Moody (1837–99) and singer and organist Ira David Sankey (1840–1908) were probably the most famous evangelists of the last quarter of the nineteenth century in both America and Britain.

166.18 Brooklyn preacher . . . Talmage] Thomas De Witt Talmage (1832–1902) was for many years minister of the Central Presbyterian Church in Brooklyn. A popular preacher, he regularly contributed to the New York *Independent*, a religious weekly. In early 1870 Mark Twain's antipathy had been aroused by a quotation from Talmage in the Chicago *Advance* for 6 January, in which the Brooklyn preacher seemed to be arguing that the cultured among his parishioners would be offended by the odors if forced to sit near working-people. Enraged, Mark Twain excoriated Talmage for his elitism in a piece entitled "About Smells," in the *Galaxy* magazine for May 1870.

Actually, the *Advance*, an unfriendly rival weekly, in order to discredit the *Independent*, had quoted out of context a paragraph from Talmage's discussion of a current controversy over whether there should be free pews in the church (*Independent*, 9 December 1869). Talmage in fact favored free pews, but was trying to conciliate advocates of both sides of the issue through gentle satire. His chief argument was that each side had a right to a preference, but neither had the right to impose it on the other. Hence he was really caricaturing those who advocated exclusiveness. But even after he read the whole article, Mark Twain would not apologize. Rather he sought to justify himself (in the Buffalo *Express* for 9 May 1870) by criticizing Talmage for ambiguity and other stylistic faults. And the treatment of Talmage here makes it obvious that his antipathy was long-lasting (see *WIM*, 48–50 and notes).

166.24 Abraham, Isaac, and Jacob] Abraham, a descendent (in the 9th generation) from Shem, Noah's eldest son, was the first patriarch and ordained by God to be the progenitor of the Hebrews. Isaac, son of Abraham and Sarah, was the father of Jacob, whose twelve sons became ancestors of the twelve tribes of Israel (Genesis 12:17–Genesis 50; Exodus 1–6).

167.20 Job] A contemporary of Abraham; Job's life and suffering constitute the biblical Book of Job.

167.21 Ham and Jeremiah] Ham was the youngest of Noah's three sons, in some traditions considered the ancestor of the Egyptians and other North African peoples. Jeremiah was one of the four major biblical prophets (along with Isaiah, Ezekiel, and Daniel).

167.22–23 Charles Peace's . . . Bannercross Murderer] Charles Peace (1832–79), a notorious burglar, escaped after murdering Arthur Dyson at Bannercross, England, on 29 November 1876, and eluded capture until 10 October 1878. Before his execution on 25 February 1879, he also confessed to killing a policeman, thus freeing a man who had been wrongfully convicted of the crime (Frederic Boase, *Modern English Biography*, 6 vols. [London: Frank Cass & Co., 1965], 2:1,410). The Clemenses were traveling in Italy at the time of Peace's capture, and were just completing an extended stay in Munich when the execution occurred (*N&J2*, 48). The fact that Sandy says that the reception of Peace occurred "a year or so ago" suggests that this section of "Stormfield" was written in 1880 or 1881. In chapter 47 (vol. 2, chap. 18 in Author's National Edition of *A Tramp Abroad* [1880]), also, Mark Twain sarcastically tells of a condemned murderer who, while awaiting the gallows, " 'got religion'—after the manner of the holy Charles Peace, of saintly memory." Twain was obviously struck by the ironies of this sort of "eleventh-hour conversion." He had earlier satirized such happenings in "Lionizing Murderers" (*A Curious Dream and Other Sketches* [London: Routledge, n.d. (1872)]; *Sketches New & Old* [1875]), and, close to the same time as the "Stormfield" segment, in "Edward Mills and George Benton: A Tale," written between late January 1879 and early June 1880 (*Atlantic Monthly*, August 1880).

167.25 Captain Kidd] William Kidd (1645?–1701). Notorious British pirate who became legendary through tales of his buried treasures, which were never recovered. In 1897 Kidd was given command of a privateer, and commissioned to capture pirates preying on British shipping. According to his story, famine and disease caused his crew to mutiny, and to save himself, he was forced to turn to piracy. Tried in London, he was convicted of murder and piracy, though the evidence was inconclusive, and was hanged there in 1701.

168.36 Cabinet of Russia] Sandy errs here in referring to a "Cabinet." During the nineteenth century in Russia, the nearest thing to our cabinet was the Council of State, established in 1810 and composed of a number of elder statesmen, appointed as closest advisers to the emperor (Seton-Watson, 105).

168.37 Prince Gortschakoff] Prince Alexander Mikhailovich Gorchakov (1798–1883), also spelled Gortchakoff or Gorschakov. A career diplomat and one of the top statesmen of nineteenth-century Europe, Gorchakov served under Tsar Alexander II (1818–81; reigned 1855–81) as foreign minister, vice-chancellor, and chancellor of the Russian Empire (*Modern Encyclopedia of Russian and Soviet History*, 13:44–45).

169.36 slush-boy] On shipboard, the cook's assistant, who cleans up used or spilled grease and cooking-fat (*Slang and Its Analogues, Past and Present*, 7:260).

170.9 Billings] A character name possibly inspired by Josh Billings (the pseudonym of Mark Twain's fellow humorist and friend, Henry Wheeler Shaw [1818–1885]). Characters named Billings appear (with different given names) in some eight other Mark Twain stories. Here Billings is also a poet who, though unrecognized on earth, wrote poetry greater than that of Shakespeare. Ben Harris McClary has noted, without arguing for specific influence, that Herman Melville, in chapter 1 of *Moby Dick* (1851), also refers to a "poor poet from Tennessee" (McClary, 63–64).

170.9 horse-doctor named Sakka from Afghanistan] In Hindu and Indo-Chinese mythology, Sakka (also Sakra or Sek-ya) corresponds to Indra, the foremost deity in the oldest sacred Hindu writings (called the Veda); a warlike god of sky and storms ("Indo-Chinese Myths and Legends" in *The Mythology of All Races*, ed. Louis Herbert Gray [Boston: Marshall Jones, 1918], 12:285). There may possibly be a connection, however, with the Sakyas, the warrior caste tribe of northeast India and Tibet into which the Buddha was born. See following note.

170.10 Buddha] Gautama Buddha (ca. 563–483 B.C.), the founder of Buddhism, was a prince named Siddhartha from northern India who renounced all worldly goods to follow a life of study, meditation, and teaching. His teachings won him the title of Sage of the Sakyas (Sakya-muni), referring to his birth tribe.

170.12 Daniel] Biblical prophet during the Babylonian captivity, probably most remembered for his experience in the lion's den. See Book of Daniel.

170.12 Confucius] Long known in China as Kung Fu-tse, Confucius (551–479 B.C.) was a philosopher whose teachings influenced the civilization of all of eastern Asia. Confucianism emphasized personal virtue, devotion to family (including the spirits of one's ancestors), education, and justice.

170.13 Ezekiel, Mahomet, Zoroaster] Ezekiel was one of the great biblical prophets (Book of Ezekiel). Mahomet, Muhammad, or Mohammed (ca. 570–632 A.D.) was the founder and chief prophet of Islam, the religion of the Moslems (or Muslims), whose visions are recorded in the Koran, the holy book of Islam. Zoroaster (Greek form of Zarathustra), founder of Zoroastrianism, was a Persian religious leader, who according to tradition lived for 77 years from the late 7th century to mid 6th century B.C.

170.15–16 shoemaker named Marais] Mark Twain probably borrowed this name from the Quartier du Marais in Paris. He would have been particularly interested in the Musée Historique de la Ville in that Quartier, for its collection is devoted to the history of Paris and particularly to the French Revolution. The Clemenses lived in Paris from 28 February until 19 July 1879 and from early November 1894 until early May 1895, and, particularly during the earlier stay, made a special study of sites connected with the Revolution; many of these, including the Place de la Bastille, were in the Quartier du Marais. Moreover, since *marais* is the French word for "swamp," the name would be appropriate for a genius of lowly birth.

171.5 mudsill] Literally, the lowest sill, block, or timber supporting a building at or below ground level. The sense, here, of a person of low social status is enhanced by the original meaning current during the nineteenth century, pertaining only to bridges: the sill that is laid at the bottom of a river, lake, etc. (*American Dictionary of the English Language*, Springfield: George and Charles Merriam, 1863).

171.20 Saa, Bo, and Soof] Possibly invented names, but Mark Twain could well have been playing with the first syllable of two famous earthly men, as well as a religious philosophy. We are grateful to Mrs. Jane Gladden for this suggestion.

Saadi (or Sadi) Muslih-ud-Din (1184?–1291) was one of the most famous Persian poets, best known for collections called the *Gulistan* or Rose Garden, and the *Bustan* or Tree Garden. Mark Twain owned a copy of *The Gulistan; or, Rose Garden, by Musle-Huddeen Sheik Saadi of Shiraz* (trans. by Francis Gladwin, biographical essay by James Ross, preface by Ralph Waldo Emerson, [Boston: Ticknor and Fields, 1865]), signed on the pastedown front endpaper, "S. L. Clemens, Hartford, 1875" (Gribben, 2:597). According to Emerson's preface (p. iii), this was the first translation of an Eastern poet to appear in America.

"Bo" could have been derived from Bohaddin, or Baha Al-Din (1186–1258), an Arabian serving as secretary and court poet in the Egyptian government and noted for his polished and delicate verse (*Webster's Biographical Dictionary*, 88), or perhaps from "Bodhisattva" (literally "enlightenment being," i.e., "Buddha-to-be," a term often used by Buddha to describe himself in early years.

"Soof" seems to suggest "Sufi," one who practices the Islamic mystical philosophy "Sufism," which developed principally in Persia beginning as early as the eighth century, and is still prevalent in Islamic countries. Its symbolism was widely used by Persian poets, including Saadi and also Omar Khayyam (1050?–1123?), whose *Rubaiyat*, as translated by Edward Fitzgerald, was one of Mark Twain's favorite works from the late 1870s for the rest of his life. Interestingly, though the spelling "Sufi" appears a number of times in both introduction and text of the *Gulistan*, in Tale XXV (p. 192), the Sheik of Damascus is asked about the condition of "the sect of the *Soof*ies" (our italics). His reply, too, might well have struck Mark Twain's interest: "They formerly were, in the world, a society of men apparently in distress, but in reality contented; but now they are a tribe in appearance satisfied, but inwardly discontented."

171.30 Longfellow] Henry Wadsworth Longfellow (1807–82) during his lifetime and for some years thereafter was probably the most famous American poet both at home and abroad.

172.5 screw a glass into their eye] This passage reflects one of Mark Twain's attitudes toward tourists and pompous observers of other sorts, especially among the British. In a journal kept during his first trip to England in 1872, he described a visit to the Doré Gallery, where he was particularly taken with the excellence of Doré's *Christ Leaving the Praetorium*. Overhearing a monocled Englishman pronouncing the work, "capetal" (capital), he sneered at the English use of that term to indicate approval on almost every occasion, often in circumstances preposterously out of place, and suggested that anyone who would praise Doré's great painting so inadequately would very likely "screw his window glass into his eye and admire the day of judgment" (quoted in Baetzhold 1970, 21).

173.16 off Sandy Hook] Sandy Hook, in east-central New Jersey about 15 miles south of the southern tip of Manhattan Island, is a six-mile-long peninsula enclosing Sandy Hook Bay on the west, and is the site of a famous lighthouse.

173.17–18 up the Bay] The heavenly equivalent of New York Bay.

174.18 Aztecs] An Indian people of central Mexico, the Aztecs established an empire there during the fourteenth and fifteenth centuries, before being conquered by the Spaniards under Cortés in 1521.

174.36–38 touring . . . write a book of travels] This passage reflects Mark Twain's reactions to the many books about the United States, often uncomplimentary, written by British tourists during the first half of the nineteenth century. See especially chapter 27 of *Life on the Mississippi* (1883).

175.25 Digger Injuns] A name originally applied to one Paiute tribe, the only such tribe to practice agriculture. In time it came to designate instead a number of root-eating Paiute tribes in several western states, including California, Nevada, and Utah. Because these root-eaters were considered a low type of Indian, the epithet rapidly became a term of scorn (Frederick Webb Hodge, ed., *Handbook of American Indians North of Mexico*, Smithsonian Institution Bureau of American Ethnology Bulletin No. 30, 2 parts [Washington, D.C.: Government Printing Office, 1912], 1:390). Mark Twain also referred to Digger Indians—uncomplimentarily—in chapter 19 of *Roughing It* (1872).

175.34–35 look at a Frenchman . . . indelicate] French "indelicacy" was a particular bugbear of Mark Twain. See especially *N&J2*, 307–26, *passim*, and "The French and the Comanches," one of several chapters on French civilization omitted from *A Tramp Abroad* (1880), first published in *LE*, 183–89. And early in August 1880, in a notebook entry containing his first use of the name Stormfield, he wrote:

> Early, in heaven Stormfield is delighted with the social equalities—a nigger, a ⟨Chinaman,⟩ Digger, an Esquimaux, & a ⟨nasty Frenchman⟩ Fejeean invite themselves to dinner with him —"if we had another animal or two we could start a menagerie." Next time, they bring also an orang-outang. "The ⟨mag⟩ menag. progresses." Next time they bring also a Frenchman. "The menagerie is complete" says Stormy. But next time they brought also a French married lady. "This is carrying it too far; this will not answer; I have read enough French novels to know that a French married lady cannot enter even a menagerie without bringing the purity

of that menagerie under suspicion." It was proposed to ⟨bring⟩ substitute a French maiden of 12, or one of 75. "No, it would not be best for the menagerie. The French confess, by the strict guard they keep ⟨of⟩ over their maidens of all ages, ⟨& all stages of⟩ that they cannot be trusted. Their novels are everywhere—nothing could prevent their girls from reading them; they do read them; consequently, whilst they are chaste in body, through compulsion, they are unchaste in mind. Let us keep the menagerie pure, from the American point of view, not the French. ⟨No, we will have no⟩ That is to say, let us have real, not sham, purity."

The menag. continued to grow, till it had in it cannibals, Presbyterians, pariahs, politicians, ⟨teetotalers,⟩ Turks, tramps,—indeed, all sorts of disagreeable people; & they all called him 'Brother Stormfield' & kept falling on his neck & weeping down his back in pious joy. Finally he said "Heaven is a most unpleasant place; there is no privacy in it. I must move" (*N&J2*, 368–69).

176.4 one Langland] William Langland (perhaps ca. 1330–86), a contemporary of Chaucer, was the author of *Piers Plowman*, one of the greatest works in Middle English. Both the original manuscript and the January 1908 *Harper's* edition of "Stormfield" at this point read "Mr. Spenser," that is, Edmund Spenser (ca. 1552–99), the English poet most famous for his long allegory, *The Faerie Queene* (1590, 1596). When preparing the 1909 book version, however, Mark Twain apparently realized, or was advised, that Spenser did not write "back of Elizabeth's time," but was a contemporary, and so chose the medieval author Langland as one of the "old-time poets."

176.4 Chaucer] Geoffrey Chaucer (ca. 1343–1400), the greatest author of the Middle English period of literature, is most famous for his masterpiece, *The Canterbury Tales* (designed ca. 1387).

176.24 Charles the Second] Charles II (1630–85) ruled Great Britain from 1660 to 1685. For Mark Twain he and his several mistresses became vivid symbols of royal profligacy.

176.28 Richard the Lion-hearted] Richard I, or Richard Coeur de Lion (1157–99) reigned for ten years (1189–99), though he was in England for only six months during that time. A leader of the Third Crusade, he became a romantic hero in England through such works as the Robin Hood legends and Sir Walter Scott's *Ivanhoe* and *The Talisman*.

176.29 Henry the Eighth] Henry VIII (1491–1547), who ruled England from 1509 until his death, became legendary both because of his break with the Church of Rome and, more so, by marrying six wives, one of whom died, two of whom were executed, and two of whom he divorced.

176.30 Henry the Sixth] Henry VI (1421–71), king in England from 1422–61 and 1470–71, was an ineffective leader, more interested in religious and educational matters than in affairs of state. His reign was marked by civil war and other strife, and by his own mental breakdown. After his death—he was murdered in the Tower of London—he was venerated as a saint by the populace because of his many virtues, and in Henry VII's reign, there was even begun a process for his canonization.

176.32 Napoleon] Napoleon Bonaparte (1769–1815), the French emperor, born on the island of Corsica, who ruled from 1804 to 1811, and again for 100 days in 1815, was one of the world's greatest military geniuses. At the peak of his power, his armies had conquered most of Europe.

177.5 Caesar] Gaius Julius Caesar (100–44 B.C.), great Roman general and statesman, whose campaigns (described in his *Commentaries*) and subsequent leadership laid the foundations for some six centuries of imperial rule.

177.5 Alexander] Alexander the Great (356–323 B.C.), king of Macedon, eventually conquered most of the Middle East and territories eastward to India.

177.8 Absalom Jones] The first black priest in the Episcopal Church, Absalom Jones (1746–1818), was born a slave in Sussex, Delaware, and at sixteen was taken to Philadelphia where he worked in his master's store, educated himself during the evenings, and eventually bought his freedom in 1784. Together with Richard Allen, he became a lay preacher for the black members of St. George's Methodist Episcopal Church. When their efforts increased the black membership considerably, church officials decided to segregate all blacks to the church balcony. As a result the blacks left the church, and Jones and Allen organized the "African Church." Ultimately Allen and a few others affiliated once more with the Methodists, but Jones and the majority favored the Episcopal Church, to which the African Church was joined in 1794 as St. Thomas African Episcopal Church. Jones was ordained deacon the same year, served well, and was admitted to the priesthood in 1804. Since there were no state-supported schools for negroes at the time, he soon established one. He was also an active Mason, an abolitionist, and a devoted worker for improvement of conditions for blacks in Philadelphia (*Dictionary of American Negro Biography*, 362–63).

If Mark Twain knew of Jones's career, he made an excellent choice of names for his supreme military genius, for Absalom Jones was a superb organizer. If not, he probably chose the name Jones because of its commonness in contrast to the other universally known great generals. Some have suggested that the first name, Absalom, may have been borrowed from Clemens's old acquaintance Absalom "Ab" Grimes, whom he encountered during his own Civil War experience, as described in "The Private History of a Campaign that Failed" (*Century*, December 1885). There Mark Twain mentions seeing Grimes, "an Upper Mississippi pilot, who afterwards became famous as a dare-devil rebel spy," among another group of recruits.

In May 1907, when news of the death of Jim Gillis reminded him of his California friend's genius for story-telling, he remarked in his autobiographical dictation on the 26th that great numbers of geniuses "live and die undiscovered—either by themselves or others," and continued:

> I have touched upon this matter in a small book which I wrote a generation ago and which I have not published as yet—*Captain Stormfield's Visit to Heaven.* When Stormfield arrived in heaven he was eager to get a sight of those unrivaled and incomparable military geniuses, Caesar, Alexander and Napoleon, but was told by an old resident of heaven that they didn't amount to much there as military geniuses, that they ranked as obscure corporals only by comparison with a certain colossal military genius, a shoemaker by trade, who had lived and died unknown in a New England village and had never seen a battle in all his earthly life. He had not been discovered while he was in the earth, but heaven knew him as soon as he arrived there, and lavished upon him the honors which he would have received in the earth if the earth had known that he was the most prodigious military genius the planet had ever produced" (*MTE*, 360).

Mark Twain dictated this passage some seven months after he had entered "Stormfield" into the *Autobiography.* It may, of course, have been a simple lapse of memory, but it is interesting that he should have recalled his "military genius" as a *shoemaker.* In the story, Absalom Jones is a "bricklayer from somewhere back of Boston." But early in the 1900s Mark Twain did describe another great military genius, the "shoemaker-prodigy," who appears in both "Autobiography of Eve and Diaries Antedating the Flood," and "Passage from 'Outlines of History' (suppressed.)."

177.16 Hannibal] The great Carthaginian general Hannibal (247–183 B.C.) is most remembered for crossing the Alps with elephants to attack the Romans in Italy.

177.18–19 off quarantine] Quarantine originally was a period of time, usually 40 days, during which a ship suspected of carrying an infectious disease must refrain from landing at or from any intercourse with a port. Later, to avoid a waiting period, a ship's medical officer could attest to the ship's being free of contagion. Being "off quarantine" therefore indicates that the ship has been properly cleared.

178.17 "We long to hear thy voice . . .] Mark Twain probably created this hymn for the occasion. If the lines are from an actual hymn, the original has not been identified.

179.11 Moses and Esau] Moses, a prophet and the lawgiver of Israel, led the Israelites out of Egypt to the borders of the Promised Land (See Exodus, Leviticus, Deuteronomy, and Numbers). Esau was the son of Isaac and twin brother (though born first) of Jacob. Here he is an archangel, even though on earth he had sold his birthright to Jacob for "a mess of pottage" (Genesis 25:25–34).

179.28 scribble their names on it.] These are the last words on page 114 of the American Academy manuscript. There follows an unnumbered page (in TS numbered 1187 [82], with "m" of "whom" corrected to "who"). That passage, doubtless deleted from the *Harper's Monthly* proof, reads: "[The bar-keeper sinks into immediate obscurity instead of being and remaining the lion of heaven—& moreover, has to do 30 weeks penance in carrying torches and shouting nightly to do honor to other incoming scrubs who he wishes had gone to hell.]"

Chapter 5

180.12–17 Professor Higgins . . . astronomical professor of astronomy at Harvard] Higgins was a favorite fictional name, which Mark Twain used in at least 19 works, possibly influenced by his vivid memory from Hannibal days of a one-legged slave named Higgins, who belonged to the Garth family (*Tom Sawyer and Huck Finn Among the Indians and Other Unfinished Stories*, 324–25). At this time, however, he perhaps was remembering the famous astronomer William Huggins (1824–1910) whose name he would have encountered fairly often in the books of astronomy that he read. The actual "astronomical professor" at Harvard at the time was Charles Edward Pickering (1846–1919), who directed its observatory from 1876 to 1919. The following discussion of light-years, however, almost certainly resulted from Mark Twain's reading (probably close to the time he wrote this segment) in *Sidelights on Astronomy and Kindred Fields of Popular Science* (New York: Harper, 1906) by Simon Newcomb (1835–1909), who superintended the American Nautical Almanac office in Washington from 1877 until his death and (1884–93) was professor of mathematics and astronomy at Johns Hopkins. See also notes to headnote of "Stormfield."

180.16 tell me his game . . . look at my hand] Stormfield here borrows his metaphor from card playing.

180.22 dead soldiers drawing pension] During the early 1900s Mark Twain often referred to abuses of the pension system for war veterans, notably in "Passage from 'Outlines of History' (suppressed.)" included in this volume, and in a passage from the Autobiographical Dictations, 15 January 1907, which Bernard DeVoto titled "Purchasing Civic Virtue" (*MTE*, 66–70).

181.10 "Six thousand million miles"] This should read "Six thousand billion." Here Mark Twain may have misread his own calculations in Newcomb's book, for after multiplying out the astronomer's observation that the distance traveled in a light-year would equal about 63,000 times the distance from the earth to the sun, his product came to 5,859,000,000,000. And a few lines below, he wrote: "Is it about 6,000,000,000^000 (six thousand billion)^ miles, a light-year?"

(*MTB*, 3:1,510). The last three zeros of the figure and "(six thousand billion)" he added above the line with a caret.

181.13–14 *four* light-years . . . to the nearest star] The star nearest to earth is Alpha Centauri, 4.3 light-years distant.

181.30 any 'Gates Ajar' proportions] Again a slap at Elizabeth Stuart Phelps's best-seller, which though it does not envision a heaven nearly as vast as Mark Twain's, does posit a heaven much larger than the "heavenly city, the New Jerusalem" described in *Revelation* (21:16) as being "twelve thousand furlongs" (1,500 miles) on a side.

181.36 try an asterisk, or asteroid] In planning an acceptance speech for an honorary Master of Arts from Yale in 1888, Mark Twain wrote, in part:

> "I found the astronomer of the University gadding around after comets (& things?) instead of attending to business. I told him pretty plainly that we couldn't have that. I told him ⟨that⟩ it was no economy to go piling up & piling up raw material in the way of new stars & comets & trash that we couldn't ever have any use for till we had worked up the old stock. I said if I caught him scouring around after any more ⟨of⟩ asteroids, especially, I should have to scour him out of the place. Privately, prejudice got the best of me there, I ought to confess it. I don't mind comets so much, but ⟨from my earliest⟩ somehow I have always been down on/never could stand asteroids. To my mind ⟨theyre only just⟩ there's nothing mature about them—only just pups/whelps out of some planet. Well, then, of course it annoyed me to hear him say he preferred asteroids to anything else,/they were just pie to him, & I said it was pretty degraded taste. . . . I said it was pretty low-down business for great universities to be in—Rochester always raking the deeps of space for comet spawn & trading it to Yale for ⟨asteroids⟩ planet pups" (*N&J3*, 472).

182.13 Gulliver's Lilliput people] The tiny people encountered by Gulliver in "A Voyage to Lilliput," part one of Jonathan Swift's *Gulliver's Travels* (1726), a book Mark Twain knew well (See Gribben, 2:679–81).

182.21 noblest work of God] In his autobiographical dictation for 5 April 1906, Mark Twain "furnished a sentiment in response to a man's request—to wit:

> 'The noblest work of God?' Man.
>
> 'Who found it out?' Man" (*MTA*, 2:316).

182.25–28 savage country that needed civilizing . . . went there . . . and civilized it . . . generally with Bibles and bullets] This detail reflects the attitudes toward imperialism, which Mark Twain had earlier expressed in works published in the *North American Review:* "To the Person Sitting in Darkness" (February 1901), "To My Missionary Critics" (April 1901), and "In Defence of General Funston" (April 1902). One of his most damning unpublished attacks during that period was "The Stupendous Procession," written in January or February 1901 (*FM*, 403–19). See also Gibson 1947, 435–70.

Chapter 6

183.8 Slattery] Mark Twain may well have borrowed this name from Martin J. Slattery, a printer involved in the testing of the Paige typesetting machine 1889–91 (*N&J3:* 547, 568, 593).

Captain Simon Wheeler's Dream Visit to Heaven

The copy-text for this sketch is a passage from "Simon Wheeler, Detective," *Mark Twain's Satires & Burlesques*, edited by Franklin R. Rogers (Berkeley: University of California Press, 1967), 432–37. We have supplied the title.

192.6 shad-belly coat] A coat that sloped smoothly and gradually from the neck to the skirt in a line presumably resembling the belly of a shad. Drab coats of this sort were often worn by Quakers, who were hence called, usually as a term of contempt, "shad-bellies" (*Dictionary of Americanisms*). Mark Twain also later used the term as a nickname for John Wharton "Shad-belly" Billson, deacon of the church and one of the nineteen "incorruptibles" in "The Man that Corrupted Hadleyburg" (first published in *Harper's*, December 1899) and for Shadbelly Higgins, one of a gang of toughs in "A Double-Barrelled Detective Story" (first published in *Harper's*, January and February, 1902).

A Singular Episode: The Reception of Rev. Sam Jones in Heaven

The manuscript in the Mark Twain Papers is copy-text for "A Singular Episode." The story was first printed as "The Late Rev. Sam Jones's Reception in Heaven" in *Mark Twain's Quarrel with Heaven*, edited by Ray B. Browne (New Haven, Conn.: College and University Press, 1970), 111–16.

198.16 Archbishop of Canterbury] In 1891, the Archbishop of Canterbury was Edward White Benson, who served in that capacity from 1883 to 1896. In 1897, the internal date of the story, Frederick Temple was archbishop, having assumed the position the year before. He served until 1902. In "Mental Telegraphy?" (1907) Mark Twain wrote:

> I was ever so fond of that "Reception" article and dearly wanted to print it, but it was hilarious and extravagant to the very verge of impropriety, and I could not beguile my wife into consenting to its publication. In that day Sam Jones was sweeping the South like a cyclone with his revival meetings and converting the unconverted here and there and everywhere with his thundering torrents of piety and slang. I represented him as approaching the New Jerusalem in the through express, and in the same pullman in which he and his feet together were occupying two chairs, sat his grace the late Archbishop of Canterbury (Mr. Tait), and I.

At the time Mark Twain wrote the sketch, Archibald Campbell Tait (1811–62), archbishop from 1868 to 1882, had been "late" for some nine years.

201.30–31 Pope Alexander VI . . . Torquemada . . . Catherine de' Medici] Of these symbols of cruelty and intrigue, Rodrigo de Borja y Doms (1431?–1503) served as Pope Alexander VI from 1492 to 1503. He holds a high place on the list of the so-called "bad popes." He was the father of the ruthless Cesare Borgia [1475 (or 76)–1507] and the infamous (perhaps unjustly) Lucrezia Borgia (1480–1519). Tomas Torquemada (1420?–98), adviser to Ferdinand and Isabella of Spain, became inquisitor general of Castile and Aragon in 1483, and then of Léon, Catalonia, Valencia, and Majorca, and was charged with centralizing the Spanish Inquisition. His reputation for cruelty resulted from the harsh rules of procedure that he established and from the rigor of their enforcement. The number of burnings at the stake during his regime, somewhat fewer than 2,000, were at one time thought to be some 8,800. Catherine de' Medici (1519–89), daughter of

Lorenzo de' Medici ("Il Magnifico"), Duke of Urbino, and Madeleine de la Tour d' Auvergne, was Queen Consort of France, with Henri II (1547–59), from 1560 to 1574. She was most notorious for the persecution of the Huguenots, particularly her part in planning the St. Bartholomew's Day Massacre (1572).

202.13 the papal Borgias] The Borgias were a Spanish-Italian noble family, originally from Aragon. Shortly after becoming pope, Alfonso de Borgia (1378–1458), Cardinal-Archbishop of Valencia, went to Rome as Pope Calixtus III (1455), with other members of his family following. Some 34 years after Alfonso's death his nephew Rodrigo became Pope Alexander VI. Mark Twain's reference here would probably include Alexander VI's illegitimate children, Cesare and Lucrezia, the former famous for his ruthlessness in eliminating rivals and Lucrezia (though most of the allegations have been disproved) for her participation in poison plots and for incestuous relations with her father and brother.

Mental Telegraphy?

Copy-text for "Mental Telegraphy?" is the manuscript in the Mark Twain Papers. This sketch was first published in 1970 by Ray B. Browne in *Mark Twain's Quarrel with Heaven* (117–19). It was also reprinted, along with Shaw's "Aerial Football: the New Game," by Rodelle Weintraub, in " 'Mental Telegraphy': Mark Twain on G.B.S.," *The Shaw Review*, 17, no. 2 (May 1974): 68–77.

205.2 sketch by Bernard Shaw] Shaw's "Aerial Football: the New Game" was published in England in *The Neolith* for November 1907, dated at the end, probably by Shaw, "July 31, 1907." Mark Twain and Shaw had lunched on the third of that same month, but, as Twain later says in the sketch, they had not spoken of "Stormfield" or "Sam Jones."

205.2–3 Collier's Weekly] Founded by Peter F. Collier in 1888, the magazine soon became an important illustrated literary and critical journal and, in the first two decades of the twentieth century, a leading liberal and muckraking voice. Thereafter it concentrated more on popular fiction and articles for a general audience, and was until the early 1950s widely popular. Hard times thereafter forced it to cease publication in 1957 (Mott, 453–70).

205.5–6 Once I wrote an account . . . uncultivated old seaman] See headnote to "Captain Stormfield's Visit to Heaven" for the course of composition of that story.

205.8 "The Gates Ajar"] A best-selling novel by Elizabeth Stuart Phelps, copyright 1868, but issued early in 1869. See headnote and notes to "Captain Stormfield's Visit to Heaven."

205.11 Dean Stanley] Arthur Penrhyn Stanley (1815–81), dean of Westminster Abbey from 1863 until his death, was a prolific writer, famous in both literary and religious circles as perhaps the leading liberal clergyman of his times.

206.6–7 remarkable episode of about 1875] In "Mental Telegraphy," mentioned in the headnote, Mark Twain described how he and his old friend from Nevada days, William Wright ("Dan DeQuille"), had almost simultaneously in March 1875 conceived of a book that would tell the story of "the Great Bonanza" following the discovery of the Comstock Lode (silver) in Nevada. Although he "stretched" some of the dates just a bit, the coincidences of that experience were indeed remarkable. Subsequently, Wright came to Hartford in June 1875, where the pair worked together every day (Twain was finishing *Tom Sawyer*) until he completed *The History of the Big Bonanza* sometime that August. Wright's book, with an introduction by Mark Twain, was published in Hartford the following year by Twain's publisher, the American Publishing Company. The fullest account of this joint venture is in Oscar Lewis's introduction to the A. A. Knopf reprint of *The Big Bonanza* (New York, 1947).

206.28 late Archbishop of Canterbury (Mr. Tait)] Archibald Campbell Tait (1811–82), head of the Anglican Church from 1869 to 1882 and one of the most famous and influential of all the archbishops of Canterbury. See also notes to "A Singular Episode."

Etiquette for the Afterlife: Advice to Paine

The copy-text for this piece is the manuscript in the George N. Meissner Collection, Washington University, St. Louis, Missouri.

208.5–6 "Hochwohlgeborene"] German: "High born," hence, "Honorable." In the manuscript after this word, which comes at the end of a line, there are four lines of a shorthand which, translated, read as follows:

> The Assyrian came down like the wolf [MT has "rollf"] on the fold,
> And his cohorts were gleaming with purple and gold,
> And the sheen of his spears was like stars on the sea,
> When the blue wave rolls nightly on deep Galilee.

These are the opening lines from Byron's "The Destruction of Sennacherib," Mark Twain's favorite stanza from a favorite poem, slightly misquoted ("with" for "in" in l. 2; "his" for "their" in l. 4). As he told readers of the *Alta California* in 1867, he had learned the piece by heart in Hannibal, its rhythmic lines having been impressed upon his mind "by the usual process, a trifle emphasized." It is perhaps natural, then, that he found a place for it among the "Examination Evening" declamations in chapter 21 of *Tom Sawyer* (1876). He also quoted from the poem on a number of other occasions, both humorous and serious (Baetzhold 1970, 280). But why these lines occurred to him at this point, and why he included them here—in shorthand—remains a mystery. Our thanks to Lin Salamo and Michael Frank of the Mark Twain Project for providing this translation.

209.17–18 Send the Lyon-Ashcrofts a fan] The objects of this satiric jibe were Isabel V. Lyon (1868–1958), Clemens's personal secretary since 1903, who also increasingly managed the running of his household, and Ralph W. Ashcroft, whom he had hired in 1907 as business manager. The pair married in 1909, primarily—so Isabel Lyon later claimed—to remove any suspicion of alleged improprieties between herself and Clemens. Meanwhile, Clara Clemens, possibly because of jealousy—and on very flimsy evidence—accused these trusted friends (to whom Clemens had given his power of attorney) of mismanaging her father's affairs and embezzling his money. Though Clemens resisted her arguments for a time, Clara finally convinced him that the two were scheming to swindle him out of all his wealth. Much bitterness followed, which Clemens partially spilled out in a 427-page diatribe cast as a letter to Howells, the "Ashcroft-Lyon Manuscript" (MTP). Reciprocal lawsuits further increased the animosity, which, as evidenced here, lasted for the rest of his life. Interestingly enough there seems to be no real proof of serious wrongdoing or evil intent on the part of Lyon and Ashcroft. (For a fuller account of this matter, see Hill, 218–43).

209.19 Explain to Helen] Helen was Helen Allen, daughter of William H. Allen, United States vice-consul to Bermuda, and one of the "Angel-fish" in Mark Twain's "Aquarium Club" of teenage girls. Clemens first became acquainted with Helen when she was 13, during one of his 1908 trips to Bermuda (25 January–6 February; 27 February–11 April), but came to know her much better on successive trips in 1909 (21 November–18 December) and 1910 (7 January–12 April), when the Allens prevailed upon him to stay at their home. For further information see Cooley, *Mark Twain's Aquarium*, 267–81 passim.

209.31 throw herself over . . . to join her child] Sometime in January 1897, at a time when he was also engaged in writing a tribute to his daughter Susy who had died the preceding summer, Mark Twain jotted the following into his notebook:

> Write a novel in which part of the action takes place in heaven & hell, the rest upon earth. Let a woman in heaven watch the sweep of the ocean of fire at close quarters—a person passes by at very long intervals only, the ocean is so large. It is a solitude—so is heaven. She has sought her daughter for a long time—she is watching hell, now, but not expecting her daughter to be there. Musing, she hears a shriek & her daughter sweeps by—there is an instant of recognition by both—the mother springs in, perceiving that there is no happiness in heaven for her any longer (quoted by Browne, *MTQH*, 72, n.6, from Notebook 41 [formerly 32aI, Jan 7–June 15, 1897], TS p. 3, MTP).

209.37 isn't the place for humor.] One of the maxims from *Pudd'nhead Wilson's New Calendar* notes: "Everything human is pathetic. The secret source of Humor itself is not joy but sorrow. There is no humor in heaven" (epigraph, chapter 10, *Following the Equator* [1897]).

Letters from the Earth

The text in this volume is that of the printing in *What Is Man? and Other Philosophical Writings*, edited by Paul Baender, 401–54. Baender's text is based on two manuscripts in the Mark Twain Papers, each paginated separately. The title is taken from the second manuscript; the first is untitled. An asterisk after the page and line number in the following annotations designates notes (occasionally slightly modified) from Baender's edition; the other notes were developed for the present edition.

221.13–14 since in heaven a day is as a thousand years] For biblical sources see 2 Peter 3:8 ("one day with the Lord is as a thousand years") and Psalms 90:4 ("For a thousand years in thy sight are but as yesterday when it is past, and as a watch in the night"). See also the related treatment in the segment from "Schoolhouse Hill" and its accompanying note.

227.22–27 This Bible . . . told you about] Mark Twain expands on this idea in the segment from the "Autobiographical Dictations" dated 10 June 1906. See the notes for that selection.

228 *footnote* the nearest star] Mark Twain's error. The star labeled 61 Cygni is the fourth closest star to the sun at a distance of 11.2 light-years. Alpha Centauri, at a distance of 4.3 light-years, is the closest. Arcturus, the fourth brightest star in the sky and the brightest in the northern hemisphere, is 36 light-years distant. Baender partially corrects Twain's error in his notes to "Letters from the Earth" (n. 578), but mistakenly suggests Twain's reading of Samuel G. Bayne's *The Pith of Astronomy* (1896) in 1909 as the source of Mark Twain's knowledge of light-years and the distance of Alpha Centauri. Actually, Twain's knowledge almost certainly resulted from his reading of Simon Newcomb's *Sidelights on Astronomy and Kindred Fields of Popular Science* (1906). For a related treatment of Mark Twain's fascination with the concept of a light-year, see "Captain

Stormfield Resumes" (180.26–181.30), along with the accompanying expanded explanatory note.

229.16–17 he said that if they ate of it they should surely die] Genesis 3:3—"But of the fruit of the tree which is in the midst of the garden, God hath said, Ye shall not eat of it, neither shall ye touch it, lest ye die." Cf. "Autobiography of Eve" (57.30–31) and "Passage from Satan's Diary" (63.1).

229.36 Moral Sense] For a discussion of Twain's attitude toward the Moral Sense, see note to "Passage from Satan's Diary" (66.14).

230.19–23 In that memorable moment . . . . They have entered it modest] See Genesis 3:7–8.

231.30–31* forgive them seventy-and-seven times] See Matthew 18:22—"Jesus saith unto him, I say not unto thee, Until seven times: but, Until seventy times seven."

232.23–25 the sweeter sex . . . hot young blossoms] Specifically refers to a frequently cited ambiguous passage in Genesis 6:1–2—"And it came to pass, when men began to multiply on the face of the earth, and daughters were born unto them, That the sons of God saw the daughters of men that they were fair; and they took them wives of all which they chose." This passage appears to be one of those which Paul uses as his source to argue that women should wear veils in church "because of the angels" (I Corinthians 11:10), perhaps a harkening back to the passage in Genesis, which, in Jewish tradition, is the basis for the fall of the angels, brought about because of the demonic angels' lust for human women.

233.13–29 He saved out Noah . . . land animals could not drink it] For the story of Noah, see Genesis 6:5–9:29. See also "Adam's Soliloquy" for a similar treatment of this story from Noah's point of view.

234.6* Symmachus] Quintus Aurelius Symmachus (d. 405) was a Roman senator. See, for example, Ludwig Friedländer, *Roman Life and Manners under the Early Empire* (London: G. Routledge & Sons, [1908]–1913), 2: 33–34.

234.16* it was Titus] See Suetonius, *The Lives of the Twelve Caesars*, Bohn's Classical Library (London, 1876), 470. A copy with Mark Twain's marginalia is in MTP.

235.25–26 They all got drowned . . . eight million years ago] Twain continues to question not only the biblical account of the Flood, but also the actual account of creation here by suggesting that the dinosaurs and other creatures existed long before the time of biblical creation.

237.20* I the Lord thy God am a jealous God] Exodus 20:5—"Thou shalt not bow down thyself to them, nor serve them: for I the Lord thy God am a jealous God, visiting the iniquity of the fathers upon the children unto the third and fourth generation of them that hate me."

237.32* "Thou shalt have no other gods before me"] Direct citation from Exodus 20:3.

239.3 Disease! that is the main force, the diligent force, the devastating force] For Twain's preoccupation with the presence of diseases in the world, compare similar treatments in "Adam's Soliloquy," "Diaries Antedating the Flood," and the selections from the "Autobiographical Dictations" in this volume.

240.19* Constipation, O constipation] Based upon the lines of Reginald Heber's "From Greenland's icy mountains":

> Salvation! oh, Salvation!
> The joyful sound proclaim,
> Till each remotest nation
> Has learn'd Messiah's name!

Heber's hymn was one of Twain's favorites. In *Following the Equator* (chapter 55), he quoted the opening lines and said they were "beautiful verses, and . . . have remained in my memory all my life."

241.4 minister plenipotentiary] a principal diplomatic agent ranking below an ambassador, but possessing full power and authority as the representative of his government or seat of government.

242.9* Eye that never sleeps] Probably an allusion to the slogan of the Pinkerton Detective Agency, "We Never Sleep," which commonly appeared beneath a large open eye on the covers of Allan Pinkerton's books. Twain had burlesqued Pinkerton many years earlier; see "Simon Wheeler, Detective" (in *S&B*, 307) and "Tom Sawyer's Conspiracy" (in *HH&T*, 152).

242.35* Dr. Charles Wardell Stiles] A zoologist, Stiles (1867–1941) discovered the cause of hookworm disease in 1902 and from 1909 to 1914 served on the Rockefeller Commission for Eradication of Hookworm Disease in the southern states.

243.2* This morning's journals] From a public statement by the Rockefeller Commission. The quotation is in a clipping from the New York *Sun*, 29 October 1909, p.1, pinned to the manuscript leaf. The closing phrase—"with God's help"—was Mark Twain's addition, and he changed "in fact largely due" to "in fact due."

244.3* Science has this to say] Source unknown; the quotation is in Twain's hand. Sleeping sickness was a common news topic in that period, for the cause of the disease had recently been discovered, and there were serious epidemics in Africa. Starting in 1903 the Sleeping Sickness Commission of the Royal Society issued a series of reports, from which Mark Twain's immediate source probably derived. See *Reports of the Sleeping Sickness Commission*, no. 2 (London: Harrison and Sons, 1903), pp. 18–19.

244.22* *Man's* inhumanity to man] From Robert Burns, "Man Was Made to Mourn." Compare *MTN*, p. 344: "God's inhumanity to man makes countless thousands mourn."

248* *footnote*] The princess was Victoria Kamamalu (1838–66). For details of her funeral see *Roughing It* (chapter 68), and *MTH*, 328–34, 348–61. In an 1866 notebook Twain wrote: "Pr. V. died in forcing abortion—kept half a dozen bucks to do her washing, and has suffered 7 abortions" (*N&J1*, 129).

249.7–8 Solomon . . . 300 concubines] I Kings 11:3—"And he had seven hundred wives, princesses, and three hundred concubines: and his wives turned away his heart."

250.4 Noah planted a vineyard . . . was overcome.] Genesis 9:20–21—"And Noah began to be an husbandman, and he planted a vineyard: And he drank of the wine, and was drunken; and he was uncovered within his tent."

252.3* And Israel abode in Shittim] Numbers 25:1—"And Israel abode in Shittim, and the people began to commit whoredom with the daughters of Moab." The verse following in the text is a direct citation from Numbers 25:4.

252.30* And the Lord spake unto Moses] Through verse 47 (with some verses missing) the quotations are from Numbers 31. They are in pages from a book of biblical selections which Mark Twain attached to the manuscript.

254.15* When thou comest nigh] This and the next four verses in the text are from Deuteronomy 20. Through the first half of verse 15 they are from the same book of biblical selections; the rest is in Mark Twain's hand.

254.28* *Thou shalt not kill*] Directly cited from Exodus 20:13.

255.3* the conduct of one Onan] Genesis 38:9–10—"And Onan knew that the seed should not be his; and it came to pass, when he went in unto his brother's wife, that he spilled it on the ground, lest that he should give seed to his brother. And the thing which he did displeased the Lord: wherefore he slew him also."

255.32* I will cut off from Jeroboam] I Kings 14:10—"Therefore, behold, I will bring evil upon the house of Jeroboam, and will cut off from Jeroboam him that pisseth against the wall, and him that is shut up and left in Israel, and will take away the remnant of the house of Jeroboam, as a man taketh away dung, till it be all gone."

255.35* The same with the house of Baasha] I Kings 16:11—"And it came to pass, when he began to reign, as soon as he sat on his throne, that he slew all the house of Baasha: he left him not one that pisseth against a wall, neither of his kinfolks, nor of his friends."

256.16* Thou shalt have a paddle] Direct citation of Deuteronomy 23:13. The following verse is from Deuteronomy 23:14.

257.33* Père Hyacinth] Charles Jean Marie Loyson (1827–1912), commonly known as Père Hyacinth, before 1870 a well-known Carmelite, resigned his Church positions in protest against the decree of Papal Infallibility (1870). In 1872, with episcopal dispensation, he married an American widow. Thereafter, in Europe and America, he continued to be a popular lecturer and writer on religious and secular subjects. The charges adduced by Twain have not been found in his works.

258.19* Twelve Indians broke into a farm house] The source was probably Col. Richard Irving Dodge's account of a very similar episode in *The Plains of the Great West and Their Inhabitants, Being a Description of the Plains, Game, Indians, Etc. of the Great North American Desert* (New York: G.P. Putnam's Sons, 1877), 420–22. A copy with Twain's marginalia is in the Redding (Connecticut) Public Library. See also note to related passage in "From the Diary of a Lady of the Blood, Third Grade" (73.10).

259.9* Blessed are the poor in spirit] The group of verses is from Matthew 5:3–11.

Appendix 1 Original Continuation of "Autobiography of Eve"

(There are no notes for appendices 2, 3, 4, and 5)

The copy-texts for the material in boldface type are deleted passages from the original manuscript of "Autobiography of Eve" in the Mark Twain Papers.

264.14–265.23 From all the islands . . . she was dead.] The description of the outpouring of condolences, and the kindly feelings they inspired, both in their sincere and satiric elements, doubtless reflect the Clemenses' own responses after the loss of their daughter Susy in 1896. In fact, on a cover of a Par Value tablet containing some of his working notes for the "Autobiography of Eve," Twain printed "SUSY" in capital letters, later scribbling over it with pencil lines. Tuckey mistakenly included these notes among the Working Notes for "Eddypus" (which deals with the related theme of the fall of the Great Civilization and the rise and dominance of Christian Science. See *FM*, 471–72).

265.17–18 Adam is gone from us, now] Shows that Twain was then still proceeding from the present time of 1012 AC when Adam was dead. Later, he changed the time to 920 in the portions of the manuscript which he retained in order to have Eve's story told roughly ten years before Adam's death in 930.

265.37 I was talking with Reginald Selkirk, the Mad Prophet] This conversation of Eve with Selkirk (original manuscript pages 68–78) was recast to incorporate part of Selkirk's original discussion about the problems of overpopulation as "Extracts from an Article in 'The Radical.'" Then—or at least some time during the restructuring process—Twain pinned the bottom half of the original p. 78 to a new sheet which he labeled "C," numbered "78—(page 1 of this)" and provided the new title "From the Diary of a Lady of the Blood, Third Grade" (i.e., one in the third generation of direct descent, hence a great-grandaughter of Adam and Eve. In the new version, then, the "Lady of the Blood," instead of Eve, receives and listens to the exhortations of the Mad Prophet. Throughout the text, the Prophet is variously called the Mad Philosopher, the Mad Prophet, the Philosopher, Reginald Selkirk, and in "Passage from a Lecture," Angina Pectoris. In that piece someone else, probably DeVoto when preparing it for the "Papers of the Adam Family" in *Letters from the Earth*, changed "Angina Pectoris" to "Reginald Selkirk."

271.28 Your civilization has brought the flood . . . before the rains begin?] See Genesis 6:1–8:22 for the full treatment of Noah and the Flood.

272.15 bone of my bone, flesh of my flesh] Cf. Genesis 2:23—"And Adam said, This is now bone of my bones, and flesh of my flesh: she shall be called Woman, because she was taken out of Man."

273.32 Peerpontibusmorganibus] Another of Twain's use of wildly extravagant names and puns, here a play on the name of J. Pierpont Morgan and, as mentioned in a related note to the "Autobiography of Eve," his reputation for collecting large numbers of books and manuscripts, which were ultimately placed in the Pierpont Morgan Library in New York City.

273.35 found a clover] The reference to clover and other notations here clearly indicate that the group of Mark Twain's planning notes, referred to earlier, belong to the "Autobiography of Eve" rather than to "Eddypus" as Tuckey had thought (*FM*, 471–72). Those notes begin: "Clover. Be another flood and others. Average of life 1000 yr. Geology shows 1,000,000 years—fossils to tell its age by. Webster, Snakspeer, Appolyon Prodigy, Pitt." See appendix 2 for full text.

Appendix 6 Discussion of the Fall from "Schoolhouse Hill"

The copy-text for this selection is the segment on pages 251–57 of *Huck Finn and Tom Sawyer Among the Indians and Other Unfinished Stories*, Mark Twain Library Edition, which reprints (and slightly emends) "Schoolhouse Hill" as published in *Mark Twain's Mysterious Stranger Manuscripts*, edited by William M. Gibson.

307.8 The boy] The boy's name, as he has told Hotchkiss, is Quarante-quatre, or Forty-four. Working notes for this story indicate that he was only one of the myriads of offspring of Satan, and that Twain thought of calling him "404" or "94" or "No. 45 in New series 986,000,000," before settling on Forty-four. The significance, if any, that these numbers had for Twain, has not been satisfactorily explained (see *MSM*, 435–36, 444, 472–73).

308.10 "A day, with us, is as a thousand years with you."] For biblical sources see 2 Peter 3:8 ("one day is with the Lord as a thousand years") and Psalms 90:4 ("For a thousand years in thy sight are but as yesterday when it is past, and as a watch in the night"). Twain included this notion of the disparities of time between the two realms in "From Captain Stormfield's Reminiscences," one of the last episodes of "Stormfield," and would develop it further in "Letters from the Earth."

310.5–6 *man is prone to evil as the sparks fly upward*] Compare Job 5:7—"Yet man is born unto trouble, as the sparks fly upward."

311.28 phonographic shorthand system.] Twain probably had in mind *A Manual of Phonography, or, Writing by Sound*, by Isaac Pitman, the Englishman who invented that form of shorthand. The first of many American editions of Pitman's manual was published in 1844. The system is still in use today (see Gribben, 2:548).

Appendix 7 God of the Bible vs. God of the Present Day (1870s)

Copy-text for this piece is the manuscript in the Mark Twain Papers. Though Albert Bigelow Paine published three paragraphs of this essay in *Mark Twain: A Biography* (1:412–13), it is here first published in full.

315.1–3 earth and moon . . . 400,000 miles . . . eleven miles] In the manuscript after "eleven" Paine added "hundred" (above the line, with a caret) but did not change Twain's text when he quoted the passage in the *Biography*. Instead, to explain the error, he provided a footnote, which read: "His figures were far too small. A map drawn on the scale of 400,000 miles to the inch would need to be 1,100 miles long to take in both the earth and the nearest fixed star. On such a map the earth would be one-fiftieth of an inch in diameter—the size of a small grain of sand" (1:412).

We also have retained Mark Twain's original text. Although Mark Twain erred in making 400,000 miles the distance from the earth to the moon (about 221,600–252,950 miles at its nearest and farthest points), the distance from Earth to Alpha Centauri, the nearest fixed star—about 23.5 trillion miles—is fairly close (in astronomical terms) to the 20 trillion miles mentioned later in the essay (see note to "20 trillions . . ." below). In that later passage in the manuscript Paine changed Mark Twain's "20 trillions" to "26 trillions" (though he did not ultimately use that passage in the *Biography*). Perhaps he made the change to make his earlier emendation (the "eleven ^hundred^ miles") more accurate, for to represent 26 trillion miles at 400,000 miles to the inch, the map would actually have to be 1,025.8 miles long—pretty close to 1100. If the distance were 20 trillion miles, however, the map would have to be only 789 miles long. In any case Mark Twain's estimate for the size of the map was very wrong.

315.29–30 unfair in punishing Adam . . . could not know it was wrong.] This argument shows that by the early 1870s Mark Twain had already adopted the view of Adam's and Eve's guiltlessness that he would develop much more fully in the "Passage from Satan's Diary" and "Passage from Eve's Diary" in the "Autobiography of Eve and Diaries Antedating the Flood" and in "Letters from the Earth."

316.7 ark was a peculiarly fantastic device.] Mark Twain would continue to argue the irrationality of the account of the flood. See especially "Adam's Soliloquy" and "Letters from the Earth."

316.38 star-light created . . . 50,000 years before it was needed] This detail, probably based on the article "The Early History of Man" mentioned in the headnote (*Eclectic Magazine*, 11 [January 1870]: 112–14), repeats the similar time-span cited in the 8 January 1870 letter to Livy quoted in the introduction to this volume.

317.9–12 twenty trillions of miles away. To merely *count . . . four hundred thousand years.*] Mark

Twain originally placed the distance of the nearest fixed star (Alpha Centauri) at "twenty trillions of miles." This is the place where Paine later changed the figure to twenty-six by adding above the line (with a caret) "six trillions." But whether at 20 or 26 trillion, Mark Twain, as he had with the size of the map, drastically underestimated the time involved for counting the miles. He had been somewhat closer, at first, for he had originally written "five hundred thousand years" but then changed it to "four." At the rate specified, however, it would take 791,476.4 years to count to 26 trillion (26,000,000,000,000), or 608,828 years to count to 20 trillion.

Appendix 8 Selected Passages on God and the Bible from Autobiographical Dictations of June 1906

The copy-text for these dictations is the typescript in the Mark Twain Papers. These dictations were first published in "Reflections on Religion," edited by Charles Neider, *The Hudson Review*, 16 (Autumn 1963), 329–52.

319.18 Nero and Caligula] Emperors of Rome known for their deeds of atrocity. Nero (Lucius Domitius Nero Claudius Caesar), the sixth emperor, who reigned fourteen years from A.D. 54 to 68, murdered his own mother and was held responsible for the conflagration of Rome in A.D. 64. He died in A.D. 68 at the age of 31. Caligula, or "little boots," at first was a moderate ruler but became a bloodthirsty, vicious tyrant and mass murderer after an illness (possibly epilepsy) that affected his sanity. During his four-year reign he declared himself a god. Caligula was assassinated in A.D. 41 at the age of 29.

319.29 To Adam is forbidden the fruit of a certain tree . . . he shall die.] See Genesis 2:17—"But of the tree of the knowledge of good and evil, thou shalt not eat of it; for in the day that thou eatest thereof thou shalt surely die."

322.11 Immaculate Conception] A belief of the Catholic church that the Virgin Mary was free from original sin from the beginning of her life, understood here as her conception. She was, by a unique grace, preserved from ever contracting original sin; she inherited human nature in an untainted condition and hence is said to be conceived immaculate, making her a suitable mother for Christ. As Bernard DeVoto has noted, "throughout Mark Twain's writing, he confuses the doctrine of the Immaculate Conception with that of the Virgin Birth of Christ" (*MTE*, 317). Though we have retained Mark Twain's title of this dictation, we have omitted his comments on the Immaculate Conception because they are not pertinent to the theme of this volume. See "Reflections on Religion," *Hudson Review* 16 (Fall 1963): 335–38.

322.18 We borrow the Golden Rule from Confucius] The Christian statement of the golden rule is from Jesus' Sermon on the Mount, Matthew 7:12—"Therefore all things whatsoever ye would that men should do to you, do ye even so to them: for this is the law and the prophets" (see also Luke 6:31). Confucius (Chinese philosopher 551–479 B.C.) put it somewhat negatively: "What do you not like if done to yourself, do not to others."

322.20 hoary Babylon] Babylon was the capital of southern Mesopotamia from the early second millennium to the early first millenium B.C., divided at that time by the Euphrates River. The Babylonian flood myth is of Sumerian origin, based on historical floods of 4000 B.C. and 3300 B.C. According to the myth the gods Enu and Enlil (Heaven and Earth) planned to drown mankind. Another god, Enki, discovered the plan and revealed it to a man, instructing him to build an ark.

322.31–32 distant Neptune is merely an outpost] During Twain's lifetime Neptune was the farthest-known planet from the sun, discovered in the autumn of 1846 by the French astronomer Urbain Jean Joseph Leverrier (1811–77). He named the planet Neptune because of its supposedly sea-green color. Leverrier's calculations leading to the assumption that a planet existed beyond Uranus were confirmed by Johann Gottfried Galle (1812–1910) of the Berlin Observatory on 23 September 1846. John Couch Adams (1819–92), an English astronomer, had made the same calculations with the same results some months earlier, but unfortunately his superiors at the time neglected to act on the matter until after Leverrier's figures were published.

Twain mentions these men in "Mental Telegraphy" (1891), and in "The New Planet" (1909) humorously discusses the "perturbations" which led to the discovery of Neptune. A. B. Paine remarks that Clemens was excited by reports in 1909 that additional perturbations of Neptune suggested the presence of a new planet: "Clemens said that heretofore Neptune, the planetary outpost of our system, had been called the tortoise of the skies, but that comparatively it was rapid in its motion, and had become a near neighbor" (*MTB*, 3:1,542). It was not until 1930, however, that the new planet was actually discovered and named Pluto.

323.7 Sirius] A star of the constellation of Canis Major, the brightest star in the heavens; also called "Dog Star."

323.7 choose our potato for a footstool] Compare Matthew 5:35–36—"Swear not at all; neither by heaven; for it is God's throne: Nor by the earth; for it is his footstool."

324.16 When Mr. Garfield lay near death] James A. Garfield (1831–1881), 20th president of the United States, elected in November 1880, served only four months of his term before being shot while at the Washington, D.C., railroad station on 2 July 1881. He lived until 19 September 1881, retaining presidential power until his death. Whether or not he was officially incapacitated (as prescribed by constitutional guidelines) was never determined, leaving the country under questionable governance.

324.25–29 The Boer population . . . South Africa the victory.] Boer: a South African of Dutch or Huguenot descent. The Boer War (or South African War), 12 October 1899–31 May 1902, was waged between Great Britain and two Boer (Afrikaner) republics, the South African Republic and the Orange Free State. British troops outnumbered the Boers 500,000 to 88,000. Early victories went to the Boers, but the British sent in reinforcements, and the Boers sued for peace in March 1901, finally accepting the loss of their independence in the Peace of Vereeniging in May 1902.

329.12 King Leopold II, the Butcher] Leopold (1835–1909), King of the Belgians from 1865 to 1909, led the first European efforts to develop the Congo Basin, founding the Association Internationale du Congo in 1876 to open the region for exploration. In 1884–85, he defeated an Anglo-Portuguese attempt to conquer the Congo Basin and gained recognition as the sovereign of the État Independent du Congo (Congo Free State), an area eighty times the size of Belgium. He was criticized for his cruel treatment of the natives involved in the lucrative rubber industry. Mark Twain expressed his horror and anger at Leopold's atrocities in *King Leopold's Soliloquy: A Defence of His Congo Rule*, issued as a pamphlet in September 1905 by the Congo Reform Association, with proceeds going to the association. See the headnote to "Adam's Soliloquy" for additional discussion of Twain's views on this and related subjects.

WORKS CITED

Works by Mark Twain

The Autobiography of Mark Twain. Ed. Charles Neider. New York: Harper, 1959.

Early Tales & Sketches. Volume 1, 1851–1864. Ed. Edgar M. Branch and Robert H. Hirst. Berkeley: U of California P, 1979.

Early Tales & Sketches. Volume 2, 1864–1865. Ed. Edgar M. Branch and Robert H. Hirst with the assistance of Harriet Elinor Smith. Berkeley: U of California P, 1981.

Europe and Elsewhere. Ed. Albert Bigelow Paine. New York: Harper, 1923.

Extracts from Adam's Diary. New York: Harper and Brothers, 1904.

Frear, Walter F. *Mark Twain and Hawaii*. Chicago: Lakeside P, 1947. [Contains all of Mark Twain's letters to the Sacramento *Union*.]

Huck Finn and Tom Sawyer Among the Indians and Other Unfinished Sketches. Ed. Dahlia Armon and Walter Blair. Berkeley: U of California P, 1989.

Letters from the Earth. Ed. Bernard DeVoto. New York: Harper, 1962.

The Love Letters of Mark Twain. Ed. Dixon Wecter. New York: Harper, 1949.

Mark Twain, Business Man. Ed. Samuel L. Webster. Boston: Little Brown, 1946.

Mark Twain in Eruption. Ed. Bernard DeVoto. New York: Harper, 1940.

Mark Twain–Howells Letters. 2 vols. Ed. Henry Nash Smith and William M. Gibson, with the assistance of Frederick Anderson. Cambridge: Harvard University P, 1960.

Mark Twain to Mrs. Fairbanks. Ed. Dixon Wecter. San Marino, Calif.: Huntington Library, 1949.

Mark Twain Speaking. Ed. Paul Fatout. Iowa City: U of Iowa P, 1976.

Mark Twain's Autobiography. Ed. Albert Bigelow Paine. 2 vols. New York: Harper, 1924.

Mark Twain's Correspondence with Henry Huttleston Rogers 1893–1909. Ed. Lewis Leary. Berkeley: U of California P, 1969.

Mark Twain's Fables of Man. Ed. John S. Tuckey. Berkeley: U of California P, 1972.

Mark Twain's Hannibal, Huck & Tom. Ed. with an introduction by Walter Blair. Berkeley: U of California P, 1969.

Mark Twain's Letters. 2 vols. Ed. Albert Bigelow Paine. New York: Harper, 1923.

Mark Twain's Letters to His Publishers. Ed. Hamlin Hill. Berkeley: U of California P, 1967.

Mark Twain's Letters to Mary. Ed. with a commentary by Lewis Leary. New York: Columbia University P, 1961.

Mark Twain's Letters. Volume 1: 1853–1866. Ed. Edgar Marquess Branch, Michael B. Frank, Kenneth M. Sanderson, Harriet Elinor Smith, Lin Salamo, and Richard Bucci. Berkeley: U of California P, 1988.

Mark Twain's Letters. Volume 2: 1867–68. Ed. Harriet Elinor Smith, Richard Bucci, and Lin Salamo. Berkeley: U of California P, 1990.

Mark Twain's Letters. Volume 3: 1869. Ed. Victor Fischer, Michael B. Frank, and Dahlia Armon. Berkeley: U of California P, 1992.

Mark Twain's Mysterious Stranger Manuscripts. Ed. William M. Gibson. Berkeley: U of California P, 1969.

Mark Twain's Notebook. Ed. Albert Bigelow Paine. New York: Harper, 1935.

Mark Twain's Notebooks & Journals. Volume 1 (1855–1873). Ed. Frederick Anderson, Michael B. Frank, and Kenneth Sanderson. Berkeley: U of California P, 1975.

Mark Twain's Notebooks & Journals. Volume 2 (1877–1883). Ed. Frederick Anderson, Lin Salamo, and Bernard L. Stein. Berkeley: U of California P, 1975.

Mark Twain's Notebooks & Journals. Volume 3 (1883–1891). Ed. Robert Pack Browning, Michael B. Frank, and Lin Salamo. Berkeley: U of California P, 1979.

Mark Twain's Quarrel with Heaven. Ed. Ray B. Browne. New Haven: College & University P, 1970).

Mark Twain's Satires & Burlesques. Ed. Franklin R. Rogers. Berkeley and Los Angeles: U of California P, 1967.

Mark Twain's Travels with Mr. Brown. Ed. Franklin Walker and G. Ezra Dane. New York: Knopf, 1940.

Mark Twain's Which Was the Dream? and Other Symbolic Writings of the Later Years. Ed. John S. Tuckey. Berkeley: U of California P, 1967.

Report From Paradise. Ed. Dixon Wecter. New York: Harper, 1952.

Sketches, New & Old. Hartford: American Publishing Company, 1875.

What Is Man? and Other Philosophical Writings. Ed. Paul Baender. Berkeley: U of California P, 1973.

Other Works Cited

Baetzhold, Howard G. "Found: Mark Twain's 'Lost Sweetheart.'" *American Literature,* 44 (November 1972): 414–29.

———. *Mark Twain and John Bull: The British Connection.* Bloomington: Indiana UP, 1970.

Baetzhold, Howard G., Joseph B. McCullough, and Donald Malcolm. "Mark Twain's Eden/Flood Parable: The 'Autobiography of Eve'." *American Literary Realism,* 24 (Fall 1991): 23–38.

Bartlett, John. *Familiar Quotations.* 12th ed. Boston: Little, Brown, 1951.

Brashear, Minnie M. *Mark Twain: Son of Missouri.* Chapel Hill: U of North Carolina P, 1934.

Browne, Ray B. "Mark Twain and Captain Wakeman." *American Literature,* 33, no. 3 (November 1961): 320–29. [See also *Mark Twain's Quarrel with Heaven,* above.]

Budd, Louis J., ed. *A Listing of and Selection from Newspaper and Magazine Interviews with Samuel L. Clemens, 1874–1910.* Arlington, Tex.: American Literary Realism, 1977.

Cooley, John, ed. *Mark Twain's Aquarium: The Samuel Clemens Angelfish Correspondence, 1905–1910*. Athens: U of Georgia P, 1991.
Cummings, Sherwood. *Mark Twain and Science: Adventures of A Mind.* Baton Rouge: Louisiana State UP, 1988.
Dictionary of American Negro Biography. Ed. Rayford W. Logan and Michael R. Winston. New York: Norton, 1982.
Emerson, Everett. *The Authentic Mark Twain.* Philadelphia: U of Pennsylvania P, 1984.
Ensor, Allison. *Mark Twain and the Bible.* Lexington: U of Kentucky P, 1969.
Gibson, William M. *The Art of Mark Twain.* New York: Oxford UP, 1976.
———. "Mark Twain and Howells: Anti-Imperialists." *New England Quarterly*, 20 (December 1947): 435–70.
Gribben, Alan. *Mark Twain's Library: A Reconstruction.* 2 vols. Boston: G. K. Hall, 1980.
Guillemin, Amédée Victor. *The Heavens: An Illustrated Handbook of Popular Astronomy.* Ed. Norman Lockyer, rev. by Richard Proctor. London: Richard Bentley & Son, 1878.
Hill, Hamlin. *Mark Twain God's Fool.* New York: Harper & Rowe, 1973.
"Indo-Chinese Myths and Legends" in vol. 12 of *The Mythology of All Races.* Ed. Louis Herbert Gray. Boston: Marshall Jones, 1918.
Kahn, Sholom. "Mark Twain's Philosemitism: 'Concerning the Jews'," *Mark Twain Journal*, 23, no. 2 (Fall 1985): 18–25.
Kurian, George Thomas. *Historical and Cultural Dictionary of India.* Metuchen, N. J.: Scarecrow P, 1976.
Mason, John A. *The Ancient Civilizations of Peru.* New York: Penguin, 1968.
McClary, Ben Harris. "Melville, Twain, and the Legendary 'Tennessee Poet.'" *Tennessee Folklore Society Bulletin*, 29 (September 1963): 63–64.
McCullough, Joseph B., and Donald Malcolm. "Mark Twain's Creation Myths: 'Captain Stormfield' and 'Letters from the Earth.'" *Studies in American Humor*, 2 and 3 (Summer–Fall, 1986): 168–76.
Modern Encyclopedia of Russian and Soviet History. Ed. Joseph L. Wieczynski. New York: Academic International P, 1979.
Mott, Frank Luther. *A History of American Magazines 1885–1905.* Cambridge: Harvard UP, 1957.
New Dictionary of Quotations. Ed. H. L. Mencken. New York: Knopf, 1942.
Paine, Albert Bigelow. *Mark Twain: A Biography.* 3 vols. New York: Harper, 1912.
Pringle, Henry F. *Theodore Roosevelt: A Biography.* New York: Harcourt, Brace, and World, 1956 (orig. pub. 1931).
Quick, Dorothy. *Enchantment: A Little Girl's Friendship with Mark Twain.* Norman: U of Oklahoma P, 1961.
Racevskis, Karlis. *Voltaire and the French Academy.* Studies in the Romance Languages and Literatures 4. Chapel Hill: U of N. Carolina P, 1975.
Roske, Ralph J. *Everyman's Eden: A History of California.* New York: Macmillan, 1968.
Schultz, Stanley K., and Clay MacShane. "To Engineer the Metropolis: Sewers, Sanitation, and City Planning in Late Nineteenth-Century America." *Journal of American History*, 65 (September 1978): 389–411.
Seton-Watson, Hugh. *The Russian Empire 1801–1917.* Oxford: Oxford UP, 1967.

Slang and Its Analogues, Past and Present. Comp. and ed. John S. Farmer. New York: Krause Reprint, 1965.

Stoneley, Peter. *Mark Twain and the Feminine Aesthetic.* Cambridge: Cambridge UP, 1992.

Underhill, Charles S. "Is the Garden of Eden at Niagara Falls? Mark Twain Said Yes," *The Gleaner,* 1, no. 8 (March 1928): 14–19. A publication of Nichols School, Buffalo, N.Y.

Warner, Charles Dudley. *Backlog Studies.* Boston: Houghton, Mifflin, 1886 (orig. pub. 1873).

Zwick, Jim. *Mark Twain's Weapons of Satire.* Syracuse, N.Y.: Syracuse UP, 1992.